Rome and the Ca... Mesopot...

Book eight of the Vetera... ... ...

By: William Kelso

Visit the author's website **http://www.williamkelso.co.uk/**

William Kelso is also the author of:

The Shield of Rome

The Fortune of Carthage

Devotio: The House of Mus

Caledonia - Book One of the Veteran of Rome series

Hibernia - Book Two of the Veteran of Rome series

Britannia – Book Three of the Veteran of Rome series

Hyperborea – Book Four of the Veteran of Rome series

Germania – Book Five of the Veteran of Rome series

The Dacian War – Book Six of the Veteran of Rome series

Armenia Capta – Book Seven of the Veteran of Rome series

Published in 2018 by KelsoBooks Ltd.

Copyright © William Kelso. Second Edition

The author has asserted their moral right under the Copyright, Designs and Patents Act, 1988, to be identified as the author of this work.

All Rights reserved. No part of this publication may be reproduced, copied, stored in a retrieval system, or transmitted, in any form or by any means, without the prior written consent of the copyright holder, nor be otherwise circulated in any form of binding or cover other than that in which it is published and without a similar condition being imposed on the subsequent purchaser.

A CIP catalogue record for this title is available from the British Library.

To: Private John Kelso, Royal Engineers, North Staffordshire Regiment, 1883 - 1960

ABOUT ME

Hello, my name is William Kelso. I was born in the Netherlands to British parents. My interest in history and in particular military history started at a very young age when I was lucky enough to hear my grandfather describing his experiences of serving in the RAF in North Africa and Italy during World War 2. Recently my family has discovered that one of my Scottish and Northern Irish ancestors fought under Wellington at the Battle of Waterloo in 1815.

I love writing and bringing to life the ancient world of Rome, Carthage and the Germanic and Celtic tribes. It's my thing. My aim is to write 100 books in my lifetime. After graduation, I worked for 22 years in financial publishing and event management in the city of London as a salesman for some big conference organizers, trying to weave my stories in the evenings after dinner and in weekends. Working in the heart of the original Roman city of Londinium I spent many years walking its streets and visiting the places, whose names still commemorate the 2,000-year-old ancient Roman capital of Britannia, London Wall, Watling Street, London Bridge and Walbrook. The city of London if you know where to look has many fascinating historical corners. So, since the 2nd March 2017 I have taken the plunge and become a full-time writer. Stories as a form of entertainment are as old as cave man and telling them is what I want to do.

My books are all about ancient Rome, especially the early to mid-republic as this was the age of true Roman greatness. My other books include, The Shield of Rome, The Fortune of Carthage, Caledonia (1), Hibernia (2), Britannia (3), Hyperborea (4), Germania (5), The Dacian War (6), Armenia Capta (7) and Devotio: The House of Mus. Go on, give them a go.

In my spare time, I help my brother, who is also a Winston Churchill impersonator, run his battlefield tours company which takes people around the battlefields of Arnhem,

Dunkirk, Agincourt, Normandy, the Rhine crossing and Monte Cassino. I live in London with my wife and support the "Help for Heroes" charity and a tiger in India.

Please visit my website http://www.williamkelso.co.uk/ and have a look at my historical video blog!

Feel free to write to me with any feedback on my books. Email: william@kelsoevents.co.uk

Rome and the Conquest of Mesopotamia

Book eight of the Veteran of Rome series

Chapter One – Praefectus Annonae

February 115 AD – The City of Rome

"They are all here," Kyna said as she came up to Marcus, who was standing in the bedroom. "Cassius is with them. But I don't think they are happy about the meeting taking place in the garden. It's freezing out there. Even with the comfort of the fire."

Marcus ignored his wife and said nothing, as a slave silently proceeded to adjust his senatorial toga and Kyna sighed and lowered her gaze.

"Would it not be better to hold the meeting inside," she blurted out.

"No," Marcus said sharply. "A bit of discomfort will make them ready to listen and my garden is one of the finest in Rome. They can enjoy the views. I need them focussed on the job. This is an important meeting and if they can't stand the cold then that is their problem."

"So that's your plan," Kyna replied, raising her eyebrows. "Manoeuvre the enemy into an unfavourable position. Then force his surrender. This is not the army Marcus. You are not fighting a war. These men are not under your command. You can't order them about as if they were your soldiers. You are a politician now and those men out there are civilians; wealthy businessmen. You need their cooperation, not their surrender."

"I know," Marcus said stoically, "and I know what I am doing. It never hurts to have an advantage when negotiating."

Kyna sighed again, and with a little flick of her hand, she dismissed the slave and waited until he had left the room. Then she turned to Marcus, stepped towards him and slowly ran her fingers down his white senatorial toga.

"All right husband," she said quietly looking up at Marcus with a little fond smile. "All right, I am with you. Do this your way then. I know that this is important and I am sure you will do your duty and make a fine politician. If they are to freeze their balls off in the garden, then so be it. Just remember you are no longer a young man yourself."

Marcus didn't reply as Kyna quickly left the room. Then slowly he turned to look down at the two remaining fingers on his left hand. He'd lost the other three fingers in the first Dacian war, during the fighting along the Danube. The wounds had resulted in his honourable discharge from the 2nd Batavian Auxiliary Cohort after twenty-three years' service. Kyna had a point. He was no longer a young man. At fifty-two years of age he was getting old and starting to feel it every day, despite a healthy diet and a vigorous exercise regime. And just recently Kyna had started to raise the subject of retirement and a permanent return to his estate on the Isle of Vectis in Britannia. The farm, under Dylis's capable management, was doing well and Kyna had argued that maybe it was time he slowed down and retired. Slowed down, he thought with sudden scorn. He'd told her, no. His red hair had not faded and he still had the energy for a challenge. Annoyed, he turned to glare at the black cat which sat on the bed, silently watching him with its yellow eyes.

It had been two weeks since he had been appointed as Praefectus Annonae, government minister in charge of the grain supply to the city of Rome. Nigrinus had organised it, of course, and had used his influence to persuade Similis, the prefect left in charge of Rome by emperor Trajan, to appoint him to the job. Marcus had not asked for the position, but Nigrinus had said that it was an important job and that the War Party needed their supporters and members in high governmental places. Especially now that Trajan and most of the senior members of his council were faraway in the east, fighting in the Parthian war. Marcus sighed. He'd been a little reluctant at first, but he would do his duty. He would be a politician if that was what Nigrinus and the War Party wanted. But most satisfying of all it gave him the chance to prove his wife wrong for he had no intention of retiring. The new job had meant, of course, that he had far less time to spend on his military veteran's charity work. The charity however was doing well, and with the additional resources that his colleagues in the War Party, Quietus, Palma and Celsus had promised, he'd been able to expand the premises and hire a manager.

Prefect in charge of the grain supply for the city of Rome. It didn't sound very exciting, but it was, as he had quickly learned, a most important government position. Two hundred thousand people in the city of Rome qualified for a free dole of grain and it was now his responsibility to keep the flow of grain from Egypt and Africa coming without interruption. The new job had led to a considerable increase in his personal visibility in the city and he was not yet sure whether he enjoyed all the new attention. Not only did he now report to Similis, his boss and prefect of Rome, but he was also accountable to the senate with its multitude of ambitious men, warring factions and troublemakers. And then there was Nigrinus - the leader of the War Party, and a leading contender to succeed Trajan as the next emperor. Nigrinus had told him to use his new position to win the loyalty and support of the shipping and business guilds, associated with the vast maritime grain supply operation. Nigrinus wanted the business and industrial guilds to become firm supporters of the War Party. That was the real reason Marcus had been appointed.

And so, Marcus thought, with another sigh, he now had twelve private owners of the largest shipping companies in the world waiting for him in the garden of his modest villa on the summit of Janiculum hill. Together these men, all wealthy and well-connected businessmen, owned and operated nearly ninety percent of the huge fleet of grain ships, that ploughed the sea between Alexandria, Carthage and Rome, providing the means by which over sixty million modii, four hundred thousand tons of grain was shipped to Rome each year to feed a hungry and ungrateful population.

***

Indus was waiting for him, as he came into the main room of his house. His big, burly Batavian bodyguard was clad in a simple brown tunic over, which he was wearing a winter cloak. A gladius was hanging from his belt. As Marcus, clad in his splendid white senatorial toga went out into the garden, Indus turned and silently followed him. Outside it was cold. The dull February skies were covered in grey clouds and it looked like it was about to rain. But it was nothing compared to a proper winter in Britannia or on the Danube frontier Marcus thought. A wood fire, carefully tended to by a slave, was burning in the middle of the garden and around it the shipping magnates were huddled in their winter cloaks. They didn't look pleased. As Marcus approached, his young secretary Cassius, Elsa's husband, rose quickly to his feet and hastily came towards Marcus.

"Maybe we could..." Cassius said.

"No, the meeting will be held here in the garden," Marcus interrupted, before Cassius could finish his sentence.

"They are not happy about this Sir," Cassius said in an urgent whisper. "Would it not lead to better results if we did this indoors?"

But Marcus shook his head and, moving past Cassius, he strode up to the assembled men and as he did, the shipping magnates rose to their feet and inclined their heads in a respectful greeting.

"Gentlemen, thank you all for coming," Marcus said in a stern and clear voice, as he motioned for them to sit down. "We have important business to discuss."

From the corner of his eye Marcus noticed that Cassius had sat down again and was smiling broadly at the shipping company owners, doing his best to make them feel at ease. It made Marcus want to laugh. Elsa was besotted by her newly-wed husband and even though Cassius was all right, Marcus could not help feeling that she could have done better. But maybe Kyna was right he thought. Maybe he was just jealous of the young handsome doctor, who had taken his Elsa away from him.

"Let us start our meeting with a prayer of thanks to Ceres, goddess of the harvest," Marcus said as, he turned to the shipping magnates. And as he spoke the words, he motioned for the slave to start burning the incense. As the powerful scent of jasmine spread across the garden, the uncomfortable silence around the fire continued.

"As you all know I have only recently been appointed prefect in charge of the grain supply," Marcus said, as he remained standing. "And this is my first chance to speak to you all. I take this responsibility very seriously. The core competency and responsibility of good government is the transport and distribution of grain to the people of Rome. Rome needs stability in the grain supply. We have import targets. It is of vital importance to the city and to the emperor. Most ordinary citizens in the city cannot afford to purchase grain on the open market. It must therefore be subsidized if we are to avoid civil unrest. The unity and power of the Roman state will fall apart if we don't do this. So, I want you all to know that, with your help, I intend to make sure that the people of Rome will not go hungry. We must all work together to maintain this objective."

"We know this," one of the shipping magnates interrupted irritably. "Some of us have been involved in this trade for generations."

Marcus nodded as he turned to the man who had spoken out.

"It is good to see such loyalty," he replied raising his chin. "And no doubt your family have prospered from the imperial grain trade."

"Prospered," the magnate replied, turning to glance at his fellow owners with an incredulous look. "Sure, transporting grain from Egypt to Rome is important but it's hardly the most profitable commodity. All of us here could make much more money if our ships were laden with higher end products, such as wine, silk, spices or luxury goods."

"Or, if we were allowed to sell our grain at market prices," another magnate said in a determined voice, shivering as he did.

"All of you are well compensated for your efforts," Cassius said suddenly, in a sharp voice that took Marcus by surprise. Glancing round at the young man Marcus saw that his secretary had risen to feet, his face resolute, fearless and impassioned as he gazed around at the group of shipping company owners.

"The fiscus pays you well for your labour and investment," Cassius said, in the voice of someone convinced that he was right. "Grain may not be the most profitable commodity but your participation in the trade brings you great benefits. Your ships are exempt from harbour taxes and other taxes. You are granted Roman citizenship. You can apply for cheap state loans to build new grain ships. You are exempt from the law that penalises celibacy and Tutela, the duties of guardianship and if you are a female ship owner you get the same legal privileges of a woman who has had four children. That is not nothing. These are great privileges."

Cassius came to an abrupt stop, his cheeks flushed with youthful emotion and, for a long moment the meeting remained silent and the only noise was the crackle and hiss of the wood fire.

"I don't see any women here today," one of the magnates muttered sourly, as he glanced around the gathering.

Marcus hastily gestured for Cassius to sit back down and then cleared his throat.

"In principal I admit that I am against the whole idea of free grain handouts," Marcus said in a grave voice, as he turned his attention back to the gathering. "Free grain handouts ruin the agriculture of Italy and why should we give away something for free when others work hard to provide their families with food. The principal sucks and, if I were you, I too would want to get involved in more lucrative trade ventures. But," Marcus sighed and held up his hand for silence, "It is a necessity. An ugly necessity and if we are to avoid civil unrest, we must do it. The prestige of the emperor will suffer if he is unable to feed his own people."

"Agreed," one of the shipping magnates cried. "But why force us to transport all the grain during the winter months. The winter is a dangerous time to be at sea. Our ships continually run the risk of being struck by storms and lost. Why can we not sail during the calmer months?"

"Your ships are well insured by the state," Marcus retorted. "You know this. We will not allow risk to move down the supply chain. If they are lost, we will compensate you. The Roman state is guaranteeing you a steady profit without any risk. That is a wonderful position to be in. Now," Marcus said moving on swiftly to the main purpose of the meeting. "I have not called you all here to complain about the system. The system is fair. It works, but from time to time we do need to make adjustments. Today is such an occasion when we need to make a change. So, I need to tell you that it is the imperial wish that all privileges enjoyed by ship owners involved in the state grain trade will only continue to be granted, if at least two thirds of the shipper's capital is invested in the grain-shipping transport business."

"Two thirds of our capital," one of the magnates exclaimed in horror.

"You can't be serious," another cried out in surprise.

"That is what Trajan wants," Marcus said sternly. "The grain supply to the city of Rome is of vital importance to the stability of the empire. We need all participating shipping companies to be fully committed to the cause."

"We are fully committed; we have been for decades," an outraged voice squealed. "Who the hell does Trajan think he is, making such demands. We are honourable businessmen. We pay our share of taxes and provide a vital service, but if we are forced to commit two thirds of our capital to the transport of grain, it will ruin us. You may as well slap us with another tax."

"It's not going to ruin you," Marcus snapped, shaking his head. "Consider this as part of your patriotic duty."

The meeting broke out into bad-tempered muttering and protests and, as the chorus of voices filled his garden Marcus turned away to look out towards the vast city of Rome that lay half shrouded in February mist and cloud. Nigrinus had instructed him to win the support of these men, but right now all he wanted to do was kick their arrogant arses out of his garden.

"All right, all right, silence, all of you," a voice suddenly called out and Marcus turned to glance at the gathering of magnates. Had they come to their senses? One of the shippers had risen to his feet and was looking at Marcus.

"We have heard your request, prefect," the man said in a calm voice. "It is a contentious issue and we will need some time to discuss this amongst ourselves. Please be assured that we mean no offense to the emperor, but we do have commercial considerations and we must work out what is best for us. I am sure that you will understand, prefect."

"I understand," Marcus said graciously. "Let us reconvene this meeting in a week's time then."

In response the shipping company owner dipped his head in a polite reply. "Let's do that," the man said, "and maybe next time we could choose a more suitable location for our meeting."

***

"That seemed to go well," Cassius said, breathing a sigh of relief as the last of the shipping magnates departed.

Marcus did not reply as he walked over to the low wall, that marked the edge of his garden, and gazed out over the city of Rome. On a clear day the views of Rome from up here on the Janiculum hill were fantastic and had been one of the reasons he'd purchased the small villa. The other being that the location was far enough away from the dreadful stink produced by the million plus inhabitants of Rome.

"That was bold of you," Marcus growled disapprovingly as Cassius came to stand at his side. "Some may feel it was disrespectful and it was not your job to speak out."

"I am sorry Sir if I caused offense," Cassius said quietly, "but I was right. Those men knew all those things. They were testing you. They were being arseholes."

Marcus turned his head to examine Cassius for a long moment in silence.

"Yes, I know," he snapped. "I am aware of their privileges. But it was not your place to speak and we need their cooperation. You undermined me in front of our clients. There will be no repeat of this. Do I make myself clear?"

"I will do as you wish," Cassius replied, looking straight ahead with a wounded but defiant expression.

Marcus sighed and turned to gaze down at the Tiber and the bridges spanning the river. Cassius was related to Paulinus, minister in charge of the fiscus, the emperor's personal treasury. He was a good and close friend and he was also Elsa's husband. He could not sack the young man, nor did he really wish to, but now and then he had doubts about Cassius. It was just instinct, but he could not shake it. Cassius was a doctor by training, but he was also a dreamer. There was something deeply idealistic about his young secretary that could, if unchecked by a healthy dose of realism, lead to trouble.

"For what it is worth Sir," Cassius said quietly, "I agree with you when you said that you are against the free handout of grain to the people. During the Republic there was no need for this."

"The Republic?" Marcus frowned.

"When Rome was ruled solely by the senate and the will of the people of Rome," Cassius replied with a little sigh, "A time of true greatness; not like now."

"Good god," Marcus muttered with a little disapproving shake of his head. "You sound just like Ahern. Republic, Republic, that's all he can talk about these days. Well emperor Trajan is a good ruler and he has brought peace to the world. I should know, I fought for him in Britannia and on the Danube."

Cassius said nothing as he gazed at the views with a faraway look and, as the silence lengthened, Marcus grunted and shook his head again.

"So, what does my schedule look like?" Marcus snapped.

"Uh the next meeting is tomorrow with the Pistorum at their offices by the temple of Minerva on the Aventine hill," Cassius replied hastily, blinking back to reality. "The college of bakers are demanding that we raise the bread price. No surprises there. They have been demanding that for years, but the guild does have some political power. The bakers also mentioned the preparations for the festivities on June the 9th to honour the oven goddess. They want to know what their budget will be for the celebrations. Then let's see," Cassius looked down at his fingers. "On Friday we are meeting the haulage firms and inland barge companies. They want to talk about traffic congestion on the Tiber. Then on Monday, next week, we are meeting the priests of Ceres at their temple. The priests are complaining that someone has repeatedly tried to open the stone that blocks the entrance into the Mundus Cereris without their permission. They have been forced to place a permanent guard." Cassius glanced quickly at Marcus. "The Mundus Cereris is the pit that contains the entrance to the underworld Sir," Cassius explained helpfully. "It's only ever opened on three days of the year, in August, October and November. It is done to allow the spirits of the dead to lawfully wander amongst the living for a short time."

"I know what it is," Marcus growled. "Holidays for the dead," he muttered with a little disbelieving shake of his head. "But what has this got to do with us? It seems to be a simple security matter for the priests. They should speak to Similis."

"The priests say that it is a bad omen Sir," Cassius replied. "They are demanding that we double the offerings we place in the pit."

Marcus's face soured. "It is only a bad omen if those trying to move the stone are doing so from the inside of the pit," he snapped. "All right," he added, before Cassius could speak, "I will discuss the matter with them. Is that all?"

"Yes, that's all the arrangements so far," Cassius replied, with a stiff nod.

"Good," Marcus said, "Good. We made progress today," he said in a more upbeat voice. "Now I want you to go to Paulinus's house and tell him that I need to discuss our funding from the fiscus. I know he is a busy man. Arrange a time for when I can meet him."

"Cassius," a soft woman's voice suddenly called out, and as she did, both men turned. It was Elsa. She was clad in a long white stola over which she had draped a grey winter cloak with a hood covering her head. One of her hands was clasped around her prominent and protruding belly. The baby was due in three months. Marcus mellowed abruptly at the sight of his adopted daughter. Elsa looked lovely as always and at twenty-three, she seemed to have everything going for her. A skilled healer, beauty, grace, intelligence, a husband and now soon she was going to become a mother. How far she had come, Marcus thought with sudden pride. How much she had accomplished since that day he'd found her and her little brother Armin, half abandoned in that miserable hut near the Charterhouse lead mines in Britannia. He had been right to adopt her and her brother Armin, after killing her father. The mess with Lucius had been unpleasant and painful, but at least some good had come from taking care of his children.

"Cassius," Elsa called out again as she came towards them, her eyes fixed on her husband. "We must go. Remember we have an appointment."

"Will you not stay for a while" Marcus interrupted. "The slaves are preparing dinner. You and Cassius are welcome to stay. It would be good to hear your news."

Slowly Elsa turned to look at Marcus.

"That is very kind, but we must go," she replied. "I am sure that you are a busy man and will have much on your mind. We do not wish to intrude."

Marcus looked disappointed, but he managed a little graceful nod. It had been hard to watch Elsa leave and go to live in Cassius's house, but he had to accept it. She was Cassius's woman now.

"Another time then perhaps," he said. "One of these days we must sit down together and discuss what to do with your little brother Armin, back on Vectis. He is getting to the age where I must decide what he is going to do with his life. I would like your thoughts on this Elsa."

Elsa paused.

"Thank you," she said in a formal and neutral voice. "Your kindness and respect for me reflects well on you and I am sure that you will make the right choice for Armin." Elsa hesitated. "Make the right decision, Marcus."

Marcus frowned as Cassius and Elsa disappeared into his house. That was odd. Elsa and Armin were very close. She had always been concerned for her little brother's welfare. When he'd first met Elsa, she had made him swear that he would never do anything to separate her from her brother. But now suddenly, she seemed indifferent. That was not like her.

As Cassius and Elsa left the house Kyna came up to Marcus and affectionately laid her hand on his shoulder. "Elsa told me that she has a new hobby," Kyna said with a little smile. "She is so bored waiting for the baby to arrive that she has started studying painting. Not that she will ever have her walls painted. She is far too frugal for that."

"Well we need to make decisions regards Armin's future," Marcus growled. "If she doesn't want to be involved in that process then I will make the decisions myself. But she can't complain I didn't try and involve her. The boy will reach manhood soon and he needs a profession."

"I am sure that you will make the right decision," Kyna replied with a sigh.

***

It was growing dark outside when Indus suddenly appeared in the doorway leading to the hall and caught Marcus's attention.

"Visitor for you Sir," Indus said quietly in his native Batavian language. "He is waiting for you outside in the street. Won't come into the house. Says he needs to speak to you. Says it's important."

"Who is he?" Marcus asked, but Indus just shrugged.

Marcus muttered something to himself and then, with his bodyguard following closely on behind, he strode into the hall and towards the door. Outside in the gathering gloom he quickly caught sight of a hooded figure sitting on a horse. The man's hood covered most of his face and in the twilight, it was hard to make out his features.

"I am Marcus, who are you? What do you want?" Marcus growled as he paused outside his front door.

For a moment the stranger said nothing, but from under his hood Marcus was aware of keen, quick eyes studying him, and as the silence lengthened, a sudden chill of unease ran down Marcus's spine.

"I have a message for you Marcus," the stranger said, in a quiet but clear voice. "Listen carefully. You have been given one chance to save yourself and your family from harm and suffering. Follow my instructions. Resign from your job. Resign from the senate. Abandon your friends in the War Party and go to the temple of Invidia and provide the god with a gift of no less than half a million denarii in gold coins. Do this and you shall be spared. Get yourself and your family out of Rome whilst you still can. A storm is coming. A storm that will sweep you away."

And as the stranger finished speaking, he urged his horse forwards and with a clatter of hooves disappeared off into the gloom.

Chapter Two – Old Friends

"The temple of Invidia," Paulinus Picardus Tagliare exclaimed with a startled look. "Half a million denarii in gold coins. Great gods, Marcus."

Marcus nodded solemnly as the two senators, dressed in their fine white senatorial toga's, ambled across the Pons Fabricus that connected Tiber island to the eastern bank of the river. It was morning, and around them in the dawn light, the bridge was crowded with noisy, impatient and aggressive rush-hour commuters, pedestrians and oxen and horse drawn wagons. The greenish waters of the Tiber were high, flush with fresh, winter snow melt, but the river and the great city beyond still stank like a sewer. Indus followed the two men at a respectful distance, a gladius stuffed into his belt and in one hand the Batavian bodyguard was holding a stout stick. At his side young Cassius was staring straight ahead with a faraway look, as if he was in a world of his own.

"Do you know who this man was? Did you get a look at his face?" Paulinus asked with a little indignant shake of his head.

"He was on a horse and he'd taken care to obscure his face," Marcus growled, as he pushed on across the bridge. "But he knew my name. Kyna is worried. She says that maybe we should do as he says."

"And what do you think?" Paulinus said, glancing sideways at his friend.

"There is no way I am going to be run out of Rome, by a coward who hides his face," Marcus replied. "Fuck that. I have a job to do."

Paulinus nodded in agreement. "And yet it is troubling," Paulinus said, turning to glance quickly at Indus. "Are you confident your man back there can handle your security?

Maybe you should hire some more men and keep a guard at your house."

Idly, Marcus glanced across at a group of beggars sitting on the ground and holding up their hands in a miserable and pathetic plea for help.

"Indus can handle my security," Marcus said breezily. "And I can call on a few good solid men from the veteran's charity, if I need to. Don't worry. This is probably nothing more than an attempt to squeeze some money out of me. It would not be the first time. I have already reported the matter to Similis. The prefect has promised to alert the commander of the urban cohorts. They will ask around if anyone knows of troublemakers capable of these kinds of threats. I can handle it," Marcus said, turning to give Paulinus a little confident smile. "We are going to be all right. But there is a business-related issue that I need to discuss with you."

The head of the imperial fiscus sighed. "Nigrinus is still at his estate in Faventia," Paulinus said, changing the subject as the two of them struggled towards the gate into the city of Rome and the cattle market, that lay just inside the old city walls. "I think he will be there for a while. He has no plans to come to Rome. But the last time that I spoke to him, he told me to impress on you the importance of winning the loyalty and support of the shipping and business guilds to our cause. What was the outcome of your meeting yesterday?"

"That's hardly news," Marcus replied. "I am working on it. But it will take time. The shipping companies are going to consider the proposal to have two thirds of their capital invested in the grain trade. I have another meeting with them next week."

"Good, they will come around," Paulinus said, with a little nod. "Nigrinus is worried that Hadrian's influence is growing amongst the army," Paulinus added. "The grain supply to the city of Rome is a key strategic interest. We must have complete control. Trajan must understand the consequences if he decides to nominate Hadrian as his successor. If Rome starves, then that is going to create some serious problems for anyone in charge."

The gate into the city of Rome was guarded by a squad from the urban cohorts and as the two senators passed on through, the soldiers on duty, recognising them, gave them a polite and respectful greeting. Beyond the walls, the Forum Boarium market was a riot of yelling and shouting merchants and shoppers, as a brisk trade took place under the watchful eye of a stone statue of Mercury.

"Is that why Nigrinus had you promoted from the prefect of the public treasury to the man in charge of the fiscus. So that you could cause trouble?" Marcus asked with a sudden mischievous grin.

"I am a money expert," Paulinus replied in a serious, slightly offended voice as he ignored the gentle jibe. "And I am the very best. There is no one else with my experience, talent and skills. That's why I was promoted to the fiscus. And it is good news for Rome that I oversee the taxes from the imperial provinces. Without a sound financial base, the empire will collapse."

Paulinus paused for a moment and glanced at Marcus. "I forget that you are from one of the more backward provinces," Paulinus said with a sudden mischievous expression of his own, as he raised his voice above the din. "So, let me educate you my friend. The power of the emperor rests on three pillars. The loyalty of the army; the support of the senate and finally the docility of the mob. My friend Tacitus may call them the plebs sordida, the great unwashed, but every emperor has an unspoken duty to provide for his people." Paulinus paused, as he struggled on through the crowds in the direction of the temple of Saturn and the Capitoline hill. "The Roman people have a right to free bread, to gladiatorial games, running water and the odd coin donative," he called out. "The bellies of the people of Rome must always be kept full."

"Well if you keep paying my shipper's and bakers, I will keep the grain flowing into Rome," Marcus said with a little wry smile. "But I need to discuss our funding for the next year," he added, in a more serious voice. "There is pressure on me to raise prices. I intend to resist the pressure but if the guilds take this issue to the senate. I need to know if I can rely on the fiscus to back me up. I need your support. If we raise the price of grain, there could be trouble on the streets."

"You have the full support of the fiscus," Paulinus replied. "The last thing that Trajan wants is to face trouble at home. I will back you up in the senate. You have my word."

"Thank you," Marcus replied in a grateful voice.

As the two of them entered the Forum of the city of Rome, Marcus turned to look up at the great imperial state buildings and ageless monuments that dominated the valley between the Capitoline and Palatine hills. Despite the years in which he had spent in Rome, he had never been able to shake a humbling sense of awe for the majestic Forum Romanum. For it was from here that Rome ruled the world and had been doing so for over two hundred and fifty years. It was from here that the great toiling masses of the earth were managed; the immortal gods honoured, and the destiny of man determined. The narrow Forum, filled by the senate house, temples, triumphal archways, statues, colonnaded shops and palaces, was like no other place on earth and the smell of power and money was tangible.

"What news from the east?" Marcus called out, raising his voice as the two of them pushed their way through the crowds towards the temple of Saturn. "Has there been any word from Trajan? The last I heard was that we had captured Armenia, taken Nisibis and that the Parthians were on the run."

"Then you know as much as I do," Paulinus shrugged. "The war seems to be going well, thank the gods. You must be worried about your son, Fergus. He is serving out there isn't he? An auxiliary unit, was it?"

At the mention of Fergus's name, Marcus's expression instantly became guarded. He had told no one about the position that Fergus occupied on Hadrian's staff, for that would not go down well with his own War Party. It would be a disaster if Nigrinus found out that Fergus was head of security for Hadrian, and had probably prevented the assassination of Hadrian some eighteen months ago. Hadrian and his Peace Party supporters were the arch rivals of his own War Party, locked in an increasingly bitter and murderous struggle for power. Both Hadrian and Nigrinus were competing fiercely with each other to be nominated as Trajan's successor to the imperial throne. No, there could be absolutely no mention of what Fergus did or whom he served. It had to be kept secret even from close friends, Paulinus and Lady Claudia. At his side Marcus clenched his right hand into a fist. If it ever leaked out that he had tried to warn Fergus about the assassination attempt on Hadrian, his life and that of all his family would be forfeit. Nigrinus would have him killed for such treachery. So Kyna and he had told no one. There was only one man outside his immediate family, who knew about Fergus, and Marcus had sworn to kill him if he as much as opened his mouth.

"Seventh Auxiliary Cavalry of Numidians," Marcus said lightly. "He's been made prefect of the whole unit. It's a promotion. The last news that I have is that they posted him to some Syrian fort, out on the desert frontier."

"That's good news," Paulinus called out, his eyes fixed on the temple of Saturn that stood ahead at the base of the Capitoline hill.

"It will be good news if he returns home alive," Marcus growled but his words were lost in the din and noise of the street.

Eighteen months ago, as news of the failed assassination attempt on Hadrian had filtered back to Rome, he'd been greatly relieved to learn from Galena's regular letters to Kyna that Fergus had survived and that he was being posted to Antioch in Syria. It however was not clear from Galena's letters whether the assassination had failed because Fergus had understood his warning letter. But Fergus had survived and that was all that mattered. There was just no way he could watch his son become collateral damage in one of Nigrinus's plots. In her letters Galena had initially expressed concern for Kyna's health, which his wife had found rather odd as there was nothing wrong with her. At his side Marcus clenched his right hand tighter. It had forced him to reveal to his wife what he'd been up to. Kyna had been furious and upset, lambasting him for his secrecy, for not caring about Fergus and for not making his warning to Fergus much clearer. It had been no use trying to tell her that he had to tread a delicate path. That he could not be seen to betray his own party, or what the consequences would be if that came out. Kyna had refused to speak to him for nearly a month. It had taken her a long time before she had been ready to understand the huge risk he'd taken, by writing to Fergus with his subtly worded warning about the assassination plot.

Galena's letters to Kyna had made no mention of his warning, or indeed the assassination attempt and, he had guessed that she was saying nothing on purpose, in case her letters were being intercepted. But then in her last correspondence to Kyna - received several months ago and dated to the late summer of last year, Galena had boldly revealed the news that Hadrian had placed him, Marcus, on a death list, for his apparent and prior knowledge of the assassination plot and that Fergus was doing everything he could to get his name scrapped from the list. Somehow Hadrian must have discovered who he was. It had been an unsettling development but not unexpected. If Hadrian did become the next emperor, there were going to a shed load of important people, who were going to lose their lives. It was a threat that all his colleagues in the War Party accepted. There had been no news from Fergus or Galena since.

"I must leave you here," Paulinus said, as he came to a halt before the great doors to the temple of Saturn at the base of the Capitoline hill and turned to face Marcus. "Business with the Aerarium I'm afraid. But let's grab a bite to eat, one of these days, and you can tell me all about your dealings with the business guilds."

"Sounds good," Marcus said, hastily forcing a smile onto his face as the two senators gave each other a brief farewell embrace.

***

Gesturing for Cassius to come and walk alongside him, Marcus stepped out onto the Sacred Way and started off in the direction of the coliseum. Around him, in the open spaces of the Forum, the money lenders, lawyers, religious-nuts, fortune-tellers, entertainers and business men, were touting for work in loud, brash voices as people of all social classes milled about. In a corner, a bawdy, puppet show was attracting a lot of attention and shrieks of laughter from the crowds. A squad of heavily armed men from the urban cohorts stood on watch. Ignoring the stench seeping out from the cloaca maxima, the network of sewers that ran beneath his feet, Marcus thoughtfully glanced sideways at the tall and newly built column of Trajan. The column, some hundred and fifteen feet high, had been erected by the emperor to commemorate victory in the Dacian wars. The column belonged to all the veterans of the Dacian wars. It was their monument. And, as he marvelled at the fine engraved stonework, Marcus suddenly remembered that Kyna had asked him to speak to Ahern.

At the thought of Ahern, Marcus sighed. A few days ago, seventeen-year old Ahern, Kyna's son by another man, a brilliant student with a gifted scientific mind, had been arrested for drunk and disorderly conduct by the urban cohorts during a night-out on the town with friends. Marcus had been forced to use his influence to get him freed. It had been an embarrassing moment for both, but Ahern had claimed he'd done nothing wrong and had been unrepentant and rebellious. He'd refused to apologise to Lady Claudia, under whose patronage and in whose school he'd been enrolled as a student and where he was being taught by a prestigious, expensive tutor. Ahern had threatened to do whatever he liked at any time he liked. The boy needs to be taught some boundaries, discipline and respect Kyna had snapped angrily. That was his job, as father of his family, Marcus thought sourly. But there had been no time to deal with the rebellious youth.

***

The temple of Minerva stood on the summit of the Aventine hill, a splendid rectangular construction with six towering stone columns at one end. A magnificent statue of the goddess adorned the front of the temple, competing for splendour it seemed with the temple of Diane, the goddess of the hunt, which stood next door. The doors into the complex were open and around the entrance steps, a few prostitutes, beggars and priests were going about their business. Marcus looked visibly annoyed as he marched down the temple steps and headed back towards the Forum. At his side Cassius, looking anxious, hastened to keep up with his boss. The meeting with the baker's guild had not gone well. The bakers had been more stubborn than he'd expected.

"It's a disgrace," Marcus hissed angrily. "Greedy, useless bastards. Who do they think they are? There is going to be no rise in the price of grain. What part of that don't they understand?"

"Yet we must be careful Sir," Cassius said, as he quickly strode along at Marcus's side. "The bakers have some political power. They are a special interest group. There are senators in the senate who will stand up for their interests."

"I am not afraid of them," Marcus growled, as he stormed on down the narrow street.

"Sir," Cassius said hastily, as he caught hold of Marcus's sleeve and tried to slow him down. "I have a plan to handle the baker's guild. If I may explain."

Marcus came to a halt and his eyes narrowed suspiciously as he glared at Cassius.

"A plan," he snapped. "What kind of plan? What are you talking about?"

Cassius quickly turned to look around at the pedestrians in the street. Then the young doctor took a deep breath.

"I was going to tell you yesterday but there was never a good moment," Cassius said, lowering his gaze. "I know how we can handle the bakers Sir. Nigrinus has provided me with a personnel file on the guild and a special fund, a slush fund, on which we can draw if necessary." Cassius lowered his voice as he turned to gaze around in a conspiratorial manner. "If the bakers continue to be difficult, Nigrinus says that we can threaten, blackmail or bribe their leading members. Nigrinus knows stuff about them that is compromising."

Marcus stared at Cassius in stunned surprise unable to say anything. Then slowly the corner of his mouth began to twitch.

"Nigrinus gave you this information," Marcus said with growing incredulity. "You are speaking to Nigrinus directly? He has contact with you? Behind my back? Without my knowledge?"

"It's not like that Sir," Cassius stammered. "He wrote to me with the information some time ago. I don't know why he came to me. What was I supposed to do?"

Dismayed, Marcus shook his head. He had not expected this. What the hell was Nigrinus playing at, by going behind his back like this? Why had he not been informed? He was the praefectus annonae after all. It was insulting. Did Nigrinus not trust him? Did he think he could not handle the job? Or was this a subtle message from Nigrinus to remind him who was ultimately in charge of things?

"Are you working for him?" Marcus hissed, his face suddenly darkening with rage, as he rounded on Cassius. "Are you spying on me; providing Nigrinus with reports on my progress? Well, what is it boy?"

But before Cassius had a chance to reply, a hand slapped Marcus on the shoulder and a deep voice boomed out.

"There you are old friend. I have been looking all over for you," Alexandros cried-out as a broad smile lit up his bearded, one-eyed face.

Chapter Three – "To the day that the Hermes sails again"

"She's not in good shape I'm afraid," Alexandros said, as he eagerly reached for the dried beans on his plate and wolfed them down.

Marcus nodded with a sour expression, as he waited for Alexandros to finish eating. From the way the big, one-eyed Greek captain was attacking the plates of food, it looked like he'd not eaten in days. And he didn't seem to have washed recently either. The captain of the Hermes, with his black eye patch and dirty beard, looked old, scruffy and worn-out. The two of them were sitting at a small corner-table in a Popina, one of the many public wine bars that lined the narrow, busy and congested streets around the temple of Minerva. Behind Marcus, at the next table, Indus sat alone, his back against the wall, his eyes on the noisy, boisterous customers. A selection of small dishes containing cuts of meat, dried beans, olives, green vegetables, olive oil and bread had been placed on the table, but Marcus wasn't hungry. Patiently he raised his cup of watered-down wine to his lips. He'd sent Cassius away, telling him that he would speak to him later. But his anger at discovering that Nigrinus was going behind his back had not abated.

"So because the Hermes is not seaworthy enough to leave Portus I had to sign on as a crewmember with the Egyptian grain fleet," Alexandros continued, as he wiped his mouth with the back of his hand and hastily reached for a piece of fish. "That was tough after being the captain of one's own ship. Had to leave Cora and Calista behind on the Hermes for a few months. But I needed the job, so I had to do it. I gave up drinking as well. Got to pay the bills. A man must support his family, right?"

"It's good to see you again Alexandros," Marcus muttered in a genuine voice and, as he spoke, Alexandros's rugged face lit up.

"And you Marcus, and you," the Greek sailor exclaimed hastily with sudden emotion. "It's been a tough time recently," he continued looking away, and as he did, Marcus was suddenly aware of the tension on Alexandros' face and in his voice. "Money is tight. Cora is deeply unhappy. She says she is fed up living on a rotting piece of wood in a violent, stinking harbour. She is threatening to leave me." Alexandros sighed. "But I don't know what else to do. The Hermes is all that I have got. I will not sell her. Times are hard Marcus, hard as nails. That's why I came looking for you."

"How are Calista and Jodoc and their child?" Marcus asked quietly.

"Oh, they are doing all right," Alexandros replied, as he reached for the bread and dipped it into the olive oil, spilling some onto the table. "They are still living on the Hermes with Cora. Can't afford anywhere else. Jodoc has a job in the harbour as a longshoreman. But the pay is shit and its backbreaking work. They survive."

Marcus nodded as he lifted his cup to his lips and took a sip. The memories of his epic voyage across the western ocean to Hyperborea were still vivid.

"When I got back to Portus a few weeks ago I heard that they had appointed you as prefect in charge of the grain," Alexandros said, as he paused for a moment to digest his food. "Congratulations Marcus. That's a very important position. You must be pleased. Things are going well."

"Thank you," Marcus replied. "It's an important position all right but so far all I have had to deal with is a load of arrogant, moaning businessmen."

Hungrily Alexandros turned to look at the remaining pieces of meat on the table, but hesitated to reach out to them.

"You need some help, don't you?" Marcus said quietly.

Across from him Alexandros lowered his gaze and nodded silently, his face suddenly blighted by embarrassment and humiliation.

"I need a loan," the Greek captain of the Hermes blurted out. "I need the money to repair the Hermes and get her seaworthy. If I can get the ship repaired, then the Hermes can join the grain fleet and do some proper business. I can start my own company again and we can finally leave Portus. But no banker will lend me the money. They say that I am too risky. Believe me, I have tried everywhere, and the answer is always the same." Alexandros slowly shook his head in bewilderment. "It's crushing," he stammered with sudden emotion; "It is sapping my will to live."

Marcus sighed and looked away and, for a while the two of them sat together in awkward silence and as they did Marcus was reminded of something. The idea was crazy and risky, but it had never really gone away. It had always been there in the back of his mind, patiently waiting to be considered once again. Marcus grunted. He would probably lose his investment, but he really did owe the Greek captain; his friend. Without Alexandros he would likely have died and Corbulo's spirit would have been lost forever in a foreign land. Boldly making up his mind, he lifted his chin and looked at Alexandros.

"I remember the first time we met, back on the Thames at Londinium," Marcus said, as a little careful smile appeared on the corners of his mouth. "You told me that you had a dream. A bold plan. You wanted to sail west across the ocean to the land of the Chin and bring back silk. You said the empress Plotina and the ladies of Rome would make you rich if you managed to establish such a trade route. Is that still your dream? To sail west across the outer ocean."

"West," Alexandros replied refusing to look up at Marcus. "That was a long time ago. I would be just content for the Hermes to have a place on the grain fleet."

"All right," Marcus growled, "here is what I will do. I am going to give you some of my own money so that you can fix the Hermes. Get her repaired and seaworthy. After that it is up to you what you do. But," Marcus paused, his eyes gleaming with sudden excitement. "If you decide you want to take the Hermes westwards across the ocean I, in my capacity as prefect in charge of the grain supply for the city of Rome, will officially commission you and the Hermes to explore and open a new western maritime trade route with the land of Chin. I shall make public funds available for you to hire a crew and buy provisions for the journey. How does that sound?"

"You would do this," Alexandros exclaimed, gazing up at Marcus with growing surprise. "You would really do this for me? This is too much."

"That's what I just said," Marcus growled. "Well, what do you say? Or have you lost the stomach for the open seas?"

For a long moment Alexandros seemed too stunned to answer as he stared at Marcus. Then with a fierceness and aggression, that had Indus half out of his seat with his knife drawn, Alexandros banged both of his fists onto the table, making the plates of food jump, before raising his arms above his head with a fierce and loud roar of pure delight.

"Me, scared of the open sea. Pigs may fly," Alexandros boomed, his face flushed with sudden emotion. "Fuck that. Here is to the day that the Hermes sails again."

Chapter Four – Punishment

The school building on the Quirinal hill had not changed much since he'd first come here nine years ago Marcus thought, as he and Indus strode on through the entrance gates. On that first occasion he'd been new to Rome and had hung around, hoping to have a word with the Augusta, the empress Plotina; whose family's children had once attended the prestigious school. He had been hoping to argue the case for the care of destitute army veterans, but it had been a vain hope. Instead however he'd ended up being reunited with Lady Claudia.

A few days had passed since his unexpected meeting with Alexandros and Cassius's admission that he was in contact with Nigrinus behind his back. As Marcus strode into the school courtyard, clad in his senatorial toga, a slave hastily bowed and hurried away to announce his arrival. From inside the building, the sounds of playful and excited children's voices were clearly audible, and a strong smell of burning incense was trying to overpower the pong of the city. At the steps leading into the school, Marcus paused to look around. There was a long history between himself and Lady Claudia that stretched all the way back to the days of the great northern rebellion in Britannia, some twenty-six years before, when for a short period he'd been prefect and in command of the 2nd Batavian Auxiliary Cohort. Little had he realised then how important Claudia would be to him. It had been Lady Claudia who had introduced him to Paulinus and Nigrinus. It had been her influence that had got Ahern a place as an apprentice to one of the leading scientists in the city. Without her, Marcus thought, he would never have risen to become a senator of Rome.

A few moments later Lady Claudia appeared in the entrance to her school and, as he caught sight of her, Marcus's stern and hard expression mellowed. Claudia was older than himself but had still managed to maintain her elegance. She was clad in a light-blue stola, the hood of which was lowered around the back of her neck and she was wearing fine silk gloves. She greeted him with a gracious smile.

"Marcus, I am glad you have found time to come," Claudia said, as he kissed her lightly on her cheeks. Then she motioned for him to follow her into the building. "I am sure your new job is keeping you busy. Come, he is in the class room."

"Has he apologised to you yet?" Marcus growled, as he followed her into the school.

Claudia sighed. "You had better speak to him," she replied in a weary voice.

Ahern was sitting on a chair in a stubborn, rebellious posture as Marcus entered the classroom. The beginnings of a beard was just visible across his chin and for a seventeen-year old, he was thin and lanky. Ahern groaned and rolled his eyes as he caught sight of Marcus.

"Oh, look who it is," the youth muttered in a sarcastic voice. "Must this take long? I have an important project to finish."

Marcus did not reply. In the doorway Claudia sighed and folded her arms across her chest. Turning to her, Marcus carefully cleared his throat.

"Maybe it is best if you leave me alone with him for a while," he said quietly. "This is going to be a man to man talk."

Claudia nodded. "As you wish," she said lightly before leaving. As she departed, Marcus gestured for Indus to close the door behind her and then slowly he turned to face Ahern, his face hard and cold as stone.

"What?" the youth blurted out defensively, as he caught the look on Marcus's face.

For a while Marcus said nothing as he stared at Ahern and, as he did, the atmosphere in the room grew increasingly uncomfortable and awkward. There had been a time not so long ago, Marcus thought, when he and Ahern had enjoyed going for walks together. They would cross the Tiber into Rome in search of army veterans sleeping rough on the streets, with the aim of telling them about Marcus's army charity. Those had been good days. A time when Ahern had nearly been like another son to him. It had been his chance of catching up with the young student and finding out what he was doing. But those days had stopped as Ahern had grown older and had started to discover the hedonistic delights of Rome.

"Do you know how disappointed I am in you," Marcus hissed, breaking the silence. "Kyna and I have done our best to raise you as a decent, honourable young man and this is how you repay us! With insolence, rebellion and disgrace. Why have you not apologised to Lady Claudia yet? What is the matter with you boy?"

"I did nothing wrong," Ahern cried out defiantly. "I've told you so many times already. I was out with the boys in a tavern in the Aventine district. We had a few drinks and the next moment I was being arrested, by those stupid pricks from the urban watch. I did nothing wrong. How many times do I have to tell you that."

"That's not what the watch commander told me," Marcus snapped, his eyes blazing. "He says his men caught you pissing on a statue of the emperor and making obscene remarks about the imperial family. He also says you were drunk and that you tried to resist arrest."

"So, you are going to believe a policeman over your own family," Ahern retorted. "It's their word against mine."

"You still don't get it," Marcus replied raising his voice. "This is about your reputation. In this city, reputation is everything. Lose it and you lose it forever and with it, the chance to make a career." Angrily Marcus pointed a finger straight at Ahern. "You boy, you occupy a privileged position in society. You have never known what it is like to be at the bottom of the ladder. When I was your age I ran away from home to join an auxiliary unit. It was tough leaving my mother on her own, but it was nothing compared to life in the regiment as a soldier. But you have been given a chance to make something of yourself. A great opportunity. A chance most people do not get. So, when you are out and about in public, the least I expect from you is that you conduct yourself with dignity. People are watching. People are always watching and your arrest outside that tavern is just what your enemies need. They will use that against you one day if you are not careful."

"Enemies," Ahern sneered bitterly. "The only enemies I have are the ones who do not want Rome to become a republic again." Boldly Ahern raised his arm and pointed his finger at Marcus. "And this is not about my reputation. You are only here because you are concerned about your own reputation. You don't give a damn about me. You don't give a damn about the steam engine that I am building. You are just like the rest of the mindless sheep walking the streets out there."

"Are you going to apologise to Lady Claudia or not?" Marcus hissed.

"No, I have said all that I am going to say," Ahern retorted.

Reaching into the folds of his toga, Marcus produced a centurion's vine staff and banged it loudly onto the table, his face dark with rage.

"Hold him down," Marcus snapped, turning to Indus. "It's time to teach the boy some discipline and respect; the old-fashioned way."

At the sight of the vine staff Ahern's face went pale and his eyes widened in shock.

"What is this? You are not serious? You are going to flog me," the youth cried out in mounting alarm.

"I have been too lenient with you for too long," Marcus growled as Indus caught Ahern's arms and effortlessly spun the youth around, so that his back was facing Marcus. "That is going to change. You are going to learn the meaning of respect the hard way. In the army if you had spoken to your commanding officer like you just did, then this is the punishment you would receive."

"No," Ahern cried out and his cry ended with a piercing howl of pain, as Marcus wacked the vine staff across his back.

"Are you going to apologise to Lady Claudia?" Marcus cried out, as the room filled with Ahern's anguished cries.

"No," Ahern groaned defiantly.

Another strike from the vine brought a renewed outburst of howls.

"Marcus, stop this at once," a woman's voice suddenly cried from in the doorway to the classroom. It was Claudia. There was a disapproving look on her face. "He is your son and you have the right to do with him what you like," Claudia said sternly, "but you shall not beat him whilst he is here in my school."

Marcus hesitated and then gestured for Indus to release Ahern. As the Batavian bodyguard let the youth go, Ahern shot away into the corner, his face terror-stricken and his body shaking and wracked with pain.

"These youths these days are soft," Marcus snapped as he looked at Claudia. "The army teaches a young man how to behave. That's what he needs. A healthy dose of army punishment. It will make a man out of him."

"Not in my school Marcus, in your own home, but not here," Claudia said stubbornly as she placed her hands on her hips.

Marcus sighed but said nothing as, looking displeased, he lowered the vine staff and slipped it back into his toga.

"You are a monster," Ahern suddenly shrieked, from the corner of the room to which he had retreated. Tears were rolling unashamedly down his cheeks as he rounded on Marcus. "But your time and that of your kind is coming to an end. A storm is coming. A storm that is going to blow you away. Go back to Vectis where you belong and leave me alone. You are not my father. You are a tyrant. I never wish to see you again."

***

The stone fountain in Claudia's small private garden in the school grounds had been fashioned to resemble a leaping fish, but Marcus was not admiring the craftsmanship as he peered grimly at the gurgling jet of water coming from the fish's mouth. At his side Claudia was picking tensely at her fingernails.

"Ahern's project is coming on well," Claudia said, as she looked down at her nails. "His tutor is impressed and has consistently given him a good report. He thinks the steam machine will be ready by the summer. There is talk of a demonstration of the machine being given to the senate. He is making good progress Marcus. He is a bright student with a great future as a scientist."

"I cannot just ignore his recent behaviour," Marcus growled. "Gifted or not he must understand that he cannot treat everyone with disrespect. If he keeps on going down this path, then one day he is going to find himself floating down the

Tiber, with a knife in his back. I am just trying to help him, to protect him."

"I know," Claudia said smoothly, "I know. We all are. He is a lucky young man even if he doesn't appreciate it yet."

Claudia sighed and folded her arms across her chest and turned to look in the direction of her school building.

"I have spent a lot of time with Ahern since you first brought him to my school in Londinium all those years ago," she said wearily. "He's not a bad young man, but I fear that he is being led astray by that new group of friends he made last year. I think they have a bad influence on him. I have noticed his behaviour has deteriorated since meeting them."

"The Republicans," Marcus snorted contemptuously. "Those boys who want to do away with the emperor and restore the republic. Sheer madness. No one supports those ideas, least of all the army."

"It's not their radical ideas that concerns me," Claudia said carefully. "Those youths come from wealthy patrician families, but they are mostly harmless. This talk of a restoration of the republic. It's a phase of life for them and they will grow out of it. But what if someone was manipulating them from behind the scenes. Getting them to do his bidding. Someone who truly does want to start a revolution and overthrow the existing order and is planning to do so. Someone with the guile and ability to do so. What if Ahern and his friends are just pawns in this game? Pawns get sacrificed, Marcus; pawns are expendable."

Marcus's face darkened as he stared at the fountain.

"What is it?" Claudia said as she sensed his sudden unease.

"I am not sure," Marcus replied with a troubled frown. "It's just something Ahern said just now. He said that a storm was coming. A storm that is going to blow me away and he told me to leave Rome." Slowly Marcus shook his head. "It could be a coincidence but those are the same words which that stranger used, to threaten me outside my home a few days ago. It's odd that he would use the same phrases."

Claudia looked surprised and for a long moment she did not reply.

"Are you suggesting that Ahern may be connected to the incident outside your house," Claudia said sharply.

"I don't know," Marcus exclaimed in a sudden weary voice. "The boy refuses to talk to me and you heard what he said. I am a tyrant. He never wants to see me again. But I doubt that he has got the balls to get himself involved in an extortion racket. His heart is with making this steam engine. I think that is all he cares about right now."

"I think you are right," Claudia nodded. "We should let matters quieten down for a while. I shall urge Ahern to focus on his machine."

"If he does get into trouble again," Marcus said, turning to look at Claudia. "I have in my mind the idea to send him away from Rome, back to Londinium or Vectis. Maybe you can impress on him, that if he screws up again, he will not be able to continue working on that machine of his. Maybe that will teach him some sense."

"A good idea Marcus," Claudia said, as a faint smile appeared on her lips. "You always manage to find a suitable solution in the end." She was just about to add something when she was interrupted by a loud cry.

Turning around Marcus was surprised to see Cassius hurrying towards him. But surprise swiftly turned to alarm. His young secretary was sweating and gasping for breath as if he had been running. But that was not what alarmed Marcus. It was the sheer look of horror on Cassius's face.

"Marcus, Marcus," Cassius cried out, as he came towards the fountain. "There is news. Terrible news from Portus. I came to find you as soon as I heard. The Egyptian grain fleet - there was a storm out at sea and the fleet is lost. The whole fleet and its cargo of grain, sunk and scattered by a storm. It's a catastrophe, an utter disaster! We were relying on that grain for our programmes and now it's gone."

Slowly the blood seemed to drain from Marcus's face, as he stared at his secretary in sheer disbelief.

"Great gods," he muttered at last.

Chapter Five - Civilisation is skin deep

Marcus looked worried as he hurried on down the narrow city street. It was around noon and in the noisy and bustling alleys all seemed normal. In the doorways to their simple two room dwellings, shopkeepers were advertising their wares in loud brash voices. The trader's products were displayed along the edge of the tall apartment blocks that hemmed in the street on both sides. Leather shoes, loaves of bread, cuts of meat, dried fish, apples, olives, cheap trinkets, religious ornaments, figs and iron tools. The smell of leather from the shoemaker's workshops, garum rotting fish sauce, the sweet smell of freshly-baked bread and the stink from the sewers beneath their feet, created a heady pong but Marcus no longer noticed it. A couple of wealthy businessmen, easily identifiable by the quality of their clothes and appearance, were concluding a deal on a street corner and in a barbershop, a young man was having his beard trimmed. Glancing up, Marcus caught sight of a group of young children watching the street from the third floor of a crumbling tower block.

Spotting a baker's shop, Marcus swerved across the street, narrowly avoiding being run over by a horse drawn wagon, laden with terracotta amphorae. Ignoring the swearing cart driver, Marcus picked up a loaf of dark, hard bread and turned to the baker who was standing beside his produce.

"How much for the bread?" Marcus growled.

"Twenty loaves of bread for two denarii. Individual loaf costs two asses," the baker replied swiftly, with a well-practised sales patter.

Marcus grunted and replaced the loaf and started out again down the crowded street. At his side Cassius looked ashen.

"The price of grain has not yet risen," Marcus snapped, turning to his secretary as he pushed his way on through the crowd, with the silent Indus following him discreetly. "We still have some time but not much. Once the news of what happens to the Egyptian grain fleet spreads across the city, the price of bread is going to shoot up."

"It's too late to contain the news," Cassius blurted out, as he struggled to stay level with Marcus in the crowd. "In Portus everyone seemed to know. How long do you think we have got?"

Marcus's face darkened but he said nothing as he stubbornly fixed his gaze on the street ahead. Down an alley, a small crowd were listening to a man standing atop of a barrel - one of the many street prophets, who was lecturing them on morality and the dangers of Bacchus, the god of wine. Cassius was right Marcus thought. It was already too late to contain the news of the disaster. Soon the whole city of a million plus people was going to know about the looming grain shortages. This was a bad day. This was a really bad day. A fucking nightmare.

"What is going to happen Sir? What should we do?" Cassius said hastily, his voice quivering and close to panic, as they pushed their way down the street in the direction of the Forum.

Quickly and roughly Marcus caught Cassius by the arm and yanked him into the entrance to a dingy, rubbish-strewn alley.

"What do you think is going to happen?" Marcus hissed as he rounded on the young man. "Once the news spreads that the bulk of the Egyptian grain fleet has been lost at sea, how long do you think it will be before the price of grain starts to rise. How long do you think it will be before people realise that they are not going to get their free handouts of bread? Look around you. Two hundred thousand citizens completely rely on the grain dole to survive. Thirty percent of this city is made up of slaves and most of the remainder of the population spend half their annual salary on food and most of that is on bread. If they can't get their dole or afford to buy bread anymore, then they are going to starve. The whole city is going to starve. So, there is going to be trouble. That's what is going to happen. I am going to the urban prefect's HQ to warn Similis about the situation and to ask him to put the urban and praetorian guard units on alert."

Cassius's eyes widened in growing horror as he stared at Marcus and, as he did his lower lip started to tremble.

"Similis, the urban prefect," Cassius stammered. "He's not here Marcus. He left a few days ago taking all the remaining praetorian and one of the urban cohorts with him. There has been trouble in Umbria. He and his men are a hundred miles away. Didn't you know?"

"What? Oh dear gods," Marcus muttered, as he took a step backwards, his eyes widening in shock as he stared at Cassius. "Similis is not here? Who has he left in charge of the security of the city?"

"That would be the prefect of the night watch," Cassius croaked. "There are three urban cohorts left in the city, plus the vigiles, the night watchmen and firefighters. That's about it."

Marcus raised both his hands to his head and ran his fingers through his hair as some colour shot into his cheeks.

"Three urban cohorts," he exclaimed, "That's fifteen hundred men to police a city of a million. And the urban prefect is a hundred miles away." Marcus groaned. "It will take Similis and his men at least five days march to get back to the city. Oh, this just gets better and better. We're fucked."

For a moment Marcus was unable to speak as he turned to gaze at the people passing by in the street. Then with an effort he forced himself to look at Cassius.

"All right, look," he said, speaking quickly, "most people haven't heard the news yet, so we have some time, but we must move fast. This is out of our hands now. I want you to go home at once Cassius. Hurry. Your duty is to look after Elsa. Look after your wife. Make sure that she and your family are safe. Barricade your home, make sure you have some supplies of food and water and do not venture out onto the streets. We are about to be hit by a shit storm, like nothing we have experienced before. Do I make myself clear?"

"Yes Sir," Cassius nodded hastily.

"Look after Elsa," Marcus snapped fixing his eyes on his young secretary, "nothing else matters now."

"I will," Cassius repeated, "What are you going to do Sir?"

Marcus took a deep breath and turned to look past the stoic Indus and out into the bustling street.

"Poseidon has made his move and we must device a counter move," he growled. "But first I am going home to look after my family. I must protect them."

***

Marcus stood in the garden of his villa on the ridge of the Janiculum hill, gazing out over the huge imperial metropolis that stretched away along the banks of the Tiber. He had discarded his senatorial robes and was clad in a common white tunic, over which he was wearing a long, grey winter-cloak. A sheathed gladius hung from his belt. It was growing dark and on the river, the cargo barges from Portus were moving up and down as normal. A few lights were beginning to twinkle in the great city and for a moment Marcus had the feeling that he was gazing down at a surreal picture, a vast, magnificent painting of something immortal. But the sickening sense of impending disaster that had started to gnaw away at him was growing worse. It was all going wrong for him. From his vantage point he had a splendid view of the temple of Jupiter that crowned the top of the Capitoline hill and, to the south the distinctive shape of the coliseum was unmissable. Kyna had not been at home when he'd come back and after a brief moment's panic, his slaves had informed him that she was out shopping for books in the Argiletum. He'd sent Indus into the city to find her and bring her back at once. Now his wife stood beside him holding a cup of Posca, sour wine mixed with herbs as she too gazed out over the city.

"Maybe it won't be as bad as you fear," Kyna said with a frown. "I mean ships are lost in storms all the time, aren't they? Surely this has happened before. Can't we buy the grain from some other place?"

"Let's hope so," Marcus growled. "But it is better to be prepared than to be caught with your pants down at your ankles. And there are no other significant sources from which we can get the quantities of grain that we need. Egypt is the empire's fucking bread basket. The loss of the grain fleet is a fucking catastrophe. There is no other way that I can put it and I don't know what to do about it. The grain supply to the city of Rome is my responsibility. I am supposed to be in charge."

"Are we safe here?" Kyna said turning to him with a troubled look. "I mean if you think it's going to be as bad as you say, should we not just leave Rome altogether? Get out now whilst we can. Maybe we should go back to Vectis, Marcus. Maybe now is the time to retire to the farm."

"I am not leaving my house," Marcus growled. "I told you once before; I will not be run out of town by anyone. This is my home and I will not abandon it. I am too old to run Kyna. We are going to stay and sit it out and that is the end of this discussion. My decision has been made. I must try and sort out this mess. That's my fucking job and I am going to do it."

At his side Kyna sighed.

"You are a stubborn old man, Marcus," she said with a hint of bitterness; "so stubborn and proud."

"I have closed down the charity," Marcus said, ignoring his wife. "At least temporarily just for a few days until the situation becomes clearer. They will not be accepting any new arrivals and I have brought Numerius and Cato here into the house to provide us with some extra security. They are good men. They know how to handle weapons." Marcus turned to Kyna and fixed her with a determined look. "I also called the slaves together and gave them a choice. They have my permission to leave the city and go to their loved ones or stay with us. They all decided to stay."

Kyna raised her eyebrows in surprise as she looked at her husband.

"You gave the slaves a choice," she remarked.

"Yes," Marcus nodded, as he turned to gaze at the sprawling city across the river. "If it comes to it, I will need to arm them. Slave or not, they have a right to choose how they die and personally I much prefer to know that they are standing beside me out of their own free will. Like I said, they all chose to stay with us. Now there is loyalty for you."

Kyna shook her head in bewilderment and looked away.

"Maybe they just decided to stay because they are afraid of you Marcus," she said. "Have you considered that?"

Marcus did not reply as he gazed out across the city.

"And what about Ahern," Kyna said sharply. "Should we not bring him back here. I mean this is his home. I am his mother."

"Lady Claudia is well protected," Marcus replied. "She knows how to look after herself. She will take care of that insolent whelp."

"I would feel better if he was here with us," Kyna said, nursing her cup. "I take it you had a talk with him today. How did it go? Did he apologise?"

"He will," Marcus growled as his face darkened. "He will when I am done with him. The boy doesn't know how lucky he is."

***

It was just after dawn when a hand shook Marcus awake. It was Indus.

"Sir," the burly Batavian bodyguard muttered in his Batavian language. "I think you had better come and have a look."

Hastily and without saying a word, Marcus rose from his bed where he'd slept fully clothed and grabbed his belt with the sheathed gladius hanging from it. Kyna too quickly slipped out from under the covers as Marcus, still fixing his belt around his waist, followed Indus out onto the terrace of his garden. The Batavian paused at the edge of the terrace and Marcus grunted. In the strengthening light a dozen or so plumes of smoke were rising from within the city of Rome. For a long moment he stared at the columns of smoke in silence.

"Fuck," Marcus swore at last. The plumes of smoke were unusual. They had no right to be where they were.

"All right," Marcus snapped turning to Indus. "Tell the others to keep their eyes open. If there is any sign of trouble you come and tell me right away."

Indus nodded and hastened away into the house and, as he did he passed Kyna coming the other way. She was about to say something when she stopped abruptly, and her face grew pale as she caught sight of the plumes of smoke rising from within the city.

"What do we do Marcus?" she exclaimed in a fearful voice.

"We wait," Marcus snapped. "Go back inside."

It was an hour later when a warning cry from Numerius, who had been posted out on the road that ran alongside the villa, caused Marcus to appear at the front door to his property. Numerius was slowly retreating towards the doorway, one hand on the pommel of his sword and, coming up the hill towards the house was a small party of horsemen. Marcus stepped out into the road and peered at the party as he tried to make out who they were and then, as the horsemen drew closer, one of them hastily raised his hand in greeting.

"Marcus, Marcus is that you," a tense voice cried out.

"Yes, it's me," Marcus called out as he suddenly recognised one of the youthful senators who supported Nigrinus's faction in the senate. "What are you doing here at this hour?"

"Have you not heard," the young senator cried out in alarm, as he trotted up to the house followed by his companions. "The city is on fire. Rioting has broken out everywhere. There is no fucking law and order. It's chaos. They say that the Egyptian grain fleet has been destroyed by a storm. The price of bread has gone through the roof. Most bakers have closed their shops. People think they are going to starve. They are taking matters into their own hands."

"I heard about the loss of the fleet," Marcus snapped as his gaze swept across the small party. Apart from the senator there were four women, one clutching a baby and two teenage boys, their faces pale with fear.

"We're leaving the city, we're heading north," the senator said as he struggled to control his nervous horse. "This is my family. It's no longer safe for us to stay. It's a fucking nightmare. We have had to abandon everything. The mob has taken the law into their own hands. They are settling scores, looting, raping and attacking people in the streets. Anyone who looks like they have some money is being set upon. It doesn't matter who you are. And that's not all," the youthful senator's eyes widened in horror. "My boys here witnessed the murder of the prefect of the night watch. The mob ambushed him and his men in the street. Slaughtered them all. Do not go into Rome, Marcus. The mob has blood on its mind and there is no one who can stop them. It's a fucking disaster. Flee now whilst you still can."

"They killed the prefect of the night watch?" Marcus called out as he took a step forwards. "So, who's in charge of security in Rome?"

"No one. It's fucking anarchy. No one is guarding the gates into the city. The praetorians at the imperial palace have barricaded themselves inside. Paulinus is at the aerarium in the temple of Saturn, trying to protect the gold and silver reserves. He says he is not leaving. He fears the mob will try to loot the state treasury. He's determined to try to protect the state's money. He's a fool," the senator cried. "Flee now, get your family out of here, that's the best advice you are going to get," the senator called out. Then raising his hand in a hasty farewell, he started to gallop away down the road with his family following close behind.

Chapter Six – Duty

"Marcus this is insane. You heard what that senator said. The city is not safe," Kyna cried out, as she tensely fiddled with her fingers, her eyes flashing with alarm.

Marcus stood in the hallway of his villa. He slipped a small bag of coins into his cloak pocket and reached towards an army pugio knife that lay on a cupboard. In a corner Indus was watching him in stoic silence.

"I must do something, Kyna," Marcus growled. "I have a job to do. It's my duty. I am the prefect in charge of the supply of grain to the city. This is my responsibility. I cannot just sit here and do nothing. People are counting on me to sort this out."

"It's not your fault," Kyna said in a voice that quivered on the edge of tears. "It's not your fault that the fleet sank. It's the work of the gods. What can you do about it? What can you do on your own? The mob will kill you. Wait until Similis returns. Let him sort this out. It doesn't have to be you - please husband, I beg you! Don't leave me here alone. Don't do this!"

"I must go," Marcus said, turning to look at her. "Paulinus is holed up in the temple of Saturn. He seems to be the only one who is doing something. He will need help." Then, sliding the pugio into his belt, he crossed the hallway and caught hold of his wife in a surprisingly affectionate embrace.

"I will be all right Kyna," Marcus said in a gentler voice. "You are safe here. Indus, Numerius and Cato will protect the house. This is not the first time that we have faced danger. You need to stay strong."

Then releasing his wife, Marcus turned towards the door and as he did, Indus started to follow him.

"Indus, I need you to stay behind here at the house," Marcus said as he turned to his bodyguard.

But Indus shook his head.

"No, Sir, I am sworn to protect you Sir. I am coming with you," the Batavian said.

"Indus, I need you to stay behind. That's an order," Marcus growled, but Indus again shook his head and stood his ground.

"No, Sir that it not an order I can obey. I have sworn an oath Sir," the bodyguard said in a calm voice, speaking in his native language. "You will have to kill me if you want to stop me from coming with you Sir."

***

There was no sign of any unrest or trouble as Marcus and Indus cautiously made their way down the road towards the bridges across the Tiber. In the distance however, a pall of black smoke hung over the city and there was no one about. The normally busy road was completely deserted. As Marcus approached the pons Cestius, the stone bridge that connected the western bank of the river to Tiber island he halted and edged up against the wall of a house. Behind him, Indus did the same, and slowly unslung the bow that he was carrying from across his back. In the middle of the approach road to the bridge, a wagon and a dead horse lay on its side. The cargo of amphorae which it had been transporting, lay smashed and scattered across the street. Carefully Marcus peered at the bridge. Three men armed with clubs and knifes were standing over something that was lying in the street. From his vantage point Marcus could however not see what it was they were looking at.

"Shall I shoot them Sir," Indus said in his native Batavian language, as he notched an arrow and raised his bow.

Marcus hesitated as he peered at the men. It was impossible to know whether they were looters or just ordinary citizens, out inspecting the damage.

"No," he said at last as he shifted his gaze towards the temple of Aesculapius on Tiber island, "but keep that bow handy. Let's go."

Boldly Marcus left the cover of the wall and started out towards the bridge. As he passed the dead horse and overturned cart, he pulled his gladius from its sheath. The cargo of red wine had stained the paving stones and, as Marcus hurried onwards, his boots crunched over the shards of broken pottery. Following closely behind him, Indus kept his bow trained on the three men standing on the bridge. The men had not moved but, as Marcus approached, they turned to face him gripping their weapons. Keeping his eyes on them, Marcus began to move across the bridge keeping to the opposite side of the walkway and, as he drew closer, he saw that the men were standing over the lifeless body of a woman. Silently he and Indus moved on past and as they did, the men remained where they were and both parties stared at each other in silence. Then Marcus was past them and approaching the boat shaped Tiber island.

The temple doors to the shrine of healers were firmly shut and there was no sign of life apart from the noise of a barking dog. But people would be watching, Marcus thought, as he hurried along towards the pons Fabricius, the bridge that connected the island to the eastern bank of the Tiber. The priests were doing what everyone else seemed to be doing. They had barricaded themselves into the temple and were preparing to sit out the rioting and lawlessness. Ahead of him, the pons Fabricius was completely deserted. It was an eerie unnatural sight for this was one of the busiest bridges in Rome and Marcus had never seen it without traffic.

As he began to hurry across the bridge, from the corner of his eye Marcus caught sight of a corpse floating in the river. The current was gently carrying the body downstream. A sudden high-pitched woman's scream drew his attention towards a shop on the banks of the river, close to the bridge. The screaming was coming from inside the building and, as he and Indus hurried across the bridge, Marcus caught sight of the corpse of a man lying in a growing pool of blood in the doorway of the shop. The man seemed to have been trying to defend his property. From inside the building men's loud, harsh voices could be heard. It was followed by a crash and the sound of something smashing onto the ground. Abruptly the woman's screaming ceased.

Grimly Marcus moved on with Indus following close behind, his arrow still notched to his bow. Up head an empty ox-drawn wagon stood abandoned in the street. The ox was still tethered to the cart, standing dumbly in the middle of the street but there was no sign of the wagon's owner. Stealthily, at a half-run, Marcus moved on past the wagon and in the direction of the city gates and, as he did he caught the distinctive smell of smoke. It was growing stronger. As the gates leading into Rome hove into view he paused and crouched against a wall. The senator had been right. The gates were wide open, abandoned and there was no sign of the usual squad of urban guards, who were supposed to be on guard duty. Instead, all he could see was the body of a smartly dressed man lying splayed out in the street. The man's white toga was soiled, and his arms were stretched out. From somewhere out of sight another dog was barking, but apart from the solitary corpse, the street looked completely deserted.

"We need to get to the temple of Saturn," Marcus said, as he quickly turned to look at Indus. "That's where Paulinus is making a stand. I don't know what it's going to be like beyond the walls, but we don't stop for anything or anyone. We keep moving, understood."

Indus nodded silently, his calm and stoic eyes already examining the terrain ahead.

"All right, let's go," Marcus said, as he started forwards with his sword in his hand. Ignoring the corpse, Marcus hurried on through the gates and into the city of Rome. As he passed through the formidable and five-hundred-year old Servian walls, he nearly tripped over an abandoned army shield. Close by, a woman was wailing in a loud, hysterical voice. She was on her knees, hunched over the body of a man who was lying in the street outside a ransacked shop. Grimly Marcus pushed on towards the cattle market with Indus, clutching his bow, close behind. As the two of them moved forwards the smell of smoke grew stronger. Then, as they rounded a corner into the Forum Boarium, the ancient cattle market, Marcus grunted as he caught sight of a building that was on fire, sending a plume of smoke billowing into the air. The roar and crackle of the flames filled the street with noise. A group of desperate people were trying to extinguish the blaze with buckets of water.

Moving hastily past the blaze, Marcus headed towards the Forum. Ahead he could see the temple of Jupiter, serenely sitting on the summit of the Capitoline hill. Glancing to his right the Palatine hill, home to the imperial palace and the most prestigious of Rome's neighbourhoods, showed no signs of life. There was no one about. The usually bustling streets of Rome were completely deserted. It was as if the whole city seemed to have shut themselves in behind their doors and suddenly he was reminded of the riot he'd caused in the Subura, all those years ago, when he'd been on the run for his life from Cunitius and his men.

As he approached the entrance to the Forum, Marcus suddenly noticed movement to his right. Coming towards him down a narrow side street, was a group of twenty or so armed men. Instinctively he shot through the doorway of a looted and abandoned shop followed closely by Indus. In the front room, with his back pressed against the wall, Marcus turned and ventured a quick peek into the street. The gang seemed not to have noticed him and were moving on down the street. They were armed with clubs, knives, swords and spears and amongst them he noticed were women. They looked savage and in a mood for violence.

A little noise behind him made Marcus whirl round, his sword ready to strike. Amongst the debris and broken household goods that lay scattered across the floor was a table that had been thrown onto its side. As he stared at the table, two small children's faces appeared from behind it, staring back at him, rigid with terror. For a moment Marcus was unable to move as he stared at the children. Then slowly he raised his finger to his mouth in a gesture that they should remain quiet.

"The mob's gone Sir," Indus whispered as he took a quick peek out into the street.

Marcus wrenched his eyes away from the terrified children. The coast seemed clear. Swiftly he emerged from the looted shop and started out down the street at a half run with Indus close behind. Ahead, the Forum seemed to be half-shrouded in smoke and somewhere nearby he could hear shouting. Keeping close to the edge of the street, Marcus moved forwards. Up ahead he suddenly caught sight of a dead man lying in the street. The man was clad in a fine toga, and as he drew closer Marcus recognised the purple stripes on the clothing. A senator. Close by was another corpse - a slave perhaps, judging from his clothing. Both had had their throats cut. In the middle of the street, lying on its side was a rudely abandoned litter with the body of a high-born woman lying half in and half outside it. It looked like she had been raped before her throat too, had been cut. A few people were scavenging amongst the corpses, pulling the rings from fingers and searching for valuable items.

One of the scavengers, catching sight of Marcus and Indus, raised a cry and without warning came at Marcus wielding a knife. But before he'd gone more than a few yards an arrow thudded into his chest and the man crashed sideways onto the paving stones.

"Get out of here, scum," Marcus roared as he menacingly lifted his sword in the air. The few remaining scavengers did not seem to have the stomach for a fight and fled down an alley, their boots pounding the pavement.

Hastily Marcus crossed the street and rolled over the senator's corpse, but he did not recognise the dead man. Gesturing to Indus he turned and headed into the Forum. The temple of Saturn was close now. He could see its great columns and sharply slanting roof standing at the base of the Capitoline hill. The building looked solid, a haven in the midst of bloody chaos. In the Forum and amongst the magnificent government buildings there was a dreadful silence. In the nearby deserted market places, nearly all the street stalls had been smashed and looted and a few of them were on fire, belching out plumes of smoke. Amongst the debris and corpses strewn across the ground, a few people were picking through the ruins, hunting for valuables and food. They paid Marcus and Indus no attention as the two of them raced towards the huge doors into the temple of Saturn.

"Friends, we're friends. I must speak to Paulinus," Marcus cried out in a loud voice as a few armed temple guards appeared at the top of the broad steps, leading to the temple entrance. The guards were armed with shields and spears and they looked very nervous. They said nothing, nor did they do anything as Marcus quickly slid his sword back into its sheath and showed them the palms of his hands.

"I must speak to Paulinus," he cried out again, as the guards showed no sign of allowing him into the temple. "I am his friend. Tell him that my name is Marcus. I am the prefect in charge of the grain supply. He knows me. Do it."

"Marcus, Marcus," a voice suddenly cried out and a few moments later a figure suddenly came thrusting through the ranks of the temple guards. It was Paulinus. Catching sight of him, the finance minister slowly shook his head, as a relieved look appeared on his face.

"I heard you were here," Marcus gasped as he strode up the steps and quickly embraced his colleague and friend. "I heard you were trying to protect the gold and silver reserves. Who is in charge in the city? Who is leading the response to the rioting?"

Paulinus looked grim.

"I think it's just us," he said.

Chapter Seven - Fight-back

"We need to restore order," Marcus insisted as he quickly followed Paulinus into the temple of Saturn. Dominating the inner sanctum, the huge, veiled image of Saturn, its legs covered with bands of wool, stood holding a gigantic scythe as it gazed serenely into space. A cluster of treasury officials had gathered around the base of the statue. They looked frightened and unsure of what to do. Further back in the gloomy, torch-lit recesses of the building, groups of civilians, including children, were huddled together sitting on the floor. Refugees from the rioting. Some of the children were crying whilst the adults were gazing at Paulinus in desperate hope.

"Yes, yes," Paulinus nodded hastily, as behind him the few nervous temple guards retreated to the doorway with its huge doors, which were still open.

Paulinus paused and then gave Marcus a cold, determined look. "The temple must not fall," he said sharply. "The public treasury is kept here. We have tons of gold and silver in our vaults and I have only twenty guards. And then there are all these people who have sought shelter here. I must protect the treasury. I must protect these people, Marcus. If the state treasury is looted it will be a crime against the millions who have faithfully paid their taxes." Suddenly Paulinus looked angry. "The mob may be moving around randomly in the streets but how long do you think it will be before they realise that this temple, the state treasury, is unprotected. How long do you think it will be before they realise that they can help themselves to all that gold and silver? It must not happen Marcus. It will not happen, not on my watch."

Marcus grunted, as he turned to look at the solid stone walls of the temple. For a long moment he said nothing as he examined his surroundings.

"You may be able to hold out for a day or two," Marcus said at last, keeping his voice deliberately low, "but no more than that; not against a determined assault; not with just twenty men. Close your doors and barricade them. Your walls are solid stone but then, after a while the mob will figure out that if they set fire to your roof they will be able to smoke and burn you out. Retreat to the vaults and the lack of water will eventually force you to surrender." Marcus looked grim as he stared at his friend. "One or two days," Marcus nodded. "That's all you have got. We can't hold this place against a determined assault. We have to think of something else."

"What then?" Paulinus snapped in an irritable voice. "What can we do?"

Marcus took a deep breath and for a moment he was silent.

"What do you know about what is happening out there?" he said.

Paulinus looked up at the huge image of Saturn and, as he did, he seemed to calm down a little.

"I know this," Rome's finance minister replied with a sigh. "The senate seem to have either fled the city or are holed up in their homes. They are incapable of action." Calmly Paulinus reached out to steady one of the young treasury clerks whose hand was trembling uncontrollably. "Law and order have completely broken down. Similis and the bulk of our security forces are a hundred miles away and the prefect of the night watch is dead, slain in the streets. The mob is in control of the whole city. Packs of them are roaming the streets at will, looting, murdering, raping. It seems that people are using this opportunity to settle personal scores and grievances and to enrich themselves. No one is stopping them. And it's all because of news that the Egyptian grain fleet has been destroyed by a storm. Is that true Marcus? Are these rumours really true?"

"I think so," Marcus muttered. "The last news that I received from Portus was that some of the survivors of the storm have managed to make it into the harbour. They seem to confirm the news."

"Shit," Paulinus swore, as he turned his eyes to the ground.

"What about the three urban cohorts that remain in the city?" Marcus said. "Where are they? Why are they not out on the streets trying to restore order?"

"I don't know," Paulinus said, raising his hands in exasperation.

"The fourth cohort is being besieged in their barracks by the mob," a woman said suddenly. Marcus grunted in surprise as, from the gloom Lady Claudia suddenly appeared. She looked calm and dignified as she came towards him, followed closely by a troop of frightened looking children and, amongst them Marcus caught sight of Ahern. The seventeen-year old youth looked out of place amongst the rest of Claudia's school children who were much younger than himself. Catching sight of Marcus, Ahern blushed with sudden embarrassment.

"The mob believe there are food supplies within the barracks," Claudia continued, as she glanced quickly at Paulinus. "They are demanding that the food is handed over to them, but the guards have no food. It's a standoff. No one is getting in or out of those barracks. That's the last I heard. As for the first and second cohorts," Claudia sighed, "I think they are still in the praetorian barracks, Castra Praetoria, on the edge of the city near the Colline gate. I don't know what they are doing. Similis allowed them to move in after most of the praetorian cohorts were sent east to join Trajan in Syria."

"Sir," an urgent sounding voice suddenly called out and a moment later one of the temple guards came hastening towards Paulinus. "Sir, looks like the mob are moving into the

Forum. There are more and more of them out there. Shall I close the doors Sir?"

"Only at the last moment," Paulinus snapped. "Only at the last moment damn it. There may still be people out there who need refuge."

"But Sir, the mob...," the guard stammered.

"Do as I say," Paulinus said irritably, and without further protest the guard turned and hastened back to his post.

"All right," Marcus said in a low and urgent voice as he glanced from Paulinus to Claudia. "We have to act. Our only hope of restoring order lies with those urban cohorts. They are the only trained, disciplined and equipped force that can handle this situation. Someone needs to get to the Castra Praetoria and lead those thousand soldiers back here to the Forum. Once here," Marcus said, as his eyes gleamed in the light from the oil lamps, "we secure the Forum and the government buildings. Then if all goes well, tomorrow at dawn we start to clear the city, one district at a time until order is fully restored. The mob may have the numbers, but they are not a disciplined or organised force. We can handle them if we isolate them into small groups. Solid training and discipline always beat numbers."

Paulinus nodded as he listened to the plan.

"We should proclaim a curfew," Claudia snapped. "A city-wide curfew. Anyone caught out on the streets will face summary execution. I know its harsh, but these are extraordinary times."

"Agreed," Paulinus snapped, "and issue a call for all loyal and able citizens to come to defend the temple of Saturn. For the moment, the treasury will have to be our command post. We will lead the fightback from here."

"That's going to be easier said than done," Marcus growled. "How are you going to get those messages out whilst under siege?"

"Leave that to me," Paulinus said with a glint of sudden hope in his eyes.

"Sir, the mob, they are starting to get close Sir," one of the guards suddenly cried out from near to the temple entrance.

"All right, all right," Marcus said hastily, as his two companions turned to look at him. "Then I suppose the only thing left to decide is on who will go to the Castra Praetoria. It can't be just anyone. The urban cohort commanders will only listen to someone in authority, so I will go." Marcus paused. "As a senator and prefect of the grain supply this mess is my responsibility. Hold the temple Paulinus," Marcus said, reaching out to lay a hand on the finance minister's shoulder. "I will be back with those soldiers. And one more thing Claudia," Marcus said as he turned, raised his finger and pointed at Ahern. "I am taking him with me."

***

Marcus shot out through the temple doors and didn't stop running until he'd reached the entrance to the Forum of Augustus. As he slowed to a walk, Indus and Ahern did the same. To his right the Senate house, the meeting place of the senate, stood abandoned and forlorn, its door closed and out in the Forum the mob seemed to be growing larger and larger. But no one paid them any attention, as he and his two companions slipped away. Snatching a glance over his shoulder, Marcus was just in time to see the great doors to the temple of Saturn slamming shut. Then he was through the entrance and into the large, enclosed and rectangular space of the Forum of Augustus. Hurrying into the shade of the colonnaded and covered walkway to his right, Marcus paused behind one of the massive columns. In the market place there was no one about, but he could see that nearly all the shops and stores that occupied both sides of the Forum had been looted and ransacked. Debris of all kinds lay scattered across the paving stones. In the middle of the Forum and open to the sky, more than a hundred marble and bronze busts of famous Romans stood on plinths, with the inscriptions of the men's deeds and achievements recorded on them. And right in the middle of the market place, as if to remind everyone of who had built this Forum and who it was who was honouring Rome's illustrious ancestors, was a statue of Augustus, the first emperor, clad in full military outfit. But Marcus was not looking at the busts. Hastily he turned his eyes towards the magnificent temple of Mars Ultor, Mars the Avenger that dominated the Forum. There was no one about. The coast seemed clear. The doors to the fine-looking colonnaded temple were closed and the solitary body of a man lay sprawled across the stone steps, that led up to the entrance. The priests of Mars would have been the first to close their doors for they had a special and unique responsibility. For in their care, inside their temple, were kept the precious Eagles, the legionary standards, from the disgraced legions that had been lost under Crassus and Varus at Carrhae and the Teutoburger Forest and which had all been recovered some years later.

Turning sharply to look at Ahern, who was crouching behind him, Marcus pulled his army pugio knife from his belt and pressed it into Ahern's hand.

"Follow me and stay close," Marcus hissed. "Use the knife to kill if you have to. Today you have permission to kill. Understood boy."

Ahern looked utterly terrified as he silently stared at the knife in his hand. Dumbly he nodded, not daring to look Marcus in the eye.

"We will get out over there," Marcus said, quickly turning to gesture down the covered walkway towards the triumphal arch of Germanicus to the right of the temple. "Beyond is an alley that will lead to the Subura. Once we get to the cross roads we will turn into Long street, Vicus Longinus. Longinus will take us to the Colline gate. From there the praetorian barracks are not far." Marcus paused as he glared at his companions. "Stay close to me. We don't pause for anything and try not to attract attention. With a bit of luck, the mob will not notice us. All right, let's go."

Rising to his feet, Marcus started down the covered walkway, his boots crunching over the shattered pottery shards and broken glass. As they passed on through the triumphal arch, Marcus turned to glance back at Ahern. The boy's face was as white as a sheet and the hand clutching his knife was shaking with fear.

As the three of them reached the end of the alley, Marcus paused. The cross roads up ahead looked deserted. A wagon lay on its side - its content of wood and building materials ransacked and strewn across the street. From somewhere out of sight a dog was barking. Carefully Marcus glanced up at the tall, cheap-looking apartment blocks that were packed close together. The Subura was a poor, densely populated neighbourhood filled with seedy bars, brothels and cheap accommodation. From behind a closed window shutter he could hear the muffled screams of a baby. Turning his attention back to the street, he saw that every shop was either closed or had been trashed and looted.

With a grunt Marcus left the cover of the alley and started out down the street towards the overturned wagon, keeping close to the edge of the street with Ahern and Indus followed closely behind him. He'd just made it to the intersection with the Vicus Longinus when behind him, Ahern tripped over a piece of discarded wood and with a startled cry went tumbling to the ground. And as he did, a shower of coins went flying from his pocket and clattered onto the paving stones. As the youth hastily scrambled to his feet a man suddenly poked his face out of the doorway to a looted store and stared at Ahern.

"Heh you," the man cried, pointing at Ahern. "What you got there?"

Ahern stood rooted to the ground staring at the man with growing horror, completely unable to move or respond. Slowly the man left the doorway and came towards him carrying an axe.

"I said what have you got there," the man growled. Then he stopped as he caught sight of the gleaming coins lying scattered across the paving stones. "Well what have we here," the man cried out, as a crooked grin suddenly appeared on his face. "Got anymore treasure like this?"

Ahern's lower lip was quivering uncontrollably, and he looked like he was about to break down completely. Then before anyone could react or say anything, Marcus came striding past Ahern and calmly thrust his sword straight through the man's neck. A spurt of blood fountained through the air as the man dropped his axe and collapsed, hitting the ground with a thud.

"Run," Marcus roared as he turned to his two companions.

Moments later an enraged cry rose from further down the street and a mob of ten or twenty armed men and women appeared, and came charging towards Marcus. Grabbing Ahern, Marcus yanked him out of his petrified state and the three of them shot away down the street with the mob in pursuit.

In the narrow street there was no place to hide and the tall tower blocks hemmed them in on both sides. Dimly Marcus was aware that Ahern had found his voice and was screaming in pure terror, as he legged it down the deserted street. Fear seemed to give the boy added strength and stamina. But they weren't going to outrun the mob behind them. Spotting an open doorway into a tall, crumbling tenement block, Marcus yelled a warning at Indus and, swerving across the street, he stormed into the dark entrance of the building. Nearly tripping over a lifeless body, Marcus leapt into the stairwell and charged up the stairs to the first floor. Ahern was still screaming in pure terror as he and Indus followed Marcus up the narrow stairs. Bursting onto a small landing, Marcus saw that all the doors to the rooms were closed. Without bothering to check them, he twisted and started on up the stairs to the second floor. Below him he could hear feet pounding on the stairs. As he reached the fifth floor and the top of the building, Marcus turned grimly to face the stairwell as Ahern, followed by Indus rushed passed him onto the small landing.

"Find a way out of here," Marcus roared at Indus. Then, as the first of their pursuers came storming up the stairs, Marcus lunged forwards with his sword, stabbing the first man in his head and kicking his dying opponent back down the stairwell. The crash of the corpse tumbling backwards down the stairs was met with a howl of rage, but on the stairs below him no new faces appeared.

Grimly Marcus glared down the narrow twisting staircase, as behind him he heard a sudden splintering crash. Snatching a glance over his shoulder, he saw that Indus had managed to kick down a door and enter one of the apartment rooms as he did the Batavian cried out in his native language; "Marcus, window - out onto the roof."

"Get Ahern out onto the roof. Then yourself. I will follow," Marcus roared in the Batavian language.

Below him he could hear men swearing and shouting. It would not be long before they worked up the courage to storm the stairs again.

Behind him Ahern's screaming ended abruptly, as if someone had slapped him hard across the face. Marcus gritted his teeth as he waited. The seconds ticked on by and below him the furious outraged voices were growing louder and bolder. He couldn't wait much longer.

"Marcus, come, we're outside," Indus roared suddenly.

Wrenching himself away from the stairwell, Marcus raced across the landing, passed the broken door and into the apartment. The single room was deserted and smelt of stale piss. Catching sight of the window, he flung himself at it, banging his knee painfully on the window ledge. Groaning and grunting, he forced himself through the opening and out onto the steeply-sloping, tiled roof. For a moment he clung to the tiles unable to move. Far below him the ground seemed to hover forwards and backwards. Then with savage determination, Marcus forced himself on all fours to clamber up to the top of the sloping roof where Indus and Ahern were lying desperately clinging to the red-roof tiles. Ahead of them the roof of the building seemed to connect with the neighbouring apartment block.

"Stick to the top of the roof," Marcus hissed, gesturing for Indus to start leading the way. "Follow it as far as it goes."

Below him, a head suddenly poked itself out of the window, first looking down towards the ground and then twisting to look up at them. With a snarl of rage Marcus yanked a roof tile free and flung it at the man's head - but missed.

"Start moving," Marcus roared at Indus.

Chapter Eight – Leadership

Stiffly and awkwardly Marcus clambered down the wooden scaffolding, landing on the ground with a relieved thud. His shoulder and arm muscles ached and his knee was badly bruised from when he'd struck the windowsill. Startled, Marcus realised that he was exhausted. There had been a time when the desperate flight across the roof tops would have been no problem, but now he could feel the toll it had taken on his body. If they would have to do that again he wasn't sure he would be able to do it. Indus and Ahern were pressed up against a door, hiding inside the cover of a vestibule. Indus had strung his bow, but down the stinking alley nothing moved. Quickly Marcus glanced up at the roof of the building from which they'd just come, but there was no sign of pursuit. The mob must have given up the chase. Maybe they had decided they had better things to do.

"Are you all right Sir?" Indus whispered loudly as he glanced over at him.

Marcus nodded as he sought to steady his breathing. In the vestibule Ahern was still clutching his knife and was peering down the alley.

"The money in your pocket," Marcus hissed at last, as he stared at the youth; "what the hell were you thinking? You nearly got us killed."

"I thought it may be useful," Ahern snapped back. "I thought maybe I could bribe my way out of trouble. I am sorry. It was an unfortunate accident."

Marcus grunted. He couldn't tell the youth off. Regarding the money - he'd had the same idea before leaving his home on the Janiculum.

"See to it that you do not have any more accidents," Marcus snapped, as he shifted his attention to the alley.

He was just about to start out down the alley, when a high-pitched scream rent the peace. Marcus stopped in mid-movement. The scream came again. It sounded like a woman and it was coming from further down the narrow twisting passageway. Gesturing for his companions to follow him, Marcus drew his sword and started out towards the noise. As he drew closer the woman screamed again and this time Marcus heard men's voices cursing. Pausing at an intersection with another alley, Marcus snuck a quick peek around the corner. In the doorway of a ransacked shoemakers, three men were in the process of raping a young woman. Pressing his back up against the passage wall Marcus swore. It was none of his business. He had a job to do. He should pass on by. This was not his problem. Then he swore again. What if that young woman had been Elsa?

"Three men. They are raping a woman," Marcus snapped, glancing sideways at Indus who was clutching his bow.

Then without another word, Marcus went around the edge of the wall and down the alley straight towards the rapists. Catching sight of him, one of the men cried out in warning. A split second later an arrow buried itself into the man's chest sending him staggering backwards and onto the ground. The second man was still in the process of pulling up his undergarments and gave a startled shout, as he saw Marcus bearing down on him. Dropping his pants, he clumsily lunged at Marcus with a knife. Evading the lunge, Marcus calmly buried his sword into his opponent's chest and flung him backwards against the wall. In the doorway the half-naked woman was screaming as she wrestled with another man, who was still lying on top of her. But before Marcus could react, Ahern jumped forwards and clumsily rammed his knife into the man's neck. With a viciousness and a frenzy that took Marcus by surprise, Ahern stabbed the man again and again until he was no longer moving. On the ground the woman was still screaming, her face, clothes and arms covered and smothered in the man's blood. Hastily Marcus knelt and slammed his hand over the woman's mouth, muffling her screaming.

"Be quiet for fucks sake. We're not going to hurt you lady," Marcus hissed, staring down at her. "But you must be quiet. Be quiet. Don't draw attention. There may be more of these arseholes about."

The woman was staring up at him with large, terrified eyes. Slowly Marcus released his hand from over her mouth and straightened up. On the ground the woman remained silent, as she gazed up at him. Then abruptly her expression changed and scrambling to her feet, she snatched up one of her attacker's knives and furiously started to hack away at the corpse. Marcus stepped back and watched the woman silently and viciously mutilate her attackers. At his side, Ahern lent backwards against the alley wall. He was breathing heavily and quickly, his eyes wide open as he gazed at the corpses lying splayed out across the blood-stained paving stones.

"We can't stay here Sir," Indus called out softly, as he pointed his bow down the alley. "We need to keep moving. The Colline gate is not far. The quickest way is to re-join the Vicus Longinus. It's that way."

On the ground the young woman cried out and gave one of the mutilated corpses a final furious kick. Then she dropped her knife and staggered backwards against the narrow alley wall and tried to wipe some of the blood from her face.

"The Colline gate," she gasped. "There is a gang. They have closed the gates. They are controlling who comes in and out of the gate. They are forcing people to pay if they want to leave the city. You won't get out through the Colline."

"How many of them are there?" Marcus asked.

Slowly the woman shook her head and closed her eyes. Her hand was trembling as she tried to scrape the blood from her face.

"I don't know. Many, many," she replied in a croaky voice. "And avoid the Vicus Longinus. There are groups of looters about. You won't get far without being spotted."

Marcus nodded and was just about to say something, when Ahern beat him to it.

"I can get us to the Colline gate without using the Longinus," the youth said quickly. "We can use the back-street alleys. I know the way."

***

Marcus leaned against the wall beside the window of the third-floor apartment and cautiously peered out into the street below. The Colline gate, set into the massive, solid, thirty-feet high Servian city walls, was indeed closed. Beyond the walls, Rome's suburbs stretched away northwards along the via Salaria and the via Nomentana. A plume of smoke was rising upwards into the sky. Just to the east and outside the old city, Marcus could see the Castra Praetoria, the huge rectangular fortress of the praetorian guard. Carefully his gaze swept along the battlements but atop the wall there was no one about, nor was there any sign of the squad of urban guards who should have been on duty. Down below however, in front of the city gates, a group of armed men and women were hanging about around a barrel of wine, which they'd dragged out into the street. They were laughing as they dipped their cups into the barrel. Turning his attention to the streets leading up to the gates, Marcus could see that they were deserted. Leaning backwards Marcus nodded at Indus, who was watching him closely. In response the burly Batavian stepped forwards, raised his bow, took careful aim and released. The arrow thudded straight into a man's chest. A shocked cry rose from the street below, as Indus swiftly moved back out of sight, notched another arrow to his bow, then stepped forwards, took aim and released again. In the streets outside a cacophony of outraged and alarmed shouts broke out, as once more Indus hastily slipped away from the window and into cover.

"Move," Marcus snapped as he hastened out of the doorway of the room and up the stairs to the fourth floor. Behind him, Ahern and Indus followed. On the top floor of the crumbling apartment block, someone had broken through the poorly constructed wall that separated the block from the neighbouring tower. Marcus ducked as he scrambled through the jagged hole of broken masonry and leapt across the small gap, separating the two tower blocks. Pausing beside the window of the abandoned room, Marcus risked a peek down at the gates from his new vantage point. The gang of armed men and women were in cover, or what they thought was cover - pressed up against the gatehouse. They were shouting at each other as they tried to spot the archer, who had felled two of their number. The bodies of their comrades lay moaning and writhing on the ground where they'd fallen. No one had bothered to drag them into the cover.

"Shoot them," Marcus hissed. Quickly and silently Indus took a quick peek out of the window. Then, raising his bow with a smooth professional movement, he took careful aim and released, before slipping back into cover. Outside beside the gates he was rewarded by a shriek.

"One, two, three, four," the Batavian counted in his native language. Then notching another arrow, he raised his bow, turned to the window, took aim and released again before swiftly moving away from the window.

"Move," Marcus snapped, as he turned towards the doorway that led out of the room. Hastily and as silently as possible Marcus went down the stairs of the tall, tower block until he reached the first floor. Most of the doors to the rooms on the floor were closed and barricaded from the inside. On the small landing, Marcus paused to listen. In the street outside, he could hear panicked yelling. Taking a peek down the stairwell, Marcus saw that someone had tried to form a barricade, for the narrow entrance leading up the stairs had been filled with broken chairs, a table and debris of all kinds. No one would be coming up that way without them hearing it. Turning away from the stairwell, Marcus launched himself at one of the doors hitting it with his shoulder and nearly taking the door off its hinges. As he barged into the room, a woman squealed in fright and a man held up his hand in a pitiful gesture. The two adults were nervously backing away into a corner of the single-room apartment desperately trying to protect a couple of young children.

Marcus raised his finger to his mouth in a gesture for the family to be silent, as he staggered painfully towards the window. A moment later he was joined by Indus and Ahern. Without having to be told what to do, Indus snatched a hasty glance out of the window at the gateway that was just across the street from the building. The position offered a perfect view of the remaining gang members. Some of the gang were still pressed up against the gatehouse, yelling at each other as they frantically searched the windows of the tall tower blocks. They had still not spotted the threat. On the ground in front of the gates, four of their number lay on the ground with Indus's arrows sticking out of them.

"Shoot them," Marcus hissed.

Without hesitating Indus notched an arrow, raised his bow, stepped forwards, took aim and released. The distance was short and unobstructed. As his arrow struck a woman in the shoulder, she screamed and slithered to the ground. But this time Indus didn't move away from the window and, notching another arrow he swiftly shot another woman. As a seventh person tumbled to the ground, the remaining gang seemed to have had enough and in panic they scattered, fleeing pell-mell down the streets and leaving the gates unguarded.

"Let's go. Hurry. They may be back," Marcus grimaced, as he quickly turned to the door, rubbing his shoulder.

***

The gates into the formidable looking fortress were open but, blocking Marcus's way into the huge praetorian barracks was a large group of urban guards and officers, clad in legionary armour and holding spears and shields. The riot police were staring at him suspiciously.

"Where is the guard commander? Where the fuck are your prefects?" Marcus cried out in an annoyed voice. "I need to speak to them at once."

Amongst the heavily-armed riot troops no one answered back. Then at last a man pushed his way through the crowd towards Marcus. He was clad in a fine horse-hair plumed helmet and cuirassed armour, over which he was wearing a red cloak. The officer looked around fifty. He examined Marcus carefully.

"I am the commander of the First Cohort," the officer said. "Who are you?"

"I am the prefect in charge of the grain supply to the city of Rome," Marcus replied quickly. "And I have just come from the temple of Saturn. Why are your men not trying to restore order? The whole city is rioting. Haven't you heard."

For a moment the officer did not reply as he looked past Marcus and in the direction of the city walls. Then calmly he turned his attention back to Marcus.

"So, this mess is your fault, prefect," the officer replied coldly.

"Yes," Marcus snarled, giving the policeman a dirty look. "But you haven't answered my fucking question. Why are your men not out there trying to stop the rioting and looting? I have a plan to regain control of the city, but I need your help. So, for the last time, why are you sitting here on your arses?"

"I have not received any orders to leave the barracks," the officer snapped back. "There is a chain of command and I haven't received the proper notification. That's why we are still here."

Marcus stared at the officer in silence, struggling to control his temper. The man was hiding behind protocol. He was behaving like a coward. This however was not the time to lose it.

"Similis is five days march from Rome and the prefect of the night watch has been murdered," Marcus growled, fixing his eyes on the officer. "We don't have time to wait for the urban prefect to return. So, I am ordering you and your men out of your barracks. We must regain control of the city and we must do it now. For fucks sake, people are being murdered and raped a stone's throw from the senate house. There are women and children besieged inside the temple of Saturn. If the mob brakes into the temple those people are all going to die. Please, the city needs its guard. We need you right now."

"I need official approval," the officer retorted. "You may be who you say you are, but I still need to receive authorisation from the urban prefect or his deputy before I can order my men to leave these barracks. There are rules, Sir."

"Damn you," Marcus hissed. "Damn your rules." Glancing upwards he saw that the battlements of the barracks walls were lined with armed guardsmen. The anxious looking men were gazing down at him and his two companions in silence. This was sheer cowardice. Everyone knew what was going on.

"Damn you, Sir," Marcus cried out suddenly in a louder voice, as he raised his hand and pointed a finger at the guard commander. "I am going back into the city right now and I am going to put an end to this madness. And if you refuse to come with me. Well then, I shall go on alone without you with just my two companions here. Rome shall remember this day; this day of shame and infamy; this day when the city's urban cohorts allowed its elected magistrate to go to his death, whilst they hid away in their barracks and did nothing. Shame on all of you," Marcus roared. "May the gods despise you to the end of your days."

***

Marcus strode along down the narrow, city street, his expression grim and hard. His hand rested on the pommel of his sheathed sword and, at his side, Ahern and Indus were gazing at the looted shops. Up ahead, a company of heavily armed guardsmen were marching down the street, eight abreast. The men were crouching behind their large legionary shields with their spears lowered before them. The riot police had formed an impenetrable, moving barrier, an armoured hedgehog, which was methodically driving every living creature before it and down the street towards the Forum and city centre. The rhythmic tramp of the riot police's hobnailed boots on the paving stones was a welcome sound Marcus thought, welcome to all those countless people who were hiding from the lawlessness, hoping for it to end. Behind him the long column of fifteen hundred guardsmen came on in disciplined silence, their weapons, shields and armour glinting in the sunlight. The shame of being branded as cowards had been too much for the guardsmen, and after a brief delay they, led by their officers, had agreed to come with Marcus. The first place he'd taken them to had been the barracks of their comrades in the fourth cohort. The mob had been besieging the barracks, but upon catching sight of the 1st and 2nd cohorts marching to their comrades' relief, the mob had swiftly faded away without putting up a fight. And now the combined force was on their way to the Forum to relieve Paulinus and Lady Claudia, holed up in the temple of Saturn. Stoically Marcus peered down the street. Plumes of smoke still hung over the city and they had encountered sporadic resistance from armed gangs, but it was impossible to know what was happening in the Forum. Had the mob already succeeded in breaking into the temple? He tried not to think about it. At least he had managed to get things moving in the right direction. It was a start. But he needed to do more. He needed to plan. He had to come up with solutions to the food shortages and fast. He had to reassure the city that all was going to be well. The really hard work was just beginning he realised. He was contemplating the decisions that still needed to be taken, when a roof tile came hurtling down and smashed into the street, narrowly missing a soldier. From the window of a tall tower block a woman was shaking her fist at the urban guards, as she subjected them to a torrent of foul-mouthed abuse.

"Once your men clear the Forum I want you to hold your positions," Marcus said, as ignoring the foul outburst he turned to the two senior cohort commanders who were striding on beside him. "We shall spend the night guarding the Forum. Then tomorrow at dawn, I need you to start clearing the city one district at a time. If anyone puts up resistance or attacks your men, you are to kill them. We are not taking shit from anyone anymore. At the same time, we are going to announce a curfew. No one is allowed out onto the streets, punishable by immediate execution."

"My men will see it done," one of the guard commanders growled, as he grimly stared down the street.

Ahead Marcus could see that the vanguard of the police column was finally approaching the entrance to the Forum. A mob of around fifty or so armed looters, men and women, were slowly retreating before the disciplined and inexorable approach, shouting and screaming at the heavily-armed guardsmen in defiance, as if to show that they were not afraid. As another roof tile crashed and shattered to pieces against a shield, one of the company Centurion's shouted an order and the foremost company paused and hastily raised their shields above their heads and began to form up into a tightly packed testudo formation.

"You had better stay here Sir whilst my men clear the Forum," one of the cohort commanders cried out, as he hastily drew his sword and turned to give Marcus a grim look. "Leave this to us soldiers. This is going to get bloody. No mercy to anyone who puts up resistance. I shall remember those words of yours, prefect. You and you alone, are going to be responsible for what happens now."

Chapter Nine – A Week is a Long Time in Politics

The dull, rhythmic tramp of the soldiers' hobnailed boots on the paving stones was continuous. It was morning and Marcus, flanked by Paulinus and Claudia, was standing on the broad, stone steps leading up into the temple of Saturn. He was gazing at the long column of praetorian and urban guards as they snaked their way through the Forum and off in the direction of the Coliseum. A week had passed since the riots had begun and Similis, the urban prefect - the man tasked with the security of the city of Rome, had finally returned with his soldiers. Marcus looked exhausted. Dark circles had formed around his eyes and his chin was unshaven. He had not been home in a week. Thankfully the security situation in the city, although fragile, had started to calm down after he had managed to clear the Forum six days ago. But that had been just the start of his task. Work had kept him busy - work, tireless, endless work - trying to figure out how to minimise the damage that the loss of the Egyptian grain fleet had caused. It had been a monumental, nearly impossible task.

"Look," Paulinus said with a little humourless chuckle, "there is the banner of the 6th Cohort again. I thought I had seen it before. Similis is having his men march around in circles. It's a show. He's trying to pretend that he has more men than he actually has. He's trying to impress the people of Rome with a show of strength."

"He doesn't look very happy," Claudia replied, as she glanced in the direction of the urban prefect who was standing watching his troops as they filed past. Then she turned to give Marcus a brief, sympathetic glance. "A week is a long time in politics. You need to go home Marcus and see your wife. You look like you could sleep for a month."

Marcus grunted and shook his head. "There is still work to be done," he muttered. "Similis wants to meet us to discuss the situation."

"I am sure he does," Claudia said cryptically, as she looked away. "No doubt he is already thinking about how he is going to protect his reputation and limit the damage to his career."

Marcus frowned. Similis was officially his boss, a supporter of Hadrian but a moderate who could be persuaded to switch sides, if the price was right. That was how Nigrinus had managed to get Marcus appointed in the first place. But since being appointed prefect of the grain supply, he'd not had much contact with Similis, which was not really a bad thing, Marcus thought, as grimly he turned to gaze at the man. He was about to turn away and re-enter the temple of Saturn, when a voice called out his name and a young man came limping towards him. Marcus paused in surprise. He didn't recognise the young man who was in his mid to late twenties and who looked like an ex-soldier. The white arm-band of the vigilante home guard, the irregular force of ordinary citizens that had formed during the riots to defend their homes, was tied around one arm and a sword was strapped to his belt. Limping towards him, the young, handsome man raised his hand in greeting and then rapped out a quick military salute.

"I have been meaning to speak to you Sir," the man said, mustering a quick smile. "My name is Aledus. I am a friend of your son Fergus. We served together in the Twentieth at Deva."

Marcus raised his eyebrows.

"You are a friend of Fergus," he exclaimed.

"That's right," Aledus called out in a cheerful voice. "Served with him in Britannia, Germania and during the Dacian war Sir, but now I am out of the army. Got injured Sir. It's my leg. I can't run and keep up on the march. The army said that I was no good anymore. So, they gave me an honourable and medical discharge." Aledus paused as he examined Marcus. "I fulfilled my vow Sir," he said in a quieter voice. "I was a good soldier. Your son will confirm that. So afterwards, I came to Rome. I heard about your veteran's charity. Fergus always spoke highly of you Sir."

Marcus nodded. "What do you want?" he asked.

"I need a job," Aledus said quickly. "A proper job Sir. I was wondering whether you could help."

***

The treasury officials stood stiffly pressed up against the wall of the room, staring into space and beside the huge veiled statue of Saturn, the temple priests had gathered and were carefully observing proceedings. Around the table in the inner sanctum of the aerarium in the temple of Saturn, above the vaults where the gold and silver from Rome's senatorial provinces was kept, Similis, Marcus, Paulinus and a few other senators had taken their seats. The mood was sombre, and the stuffy, airless room remained silent as the men around the table tensely busied themselves with nothing. Similis was looking down at the wooden table top. His stern, deeply-tanned face contrasted with his closely cropped white hair and he looked distinctly unhappy. The urban prefect had only said a few words since Marcus had initially greeted him on his return to the city that morning.

"Report," Similis snapped at last, as he raised his head and looked at Marcus from across the table.

Marcus cleared his throat.

"It has been seven days now since the rioting broke out across Rome," Marcus said, speaking in a calm but tired-sounding voice. "The security situation in the city is still volatile and fragile but it has been calm for the past few days Sir. We think we have managed to re-establish law and order. It is imperative however that the citywide curfew is maintained for a while longer and that our security forces remain out on the streets as a deterrent, and as reassurance." Marcus sighed as he looked down at the table. "The initial disturbances were caused by the news that the Egyptian grain fleet, on which we rely for most of our grain, had been lost at sea; destroyed by a storm. People believed that they were going to starve Sir. The lawlessness spread rapidly throughout the city. The mob murdered the prefect of the night watch. That was the spark that started the looting. They then went on to besiege the fourth Cohort in their barracks. Law and order broke down completely which, gave the mob the opportunity to settle scores and rob, murder and rape their way across the city. No one and nothing was spared. Effective leadership broke down but Paulinus and I managed to regain control of the Forum by the end of the first day, using the remaining urban cohorts Sir."

"Effective leadership broke down..." Similis interrupted sharply, as he stared at Marcus with a hard, unfriendly gaze.

Marcus looked up and met the urban prefect's gaze.

"Most of the senate seem to have fled the city upon the outbreak of the rioting," Marcus replied, "and with the death of the prefect of the night watch, there was no one left in charge. The breakdown in command led to paralysis amongst the urban guard units Sir, but we sorted it out in the end."

"I hope you are not suggesting that I am to blame for this disaster," Similis snapped angrily, as he glared at Marcus from across the table.

"No Sir," Marcus said hastily. "No one is to blame Sir. Paulinus and I have focussed our efforts on restoring order and planning what to do next. We imposed an all-day curfew, which we have now relaxed to allow women only to leave their homes, so that they can buy food for their families. The urban cohorts are in full control of all the city gates and are maintaining regular patrols across the city. They have been aided in this by groups of vigilantes, mostly army veterans who are keen to protect their homes, businesses and families. Paulinus organised them into district groups. We have also started looking for the ringleaders complicit in the murder of the prefect of the night watch. Once we catch them, they will be publicly executed in the Forum Sir. The city is calm Sir. We are getting back to normal."

Across the table from Marcus, Similis looked unhappy.

"And what do you intend to do about the loss of the Egyptian grain fleet, prefect," Similis snapped. "How are we going to feed Rome?"

Marcus glanced quickly at Paulinus, who was listening to the conversation with a stoical expression.

"I and my team have been putting a lot of effort into finding solutions to this problem," Marcus replied as he turned his attention back to Similis. "The loss of the grain fleet is a disaster. But there are things we can do to mitigate the loss and I am confident that, if we adopt the plan that I have drafted, all shall come right in the end. Sir, if I may explain."

Similis raised his hand with an irritable expression and silently gestured for Marcus to continue.

Hastily Marcus cleared his throat. "Sir," he said, "I have taken an inventory of all our existing grain supplies held here in Rome. I have personally been to every granary around the city and know how much grain reserves we have at this moment. Based on the current estimated population size of Rome, I have calculated how much grain we will need to provide every person in the city with a basic weekly allowance for the next year. There is obviously a large shortage of grain, but there are just enough reserves to provide the city with a free bread dole, if we were to implement a strict system of government-controlled grain rationing. This would mean about ten loaves of bread per person per week. But this rationing system must be implemented right away. There can be no delay."

Marcus paused as he tried to gage Similis's reaction, but the urban prefect was keeping his thoughts tightly under wraps.

"The most practical way in which to set up this rationing scheme is to expand and build on the existing scheme of free grain-handouts," Marcus continued. "In the army we are used to rationing. Rome is going to have to get used it to. Our first step is to take full control of all the granaries in the city and temporarily outlaw the private sale of grain and bread. Harsh penalties should be handed out to anyone who breaks these laws. We will then set up two public registration schemes. The current scheme for those poorer citizens, who already rely on free grain handouts, will remain unchanged but to this we shall add a second scheme for everyone else. Citizens will need to register with their local bakeries if they want to buy grain. I propose that we limit the purchase of grain to the father of a family who buys it for his whole family and does so just once a week. Each city bakery will then be provided with a fixed amount of grain from our granaries, depending on the number of people registered with them. Once citizens are registered, the bakeries will provide each head of household with coupons, small marked stones, similar to the ticketing system we use for the games in the Coliseum. Citizens will need to show their tickets to the bakeries before they can purchase one week's worth ration of grain. Once they have purchased their ration their names are crossed of the list for that week. This way, the government will be able to control the price of grain but also the size of the rations, meaning we can react to changing circumstances. There would be no difference between rich or poor. Everyone will be rationed. This is important point to make."

"And how will you guarantee that there will be no fraud on the part of the people," Similis hissed. "How will you prevent them from registering with two of three bakers? How are we going to handle the registration of so many citizens? This has never been done before, not on this scale."

"The registration shall be done by the bakeries with our help," Marcus replied. "As for fraud and multiple registration. We have looked at this. It will be the responsibility of the bakeries to catch out fraudsters. We can also cross reference the lists. It is a threat to the system, I admit, and we shall probably have to rely on informers to catch the worst criminals. It's not perfect but if we implement heavy punishments for those caught breaking the law it may dissuade some citizens whom are considering cheating the system."

Similis grunted and Marcus could see that he did not look impressed. Clearing his throat Marcus continued.

"There can be no suggestion that the rich are eating all the poorer people's bread. Security at the bakeries will be provided by squads of soldiers from the urban guard, who would be posted outside the bakeries to prevent trouble. Public rationing will be only limited to grain. There is no rationing when it comes to barley, vegetables, meat, wine and fish. These commodities shall continue to be freely available on the open market. We shall continuously monitor the price of these goods and if they rise by too much we shall take action to keep them affordable to the population." Marcus paused. "In effect what I am saying," he said continuing, "Is that only the free market in grain is going to be suspended. At least until the food emergency is over. We are not going to allow the city to starve."

For a long moment Similis was silent, as he looked down at the table.

"Will it work?" the urban prefect snapped at last, as he looked up.

"The rationing scheme has never been tested on this scale before as far as I am aware," Marcus said confidently. "But it will work. It is a tried and tested system in the army Sir."

"And how long will this emergency last?" Similis growled.

"I believe it will be a year before things return to normal," Marcus replied. "I have also looked at ways in which to increase our grain supplies. I have devised an incentive scheme for farmers in Italy, encouraging them to switch from ranching to wheat and grain production. The results will not however be known until the harvest time later in the year. I have also devised a similar scheme for fishermen and poultry holders. Finally, I have issued and sent orders to various provincial governors in Gaul and Hispania, demanding that they immediately despatch their excess grain supplies to Rome." Marcus paused as he took a deep breath. "The governors may of course complain and try and block the order, but if they do they will have to explain their actions to the people of Rome, when they are next in the city."

Marcus lent back in his chair and gazed across the table at Similis.

"Everything that can be done is being done Sir. To conclude, grain is going to be scarce in Rome throughout the coming year, but no one is going to starve, not if we handle the situation properly. I suggest that we make that public knowledge. If people know that they are all in this together and that everyone is being treated the same way, it should go some way to preventing any further unrest."

"And how much is this all going to cost us? Will we have to raise taxes?" Similis snapped.

Marcus shot Paulinus a quick look. "Well," he said carefully, "the cost is going to be considerable. Paulinus and I estimate it will cost the state between three and four million denarii before the crisis is over."

"The state's budget deficit is not where I would like it to be, but by moving things around and making certain cuts to other budgets, I have found a way in which we can afford the extra emergency spending without having to raise taxes," Paulinus said turning to look at Similis.

"Good gods," Similis muttered as his face went pale. "That's the cost of maintaining two legions at full strength for a whole year."

An awkward silence settled around the table. Slowly Similis turned to gaze at Marcus with a cold, unsympathetic look.

"I am the urban prefect," Similis said at last in a grave voice. "It is my responsibility to maintain law and order in the city of Rome. I shall write to Trajan. The emperor is going to have to be informed about the riots and their consequences." Similis paused and, as he stared at Marcus his face darkened. "But you are wrong Marcus. Someone is to blame for this disaster and it certainly isn't me. I will be damned if I am going to take responsibility for this mess. I wasn't here. No, this whole shit-storm is your fault Marcus. You are the prefect in charge of the grain supply and you have failed Rome. You were put in charge of managing Rome's food supplies. You are responsible for this fucking disaster and I am going to make sure that Trajan knows it. Implement your rationing plan and get out of my sight. You are a disgrace."

***

It was getting late as Marcus slowly made his way up the Janiculum hill towards his home. He looked dog tired but satisfied. Similis had given the go-ahead for his plan and that was good news. The rationing scheme would work. It had to work. The rest of the meeting had just been politics, dirty, unfair, scandalous unimportant politics for which he did not care. He would focus on his job. He had a duty to fulfil. The important thing, the only thing that truly mattered was that he was getting on with his job. That's what he was supposed to do. Ensuring the welfare and survival of real people like that young woman who'd been raped, was far more important than pandering to the weasel who'd had been left in charge of Rome. Marcus realised that he should have been furious and upset after having Similis blame him personally for the disaster at sea. But the truth was that he just couldn't give a shit.

Kyna met him just outside the door to his villa and without saying a word, flung her arms around her husband and did not let go for a long moment. When she finally did, she looked calmer.

"Look at the state of you," she muttered, as he led her into the house with the silent Indus following close behind. "I am so glad to have you back Marcus," Kyna said, as Marcus collapsed onto the couch. "I heard you have been holed up in the temple of Saturn. They say the city is calmer now. They say that the rioting is over. This is good news. Welcome news."

And as she gazed at her husband a fond look slowly appeared on Kyna's face.

"Rome owes you husband," she said with a hint of sudden pride. "They owe you for what you have done. I am going to make sure that the city knows it and remembers."

He nodded and smiled as he looked up at her.

"Have you heard from Elsa and Cassius?" he exclaimed wearily.

"They are both safe," Kyna nodded quickly. "Cassius followed your advice and barricaded himself into his home. They had a few tense moments, but they are all right." Kyna paused, as she examined Marcus. Then she sighed. "I have heard from Ahern too. He told me all about his adventures crossing the city. Why did you decide to take him? You put him in danger Marcus. The boy is only seventeen. He could have been killed."

"Ahern needs to pick a side," Marcus growled. "He has to choose whose side he is on. For too long that boy has enjoyed a pampered, expensive upbringing. It's time he grew up. It's time he learned who his family and real friends are and what the world is really like. He is either with us or against us."

Slowly Kyna shook her head as she folded her arms across her chest. Then she looked away.

"That steam machine of his," she said at last. "You know the one he has spent a year building. The machine he was hoping to demonstrate to the senate. Well it's gone. The mob destroyed it during the riots. There is nothing left. I spoke to Ahern. He blames you. He says that because you forced him to go with you, he was not there to protect his machine. It's not your fault, I know Marcus, but he is distraught." Kyna sighed. "He doesn't know whether he will build another machine and he says that he is going to make you pay for what you have done to him. Claudia has heard him muttering about taking revenge."

"Good," Marcus snapped, as he reached for a jug of wine. "Then the boy has chosen the side he wants to be on."

Chapter Ten – The Man Feared by the Gods

March 115 AD

It was noon and the sun had come out, bathing the city in warm, bright light. On the pons Fabricius, the bridge was filled with traffic. Wagons, horsemen, ox-drawn carts and pedestrians were crossing in both directions and here and there an enclosed litter, carried by a troop of slaves was moving across the bridge. Street hawkers, loudly pitching the delights of their wares and services, stood along the edge of the walkways, trying to catch punters attention. And over it all, the putrid stench of the metropolis hung thickly in the breezeless air. Out on the greenish waters of the Tiber, in the dazzling, twinkling sunlight, the river barges, stacked high with commodities, were moving up and down on their regular journeys from Portus to Rome and back. Marcus, accompanied by Cassius and Indus, pushed their way across the bridge in the direction of the city walls. Several weeks had passed since the riots and the city had returned to normal, or so it seemed. But Marcus looked unhappy. The debris and destruction wrought by the looting and rioting may have been largely cleared up but, if he looked carefully enough, he could still see traces of the bad times. They were etched into doorways and walls and stained into paving stones. There were many grim black clothed women in mourning, who were sitting out in front of their homes. And now the senate had joined the witch hunt, searching for someone to blame, Marcus thought grimly. Its members had finally had the courage to return to Rome and had launched an inquiry into the riots, summoning him and Paulinus to appear before them to give evidence. Those pompous arses in the senate had appointed themselves onto a committee of inquiry. Marcus's face darkened. This was going to be a shit day. He could sense it.

Cassius, struggling to stay level with him amongst the throng of the crowds, was talking in his quick-fire voice, briefing him on the latest developments and seemed oblivious to Marcus's mood. Sourly Marcus turned to glance across the river as he listened to his secretary. Descending the steep rocky slopes of the Janiculum and crossing the Tiber in the direction of the Aventine hill, were the magnificent, high stone arches of the Aqua Traiana, Trajan's brand-new aqueduct, which gleamed in the sunlight. And arrayed alongside the aqueduct on the slopes of the Janiculum, the state-owned complex of sixteen, wooden water mills, used to crush grain into flour, were working flat out, their ingenious wheels turned by the force of the water flowing down the aqueduct.

"There is a final piece of news, Sir," Cassius said hastily, as Marcus strode on towards the gates leading into the city. "Attianus has returned from Syria. He arrived a few days ago by ship. It's likely that he will be here today during the senate hearing." Cassius gulped in some air, as he hurried along at Marcus's side. "You should be careful with Attianus Sir," Cassius continued. "He wields a lot of power and he hates the War Party. He is Hadrian's right-hand man, his enforcer. A real hard nut. Doesn't tolerate fools and has made a lot of enemies." Cassius chuckled to himself. "It's said that even the gods fear him."

"I know who Attianus is," Marcus growled, as his eyes swept over the squad of urban guards on duty outside the gates. "He carries a death list around with him of people who he is going to have executed, if Hadrian becomes the next emperor, and I am one of the names on his list."

"Holy shit," Cassius swore, as a little colour shot into his cheeks and he turned to gaze at Marcus in horror. "How do you know this?" he gasped as the three of them swept on through the gates and into the city.

"Let's just say that I know," Marcus said, as he glanced at the shops doing business along the side of the street. "The man is a prick."

"A death list," Cassius exclaimed. "He keeps a death list."

"Do you want me to ask him if you are on his list?" Marcus growled.

Cassius's blush deepened and for a long moment he was speechless. Then he pulled himself together.

"The point Sir, that I am trying to make," Cassius said, "Is that the arrival of Attianus in Rome has prompted Nigrinus to leave his estate at Faventia. Nigrinus is here in Rome. He wants to speak to you before the senate hearing. He is going to meet us at the senate house. I honestly don't know what he wants to talk to you about."

Marcus stopped abruptly in mid-stride, so abruptly that Indus who was following on behind, nearly crashed into him.

"Nigrinus is in Rome," Marcus said frowning. "I see you are well informed as always but why didn't you tell me this earlier?"

"The message came late yesterday evening Sir," Cassius stammered. "You were busy. I thought it could wait until this morning."

Carefully Marcus studied his secretary face. Then, without saying a word, he turned and started out again in the direction of the Forum.

"Is there anything else that I should know," Marcus cried out at last in an annoyed voice. "Are you withholding anything else from me Cassius?"

"No Sir," Cassius stammered. "Nothing business related. The only other thing is that Elsa has told me, to tell you, to be careful Sir. She has been to see this fortune teller who says that you are in danger. Personally, I don't believe in all that crap, but Elsa does. She worries about your safety. She says you should have left Rome when you had the chance."

***

The Curia Julia - the senate house stood in the Forum, within sacred and ancient boundaries of the Comitium and in the shadow of the Capitoline hill. The tall brick and concrete building was decorated with slabs of marble and the whole place looked rather drab. Nigrinus was waiting on the broad steps leading up to the bronze doors. The faction leader of the War Party was dressed in his white senatorial toga and was accompanied by a single slave. As he stood waiting a constant stream of grave looking senators were filing passed him into the senate house. Marcus nodded a polite greeting, as he strode up to his political boss. Nigrinus looked tense as he returned the greeting.

"It's good to see you Sir," Marcus began. "I was told that you had returned to Rome. Rest assured that I have matters under control."

"I do hope so," Nigrinus snapped, glaring at Marcus. "I do hope that my trust in you has not been misplaced. There is a lot of political capital invested in your position. Do not forget that. The party is counting on you to defend its interests."

"I understand," Marcus nodded gravely. "I shall do my best Sir."

"Listen," Nigrinus said sharply, as he took a step towards Marcus and glanced around him to see that no one was listening in. "Attianus, Hadrian's right-hand man has recently arrived in Rome from Syria," Nigrinus said in a low, urgent voice. "He will be here in the senate today. Now the official reason for Attianus to be here in Rome is to look after Hadrian's property portfolio and business interests, but the real reason is to seek vengeance on us for the failed assassination attempt on Hadrian's life eighteen months ago. He blames us for the attack. He is out for revenge."

Marcus nodded again but said nothing as Nigrinus reached out and grasped hold of Marcus's arm, holding it in a tight grip.

"So be careful," Nigrinus hissed. "Don't let that arsehole manoeuvre us into a corner today at the hearings. The party must not be tarnished by these riots. Lie if you must, but under no circumstances are we to accept blame for this mess. The people of Rome are fickle. They can be swayed. But we will need their support when the time comes." Nigrinus paused and glared at Marcus. "Attianus may be a dangerous man but remember, so am I."

***

Marcus sat stiffly on the front bench and gazed at Paulinus, as the finance minister started to wrap up his testimony on the riots. Paulinus, holding the folds of his white toga in a statesman-like pose looked comfortable and at ease, as he stood alone in the open space that separated the benches on both sides of the house. And, as he gazed at his friend, Marcus felt a sudden flutter of nerves. Hastily he turned to look at the rows of benches that faced each other across the open central floor. The senate house was packed with over three hundred grave and serious looking toga clad senators and, apart from Paulinus's voice, the great hall was completely silent. For a moment Marcus stared absentmindedly at the benches. The senate no longer had the power or significance it had once held during the days of the Republic, but it was still an important body, a key adviser to the emperor. A wise emperor, Paulinus had told him once, did not ignore the senate, for it was the place from which rivals to the imperial power could come. And here he was, Marcus thought, the illegitimate son of a Roman legionary about to address the great and good, the lords and masters of Rome for the very first time. What would Corbulo, his father, have made of this? What indeed would Corbulo have made of it all?

Nervously Marcus's gaze swept across the magnificent, colourful and finely patterned floor towards the altar of Victory that stood at the far end of the hall. A statue of Victory stood on a globe, extending a wreath and, as he stared at the ancient altar, the eyes of the statue suddenly seemed to gleam in the light and wink at him.

Slowly Marcus turned to look at Nigrinus. His faction leader was sitting further along on the front bench, surrounded by his closest supporters and the most senior members of the War Party. As he sat listening to Paulinus, Marcus could see that Nigrinus's face was a stoic mask, behind which he was concealing his real thoughts. And sitting directly opposite and staring straight back at Nigrinus, were the massed-ranks of the supporters of Hadrian and the Peace Party, easily distinguishable by their beards. The War and Peace parties were however, not the only factions in the senate. There were other, smaller, less-influential interest groups. Factions, groups and individuals that wanted to bring in full-scale Athenian democracy, abolish slavery, restore the Republic, expel all foreigners from Rome or allow women to become senators. These fringe groups however, had very little support and were not taken seriously by anyone apart from themselves. But that did not stop Ahern and Cassius from being interested in them, Marcus thought sourly. But they were still young and impressionable. They would grow out of it. Steeling himself, Marcus hastily turned his attention back to Paulinus. The finance minister had finished his testimony and was returning to his seat and, as he did so Similis rose to his feet and called out Marcus's name.

Standing alone in the middle of the senate house and without notes, Marcus paused as he turned to gaze at the benches filled with his fellow senators. The grand hall remained completely silent as the masters of Rome waited for him to speak.

"My lords," Marcus began, raising his voice. "I am the prefect in charge of the grain supply for the city of Rome. Our great city. It is my duty and responsibility to make sure that the Annona is properly managed. That the city has enough bread to eat. And - rest assured that I take this duty very seriously. I will not repeat what my colleague Paulinus has just talked about, but I will give you an update on the grain supply. The situation is critical but not hopeless. Once the riots were put down and the city brought under control, I implemented a city-wide system of grain rationing as I am sure you are all now familiar with." Marcus paused and slowly turned to face the other side of the house. "I am pleased to confirm that the system is working. The populace has responded to the emergency by registering with the bakeries in great numbers. Our fishing fleets and farmers have promised to raise their production. There has been only minimal trouble with the registration and rationing process. There are some issues with fraud, but I am working with the state treasury and the urban cohorts to stamp this out. My lords, the good news is that the people of Rome have accepted the rations of grain they are provided with. They have accepted the suspension of the free-market in grain and they have accepted that the rationing will probably continue for another year. This is welcome. In addition, I am pleased to announce to you today, that I have just received word from the provincial governors of Gallia Lugdunensis, Gallia Aquitania and Hispania Tarraconensis. They will be sending us their grain reserves, shipments of which should start to arrive within a month. And I hope to have further good news soon."

As he finished speaking, silence descended once more upon the great hall.

"No, No, No," a deep voice suddenly boomed out. Amongst the ranks of the Peace Party supporters, an old and grave-looking senator had risen to his feet and was pointing an accusing finger straight at Marcus.

"No, there is no good news prefect. Do not try to fool us. Let's not forget what led to this crisis - sheer incompetence," Attianus bellowed. "The recent food riots in Rome are a disgrace, a stain on the reputation of the Emperor, a calamity for which you as prefect of the grain supply and a member of the War Party are solely responsible. Shame on you. Shame on you Nigrinus for allowing this to happen. The War Party have once again proved," Attianus roared, "that they are not fit to manage the affairs of Rome. Similis," Attianus snarled turning to glare at the urban prefect as he continued to point a finger at Marcus - "I ask you here, before us all, to sack this incompetent man. He has proved unworthy of the great office for which he is responsible. Sack him! Sack him now."

Attanius's cry was swiftly followed by loud cries of support from Hadrian's supporters and equally loud protests from the War Party. A little colour shot into Marcus's cheeks, but he stood his ground, gazing back at Attianus in silence. On his bench Similis seemed to shrink back into the wood and, for a long moment the urban prefect seemed unable to give a reply and as he stalled, the house descended into uproar. Gazing coolly at Attianus, Marcus suddenly understood the source of Similis's discomfort. Although a supporter of Hadrian, Similis could not sack him for he had been bribed. He had taken Nigrinus's money when he had agreed to appoint Marcus to his position. If Similis were to agree to sack him, he would be agreeing to his own downfall as well.

Across the open floor that separated the rows of benches Marcus was suddenly conscious of Attianus's cunning eyes gazing at him with sudden glee. The man was still pointing his crooked finger accusingly at Marcus.

"For if this man is not sacked," Attianus bellowed, his voice rising above the uproar. "There can be no respect. No legitimate support for any member of the War Party. There can only be contempt for their incompetence."

***

Marcus looked grim as he sat alone in the small study of his office in the building that housed his military veteran's charity. The hospice, located close to the Mausoleum of Augustus was quiet, apart from the sound of a lonely army veteran singing to him-self in a nostalgic voice. It was late, after midnight, but Marcus didn't feel like returning home just yet. Slowly he raised the cup of wine to his lips. The verbal and highly public assault on his character and reputation, which he'd endured in the senate house, had been brutal. It had left him feeling physically sick and his ordeal had not been improved by the furious look Nigrinus had given him on his departure. But it was just politics he thought. It was not important. He would ignore the political attacks. He would rise above it. He would get on with his job and let those self-important and self-serving men in the senate say what they liked. And as he pondered the day's events, he suddenly remembered the young woman who'd been raped during the riots. Picturing her bloody face, he sighed. He could not let politics undermine his ability to do a good job. People were counting on him.

"Sir, is everything all right?" a voice said from the doorway to his study. "You said you wished to see me?"

Glancing across the room, Marcus saw Aledus standing watching him. Quickly Marcus rose to his feet, his expression softening. After the ex-soldier and young friend of Fergus had approached him in the Forum, he had given him a job providing security for his charity. It had however quickly become apparent to all, that Aledus was a highly competent and experienced soldier and that his martial skills would be grossly underused at the charity.

"I have another job for you if you are interested," Marcus said, getting straight to the point. "I have a relative, a youth called Ahern. He's seventeen and I need an experienced soldier like yourself to teach him how to fight. The boy has never been trained in how to use a sword or shield. It's time he learned. It's time he started to behave like a man and not the spoilt brat that he is in danger of becoming. Would you be willing to teach Ahern? To be his trainer? You will be well paid for your time and you will be free to live here at the charity for no cost."

Aledus looked down at the floor as he seemed to think proposal over. Then he looked up at Marcus.

"I would be delighted to teach the boy Sir," Aledus said cheerfully.

***

After Aledus had gone, Marcus raised his cup of wine to his lips and finished off the contents in one go. At least something positive had come out of the day. He was about to refill his cup with wine when he heard a woman calling out his name from the hallway outside his office. A few moments later Kyna burst into his study, her cheeks red with exertion, as if she had been running. And as he caught sight of the expression on his wife's face, Marcus stiffened in alarm.

"What?" he blurted out. "What's happened now?"

Kyna paused as she struggled to regain her breath, her chest heaving with exertion. "A messenger came to our house just now," she gasped. "They were looking for you. They said it was urgent. There was no one able to warn you. So, I decided to come myself." Kyna gazed at Marcus with an apprehensive look. "The messenger came from the bakery who operate the water mills along the Aqua Traiana on the Janiculum. You know, the ones they use to grind the grain into flour. Well someone has attacked the mills. Several have been destroyed. But no one saw who did it. The saboteurs used the cover of darkness. The bakers say someone has deliberately sabotaged them, but there is something else Marcus." Kyna's eyes widened. "Afterwards when they inspected the damage they found red graffiti painted all over the aqueduct near to the mills. The slogan is scrawled repeatedly across the aqueduct. It's there for everyone to see and the graffiti is addressed to you."

"To me? What does it say?" Marcus said as he started to feel sick.

"It says that you should have gone to the temple of Invidia," Kyna exclaimed as a little horrified blush appeared in her cheeks.

Chapter Eleven – A Deal with the Devil

Marcus looked up at the high, stone arches of the Aqua Traiana and sighed. It was morning and he was standing on the rocky slopes of the Janiculum, close to the point where the aqueduct crossed the Tiber. Amongst the reed beds, that lined the banks of the swollen river, an otter inquisitively poked its head out of the greenish water and gazed at the group of men. Cassius together with a few engineers and the men from the bakery, which operated the mills, were standing beside Marcus examining the damage to the watermills. Several of the wooden mills, built into the stone and concrete structure of the aqueduct, had been destroyed by fire and others had been severely damaged.

"And no one saw anything," Marcus asked turning to gaze at the men from the bakery. "No one saw who did this?"

"It happened under cover of darkness," one of the bakers replied. "All my workers had already gone home. There was no one here during the attack. We were only alerted when the mills were already on fire."

Marcus grunted in frustration. Then gathering himself together, he turned towards one of the engineers. "How long will it take before you can rebuild them?" he asked.

"That depends on the resources that I am given," the engineer replied gruffly. "If I am allowed to do my job without constraints, then we can have the mills back up and running within a few weeks."

"And what stops these arsonists from coming back during the night and destroying them again," one of the bakers snapped angrily. "I can't grind grain without these mills, not in the quantities that are needed. You need to start paying for round the clock security. Proper security. These mills are crucial to the making of flour and bread. They cannot be left undefended."

Marcus sighed again and ran his hand across his stubbly chin. Funds were tight, especially now and it would be tough getting Paulinus to agree to more spending. But the watermills were part of the state-owned infrastructure for which he, as prefect of the grain supply, was responsible. He could not just do nothing. Turning away without saying anything, he walked over to one of the stone arches and gazed at the red, painted graffiti that defaced the fine stone-work.

"You should have gone to the temple of Invidia, Marcus," he muttered to himself as he read the graffiti out loud. "You should have gone to the temple of Invidia, Marcus," he repeated.

"Do you think it is connected to the warning by that stranger," Cassius blurted out, as he came up to Marcus and stared at the scrawled message. "You know; the man who delivered that warning, telling you to leave Rome. Didn't he tell you to pay half a million denarii to the temple of Invidia?"

"He did," Marcus growled. "He did."

Cassius remained silent as he turned to gaze at the freshly-painted red graffiti messages that were scrawled over the stone arches of the aqueduct.

"The temple of Invidia," Marcus said pronouncing each word slowly and carefully. Then he frowned. "Invidia. Known to the Greeks as the god Nemesis. God of vengeance; of revenge. Why Invidia? Why choose this god?"

At his side, Marcus's young secretary shrugged as he stared at the tall arches of the aqueduct. "Maybe the person behind all of this wants revenge Sir," he said at last. "Maybe they want to take revenge on you for some reason. Choosing Invidia would be a good way of getting that message across."

"Who the fuck would want to take revenge on me?" Marcus snapped, as his face darkened. "Is this what this is all about? Some stupid personal vendetta. Well I will be damned if I am going to let these arseholes run me out of town."

"I understand," Cassius said quickly. "But would it not be wise to take some precautions. Whoever is doing this may decide to try and strike closer to home next time. Maybe we should start to limit your public exposure; limit the number of meetings that you attend. Maybe we should hire a few more bodyguards Sir. No offence, but Indus is old."

"I am not going to change my routine and public commitments because some terrorists are trying to scare and blackmail me," Marcus retorted, as he rounded on Cassius. "No way in hell am I doing that. And as for my personal security, Indus is more than capable of handling matters. No Cassius, there will be no compromise with these terrorists whoever they are."

"Then what do we do Sir?" Cassius muttered as he looked away.

"We are going to find these bastards and stop them," Marcus growled with sudden resolve. "And to help me do that I am going to have to make a deal with the devil!"

***

The Subura neighbourhood brought forth many memories and none were pleasant, Marcus thought. Pushing his way through the crowd and accompanied by Indus, he headed deeper into the chaotic warren of dank alleys and overcrowded, crumbling tenement buildings. Most respectable people avoided the inner-city neighbourhood just off the Forum. The Subura was where the poor and the criminal classes of Rome had set up their businesses and made their homes. And it was here too, in this densely populated, squalid and overcrowded neighbourhood, that many newly arrived immigrants from across the empire came to try and make their fortune. Their presence was easily noticeable by the dozen foreign languages that he could hear being spoken around him. The stink of shit and piss was overwhelming, and rats were skittering about amongst the human refuse, that had been dumped out of windows and into the street. The voices of the shopkeepers filled the alleys and in the shadows of doorways, female and male prostitutes, some of them no more than children, were eyeing up potential customers. Keeping his hand firmly on his money bag in the pocket of his senatorial toga, Marcus paused at an intersection and tried to get his bearings. He'd been to the Subura many times before - but the place was still a bewildering labyrinth.

As he paused, a prostitute appeared from a doorway and quickly slipped her arm around Marcus's waist, as she gave him a glimpse of her breasts.

"Looking for some fun senator," she purred.

"I will give you one sesterce," Marcus replied as he patiently removed her hand from around his waist. "If you can tell me where Cunitius lives."

The girl frowned and then looked down at the silver coin in Marcus's hand. As she reached out to take the coin, Marcus's hand closed around it.

"Cunitius," he said sharply. "I am looking for Cunitius. He has an office in the Subura. He's an investigator. Do you know him? Do you know where he lives?"

A coy little smile appeared on the girls face as she looked up at Marcus.

"Two sesterces, senator," she replied. "Two sesterces, one for me and one for my baby. Then I will tell you where he lives."

Marcus raised his eyebrows as he looked at the prostitute. Then, with a sigh he reached into his toga and produced a second silver coin. He handed the money to the girl and she hastily pocketed the coins and pointed down a crowded alley. "Follow it," she said. "Then take the second alley on the left. Follow that right until the end. You will want the yellow door on the right." The prostitute paused as she studied Marcus for a moment. "When you are done come back and find me senator," she added. "You look like a good, honest man, not like the rest of them. I will give you a free ride."

Marcus did not reply but turned and started to push his way down the narrow, congested street with Indus following him. There was nothing noble about the Subura. It was a hard, dangerous place where the poor were mercilessly exploited and discarded when they no longer had any commercial value or use. The people in the Subura were slaves in all but name.

Up ahead, a crowd had gathered around a man who was standing on top of a barrel, waving his arms around in an agitated manner. People were listening in respectful silence. Another street preacher Marcus thought, as he headed towards them. Street preachers could be found on every street corner in Rome. They came from all corners of the empire, peddling their bizarre religions, ideas, salvations and prophecies to anyone who cared to listen. Most of them were harmless, out to make a quick fortune or seeking fame, but now and then the urban guard had been forced to remove trouble makers who threatened society's strict class hierarchy.

As he drew closer, Marcus could hear the man crying out and, as he did Marcus abruptly stopped and the expression on his face turned to one of alarm. The preacher standing on his barrel was speaking in good, clear Latin and he was laying into the leading politicians and senators of the War Party. As he stood listening to the man haranguing his friends and political faction, a little colour shot into Marcus's cheeks. What the hell was going on? What was this? He had never come across this before. This was bold; bold in the extreme. A street preacher criticising the War Party in public. Who the hell did the man think he was.

"Heh," Marcus shouted, as he stared at the preacher. "Heh you! Who has put you up to telling these lies? You don't know what you are talking about. Shame on you."

Catching sight of Marcus, the preacher grinned in sudden delight and, raising his hand, he pointed straight at Marcus.

"There is one of these monstrous people," the preacher roared, spittle flying from his mouth. "There is the senator responsible for our miserable grain rations. If you are hungry people, then blame him. Blame that man for your misfortune. His incompetence is the reason that we all have to suffer."

The crowd gathered around the preacher, had all turned to gaze at Marcus and, as he felt their sullen, raking, resentful glares, Marcus's hand dropped down to the pommel of his sword, which he was carrying under the folds of his toga. The smouldering hostility was unprecedented. On top of his barrel, the street preacher was sneering at Marcus, making no attempt to hide his contempt. Wrenching his gaze away from the preacher, Marcus started to move away down the street. When he'd reached the alley, the prostitute had told him to enter, he paused and turned to gaze back down the narrow street. The preacher had resumed his shouting and frantic arm waving.

"Shit," Marcus hissed to himself, with a worried look.

***

"Well, well look who it is," Cunitius exclaimed, with a genuinely surprised look, as he rose from behind a desk upon which were stacked piles of scrolls and wooden writing tablets. Marcus stood in the small entrance hall and said nothing as his former nemesis grinned, came towards him, and stretched out a hand. Looking down at the proffered hand, Marcus hesitated, then grasped it in a firm handshake. There had been a time, some years before, when Cunitius had been the enemy. He had been the implacable and relentless agent who had hunted Marcus, from the shores of Vectis to the back streets of Rome, intent on his capture and downfall. There had been a time when Cunitius had threatened everything that he had.

"I did not expect to ever see you walk through my door," Cunitius said, still grinning as he took a step backwards and carefully examined Marcus. "I thought you'd had enough of me after my man tried to mug you, down at the harbour. But here you are. Marcus, the Senator, the prefect of the grain supply. How is you son Fergus? I heard that the assassination attempt on Hadrian's life failed."

Cunitius was a big broad-shouldered man with a broken nose and a closely shaven head. He looked in his late forties.

"Fergus is doing fine," Marcus growled. "And as for the attack on Hadrian. I know nothing about that or why it failed."

"Ofcourse you don't," Cunitius said smoothly, as his eyes twinkled in delight. "Nigrinus must have been furious that the attempt failed. I have done work for that man before and you do not want to cross him. You don't want to make an enemy of Nigrinus. You may as well kill yourself if you do."

Stoically, Marcus stood his ground as he gazed at Cunitius. The last time he'd seen Cunitius had been some eighteen months ago, when the investigator had arrived at his veteran's charity and told him about the plot to assassinate Hadrian. The revelation had put him in a very difficult position, for it had forced him to choose between loyalty to the War Party or Fergus his son.

"For a man who claims to have made a fortune serving the rich of Rome," Marcus replied sharply. "You do sure still live in a shithole."

Cunitius raised his eyebrows in mock surprise and turned to look around the small dingy office on the ground floor of the apartment block.

"Maybe, maybe," he nodded. "You should see my country estate. It is in an even worse state than my office. But I don't think you have come here to criticise my taste in interior design. What can I do for you Marcus?"

"I need your help," Marcus said, forcing the words from his mouth. "I need an investigator to help me catch someone. I heard you specialise in such work."

"Ah," Cunitius said lightly as he raised his hand to stroke his chin. "You need a first-class investigator, a professional, a man who gets things done. So that is why you thought of me. I am flattered Marcus. I really am."

"Cut out the shit," Marcus growled, as he glared at Cunitius. "Can you help me or not?"

Cunitius seemed to be enjoying himself as he gazed at Marcus in silence. Then he turned and sat back down behind his desk.

"I am a businessman, Marcus," Cunitius said at last, with a weary sigh. "I told you this many years ago. I bear no grudges. I do the job that I am paid to do - and I am the very best at what I do. And this may surprise you, but I enjoy my work. So, who are you looking for?"

Marcus looked away as he spoke.

"A man came to my house back in February, just after I was appointed as prefect of the grain supply," Marcus snapped. "He threatened me. Told me to get out of Rome and leave everything behind. He told me to pay half million denarii to the temple of Invidia and warned me that a storm was coming. A storm that was going to sweep me away. I didn't take it very seriously at the time, but then yesterday an act of sabotage was carried out against the water mills on the Janiculum. These mills are part of the infrastructure for which I am responsible. Graffiti had been scrawled across the aqueduct close to the mills. The graffiti was addressed to me personally. It said that I should have gone to the damned temple." Marcus paused, as he took a deep breath. "I need this man, or whoever is behind this man, caught and caught quickly."

Cunitius nodded, as a thoughtful look appeared on his face.

"So, you think both incidents are connected," the investigator said smoothly. "You think the same man who threatened you, is also responsible for the sabotage. Did you get a look at him when he came to your house? Could you recognise him if you had to?"

Marcus shook his head. "He was cloaked and hooded and riding a horse. I didn't get a proper look at him. It all happened too fast."

"I heard about the sabotage at the water mills," Cunitius said, as he leaned back in his chair and turned to gaze at the stacks of documents on his desk. "It's unusual. Who would want to hurt the production of bread, especially now that the whole city is living on grain rations. Who would want to do that?"

"They don't want to sabotage the production of bread," Marcus replied as his face darkened. "They are out to get me. That's what this is all about. Someone is seeking revenge on me. They are trying to ruin me. That's why they mentioned the temple of Invidia."

For a moment Cunitius looked lost in thought. "All right," he said at last, as he looked up at Marcus. "I shall take the job. I am interested. Anyone who is out to ruin you Marcus, gets my attention."

"I am willing to pay your market rate for this work," Marcus said quickly. "Half now and half on the successful completion of the job. And I need you to start work on this right away."

But behind his desk Cunitius had raised his hand.

"No," the investigator said sharply. "No, I shall charge you for expenses only. This investigation will be free of charge but," Cunitius said, his eyes gleaming with sudden delight. "Once I have delivered, you Marcus, will owe me a favour, a big favour. Agreed?"

Marcus was gazing at the man sitting behind his desk. "Agreed," he replied.

"Good," Cunitius said smoothly. For a moment he remained silent as he pondered what to do. "All right I will do some digging amongst my contacts and see if anyone knows about who could be behind this," he said at last. "You will be amazed at how much the criminal classes of this city know about what's going on. They are a veritable mine of information."

Marcus nodded and turned to look around the small dingy office in silence.

"But first let's go and have a look at the damage to the watermills," Cunitius said suddenly, as abruptly he rose from his chair and reached for his cloak. "Always a good idea to see the handiwork of our fugitives. People always leave clues. They just can't help it."

***

It was getting late and the light was fading, as Marcus and Cunitius stood at the base of the Aqua Traiana on the Janiculum and gazed up at the ruined and burnt-out water mills. Indus stood a little to the side, stoical and silent as ever. Apart from him, there was no one about. On the Tiber the river barges were slowly moving to and from Rome's river harbour, below the slopes of the Aventine. For a long while Cunitius was silent as he studied the damage. Then slowly he shifted his gaze and walked over to the stone arches of the aqueduct.

"You should have gone to the temple of Invidia, Marcus," he exclaimed, reading out loud the red graffiti that was scrawled onto the stonework. "Whoever wrote this knows how to spell words and they sure did make it look personal," Cunitius added, as he took a step back and gazed up the length of the stone arch.

"It's all over the arches," Marcus growled. "Now can you see why I think this is connected to the man whom came to my house. No-one else knew about the temple of Invidia."

Cunitius suddenly frowned and took a step towards the stone arch. Reaching out to touch the graffiti, he carefully ran his fingers over the message.

"The paint," Cunitius exclaimed, as his frown deepened. "Red paint. Whoever did this, wrote their messages in red paint. Nothing unusual about that but I know a man, an expert on making paints. Maybe if he could examine a sample of the paint, he could tell us more about its composition and origin. It may give us a lead."

"Do what you have to do," Marcus snapped. "I want this bastard or bastards found and caught as soon as possible."

Chapter Twelve – Suspects

The clatter of wood striking a shield was followed by a harsh cry. Down in the small sandy playground of the school, two young men were fighting, both armed with large legionary shields and wooden training swords. Sweat was pouring from Ahern's face and an angry bruise already adorned his left eye. Wildly he lunged at Aledus with his wooden sword, which Aledus effortlessly blocked with his shield, and before Ahern could react he'd slammed his sword into the youth's side in a painful blow that made Ahern cry out.

"Keep your shield up," Aledus roared. "You think it hurts now. If that had been a real sword made of steel, you would have been dead. Now try again."

With a miserable groan, Ahern forced himself to square up to his opponent. From the open window of the second floor, half hidden from view by the curtains, Marcus and Claudia were watching the training session. Marcus looked glum. This was Ahern's first training session and it was embarrassing to watch. The boy was clearly not a fighter, not a soldier, but he was still determined that the boy should learn. The army turned youths into men, and discipline was exactly what Ahern needed right now. The boy needed to show some character.

"He fights like a girl," Marcus said contemptuously, as he studied Ahern from the window.

"Give him time," Claudia replied in a soothing voice. "Ahern is a thinker. Swords and shields are an unfamiliar world for him. He's still trying to figure it out."

Marcus grunted and his face soured. A few days had passed since he'd hired Cunitius and, despite a busy schedule, he'd cleared time to come to Claudia's school for there was something else that concerned him. A nagging worry that had been growing on him for several days now.

"I am concerned by what you told Kyna," he blurted out, without taking his eyes off Ahern. "You told Kyna that you'd heard Ahern muttering something about taking revenge for the beating I gave him?"

At his side Claudia sighed. "He was angry Marcus. Angry people say stupid things. I am sure he didn't mean it."

"Well someone is out to take revenge on me," Marcus snapped. "That's what this is all about. Someone wants to embarrass me, ruin me."

Claudia turned to look at Marcus and frowned.

"Surely you don't still suspect Ahern of having anything to do with that man who threatened you at your house, do you?"

"No," Marcus growled, looking unhappy. "I don't think he has the balls for that or for setting fire to my water mills. But he is a member of my family and he will know things, privileged information. When we last spoke about this, you mentioned your fear that someone may be manipulating these boys. That does concern me. Ahern talks about the Republic as if it were a sacred place. Where the hell does he get these ideas from? And then he gets arrested for drunk and disorderly behaviour. He never got into trouble before. No. Someone, is leading him astray. He may be a brilliant scientist, but he is also impressionable and gullible. So, I want to know everything there is to know about this group of friends he likes to hang around with. What can you tell me about them?"

Claudia turned to gaze out of the window at the two sweating, young men. In the sandy courtyard Ahern, sporting another bruise to his shoulder, had thrown down his shield and sword and was stomping away in disgust. Claudia sighed again.

"They like to go to a tavern, called the Black Lady, in the Caelian district," she said in a weary voice, "It's their favourite place." Claudia frowned. "There is also a name that they keep mentioning. The blond one. I think they mean a seer, one of these street preachers. Apparently, this seer gives speeches predicting the future, that kind of stuff. That's why they go there, to listen. That's all I have heard."

***

It was late in the afternoon as Marcus, trailed by Indus, made his way down the narrow city street towards the Subura neighbourhood. Marcus, clad in his senatorial toga, looked lost in thought, as he pushed his way through the crowd. Pressure had been growing on him to find a way in which to fund the repairs to the watermills and provide security for the industrial complex. He would have to speak to Similis regarding the security situation but Paulinus would not be happy with the additional spending. So, in the end Marcus had decided that he would personally pay to have the damage repaired, using his own money. The plan would have to be kept secret from Kyna. If she found out what he was doing she would be beyond furious. Women, he'd learned, were incredibly territorial when it came to money. And now Cunitius had sent him a message, saying that he wished to speak to him right away. The investigator seemed to have some news for him.

As he approached a busy and noisy intersection, he came to an abrupt halt and took a deep breath. Across the street from him a crowd of people had gathered around a lewd puppet show. The people were laughing. But as he stared at the puppet show Marcus's expression changed. The puppeteers, hiding behind a curtain at the back of their small cart, were poking crude fun at the War Party and the crowd was loving it. And as he stared at the show, Marcus suddenly blushed as he recognised his own puppet character. His character was being shown in a compromising and humiliating position and the hidden voices of puppeteers were happily cutting his reputation to shreds. Marcus's face darkened. The public attacks on the War Party had increased in the last few days.

They had begun shortly after Attianus had arrived in Rome. Throughout the city he'd heard reports from his colleagues that suggested that a concerted effort was underway to paint the War Party into a dark place. He had noticed too that the urban guards at the city gates no longer acknowledged him like they used to. It was all Attianus's work. There could be little doubt that he was the brain behind this propaganda war, this battle for the affection and loyalty of the mob. Attianus was skilfully using the grain rationing and current food emergency, to turn the population against the War Party. Angrily Marcus turned away, ignoring the raucous laughter of the spectators, and started to move on down the street. Politics was a truly shitty and unrewarding profession, he was beginning to realise.

***

Cunitius was sitting in his small office as Marcus came through the doorway. The letters and documents that had once been piled up on his desk had been cleared away and replaced by three little pots of reddish paint. Cunitius was gazing down at the pots with a perplexed frown. Then, as he caught sight of Marcus his expression changed. Quickly he raised a hand in greeting. As he entered, Marcus noticed another man standing in the far corner. The man was old and foreign looking with short grey hair and his fingers were stained with dried paint.

"Marcus, meet my friend Philip," Cunitius called out in a cheerful voice. "Philip is Greek and the finest paint-maker in Rome."

Marcus nodded a quick, silent greeting which Philip returned.

"I have some news for you," Cunitius exclaimed, as he gestured to the pots of paint standing on his desk. "I took a sample of the paint that was used to draw that graffiti on the aqueduct walls and asked Philip here to examine and test it.

He has some interesting conclusions that you need to hear." Cunitius glanced at Philip. "Do you want to explain?"

In his corner, Philip cleared his throat and dipped his head respectfully as he glanced at Marcus. "Senator, I heard about the damage done to the watermills," the man said, in a heavy foreign accent, "and I am more than pleased to be able to assist you in this inquiry. Cunitius is right. I am the finest paint-maker in Rome. My clients include most of the great families that rule this city. If you…"

"There is no need for a sales pitch," Cunitius interrupted sharply. "Just get to the point."

Philip hesitated. "I tested the sample taken from the aqueduct wall," he said slowly. "The pigment in the sample of red paint was made from the Cinnabar mineral. Cinnabar is toxic because of its mercury content but if ground down it makes for a fine red pigment. When finely ground you get Vermillion. Many of my clients use ground Cinnabar in their frescoes and wall paintings. Women and actors also use it as a lipstick. It is a popular colour."

"How is this useful in catching the people who damaged my watermills?" Marcus demanded as he stared at the paint maker.

In reply, Philip held up his hand, indicating that he was not finished.

"There is only one commercially viable place from which we mine Cinnabar," Philip said quickly. "That's the Almaden mine in Hispania. It produces around ten thousand pounds of Cinnabar a year. The mineral is shipped directly to Rome where it is sold to us paint makers." Philip paused. "The point I am trying to make Sir, is that Cinnabar is not cheap. The price is fixed in law at seventy sesterces or seventeen and a half denarii a pound."

"So, whoever scrawled that graffiti onto the aqueduct was using expensive paint," Marcus snapped. "Is that what you are saying?"

"Yes, they used expensive paint," Philip nodded. "But that's not all." Philip sighed and frowned as if he was struggling on how best to make a complicated matter look simple. "People who do not appreciate fine paintings and art Sir; they think that paint is all about colour," he began. "But it isn't. There is another important aspect to paint besides its colour and that is its texture. Proper, professional painters understand this. They understand that if you want to make a statement or send a message to the viewer, you can use colour or the texture of paint or both. The paint used on the aqueduct was Vermillion, but the colour red is also a sacred colour used to colour the faces of gods on paintings." Philip fixed his eyes on Marcus. "The person who wrote that graffiti was sending you two messages Sir. The obvious one, which anyone who can read, could see. And then there was the second subtler message. By using this specific paint and colour, they were telling you that this whole conflict with you is sacred, personal to them and that they don't care about the dangers or how much it is going to cost."

The room fell silent and as it did, Marcus gazed at the paint maker. Then at last he nodded his gratitude and turned to look down at the floor.

"How many paint shops in Rome sell this Vermillion?" Marcus asked at last.

"About a dozen, including my own business," Philip replied confidently.

"I am going to make some inquiries with the owners of these businesses," Cunitius said smoothly. "Ask them a few questions about their clients, that sort of thing. Shake the tree. Our graffiti artist is most likely one of their clients. Maybe, if I can draw up a list of recent buyers we can narrow down the list of suspects, but it will take some time."

"Do it," Marcus growled. "Let me know as soon as you have compiled that list," he said, as he turned for the doorway.

***

It was dark by the time Marcus reached the Forum on his way home to the Janiculum hill. The night sky was filled with a multitude of twinkling stars and in the Forum a few remaining traders were packing up their market stalls. There were few people about apart from the small army of street cleaners, who were busy cleaning up the mess left by the market traders and the public. Somewhere in the distance a dog was barking. Resisting the urge to drop in on the temple of Saturn to see if Paulinus was willing to go for a drink, Marcus continued in the direction of the old cattle market and the bridges across the Tiber beyond. In the great temples and state buildings around him, torches and oil lamps glowed in the darkness, illuminating the Forum in an eerie, dim and reddish light.

Marcus had just entered the street leading to the city gates, when a troop of twenty or thirty Vigiles from Rome's fire brigade nearly crashed into him in their haste. Marcus cursed as he sprang aside. The men came rushing past, carrying their water-pumps and wooden-buckets. "What's going on?" Marcus cried out, as he caught sight of the buckets that the fire fighters were carrying.

"There a fire's down near the river harbour," one of the Vigiles called out, as he rushed past. "One of the grain warehouses is on fire."

"Shit," Marcus hissed to himself, as his eyes widened in alarm. Stepping back out onto the street he stared in the direction down which the firefighters were disappearing. "Oh fuck," he suddenly swore in a louder voice. Then, crying out to Indus, he started to run down the street in pursuit of the firefighters.

As he drew closer to Rome's river harbour that lay just below the city walls at the base of the Aventine hill, Marcus could see that the night sky was lit by a reddish glow. Up ahead he could hear confused yelling and shouting. Panting and gasping for breath, he finally came to halt beside a warehouse and reached out to steady himself against a wall. Then he groaned in dismay. Ahead, close to the banks of the Tiber, one of Rome's largest grain warehouses was on fire. He could clearly smell and taste the smoke. The roar and crackle of the flames was a horrible sight. Around the huge warehouse, hundreds of Vigiles had formed a disciplined human chain, along which a continuous line of buckets of water were being passed up from the river bank. With a frustrated cry, Marcus slammed his fist into the wall as he stared at the unfolding scene. The firefighters closest to the blaze were doing their best to quench the inferno with the steady supply of buckets that was being passed up to them. But would it be enough to save the warehouse and its precious cargo of grain?

"There is nothing that you can do Sir," Indus cried out in alarm, as with a determined grunt Marcus pushed himself away from the wall and headed straight towards the blaze. The Batavian caught up with Marcus, just as the heat and ferocity of the fire forced him to a halt.

"This is not a good idea Sir," Indus roared and before Marcus could react, his bodyguard was pulling him back from the flames.

"The Vigiles know what they are doing," Indus yelled. "Let them do their job Sir. There is nothing that we can do."

Marcus allowed himself to be dragged backwards. Then at a safe distance, he shook himself free from Indus's grip and turned to stare at the fire, barely able to contain his rage.

"Sir, Sir, have a look at this," Indus cried out suddenly, and something in the tone of his bodyguard's voice made Marcus turn and look in his direction. Indus was standing beside the corner wall of the huge warehouse that was on fire, and pointing at something that had been scrawled onto the stone work. As he approached the wall, in the flickering light of the fire, Marcus suddenly caught sight of words painted onto the wall in red paint.

"You should have left Rome when you had the chance, Marcus," he hissed as he read the graffiti out loud.

Chapter Thirteen – The Pressure on Marcus Grows

Marcus looked grim and exhausted, his face and toga stained by soot, dirt and sweat as he slowly picked his way through the smouldering, blackened rubble of what was left of the grain warehouse. It was dawn and, across the site hundreds of Vigiles, Rome's hybrid police and fire brigade, were examining the burnt-out wreckage. The smell of smoke hung thick in the air. A few fire fighters were still bringing up buckets of water from the Tiber to dampen the debris, but most of their comrades had flung themselves onto the ground, too tired to do anything else. Leaning against the wall, upon which the red graffiti had been scrawled, watching his boss, Indus too was struggling to keep his eyes open. To the east the sun was rising, a reddish ball in the clear sky, and as he felt the sun's warm welcoming rays, Marcus realised that he should really send a message to Kyna to let her know where he was. He had stayed at the site of the fire all night, trying to do his best to help the firefighters put it out. The battle against the flames had been epic. A ferocious and stubborn struggle between man and the elements and the dedication of the firefighters had left a deep impression on him.

"There he is. Sir, Sir," a voice suddenly cried and as he turned, Marcus saw Cassius hastening towards him. His young secretary was accompanied by the fire chief in charge of the cohort of Vigiles.

"The fire is out," the chief growled as he and Cassius came up to Marcus. The fire chief wiped his forehead, sighed and turned to gaze at the blackened rubble. "The western warehouse was lost Sir," he said. "Together with the grain that was stored inside. But we managed to save the other three warehouses. My men used catapults, artillery and pickaxes to create a fire break to prevent the flames from spreading. It seems to have worked. My investigators are now searching for clues to the cause of the fire. They have spoken to the night watchman who was on duty, and who first raised the alarm, but that man claims to have seen no one on his rounds. My men think though that he may have been asleep when it started. I hope to have more answers soon Sir."

Marcus nodded silently and turned to look at the ruined warehouse.

"You did what you could," Marcus said at last. "No one here is to blame. I shall make sure that the people of Rome know about the dedication and professionalism of your fire fighters. Tell your men that Rome is proud of them."

"Sir," the fire chief muttered, as he lowered his gaze to the ground.

"Cassius," Marcus said in a weary voice. "This is not just a random fire. This was started deliberately and by the same person or people who sabotaged the water mills on the Janiculum. The graffiti on that wall over there confirms it. They are sending us a message. Their strategy seems to be to target our grain supply infrastructure, for which I am responsible. So, I want a permanent guard placed on all of Rome's grain and bread production infrastructure and I want it done right away."

"Of-course Sir," Cassius exclaimed. "I will see to it at once but how are we going to pay for this expense. We have no money for such additional expenditure. Our budget is already stretched by all the emergency measures."

"I will personally pay for the security costs," Marcus snapped irritably. "Just get it done."

Then beckoning for Cassius to follow him, Marcus carefully picked his way towards the stonewall against which Indus was leaning. Beside the wall he paused and pointed at the red graffiti scrawled across the stones.

"You should have left Rome when you had the chance, Marcus," he read aloud. Then turning to Cassius, Marcus's face darkened. "Do you know who is behind this? If you have any suspicions or theories, you need to tell me now."

Cassius blushed as he gazed at the graffiti. Hastily he shook his head. "Of-course I would Sir, but nothing comes to mind right now. If I knew who was behind this I would tell you."

Marcus grunted as he examined his secretary and then turned to stare at the graffiti. Exhaustion seemed to be making him suspicious of everyone and everybody. He needed to get some sleep. He needed to go home.

"Marcus," a voice suddenly called out and as he turned Marcus saw Paulinus standing in the street gazing at him. Rome's finance minister was clad in his senatorial toga and was accompanied by a slave.

"I heard about the fire and came as soon as I could," Paulinus called out with a grave, troubled looking expression. "The senate, Marcus. They have summoned you to a special sitting later this morning at the Curia Julia. They want to know what the hell is going on. I thought I would come and tell you in person."

***

Marcus ran his hand across his soot stained and unshaven cheek as he strode into the Curia Julia, the senate house in the Forum. He looked like shit for there had been no time to go home for a change of clothing. But it couldn't be helped. There had been barely enough time to consider what he would tell the senate. The House was only half full and the toga clad senators were spread out across the rows of benches. And as he came into the building with Paulinus in tow, he groaned. A quick cursory glance seemed to show that the house was solely packed with Peace Party supporters.

"Where are our supporters?" Marcus hissed as he rounded on Paulinus, but the finance minister just shrugged, his face a mask of concern. Turning to peer at the stony-faced and bearded senators, Marcus could see no sign of Nigrinus, nor of any of the other leading men of the War Party. Apart from Paulinus it looked like he was on his own. There was no support from his own faction.

"Don't let them humiliate you," Paulinus whispered, as he headed towards his seat on one of the benches.

"Prefect," one of the bearded senators called out as he stood up. "News of a second attack on Rome's critical infrastructure has spread throughout the city. I understand that you have come directly from the scene of the fire. What happened? What are you doing about this intolerable situation?"

"We want to know what the hell is going on? We need answers," another bearded senator cried out in an angry voice, as he too stood up.

Marcus did not immediately reply. Straightening his toga, he tried to rub off some of the dirt from his clothing. Then lifting his head, he turned to face the hundred and fifty or so senators who were waiting for him to speak.

"Late last night there was a fire in one of the grain warehouses down near the docks," he began in a tired-sounding voice. "The fire was started deliberately. The Vigiles however acted promptly and managed to contain the blaze, but we have lost one of the warehouses with all the grain inside. It will have short term consequences on the grain rationing." As he paused a gasp of dismay rose from the benches at the news. "You are right Sir," Marcus continued stoically, "that this is the second attack on Rome's grain and bread production infrastructure in a matter of days. I do not yet know who is behind these attacks but rest assured that I have people investigating these crimes. I have also this morning ordered a permanent, night and day guard to be placed on all our critical food production and distribution infrastructure and I shall be paying for these costs from my own personal funds."

"It is not so long ago that you were accused of incompetence," a senator cried out, as he rose to his feet and pointed an accusing finger at Marcus. "There were calls for you to be sacked and yet here you are again, standing before us with more bad news. Is now not the time to resign and admit that you cannot handle this important job?"

"I can handle this job," Marcus shot back. "If Similis, the urban prefect, wishes to have me replaced then let him speak now."

On the benches loud muttering broke out, but as he looked around him Marcus could see no sign of Similis.

"Is it not true that these attacks," a distinguished looking senator suddenly cried out. "First on our water mills and now on our grain warehouses are linked to you personally? Is it not true that at the scene of each crime, red graffiti has been found scrawled onto walls which suggests that these attacks are related to your own private affairs? And let me be clear. These messages are addressed to you personally. One read: You should have gone to the temple of Invidia Marcus. Another: You should have left Rome when you had the chance Marcus."

"Yes, graffiti implying that, has been discovered on each occasion," Marcus admitted with a little nod.

"So, you admit that these attacks, for which Rome is suffering, are being caused by someone having a grudge against you," an outraged senator shouted. "This is a disgrace. This is intolerable. Rome is suffering because of your incompetence. It is you who is the problem and because of you we all suffer. We need a new prefect of the grain supply and urgently."

And as the senator spoke similar outraged cries and yells rose from the benches and the house threatened to descend into uproar. From the corner of his eye Marcus caught Paulinus's shake his head in an urgent warning, as his friend seemed to guess what was about to happen, but he was too tired and annoyed to care.

"Maybe it is someone in this house who is behind these attacks," Marcus cried out in a defiant, angry voice as a torrent of resentment came rushing to the surface. "Maybe one of you is out to ruin me. Well if that is the case then let them step forwards and we shall settle this once and for all, man to man. You fine gentlemen sit and judge me here, but I am trying to do my best for this city. I have loyally and dutifully served Rome and the interests of Rome for nearly my whole life and I will be damned if I am going to let you drag my good name through the mud."

As the benches rose in near universal uproar Paulinus groaned, lowered his head and ran his hand across his face. On the floor however, Marcus stood bolt upright, defiant and unrepentant as he faced the hostility of the house. They had pushed him too far and he'd had enough. He no longer cared what they thought.

On the benches many of the senators had risen to their feet and were shouting and gesticulating wildly, but as he stood his ground a deep booming voice began to override the tumult. And as the house started to calm down, Marcus saw that Attianus. Hadrian's enforcer, was on his feet, glaring at his fellow senators.

"Order, order," Attianus bellowed and the authority in his voice was clear. As the House reluctantly quietened down, Attianus turned to gaze at Marcus.

"I do not doubt your sincerity prefect," Attianus called out in a calmer voice. "You are after all a distinguished soldier, a man who has seen the frontier and the barbarian threat for himself; unlike many here in this house today. But these attacks on the city's critical infrastructure are a cause for alarm. They must be stopped and as you are still the prefect in charge I personally look forward to hearing from you when you have a further update on the situation."

Marcus remained silent and did not move, as the session abruptly seemed to come to an end and loud, bad-tempered muttering broke out, as most senators rose from the benches and headed for the exit. What was going on? Had Attianus just defended him before the whole senate? Fighting the fatigue that threatened to overwhelm him, Marcus was suddenly aware of Attianus approaching him, accompanied by a few of his bearded supporters. And, at the same time, from the corner of his eye, Marcus noticed several Peace Party supporters swiftly engage Paulinus in conversation, physically preventing him from coming to his colleague's aid.

"Prefect, I would like to have a word with you," Attianus said in a quiet voice, as he carefully studied Marcus. "Do not worry. I give you my word that your life will not be in danger. I am not yet ready to escalate the conflict between our factions into a bloody feud of revenge killings. But it may be to our mutual benefit if we had a little private chat."

***

Attianus's house was a modest building tucked away on the Viminal hill. Leaving Indus behind in the hallway, Marcus cautiously crossed the fine-looking mosaic floor and entered the gracious large central atrium around which the rooms of the house were arranged. Here he was, he thought, in the heart of his enemy's house and the knowledge made him nervous. He could feel the tension growing in the muscles around his neck and back, but if Attianus had something important to say then he would listen. The pleasant smell of jasmine dominated the room. In the middle of the atrium a low, square stone-basin filled with rainwater and with an opening in the roof, had been set into the floor. Colourful and expensive-looking fish were swimming up and down inside it. A slave stood stiffly against the wall, staring into space and from somewhere out of sight Marcus could hear children's playful shrieks. Attianus, clutching a cup of wine, was standing beside the doorway that led out into a small walled garden. He turned as he heard Marcus come into the room and with a stern and silent expression, gestured for Marcus to take a seat on one of the comfortable couches that had been arranged around the central basin. Apart from the motionless slave there was no one else in the room.

"Thank you for trusting me and for coming here," Attianus said, gesturing to the jug of wine that stood on a table. "That was courageous of you, given the circumstances between our factions." In response Marcus politely shook his head as he turned down the offer of a drink. He was in the den of his mortal political enemy, the man who had added his name to his death list. This was no time for drink. He needed all his wits about him.

"Suit yourself," Attianus said as he turned to study Marcus. For a long moment the two men gazed at each other in tense silence.

"Life is cheap in Rome these days," Attianus exclaimed at last, breaking the silence. "Do you know how I know this?"

"I have no idea," Marcus replied.

"I keep an eye on the price that the criminal gangs charge to have someone murdered," Attianus snapped. "The price for buying murder is going down. It has been going down ever since Trajan left for the east."

"Is this supposed to frighten me?" Marcus retorted.

"No," Attianus shook his head. "If I wanted you dead you would have been dead by now. But that is the current situation. You may have heard that I keep a list, a list of death. Every name on my list is going to be executed, once Hadrian becomes emperor. Your name is on my list too. But here is my dilemma Marcus. Strange as it may seem, I have grown to respect you. Having seen you in the senate I have to say I like you. You are an honest man with a good heart."

Attianus paused as he gazed at Marcus, his face a perfect emotionless mask.

"You represent everything that makes Rome great," Attianus continued. "An accomplished and brave soldier who rose from humble beginnings, a loyal and competent commander who has gained the respect of his men. Oh yes Marcus, I have looked into your life and career. You have quite a military service record. Mons Graupius, the Brigantian rebellion, the Danube frontier, Trajan's first war with the Dacians. I know everything there is to know about you and your career with the 2nd Batavian Auxiliary Cohort."

"Then you should know that I am a member of the War Party and that I have sworn an oath of loyalty to Nigrinus," Marcus replied swiftly.

"Yes, that is a shame," Attianus nodded. "A great shame. I have spoken with Nigrinus about you in private. You are a fool if you think that Nigrinus is your friend. He told me that he agrees with the verdict of the senate – that you are incompetent. That you have mishandled the riots and the grain supply. Did you know that?"

"I think you are lying," Marcus replied.

"Sure," Attianus said quickly. "Sure. Believe what you like but it is the truth. If you don't want to believe me then ask Paulinus. He was at the same meeting. He heard Nigrinus say it. I am not lying to you."

Across the basin of rainwater that separated the two men, Attianus fixed Marcus with a cold, contemptuous look.

"You are a fool if you believe that Nigrinus is your friend," Attianus snapped. "You have made many enemies in Rome Marcus, but the ones you should fear the most are not amongst the members of the Peace Party. No, your most dangerous enemies are within the ranks of your own faction, the War Party. Can you not see that? Nigrinus doesn't give a rat's arse about you. You are expendable to him, just another soldier who must die for the greater glory of bloody Gaius Avidius Nigrinus. It is Nigrinus who will be the cause of your eventual downfall. Fear him, not me. Fear him!"

"That's hard to believe from the man who has added my name to an execution list," Marcus retorted, his face bitter and angry. "Is this the reason why you called me here for a chat? So that you can frighten me and lecture me on how awful the War Party is? How nice you are. Sorry but I have better things to be getting on with."

"Sit down prefect," Attianus growled, as Marcus started to rise to his feet. "I have not yet finished explaining why I wanted to talk to you."

Reluctantly Marcus sat back down again. "Well maybe you should get to the point," he said in an unhappy voice.

"I want to make a bargain with you," Attianus said sharply. "An arrangement that will be mutually beneficial. I want you to change sides and become a supporter of Hadrian and the Peace Party and I want you to kill Nigrinus for me. In your position you are one of the very few people who can get close enough to Nigrinus without raising suspicion. That piece of shit has walked this earth long enough."

As he fell silent Marcus stared at Attianus in growing disbelief.

"You want me to change sides. Abandon my friends and kill Nigrinus?" Marcus exclaimed.

"That's right," Attianus said. "Do this, and in return I shall promise to take your name off my death list and make sure that Fergus's army career is given a helping hand. Hadrian knows all about you and your son Fergus. It's just as well for Fergus is one of his most trusted supporters. He has saved Hadrian's life twice now. Did you know that? I take it that you still care about your son's welfare?"

For a long moment Marcus said nothing as he stared at Attianus. Then slowly he shook his head.

"I have no love for Nigrinus but I won't betray him," he growled.

"That's the wrong answer," Attianus said as his face darkened. "Why not?"

"Because I gave Nigrinus my word," Marcus hissed. "Because I swore an oath of loyalty. That still means something to me. I will not break it."

"Oh, for fucks sake," Attianus cried out raising his arms in the air. "I could have you killed. I could have you prosecuted for treason. There are a hundred ways in which I can ruin you and your family. I am not joking. This is serious. We're getting fucking serious here."

"Then what is stopping you," Marcus bellowed.

"Your son Fergus," Attianus roared back. "He is protecting you. Didn't you know? He is pleading with Hadrian to save your miserable life. That's what's stopping me. If you don't want to do this for yourself, then do this for him."

"I will not betray Nigrinus nor will I abandon the War Party," Marcus shouted, as he rose to his feet, his face white with anger. "What you are asking me to do is dishonourable and I will have nothing to do with it. I fear death like the next man, but I fear dishonour more. You will have to do your worst."

"Fine," Attianus roared as Marcus headed for the hallway. "Then I shall inform Nigrinus that you, his trusted colleague, warned us about the attempt on Hadrian's life eighteen months ago in Athens. I shall tell Nigrinus that you were directly responsible for the failure of the assassination attempt and that you did it to protect your son Fergus, who just happens to be Hadrian's head of security. I wonder how long you will last after that."

Marcus had stopped in his tracks and slowly he turned to gaze at Attianus.

"That is a lie," he hissed, as blood shot into his cheeks. "I don't give a shit about your Hadrian."

"I don't care," Attianus retorted. "But Nigrinus is going to believe me. He is going to believe me when he discovers that Fergus your son is on Hadrian's staff. And then Marcus," Attianus said in a sneering voice, "the shit is really going to start flying for you."

Chapter Fourteen – The List

Cunitius's office felt stuffy, airless and the faint pong of stale urine was seeping into the room from the squalid alley outside. In the open doorway, a dog was scratching itself against a wall, and in one of the apartments above the ground floor office a man and a woman were having a massive foul-mouthed row, but Marcus didn't notice. It was morning and a week had passed since his tense meeting with Attianus. Marcus and Cunitius were hunched over a long scroll of papyrus that had been laid out across Cunitius's desk. The neat, beautiful and stylish paragraphs seemed to have been written by a professional clerk. Marcus frowned as he studied the list.

"So, the good news," Cunitius exclaimed, as he too studied the list. "Is that the paint makers have kept records of their clients. I have been to see them all. There are thirteen businesses that sell vermillion in the city of Rome. As the paint is expensive, I expect that most of their clients will be the city's wealthier families." Cunitius paused and grinned at Marcus. "I don't think you will find many people in the Subura who are interesting in painting the walls of their homes. The most popular commodity in this neighbourhood is wine and flesh."

"Go on," Marcus replied with a grim, unamused expression.

"When a client wishes to buy some paint," Cunitius said, turning his attention back to the scroll. "They typically send one of their slaves or freedmen to place the order. The paint makers then create the paint, which may take a few days, and then they deliver it to the house of their client, where the financial transaction is also concluded. That means that our paint makers have the addresses and names of everyone who buys their products." Cunitius's eyes gleamed in amusement. "So, I persuaded them all to share their client lists with me. This list here is a record of all the families who have purchased vermillion in the last six months. It contains the names of the slaves and freedmen who purchased the paint, and the addresses to which the paint was delivered. The bad news is that the list contains four hundred and seventy-two different names and addresses."

Marcus grunted as he gazed down at the scroll and for a moment he didn't reply.

"How accurate is this?" he growled at last.

Cunitius sighed. "As accurate as I could get it," he replied. "Ofcourse there is a small chance that our saboteurs purchased the paint, without giving their address or stole it or got it from outside of Rome. Or that the paint makers have not shared their full client lists with me. But if Philip, my paint expert, is right then our saboteurs have chosen this specific paint because they want to send you a subtle message. They must have realised it would be risky to use this expensive paint instead of a more common variety, but they decided to use it anyway. That tells me something." Cunitius tapped the scroll with his fingers and looked up at Marcus. "This is as comprehensive as its going to get. I suggest that you take some time to study the list and see if anything jumps out at you."

Marcus nodded as he gazed at the paper. Then slowly he looked up at Cunitius.

"You said that this tells you something about the saboteurs," he said in a grim voice. "What do you mean by that?"

Cunitius looked thoughtful as he raised his fingers to his mouth. For a moment he remained silent. "Maybe," he said at last. "Just maybe the people we are looking for want to be found. Maybe they don't want to hide forever. It's just a theory. Just a hunch."

***

Marcus looked unhappy as he carefully unrolled the papyrus scroll onto his garden table and fixed it, by laying a heavy stone at each end. Around him in the garden of his villa, high on the Janiculum hill, the first of the spring flowers had started to appear and a fresh and pleasant scent and breeze filled the noon air. In a nearby tree a cheerful bird was singing and on a chair, the black cat was sitting contentedly watching Marcus with its yellow eyes. As Marcus straightened up and gazed down at the list of names and addresses, his mutilated left hand started to tremble uncontrollably. Silently Marcus reached across with his right hand to steady himself. Then quickly he turned to look around, but no one had noticed what had just happened. The uncontrollable trembling had started after his meeting with Attianus, a week ago. Marcus stared at his left hand and arm. He'd not told Kyna. For she would just worry and use it as another excuse to try and get him to retire to Vectis. But at some point, he would have to go and see a doctor. The trembling could just be stress but it could also be something worse.

Marcus was studying the list carefully, when Kyna appeared at his side and placed a cup of posca and some bread, cheese and olive oil on the table. Nodding his gratitude Marcus leaned back in his chair and stretched out his arms.

"I have been over this list twice now and nothing jumps out," he complained, in a frustrated voice. "It's just an endless listing of the rich and famous. Gods, there are people close to starving on the streets of the Subura and here their fellow citizens are spending vast amounts on fancy wall paintings."

"Mind if I have a look," Kyna said, as she turned to gaze down at the scroll with its neat, professionally written paragraphs.

Marcus gestured for her to do so. Reaching out to the bread, he dipped it into the oil and took a bite. The black cat was still watching him. Stiffly Marcus rose from his chair and, breaking off a little bit of cheese, he reached out to let the animal have a sniff.

"That's odd," Kyna suddenly exclaimed with a frown. "That's Cassius's address. That's the name of his freedman, Blaikisa."

"Are you sure," Marcus said, as he quickly returned to the table and gazed down at the list.

"Yes, that's Cassius and Elsa's address all right. I am sure of it," Kyna replied. "And that's the name of one of Cassius's freedmen, Blaikisa," she said, pointing at a name on the list. "What are Cassius and Blaikisa doing on this list?" Kyna looked up at Marcus. "Blaikisa was one of the Dacian prisoners of war brought back from the Dacian war. Cassius freed him about a year ago I think. He got his own apartment in the city after he was freed."

Marcus frowned as he studied the list.

"You said it was odd," he said at last. "Why is it odd?"

"I have been to Cassius and Elsa's house many times," Kyna replied. "We planned her wedding there and I am helping her prepare for the baby. The last time I was there, which was just a few days ago, they did not have any wall paintings or frescoes in their home. There was not a lick of red paint to be seen anywhere."

Marcus grunted. "But it says here that Blaikisa took delivery and paid for a large quantity of vermillion paint, less than two months ago. If they don't paint their walls, then what the hell is all this paint meant for then?" Annoyed, Marcus turned and bellowed for one of his slaves to come out into the garden.

"Go to Cassius's house at once," Marcus said as the slave appeared. "Tell him that I wish to see him right away. He is to come right away. I will not accept any fucking excuses."

***

Cassius looked nervous as he came striding out onto the garden terrace. Marcus rose from his seat as he caught sight of his young secretary.

"What's this all about Sir?" Cassius stammered as he caught the look on Marcus's face. "Has there been another attack?"

"No," Marcus growled, as he turned and gestured at the papyrus scroll that was pinned down onto the table. "I want you to explain how your address and the name of one of your freedmen appears on a sales list for vermillion paint. Kyna here tells me that you have no wall paintings in your house. So why do you need red paint? It's not like it cheap either."

A little colour shot into Cassius's cheeks, as he turned to gaze at the scroll in silence. At last he shook his head in confusion.

"Is this to do with the investigation into the recent attacks on our infrastructure," the young man exclaimed. "For if it is, then I swear I have nothing to do with them."

"Just answer the damned question," Marcus snapped.

Cassius stared at Marcus. Then hastily he turned his attention back to the scroll and slowly shook his head in bewilderment.

"We haven't bought any red paint," he protested as his blush deepened. "Kyna is right - we do not paint our walls. This must be a mistake or else," Cassius paused. "Or else someone is impersonating me; using my address for false reasons. Blaikisa is the name of my freedman. That is true. But he can't possibly have signed for that shipment of red paint two months ago."

"And why is that?" Marcus said sharply.

"Because he is dead," Cassius blurted out. "Blaikisa died four months ago. He caught a fever. I saw them burn his body with my own eyes."

Marcus stared at Cassius in silence. Then he turned to look at Kyna, who just shrugged.

"Someone is using my address and the name of my freedman without my knowledge or approval," Cassius snapped, stabbing the scroll angrily with his finger. "This is a disgrace," Cassius said as he looked at Marcus. "And for you Sir to suspect me of being complicit in these attacks." Cassius's blush grew, but mixed in with it was real anger. "Well I am disappointed Sir," the young man said sharply. "Have I not proved my loyalty to you. Have I not carried out everything you have asked of me?"

Marcus sighed and looked away. Cassius was right. Maybe he'd been too hasty, too aggressive. It was the relentless political pressure he thought. The growing and ever- present fear of what Nigrinus would do, when he heard what Attianus had to say about Fergus and the plot to assassinate Hadrian.

"You have," Marcus muttered, lowering his eyes. "And I apologise for being so blunt."

Marcus was about to say something else when a slave, accompanied by another man, came hurrying onto the terrace. Turning to face the newcomer, Marcus recognised the man as one of the priests of Ceres, the goddess of the harvest. The priest's face and neck glistened in sweat and he was gasping for breath as if he had been running.

"Oh god what is it now?" Marcus called out, as his heart began to sink.

"Prefect," the priest gasped. "I have come straight from the temple of Ceres on the Aventine. Last night a bronze statue of Ceres was stolen from the temple and a snake was left in its place. The snake is an evil sign, and without the statue we cannot bless the harvest. My colleagues are greatly upset. They believe that Ceres has abandoned us and that this is an omen, telling us that we are all going to starve. We only discovered the theft a few hours ago."

"So why come to me?" Marcus exclaimed, as his face darkened. "Similis is the urban prefect and in charge of security in Rome. He is responsible for dealing with thefts."

But the priest hastily shook his head. "Prefect you do not understand," the man stammered. "A message was left in the room where the statue was kept. It was painted onto the walls. The message was addressed to you. It reads simply - the dead cry out for vengeance and they shall receive it."

Marcus stared at the priest in horror and for a moment he could not move.

"The dead cry out for vengeance and they shall receive it," he said at last, in a weak sounding voice. "Was the message painted in red paint?"

The priest nodded. "But there is more," the priest added hastily. "One of my fellow priests is missing. His name is Evander. He was on duty last night. He was supposed to be guarding the statue but he didn't show up at the temple this morning. We have the address where he lives. It's on the Aventine not far from the temple. The high priest is waiting on you to decide what to do."

"Indus," Marcus roared, as he quickly turned towards his bodyguard. "Fetch my sword. Hurry. We are going to the Aventine hill. Cassius, you are coming with us too."

***

The Aventine, the southern-most of Rome's seven hills, was a densely packed neighbourhood of tall insulae, apartment buildings and narrow, twisting streets dominated by the magnificent temples of Ceres and Diane, the goddess of the hunt. Marcus looked grim and determined as he followed the posse of priests down the noisy, smelly and crowded street, with Indus and Cassius bringing up the rear. A single bronze statue of Ceres didn't mean much to him he thought, but to the priests of Ceres the theft was an outrage, an ominous sign of divine displeasure. Whoever had masterminded the theft must have known this. Marcus's rage deepened. If their intention was to sow discord and fear amongst the religious establishment, then stealing the statue was the way to go about it. But to link his name to the theft made his blood boil, for how long would it be before the ordinary people started to blame him personally, for their misfortune. In Rome, he thought sourly, the mob always like to find someone to blame for their misfortune.

Up ahead, the posse of finely dressed priests of Ceres had come to a halt around the doorway into one of the high, five storey apartment blocks.

"Is this the place where he lives?" Marcus growled as he came up to the doorway. The priests nodded solemnly.

Glancing upwards at the roof, Marcus noticed a few people leaning out of the windows gazing down at him. The gathering of priests in the street was starting to attract some attention. He would have to hurry. Turning to nod at Indus, Marcus quickly drew his gladius and then, leading the way, he vanished through the doorway and into the building. The lobby was deserted and dark and the narrow stairwell at the back stank of urine and rotting food. Carefully Marcus began to ascend the stairs, clutching his sword in his right hand. Behind him came Indus, Cassius and the long column of silent priests. As he climbed the stairs, he met no one and reaching the top floor Marcus paused to listen, but apart from a few distant voices, he could hear nothing unusual.

Creeping across the small landing, Marcus took a quick glance at the door to room nineteen and then, with a grunt he launched himself at the door, slamming into it with his shoulder. With a harsh cry of pain, he crashed through the flimsy barrier, before tumbling ungainly onto the floor and into the room beyond. As Marcus hastily and painfully staggered to his feet, Indus appeared at his side, his sword in hand and behind him the priests flooded into apartment. And as they did, some of them cried out in horror and clasped their hands to their mouths. Marcus grunted in surprise as he caught sight of the man hanging from a hook in the ceiling on a short rope. The corpse was stark naked, and a large pool of blood had formed on the floor directly below his feet. But it was not the corpse or the blood that horrified the priests. As he stared at the dead man, Marcus could see that someone had cut off the man's penis and had stuffed the remains into his mouth.

"Is this Evander," Marcus growled, as he turned to the priests. "Is this the priest who didn't show up for work?

"It is," one of the priests stammered, his face horror stricken.

"Someone murdered him," Cassius gasped, as he stared at the corpse hanging from the ceiling. "But why mutilate him like that. What does it mean? Who would do such a thing? It's disgusting."

Chapter Fifteen – Investigation

Quickly Marcus reached out to steady his trembling left hand. For a moment he stood still, frowning, as he gazed down at his arm and gently rubbed it with his fingers. Then hastily he glanced at Cassius and the others, but no one seemed to have noticed. In the small top floor apartment, the priests had managed to cut down their colleague and had laid the body on the floor and had covered it with a bedsheet. Some of the priests seemed close to tears. Others were muttering to themselves and praying out loud. With a sigh, Marcus turned to look around the room. Apart from a camp bed, some discarded clothes, a small wooden table and a single chair, the apartment was bare. Moving towards the window, Marcus poked his head out, looking down and then up at the roof but he saw nothing unusual. Turning back into the room, he sighed again and gazed about.

"The statue of Ceres is not here," one of the priests said, as he came up to Marcus. "Whoever murdered Evander must have taken it."

Marcus nodded. "Did Evander have any enemies?" he asked. "Did he have any issues with the criminal gangs, family disputes, any debts?"

The priests glanced at each other and then shook their heads. "No, he was never in trouble with the gangs and he lived alone," one of the priests replied. "He was frugal with his money. Never seemed to spend it on anything," another priest added. "I don't think he had any enemies. Evander was a popular man with the beggars outside the temple. I can't understand who would want to do this."

"The mutilation," Marcus replied, gesturing at the corpse. "I have seen that before on the Danube frontier. The barbarian tribes would sometimes make examples out of captured Roman soldiers. The murderer is making a statement. They are saying that they do not want the murdered man to be able to use his penis in the next world. That suggests that there was a personal motive."

Around him, the priests gasped in horror and some raised their hands to their mouths and in a corner, one of them turned away and threw up.

"Keep searching the room," Marcus growled. "They may have left clues. Anything, even the smallest thing can be important."

"What are we looking for" Cassius asked as he straightened up and peered around the small apartment.

"If the murdered priest was induced or blackmailed into stealing the statue from the temple for someone else," Marcus replied. "Then that must mean Evander had some sort of relationship with the person or people who wanted the statue. We need to establish the nature of that relationship. That will lead us to the killer and most likely to the people behind these attacks."

Crouching beside the corpse, Marcus carefully pulled back the bed-sheet and stared down at the dead man's face. Then with a sudden frown, he reached out and lifted the lifeless arm and peered closely at Evander's fingers. With a grunt he leaned back and turned to gaze at the priest's face again. The man's fingers were stained and marked by little splashes of red paint.

"Marcus, have a look at this," Indus called out suddenly, speaking in his native Batavian language.

Swiftly Marcus crossed the room to where Indus was crouching in a corner of the room beside the stone wall. The Batavian bodyguard was gazing at something that had been scratched into the wall. Kneeling beside Indus, Marcus frowned, as he stared at the small, barely visible graffiti etched into the stone. If Indus's sharp eyes had not spotted it, he would never have noticed it. The writing looked like it had been done with a knife or a coin and it looked like it had been there for a while. Peering closer, Marcus was able to discern the tiny, faded words and numerals. It looked like some sort of list formed into three long columns.

"The Horse – Laelia – Ten," he said out loud, as he read the carvings. "Reds – Corvus – Eleven. The Gladiator – Honoria – Eight. Diana – Lucius – Nine. The Black Lady – The blond one – Twelve."

Abruptly Marcus stopped reading and sat back. "The Black Lady," he muttered. "The Blond One." Where had he heard these names before? Then he remembered. Claudia had told him that Ahern liked to visit the Black Lady tavern. The boy went there to listen to the blond one, the street preacher who seemed to be filling Ahern's head with stupid revolutionary ideas.

"How long had Evander been living here?" Marcus called out sharply, as he turned to the priests. "Could he write?"

"He could write," one of the priests replied. "As for how long he'd been living here. I think it must have been over two years. That's how long he was with us."

Marcus grunted. "Cassius," he called, as he beckoned for his secretary to come over, - "see this graffiti here. Take a note of every word and numeral on this list."

Cassius crouched beside Marcus and peered at the faint graffiti scratched into the wall. Then he raised his eyebrows.

"Do you think Evander scratched this into the wall?" Cassius exclaimed, his breathing coming in excited ragged gasps. "Could it not have been a previous occupant of the room?"

"It's possible," Marcus replied, "but write it all down anyway. It may be useful."

"What do you think it means?" Cassius blurted out as he gazed at the tiny, faded words.

"The first column seems to imply the names of taverns or wine-bars," Marcus said with a thoughtful look. "The second column may be the name of a person. Fuck knows what the third column means."

Stiffly Marcus rose to his feet and, without another word he headed towards the door and the landing beyond. It was time to speak to the priest's neighbours. There was no reply from the first two doors on the floor but, as he banged on the door to apartment number twenty, a suspicious voice cried out in protest.

"Open up, I am on official business," Marcus shouted in an annoyed voice.

A moment later the door creaked open and a suspicious-looking face appeared, glaring back at Marcus. The man looked in his fifties with tufts of white hair on the sides of his bald head.

"What's going on?" the man said. "What do you want? I am a busy man."

"Your neighbour in nineteen has just been murdered," Marcus said in a harsh voice. "Someone killed him. Did you see or hear anything last night?"

"Murdered," the neighbour's eyes widened in shock and quickly he turned to peer in the direction of the doorway to nineteen. "What. Evander. He was murdered?"

"That's right," Marcus replied. "Someone hanged him from the ceiling and cut off his penis. It happened last night or early this morning. Did you see or hear anything unusual last night?"

The man blushed and, for a moment he seemed too stunned to say anything. Then hastily he nodded, his eyes avoiding Marcus's piercing gaze.

"Yes, I think I saw a man," the neighbour said, nodding again. "I heard him coming up the stairs, so I took a quick peek. He was carrying a small lamp and his head was covered by a hood. He came to see the priest late last night, but I didn't get a good look at his face. It was too dark. We are not allowed to have any oil lamps up here on the landing you see. It's to prevent a fire. Afterwards there was a commotion in the room, but it didn't last very long, so I didn't think anything more of it. Then maybe an hour later I heard someone leave. After that I went to sleep."

"This man who came to visit last night," Marcus said sharply - "Had he been to see Evander before? Is there anything else that you can remember about him?"

"I don't know. Like I told you, I didn't see his face," the neighbour replied.

Marcus sighed as he tried to hide his disappointment. Another dead end. "All right," he growled. "If you remember anything else then let the priests of Ceres know right away. I shall make it worth your time."

Giving the man a quick glimpse of a few silver coins in his hand, Marcus was turning away when the neighbour called him back.

"Evander," the neighbour called out. "He liked male companionship. He was never interested in women. He would hire male prostitutes. They would come to his room. Sometimes he had orgies. Maybe that is why they cut off his dick. I should know," the neighbour whined, his face contorted into a look of disgust. "When they constructed this block, they must have done it on the cheap. The walls in this place are so ridiculously thin."

***

It was late and dark when Marcus finally arrived back home. Kyna was waiting for him in the hall of his villa on the Janiculum and, as he caught sight of the look on her face, Marcus's expression changed.

"What's the matter?" he asked hastily, as Kyna came towards him and gave him a quick, silent welcoming hug.

"Paulinus is here," Kyna said in a tight voice. "He has been waiting for you to return. He's outside in the garden. He says he has important news. He has been here for hours Marcus," Kyna said nervously. "Is this to do with that awful man, Attianus? I fear Paulinus has not brought good news. He doesn't look happy."

Marcus grunted as he gently released himself from his wife's embrace and turned to stare in the direction of the garden.

"I will go and speak with him," he said, turning to give Kyna a brief look. "Don't worry, things will work out just fine."

"You always say that just before things go horribly wrong," Kyna replied quickly, her eyes flashing with worry. "You will tell me everything afterwards Marcus. Swear that you will not keep me in the dark on this."

Marcus didn't reply, as he left Kyna in the hallway and quickly headed out onto the terrace of his garden. Paulinus was sitting in a chair admiring the thousands of glowing lights of the city of Rome that lit up the night sky. As Marcus approached, Paulinus rose to his feet and solemnly gathered his toga around him. The garden was lit by several burning oil lamps and, in the reddish glow Marcus could see that Paulinus indeed did not look happy.

"Paulinus," Marcus said stiffly, as he acknowledged his friend.

"Marcus," Rome's finance minister replied in a grave sounding voice. "I won't beat about the bush my friend. I have just come from a meeting with Nigrinus and thought you should hear it from me first."

"Hear what," Marcus replied.

"Nigrinus has left Rome for his estates at Faventia," Paulinus said with a sigh. "But before he left this morning, he held a meeting with the inner council of the War Party. I was also called to the council. At the gathering Nigrinus told us that he'd been approached by Attianus who claimed to have scandalous information concerning you and your son Fergus. Attianus claims that you warned your son of the assassination attempt on Hadrian and that it failed because of you." Paulinus fixed Marcus with a hard look. "Well is it true? Did you betray us?"

"I did not betray the War Party," Marcus replied.

Paulinus said nothing as he gazed at Marcus. Then at last he nodded. "I was not aware that your son was head of security for Hadrian," he said. "Is it true? I thought Fergus was serving with an auxiliary unit. That's what you told me. Was Attianus speaking the truth about Fergus?"

"It's true," Marcus replied. "The last news we received from Fergus was that he'd been assigned to a Numidian auxiliary ala, out in the Syrian desert. But before that, he was in command of Hadrian's personal security detail."

Paulinus took a deep breath and looked away. For a long moment he was silent. Then he turned to face Marcus.

"You can see how bad this looks for you amongst the party. Hadrian is our arch enemy. He is likely to have many of us executed, if he becomes the next emperor including me and yourself. And now we find out that your son is protecting him.

The mood in the party is not good. Many senators are furious with you, Marcus."

"Fergus has chosen his side and I have chosen mine," Marcus replied calmly, as he sensed Kyna approaching behind him. "And that's all there is to it. I have not betrayed anyone. I serve Rome and the War Party. I have always done my duty. I have done nothing of which I am ashamed."

Across from him, clutching his toga in one hand, Paulinus was staring at Marcus and there was a sudden regret in his eyes.

"Like I said," Paulinus, said at last. "I wanted to be the first to tell you about the meeting. I owe you that much, my friend."

"What is Nigrinus going to do to my husband?" Kyna asked suddenly, as she halted beside Marcus, her eyes blazing as she gazed straight at Paulinus.

Paulinus took another deep breath and lowered his gaze. "I don't know," he replied. Then he raised his head and gazed at Marcus. "But you should know that Nigrinus has begun to see you as a liability. He blames you for the riots, the public mockery in the streets and the unpopular grain rationing. He says that you have caused great damage to our faction's reputation. That you have discredited the War Party." Paulinus raised his hand and pointed a finger at Marcus. "He is openly questioning your loyalty in front of the council. I came here to warn you. Nigrinus does not forgive those he believes have betrayed him."

Chapter Sixteen – The Net Closes

Marcus stood waiting in the shadows of the vestibule, safely hidden in the darkness. It was night and it was surprisingly cold. Carefully, he reached out and pulled his hood closer over his head and, as he did, he could feel the warmth of his breath on his hand. Earlier that evening, as soon as he'd received Lady Claudia's message, he'd given Indus the slip, and had headed out into the city alone. For this was something that he had to do on his own. Resisting the urge to stamp his feet, he leant back against the wall of the doorway. It felt as if he'd been waiting for hours, but it couldn't be so long he thought. Across the street from his stakeout, the gates to Claudia's school were still closed. No one had come in or out for a while now. Along the dark street to his left he could hear the shouts and loud merry voices coming from a nearby tavern and, down an alley an animal was rooting around in the rubbish. Had Claudia misheard? Had she got her times mixed up? But in her message, she had sounded sure of herself. Grimly he forced himself to remain patient. They would come.

A few days had passed since Paulinus's visit to his house. Stoically Marcus gazed at the school gates as he waited. Kyna had taken Paulinus's visit badly. She was growing more and more anxious and nervous. The fear of what Nigrinus may do, now that he was openly questioning his loyalty, was gnawing away at her and giving her sleepless nights. More than once she had woken him up in the middle of the night to insist that they leave Rome and retire to Vectis. Marcus grunted and, raising his left hand he gently rubbed it with the fingers of his right hand. He'd tried to calm her down, but it was getting harder. He had tried to explain that he had a job to do. That people were relying on him. That it would be cowardice to be run out of Rome like this and that he would not go. But she'd refused to listen, and her distress had added to the heavy burden he was already carrying. But he would continue, he had resolved. He would go on. He would not give up, just because Nigrinus was feeling betrayed or because someone was out to ruin him. No one was going to stop him from doing his job.

Across the street there was a sudden movement outside the school gates and, as he looked on, Marcus saw Ahern and three other young men appear and start to wander off down the street. The youths seemed to be in high spirits, as they playfully pushed each other and cried out to each other. Silently Marcus slipped away from his hiding place and began to follow them.

The Black Lady looked just like any other tavern in Rome. Pausing in the darkness, Marcus watched as Ahern and his friends entered the wine-bar and disappeared inside. From his vantage point he could hear music and laughter coming from within the establishment. Turning to look around, Marcus could see no one else about. The dark streets seemed deserted. Grimly and silently he reached out to touch the pommel of his sword that hung from his belt, before slipping his hand inside his cloak to touch the cold steel of his army pugio knife. Turning to the tavern, he hesitated. He hated and dreaded what was coming, but it had to be done. If Ahern was somehow caught up in the attacks against him - if he had a role to play in this extortion game, then he could not let that go unpunished. Seeing the Black Lady's name and that of the blond one scratched onto the wall of the murdered priest's apartment, and remembering what Claudia had told him, had got him thinking. And now the time had come to find out what Ahern was up to. Whether he was involved in the plot against him.

Crossing the street Marcus entered the tavern, keeping his hood over his head. A blast of heat hit him in the face and suddenly he was in a brightly lit, noisy and boisterous place filled with people in varying states of inebriation. In a corner, a musician was playing on a harp and a crowd of people were pressed up against the bar, some of whom were singing. Quickly Marcus allowed his eyes to wander across the tavern but there was no sign of Ahern. At the far end of the inn, a door seemed to lead on to a back room and, in a corner a ladder led up to the second floor of the building. Pushing his way towards the bar, Marcus leaned forwards and caught a bar woman's eye.

"I was told that the blond one comes here to speak," he said, raising his voice above the noise. "Where can I find the blond one?"

For a moment the woman looked confused. "The blonde one," she called out. "She's upstairs but she's busy. You will have to wait your turn."

It was Marcus's turn to look confused. "She," he cried out over the noise - "I was told the blonde one came here to speak to the crowd, to fill young minds with weasel words."

The bar woman gave Marcus a crooked half grin. "She sure has a talent for corrupting young minds, but she normally does it naked and on her back and you have to pay for it." Growing annoyed, the woman behind the bar pointed at the ladder leading up into a hole in the ceiling. "She's up there, but like I said she is busy. You will have to wait your turn. Now are you going to buy a drink or what? I am busy."

A little colour shot into Marcus's cheeks. The blonde one was not a street preacher after all. He and Claudia had been wrong. She was a prostitute. He had completely misjudged the situation. The lady behind the bar was about to give up in disgust and turn away when Marcus caught her arm.

"How much does she charge?" he cried out over the noise.

"Twelve asses," the bar woman retorted, wrenching her arm free and moving away muttering angrily.

Marcus turned away from the bar and stared at the ladder in the corner. Twelve asses. It was the same number that had been scratched into the wall in Evander's apartment. Marcus's eyes widened. The graffiti on the wall began to make sense. The writing was listing taverns, individual prostitutes and the prices they charged. But why would a priest of Ceres, a gay priest, scratch such information onto his wall? With a grunt Marcus began to push his way through the crowd towards the ladder but as he approached two big beefy-looking men rose to their feet and blocked his path. Slowly the men folded their arms across their chests.

"I will pay you two denarii for the blonde one," Marcus snapped, as he dug his hand into his pocket and showed the men the coins. "Now stand aside."

"She is busy with another client," one of the men growled as he refused to budge, "And the correct price is twelve asses."

Marcus raised his eyebrows. "Well that's a welcome surprise," he said in a sarcastic voice. "You must be the only man in Rome who cannot be bribed. But tell me has your establishment procured all the necessary licences for it to operate legally. Have all your prostitutes registered themselves with the Aediles and are your tax affairs all in order? For if they aren't, then a shed-load of shit is about to come your way. The city authorities do not look kindly on whorehouses that bend the law."

"Two denarii and be quick about it," the second man said suddenly holding out his hand. "But you will still have to wait. Blondie has another client."

Marcus dropped the coins into the man's outstretched hand, and without another word he started to climb up the ladder. As he clambered up onto the second floor he saw that he was on a dimly-lit landing with doors leading off it. Against the wall a fat and bored looking woman was sitting in a chair drinking from a cup of wine. She burped as she caught sight of Marcus.

"The blonde one," he said, as he got to his feet, and in reply she pointed with her cup at one of the doors.

"You will have to wait, she is seeing a young master," the woman said sourly, as she turned to look away.

Marcus didn't hesitate. Calmly he strode towards the door and flung it open. In the dim light he caught sight of a young woman wearing a long flowing blond wig. She was on her knees, naked except for a bra and she was kissing Ahern's bare chest. As he turned at the intrusion and saw Marcus standing in the doorway, Ahern's face went beech red and he yelped in sheer horror, stumbling backwards against the wall.

Marcus advanced into the group, ignored the outraged squeals of the prostitute and turned to face Ahern.

"So, this is what you and your friends have been up to," he hissed. "Shagging whores and using my money to do so. Pray boy that I don't tell your mother about this. You know how she feels about whores. Now get out of here."

Ahern didn't need to be told twice. Snatching up his clothes, he practically ran from the room and nearly tumbled down the ladder in his haste to get away. Slowly Marcus turned to look at the girl. She was still on her knees and was slowly shaking her head in bewilderment and disbelief.

"I am not here for sex," he said, lowering his voice as she looked up at him. "Although I have paid double the rate you charge. Now listen. I need some information. A few days ago, a priest of Ceres by the name of Evander was murdered in his apartment on the Aventine. We found your name and the amount you charge for your services, scratched into the wall. Did you know Evander? He seemed to know you, but I don't think he would be a client of yours."

On the floor the prostitute was gazing up at Marcus. Then slowly a blush spread across her cheeks and she struggled to maintain her composure.

"Evander was murdered, he's dead," the girl stammered, as a sudden tear appeared in her eye. "He was my friend." Quickly the girl looked away and took a deep breath as she dabbed at her eye with her hand. "How did he die?"

"Someone strangled him and then hanged him naked from the ceiling, cut off his penis and stuffed it into his mouth," Marcus replied. "I am trying to find out who murdered him. I need your help."

"What can I do?" the girl muttered as she looked down at the floor.

"I need to know which male prostitutes he liked to hire," Marcus said quickly. "You are in the business. You said he was your friend. Who would Evander go to for sex? I was told he only used male prostitutes."

On the floor the girl was fighting back the tears. Then sharply she looked up at him and shook her head.

"You've got it all wrong," she cried out. "Evander didn't pay for sex. He was the prostitute. He was one of us, but he was independent. Clients paid him for sex. He worked part time. He told me that it helped him top up the salary that the temple paid him."

Marcus stared at the girl in surprise. "What do you mean; he was independent," he said at last.

"No one controlled him. No one took a cut of his earnings," the girl replied, wiping the tears from her face. "He worked for himself."

"So how did he find clients?" Marcus shot back.

"I don't know," the girl sniffed as she dabbed at her eyes again. "But he always did." Then she froze, before slowly turning to look up at Marcus with wide-open and staring eyes.

"No, wait," she said quickly, "I remember now. He told me once that he kept a record of his clients and how well they performed. Yes, that's right. He liked to grade his clients. He would record their names. They must still be there."

"We went over his apartment," Marcus snapped. "We checked everything. We found no further markings on the walls. I can assure you. There was nothing there."

"Not the walls," the girl exclaimed, as she stared up at Marcus. "In the floor. He kept a small, wooden writing tablet hidden under the floor near his bed. Did you check the floor boards?"

***

"Cunitius," Marcus bellowed as he banged his fist on the door to the tall apartment block. "Cunitius get your arse out of bed right now and bring a torch. It's me. Marcus."

Outside in the dark alley, it was cold. Impatiently Marcus turned to look down the alley, but in the darkness of the night, he could not see far. In his hand he was holding a small oil lamp, which cast a fragile flickering light onto the door. Down the stinking alley and hidden in the shadows, a drunk was snoring loudly. From inside the building there was no immediate reply. Then, as Marcus banged his fist against the door again and cried out, someone poked their head out of a window in one of the higher floors and screamed at him to be quiet.

"What the hell are you doing here?" Cunitius exclaimed irritably, as he hastily pulled a cloak over his body. "It's the fucking middle of the night." The investigator stood in the doorway clutching a lit torch. He looked like he had just woken up.

"I need your help," Marcus demanded as he started out down the alley. "There is a new lead in our investigation, but we must hurry."

"Does this mean that we are friends now," Cunitius exclaimed sarcastically, as he hurried on after Marcus.

"Not friends," Marcus retorted as he kept walking. "Let's just say that I want to get my money's worth out of you."

"What's the new lead?" Cunitius replied as he caught up with Marcus. The two of them emerged from the alley and stormed down the main street. "What's so damned important that it can't wait until the morning? For the god's sake Marcus, the streets are not safe to walk during the night, especially in this neighbourhood. You are crazy; you know that."

"Are you scared?" Marcus replied.

"Shut up," Cunitius snapped irritably, as he quickly glanced around at the silent and dark doorways, alleys and vestibules.

"A few days ago, a bronze statue of Ceres was stolen from her temple," Marcus said, as he marched along the street holding up his lamp. "You can imagine the panic amongst the priests. They believe the sky is going to fall on their heads," he added in a contemptuous voice. "But at the same time as the statue was stolen, someone left a message for me on the walls inside the temple. The message was scrawled in red paint. Sound familiar?" Marcus took a deep breath as he continued walking. "Whoever stole the statue; they are the same people who attacked the watermills and set fire to the grain warehouse. This is their work. A priest of Ceres, by the name of Evander, stole the statue but I think he was doing it for someone else. Evander didn't show up to work the next day and we have just found his body. Someone murdered him; cut off his dick too."

"Shit," Cunitius exclaimed, "That must have hurt."

"It's likely that Evander stole the statue because he was asked to by his killers," Marcus said quickly. "Initially I thought he may have been paid to steal the statue and leave the message for me, but now I am not so sure. There could have been another motive. Anyway, tonight I discovered a new lead. We're going back to Evander's apartment. There is something there that may lead us to the people who are behind these attacks and these messages."

"I don't understand. What are we looking for?" Cunitius frowned as he strode on along beside Marcus.

"Evander was a part time prostitute," Marcus snapped. "He kept a record of who his clients were. He hid a wooden tablet under the floor-boards of his apartment. We missed it on our first search. The tablet may contain the name of his killer."

"You said that this priest could have had another motive for stealing the statue, other than money," Cunitius said hastily. "What do you mean? What other motive could he have?"

"Love," Marcus snapped grimly.

***

Someone had fixed two ropes across the open doorway into Evander's apartment and had hung up a no-entry sign. Marcus paused on the landing and, holding up his lamp he turned to look around, but in the darkness, all was quiet and peaceful. The whole apartment block seemed to be asleep. Carefully he ducked under the sign and entered the dark room. Evander's body had been removed but, as he held up his lamp again, he could see that all the furniture was still there. Behind him Cunitius was muttering quietly to himself, as he turned to examine the apartment.

Crouching beside the bed, Marcus placed his lamp on the floor and then carefully began to feel around the floorboards with his fingers. The blond whore had said that the hiding place was near to the bed. As his fingers moved across the floor, Marcus suddenly grunted as he felt one of the boards move. Reaching out to his lamp, he brought it closer. The floorboard was loose. Hastily Cunitius came over to him and held up his own lamp and as he did, Marcus pried away the floorboard and reached down into the small cavity below. For a moment he silently rummaged around in the small space beneath the floor.

"Shit," Marcus hissed as he straightened up. "It's empty. There is nothing here."

"A dead end," Cunitius groaned. "So much for that whore's word. She lied to you Marcus."

"Maybe there is another hiding place," Marcus growled, refusing to give up.

"What are you doing?" a voice suddenly exclaimed from the doorway into the room.

Marcus and Cunitius whirled round, caught completely by surprise and, as he did, Marcus's hand grasped hold of the pommel of his sword.

In the darkness around the doorway, he could make out the dim outline of a figure. Snatching up his lamp Marcus raised it and pulled his sword free from its sheath and advanced across the room towards the door. And as he did, in the flickering reddish light he caught sight of a face. It was Evander's neighbour, the man whom he'd questioned a few days ago. The white tufts of hair sticking out from the side of his bald head were unmistakable.

"Ah it's you," the man said, as he stood his ground. "You were here before with the priests. I recognise you. Are you a friend of Evander?"

Marcus hesitated as he glared at the man. "We are looking for the person who killed him," Marcus said at last. "That's why we are here."

"You were looking for something," the man said gesturing in the direction of the bed. "Did you find it?"

"What's it to you if we did," Marcus said sharply.

The man standing in the doorway sighed. "Evander was all right," he said quietly. "He was a kind man although I did not approve of the company he kept. He knocked on my door a few days before he was killed and asked me to look after this for him. He said it was valuable and, that if anything happened to him, I should give it to the proper authorities."

And in the faint light, Marcus saw that the man was holding a small wooden writing tablet in his hand.

"I hope this helps you catch his killer," the man exclaimed. "Evander didn't deserve to die. He was a good man."

Swearing softly to himself, Marcus handed his torch to Cunitius and hastily took the tablet from the man's outstretched hand. Then carefully he opened it. In the hissing and flickering light from the oil lamps, he peered down at the long list of names, addresses, dates and numbers that had been beautifully etched into the thin plywood.

"These must be the details of his clients," Marcus exclaimed, as his eyes went down the list of names. Abruptly he stopped talking and frowned.

"Blaikisa," Marcus blurted out, shaking his head in confusion. "The last name on the list is called Blaikisa. That's odd. That's the name of Cassius's freedman, but how can this be? Cassius told me that he was dead."

"Could it be another man with the same name" Cunitius said quickly.

"There is only one way to find out," Marcus growled, as he stared down at the tablet, his cheeks colouring with sudden foreboding. "It's not a common name. Blaikisa is a Dacian name. Come on, there's an address here, it's not far. Let's go and pay this Blaikisa a visit."

Slamming the tablet shut, Marcus turned to the man in the doorway.

"You are a good citizen Sir," he said and with that he pushed past the man, and started down the dark, deserted stairs.

***

The address was hard to find in the dark, but eventually Marcus located the building. It was another tall insulae apartment block down a narrow, twisting street. Trying the front door to the building, he found it locked. Swearing softly, Marcus turned to look up at the building, but again, in the night sky, he could see no lights in the windows.

"It's locked," he hissed in frustration.

Beside him Cunitius did not reply and he seemed to be fumbling with something in his pocket. Then with a little grin, he produced an iron latch-lifter, a simple metal rod with a hook at the end. Pressing himself up against the door, he quickly worked the latch lifter into a crack between the door and the wall and after a few moments Marcus heard the latch slide upwards. With a triumphant look, Cunitius grasped hold of the door knob and opened the door.

"They always have cheap locks in places like this," he whispered. "I never leave home without a latch lifter."

"I knew I would need the services of a thief," Marcus muttered, as drawing his pugio army knife, he hastily slipped into the dark entry hall of the building.

As he slowly ascended the stairs Marcus strained to listen, but all was quiet and peaceful. There were still a couple of hours before dawn. Reaching the fourth-floor landing, he paused and glanced at the closed doors leading to the different apartments. Behind him on the stairs, Cunitius slowly pulled a knife from his belt. The cold steel gleamed in the torch light. Silently Marcus turned and pointed at the door with a number six above it. Then quietly he crossed the landing and pressed himself up against the wall beside the doorway, clutching his knife. Cunitius followed him onto the landing and did the same on the other side of the door. For a moment Marcus waited for his breathing to calm down. Then slowly he tried the door handle, but the door would not budge. Suddenly from inside the room he thought he heard a noise. Straining every muscle, he listened and as he did, he heard the noise again. Someone was home and moving about in the room. Marcus closed his eyes as he tried to decide what to do. It was either a knock on the door, get Cunitius to use his latch lifter or suffer another bruised shoulder. Inside the room he heard a little noise again. It sounded like someone stuffing something into a bag.

With a splintering crash and a sharp cry of pain, Marcus came crashing through the door ripping the flimsy lock from the wall and sending splinters of wood and pieces of metal flying through the room. As Marcus tumbled to the floor, he was greeted by a startled cry. A man was standing beside the open window frozen in horror and staring at him. A half-packed travelling bag lay on the unmade bed and, leaning against the far wall a bronze statue of Ceres gleamed in the torch light.

"Blaikisa," Marcus shouted, as he started to scramble to his feet. But as Cunitius came charging into the room, clutching his torch and his knife the man, without saying a word, turned and leapt out of the window.

"Fuck," Marcus roared as he stumbled over towards the window and thrust his head out.

Looking down at the street below he could just make out a motionless figure lying on the stone cobbles.

"He could never survive that jump," Cunitius gasped, as he too poked his head out of the window and looked down at the street.

Marcus didn't reply, as snatching Cunitius's oil lamp, he stormed out of the room and thundered down the stairs. Bursting out into the dark street he slowed down as he approached the body. A large pool of blood was slowly spreading out onto the cobbles and, as Marcus reached out and turned the body over, he could see that the man had broken his neck and was dead.

"Shit," Marcus swore softly. "Oh, you fool."

He had just managed to drag the corpse into the hallway of the building, when Cunitius came down the stairs holding a small earthenware jar.

"Looks like our friend was packing up to leave town," Cunitius exclaimed, as he looked down at the body. "He had the statue and I found this under his bed," he added, as he showed Marcus the small pot of red paint. "There is plenty more from where this came from. Enough to paint the whole of Rome. I think we have caught our man, Marcus."

Marcus nodded and gazed down at the blood-soaked corpse. Then, as a startled-looking tenant appeared on the staircase, he turned.

"Government business, go back to your apartment and stay there," he yelled, brandishing his knife.

As the tenant swiftly fled back up the stairs, Cunitius burst out laughing and slapped Marcus across his back.

"Government business. I haven't had this much fun in ages," Cunitius blurted out. "We should do this more often Marcus. You and I make a good team."

***

It was dawn and to the east the sun was a red ball on the horizon and was growing in strength and warmth. Grimly and tiredly Marcus looked up as he caught sight of his villa, as it appeared through the trees. And as he drew closer to his home, the sense of foreboding grew. Kyna would be wanting to know where he'd been all night. She would probably be frantic with worry, but before he could settle her there was something more important that he needed to know. The answer to which he had begun to dread.

Somewhere out of sight a dog was barking, and the scent of freshly baked-bread was growing stronger. In his right hand he was grasping the reins of a horse over which he'd slung Blaikisa's corpse. The dead man's arms and legs hung limply on either side of the beast, pointing at the ground. And bringing up the rear, Indus kept his eyes firmly fixed on the horizon. He didn't look happy and had not said a word since Marcus had sent a messenger to fetch him. In his hands the Batavian was carrying the bronze statue of Ceres.

As he came up to the door of his villa it burst open and Kyna came rushing out. Her face looked ashen. She stopped abruptly, as she caught sight of the body slung across the horse's back.

"Marcus there…," she exclaimed, but he held up his hand to silence her. Bringing the horse to a halt, he reached out and pulled the corpse down onto the ground. Rolling it over with his foot, he gestured at the body.

"Is this Cassius's freedman, Blaikisa?" Marcus asked, in a quiet voice. "Do you recognise this man?"

Kyna stood rooted to the ground as she stared down at the corpse. Then quickly she raised her hand to her mouth and gasped.

"I think so," she said, her voice fading as she turned to gaze at Marcus with large eyes. "Yes, I think that is him."

Marcus nodded and grimly turned to gaze at the corpse. Cassius had lied to him.

"Marcus," Kyna said urgently and something in her voice made him turn to look at his wife. "Marcus, we received a letter," Kyna said in a shaken voice. "It was delivered late last night whilst you were out. Indus thinks that the man who delivered it was the same man who was here before, who warned us to leave Rome. The letter Marcus. It's come from Elsa."

Chapter Seventeen – The Collapse of Marcus's World

Marcus gazed in silence at the letter in his hand. The scroll of delicate papyrus had been tightly wound around a wooden stick and the wax seal, bearing the proud stamp of Cassius's house and family, was unbroken. The letter looked fragile, small and insignificant. Kyna stood facing him in the main living area of their villa. His wife's face had drained of all colour and she was furiously picking at her fingernails.

"Why would Elsa send us a letter," Marcus asked with a confused frown. "She doesn't live that far away. If she had something to say, then why not come to our house and tell us in person?"

"I don't know," Kyna whispered hoarsely. "But something is not right Marcus. I can sense it. You had better read what it says."

Marcus nodded and carefully he broke the seal, unrolled the letter and began to read the small, neatly written words out loud.

Elsa to Marcus, I have waited a very long time to write you this letter. But now that I am old and strong enough, the day has finally come - and I am glad. It feels that a burden has been lifted from my shoulders and that I am free at last.

You will remember the day that we first met all those years ago, in the depth of winter, at my father's home at the Charterhouse lead mines in Britannia. You thought you were being kind to me and Armin that day, by sparing our lives after you had so brutally murdered my father, Lucius. But you were wrong. What kind of person do you think I am? Did you really think that I would forget or forgive you for what you did to my father Lucius and my uncle Bestia? You murdered them both. I know what your family did to them. I know the whole long sordid feud between you and your father Corbulo and my father Lucius and uncle Bestia. I have not forgotten, and now is the time for vengeance. I am my father's daughter, not yours and I owe his spirit that much. The dead shall have their revenge on you Marcus. They will watch you squirm and twist, they shall laugh at you and they shall spit on you, for you deserve nothing less.

I want you to know that it is I, who has caused all your recent misfortune. This was my plan from the start and no one else's, although Cassius my husband and his freedman Blaikisa, agreed to help me. Cassius was good at fooling you Marcus, he enjoyed the part he played, and Blaikisa served us well. But I am not the heartless bitch you think I am. Many years ago, I vowed that I would punish you for what you did to my family. But you did not deserve death. That was never my intention for I know that there is some goodness in you. So, I gave you a chance. To walk away, but you ignored it. So now you shall bear the consequences. I do not seek your death. No, Marcus your punishment will not be that easy. You are going to witness the collapse of everything that you have spent years trying to build. I am going to take away everything you have, your reputation, your career, your position in society and your money. I am going to ruin you Marcus. I am going to take away everything that you love and possess. Just like you did to me and my brother. My vengeance will be complete when I see you fall. And once it is done I want you to know that I, and Cassius and our new-born child, will live out our lives in peace and happiness, far away from you, and that I shall never think of you again.

Do not try to search for us Marcus. When you read this, we will be long gone. You will never find us. The attacks on the watermills, the grain warehouse and the stealing of the statue were intended to raise the pressure on you. But what is going to finish you off is the revelation and publication of every secret that you have. And rest assured that throughout all these years spent in your household, I have come to know them all. So, I want you to know that I have sent a letter to Attianus and another to Nigrinus and a third to Similis. I am going to reveal everything. The letters list your crimes, every dirty little secret that you have Marcus. The murders of two veterans of the 2nd Batavian Auxiliary Cohort, for which you and your father Corbulo are responsible. The fact that Nigrinus had Similis bribed to get you your position in government. I shall also reveal to the senate, Fergus's role in protecting Hadrian and how you tried to warn Fergus about the assassination attempt on Hadrian. These letters are going to destroy your reputation. They are going to provide your enemies with the fuel to burn down your house. It is time Rome and your friends in the senate knew what kind of man you really are. And do not think that you can take your frustration out on my little brother Armin. For you will never see him again or the fortune in gold and silver, that you thought you had safely buried on the farm on Vectis. Both shall be gone by the time you read this letter.

I hope you spend the rest of your life Marcus, thinking and reflecting on what you have done to my family, and that your nights are sleepless and disturbed. Elsa to Marcus.

Slowly Marcus dropped the letter onto the floor. His face had grown pale and for a moment he seemed too stunned to do anything. Across from him, Kyna was staring at him in wide-eyed horror. Then without saying a word, Marcus yanked his knife from his belt, strode out of the room, found Blaikisa's corpse and viciously slashed the freedman's throat. Unsteadily he staggered back onto his feet and dropped the knife, as Kyna and Indus rushed over to him.

"Cunomoltus was right," Marcus gasped, barely able to breath, as he wildly turned to stare at his wife. "Cunomoltus, my brother was right. We were at Vebriacum near the lead mines in Britannia, eleven years ago. He warned me that keeping Lucius's children alive was just storing up trouble for the future. He told me that one day they may try to take revenge for their father's death and I ignored him. He told me that I had a good heart but a stupid head. He was right. I have been a fool. A damned fool."

"You could not have known this," Kyna said hastily. "None of us saw this coming. Elsa, she seemed so content. She fooled us all."

"Her brother Armin," Marcus muttered, as his eyes widened. "The boy, yes maybe he could have wanted revenge but not Elsa. Not Elsa. She was like a daughter to me. I tried to raise her as best as I could. I gave her everything. She was my girl."

"Elsa has chosen her path Marcus," Kyna said, with sudden strength in her voice. Coming up to his side, Kyna reached out and grasped Marcus's arm in a firm grip and, as he looked at his wife, he saw a sudden resolve in Kyna's eyes. "She has chosen her path," Kyna said, as a single tear appeared in her eyes. "And now, so must we. We must be strong, husband. We will survive this. We will survive this because we are strong."

Marcus gasped and turned to look away. Then at last he nodded, and a little colour seemed to return to his face.

***

The view of the sprawling city of Rome from his garden terrace was magnificent but Marcus did not seem to notice, as he sat morosely in his chair and absent-mindedly gazed out over the metropolis. He was unshaven, and he looked tired. Dark wrinkles had woven themselves around his eyes. Leaning upon the arm rest of the chair, he reached out to steady his shaking left arm. An untouched cup of posca sat on the table beside him. It was morning and five days had passed since he had read Elsa's letter. Grimly, Marcus stared into space. Elsa's words had struck home like physical blows. Her betrayal had been worse than the pain of losing his fingers during the Dacian wars. They had hurt more than the experience of nearly starving to death, during his captivity in Caledonia when the druids had been preparing him as a human sacrifice. Worse than Lucius's betrayal during the Brigantine uprising. How could she have done this to him? He had loved her like a daughter. How could he not have seen this coming? Slowly Marcus let go of his left arm and reached for the cup of posca. Kyna was right. Pondering endlessly about it was not going to do him any good. He needed to be strong. He would survive this betrayal. He had to. People were counting on him.

There had been much to do and keeping himself busy had taken his mind of the pain of the betrayal. Within hours of reading her letter, he'd received confirmation that Cassius's house was indeed deserted. There had been no trace of Cassius or Elsa. No one knew where they had gone. They had just vanished. But there had been more urgent business that needed his attention. If what Elsa had said was true, about her little brother Armin stealing the Dacian gold, which he'd buried for safe-keeping on the farm on Vectis, then she had financially crippled him. That would have consequences for his position as a senator if it became public. Dylis was the only one, apart from himself, who knew where the treasure was buried, but Armin would have had plenty of time to discover its location. The bulk of the gold that Fergus had brought back from the Dacian war had been kept on the farm. Taking a sip of posca, Marcus gazed grimly out across the city of Rome. He'd immediately sent a messenger to Dylis, his sister on the Isle of Vectis, warning her about what had happened. But it would take weeks before the messenger arrived. And Elsa had the advantage for she seemed to have been planning this for years.

He would just keep on going, he had told Kyna. He was still prefect of the grain supply and he had a job to do despite what had happened. Draining the cup of posca into his mouth,

Marcus reached up and wiped his lips with his hand. He'd already started making inquiries for a suitable candidate to replace Cassius, and just yesterday he'd received the welcome news that additional supplies of grain were being despatched to Rome from Sicily, Africa and Dacia. Better times are coming. His letters, appealing for aid to the provincial governors, were beginning to pay off. The welcome news had come on top of a positive response from the fishing fleets and Italian farmers, who had all promised to increase their production of food. And the day after tomorrow he would go to the senate and give them an update on the efforts that were being made to build a new grain fleet. He needed to regain the initiative. The food emergency in Rome was being brought under control. Since the return of their precious statue, the priests of Ceres had made a multitude of offerings begging for divine favour. With a good new harvest in Egypt and no further maritime disasters, the crisis would be over by the end of the year. There was no doubt about that. The time had come for the senate to recognise his work and stop panicking about the situation. He had to get them to move on. Better times are coming. He had to wrest the initiative from his detractors and he would do it. He would push on with his job, for what else should he do.

"Sir, you wished to see me," a voice said behind him. Rising stiffly to his feet, Marcus turned to see Aledus, old friend of Fergus, rap out a quick salute.

"Yes," Marcus said with a little nod. "I need you to do something for me and I need you to do it right away."

As he spoke to Aledus in a low, urgent and conspiratorial voice the young army veteran frowned. At last he nodded before saluting again and hastening away. Marcus looked pensive as he watched him leave. The young man's errand was just a precaution but in these tense, uncertain days it was the smart thing to do. Aledus was turning out to be a good, useful man. Turning away, Marcus crossed the terrace and reached out to give the black cat a tickle under its chin.

It was a couple of hours later, whilst he was working out in his garden writing a letter, when a slave came hastening towards him.

"Sir," the slave said lowering his eyes. "There is someone here to see you. It's Lady Claudia, Sir. Shall I show her onto the terrace?"

"Yes, I will meet her here and bring another cup of posca; make it two cups," Marcus growled, as he laid down his iron-tipped stylus and quickly closed the small, wooden writing tablet.

"Marcus," Claudia said stiffly, as she came up to him and reached out to touch him lightly on both hands.

"Claudia," Marcus replied with a little welcoming smile, as he quickly kissed her on her cheek. "What brings you to my home?"

Claudia sighed and for a moment she avoided his gaze, and as she did Marcus noticed a tenseness about her that was not normal.

"Listen I have some news," Claudia said as she looked up at him. "Bad news I'm afraid. I've heard that a couple of days ago Nigrinus received a letter. The letter came from an anonymous source, but whoever wrote it seemed to know you and your family very well. The letter contained an appeal to Nigrinus to have you prosecuted for the murder in Britannia of a retired officer of the 2nd Batavian Auxiliary Cohort. It also claims that you had a hand in the death of another Roman citizen, a former senator by the name of Priscinus. The author of the letter alleges that you murdered your fellow officer, and that you were complicit in the murder of Priscinus, by helping cover up the evidence. Apparently, you helped the killer, a Christian woman disappear." Claudia sighed. "The letter goes on to say that you also helped your son Fergus prevent the assassination of Hadrian. There is more…"

Claudia stopped speaking as Marcus held up his hand.

"What has been Nigrinus's reaction?" he said sharply. "What does he plan to do?"

Claudia bit her lip as she gazed at Marcus. "He has a called another meeting of the inner council," she said quietly. "They are meeting today here in Rome. I only heard about it from a friend. I am worried. I fear for your future Marcus. Nigrinus is already furious with you. He is openly questioning your loyalty to him and the party. These latest accusations against you may tip him over the edge."

Marcus nodded and lowered his eyes to the ground.

"Claudia, how nice to see you again," Kyna said suddenly, as she crossed the terrace towards them.

In response Claudia dipped her head gracefully and the two women quickly exchanged kisses, but there was no warmth in their exchange. Marcus closed his eyes and ran his fingers across his face. Ever since he'd told Kyna about his affair with Claudia during the siege of Luguvalium, the two women had been civil but utterly cold towards each other. But the affair had been over twenty-five years ago. Could they not just move on?

"Is my husband in trouble with you again," Kyna asked as she gave Claudia a bright smile. "Or has Nigrinus sent you to deliver another message?"

"Your husband is in trouble, but not with me," Claudia replied smoothly. "I shall always be your friend and a friend to your son Ahern. I came here to warn you that Nigrinus is about to make a move against you. I don't know what he is planning to do, but you need to prepare yourselves."

"We know this," Kyna said in an ice-cold voice. "How is Ahern, my son?"

"He is well," Claudia replied quickly. "He is throwing his energy into creating a new steam machine. But it's likely to take him another year to build it."

"Claudia," Marcus said, intervening with a grave voice. "If Nigrinus wishes to have my resignation then I shall of course give it to him. But I have never betrayed our faction. I have kept my vow. I am still loyal to the party and everything that I have done is in the service of Rome. Better times are coming. Will you tell him this? Will you impress on him that I can still be trusted?"

Claudia was silent for a moment, as she gazed fondly at Marcus. Then she nodded. "If I get the chance, I shall convey your message," she replied.

"I shall let you two say goodbye to each other," Kyna said sharply, as she turned and started to walk away.

When Kyna had vanished into the house, Claudia turned and gave Marcus a little wry look. "I see that you didn't tell your wife about Ahern's adventures with that prostitute in the Black Lady," she said.

Marcus grunted. "I will tell her when the time is right," he replied. "But right now, she has too many other things to worry about, as do I."

Claudia nodded. "You are a good man Marcus," she said at last. "I knew it from the first time we met at Luguvalium. You saved my life and that of my daughter twice, I recall." Claudia fell silent as a sudden sadness seemed to come over her. Then lifting her head, she gave him a quick kiss on his cheek.

"Goodbye Marcus," she said, as she hurried away without looking back.

***

A day had passed since Claudia's visit and Marcus was busy rehearsing the speech he would deliver to the senate the next day, when Indus appeared in the doorway to his bedroom. Annoyed at the intrusion, Marcus halted in mid-flow and turned to his bodyguard.

"Can't you see I am busy," Marcus growled.

"There are two senators at the door," Indus replied, in his native language. "They say that they wish to speak to you Sir."

"Senators," Marcus frowned.

"Yes Sir," Indus replied dutifully.

Laying down his speech notes on the bed, Marcus strode out of the bedroom and headed in the direction of the hallway. It was around noon and, out on the terrace he caught a brief glimpse of Aledus, flirting with one of the slave girls. With Indus following closely behind, Marcus swept across the central living space of his villa and as he approached the hallway, he spotted and recognised the two men. They were standing in the hallway still wearing their cloaks and waiting patiently for him. Underneath their cloaks the pair were wearing their fine, white senatorial toga's. The senators belonged to his own faction, the War Party. Stiffly Marcus extended his hand in greeting but neither man inclined to take it. They looked stern and unfriendly.

"Well gentlemen, what can I do for you" Marcus said as he slowly lowered his hand.

"We're not here on a social call Marcus," one of the senators said in a grave voice. "We are here because Nigrinus asked us to pay you a visit."

"I see," Marcus nodded as he looked down at the floor.

For a moment the two senators remained silent. Then quickly they glanced at each other and from the folds of his toga, one of the men produced a sheathed gladius, and with a bang he placed it on a nearby table.

Quietly Marcus stared at the sheathed sword lying on the table and, as he did the silence in the hallway started to grow ugly.

"What is that?" Marcus asked in a quiet voice, gesturing at the sword.

"We are here on Nigrinus's orders," one of the senators said sharply. "A meeting took place yesterday of the inner council and a decision has been made regarding your fate. You have betrayed us for the last time. Nigrinus has found you guilty of treason. The punishment is death. Nigrinus commands you to kill yourself, Marcus. We are here to see that you carry out his orders."

Marcus stared at the two senators. Then slowly he turned to gaze at the sheathed sword lying on the table.

"And what will happen to my family, if I obey," Marcus said quietly.

"Nigrinus is an honourable man," one of the senators replied, raising his chin. "He has offered you this death as an honourable way out. Obey his command and he shall see to it that no harm will come to your family and that your name shall continue to be honoured. Your family will be allowed to keep their estates, jobs, position and place in society. But refuse, and every member of your family will be rooted out and executed; your estates will be taken from them and your very name will be erased from history. The choice is yours Marcus. Nigrinus has been generous. He has been merciful. It could have been a lot worse."

Marcus's face had grown ashen and for a long moment he said nothing, as he gazed at the sheathed sword.

"Have you somewhere quiet where we can go and do this," one of the senators snapped, craning his neck to get a better look at the house. "It's so much easier when the family do not need to witness it."

Marcus nodded. Then slowly he walked across the hall and grasped hold of the sheathed sword. Sliding the gladius from its sheath, he gazed at the cold hard steel.

"A soldier's death," he muttered, as he gazed at the blade. "An honourable way out. That's what we used to talk about in the army. Nigrinus is indeed an honourable man to grant me a way out like this."

Then Marcus looked up. "Indus," he said in a calm voice, pointing at one of the smartly dressed senators. "Kill that man."

"What! No!" The senator cried out in horror. But it was already too late for him. Swiftly and silently Indus crossed the hall and as he did, a knife appeared in his hand and before the startled senator could raise his hand to protect himself, the Batavian had sliced open his throat. As the dying man collapsed to the floor, a fountain of blood went spraying across the fine mosaic floor-tiles. Raising the blade of the sword, Marcus calmly pointed it at the remaining senator and advanced towards him, and as he did the man stumbled back in terror.

"No, no, no," the senator cried out, his face draining of all colour.

On the floor his colleague was writhing in agony, as he choked to death with Indus standing over him.

"On your knees now," Marcus cried out, as he forced the senator down onto the floor with his sword.

"If I don't report back in a few hours," the senator wailed, holding up his hand to try and shield himself. "Nigrinus has thirty armed men ready to come to this house. They will kill anyone they find inside. You are a dead man walking Marcus. You and your whole family are already dead."

"Maybe it's already too late for me and for you," Marcus hissed. "But if Nigrinus thinks that I am going to kill myself for him, to fall on my sword for that dick, then he has badly underestimated me. No one threatens my family in my own fucking house."

"Do you want me to kill him Sir?" Indus said as he glared at the kneeling, terrified senator.

With a swift practised movement Marcus drove his sword straight into the kneeling senator's neck, killing him instantly. As he pulled his sword free and watched the corpse flop sideways onto the floor, Marcus felt his breath coming in ragged gasps. Stumbling backwards he dropped the sword and it clattered noisily onto the stone floor. At the sound, Kyna, Aledus and one of the female slaves appeared in the doorway. As she caught sight of the two corpses and the bloody mess strewn across the hall, Kyna cried out and quickly raised her hand to her mouth. Marcus steadied himself against the wall, as he too gazed down at the pools of blood that were merging and spreading out across the floor.

"They came here," he said, breathing heavily; "these fine senators came into my house to demand that I kill myself. Nigrinus has ordered me to fall on my sword but fuck that. The prick is not worth it. He was never worth it. So, I quit."

"Marcus," Kyna cried out in alarm, as she stumbled across the hall and caught hold of him with both hands, forcing him to look at her. "You killed them. These are Nigrinus's men. We can't stay here. Not now Marcus. They will kill us all. Think about Dylis's children, think about Ahern. They are all innocent."

Slowly Marcus turned to gaze at Kyna. Then at last he nodded, and his features seemed to soften, and fondly he reached up to touch her cheek.

"Yes, you are right," he said quietly. "We must leave Rome. We must leave everything behind. There is no choice now. We shall go back to Dylis, Cunomoltus, Petrus and Jowan and the farm on Vectis, but we don't have much time. Once Nigrinus discovers what has happened, he will send his men to our house and kill all of us. We are fugitives now. We must flee."

Kyna nodded vigorously and as she clasped hold of him and stared at him, tears started to appear in her eyes. Gently Marcus ran his fingers across her cheek. Then firmly he removed her hands from around his face and quickly turned to Indus.

"We must hurry," Marcus snapped. "You heard what that senator said. We only have a few hours before Nigrinus's men arrive to find out what is going on. Get the horses ready to ride. We will pack only those things we can carry on the horses. Everything else will have to be left behind. You," Marcus cried jabbing his finger at one of his slaves. "Go to Lady Claudia's school and bring Ahern back with you. If he asks you why, tell him that we are leaving Rome urgently, and that his life may be in danger. Bring him back here. Now go. Hurry."

As the slave vanished out through the door, Indus cleared his throat.

"Sir, if you are planning to escape on horseback then I hope you have a plan. Once he discovers what has happened, Nigrinus will scour all the roads leading away from Rome. He is likely to place a bounty on our heads. No offence Sir, but I don't think we are going to be able to outride him and his men. Not with a woman, a boy and baggage."

"We're not going to be travelling to Vectis on horseback," Marcus said quickly, as he glanced at Aledus. "We'll only need the horses to get us to Portus. From there we are going to be taking a ship all the way home."

"A ship," Indus exclaimed with a frown.

"Yes," Marcus nodded. "Yesterday I sent Aledus here to check on the repair work for the Hermes. It was just a precaution, but I am glad I did. Alexandros assures us that the Hermes is seaworthy. We're damned lucky that he is still in port. Now get those horses ready."

Chapter Eighteen – "We Leave Everything Behind"

The villa was in chaos as the slaves rushed around packing valuables into the few saddle bags and in the middle of it all stood Kyna, her hands in her hair, her lips trembling, as she tried to direct the frantic activity. But there was little that she could really do. Marcus could see that she was close to bursting into tears. The realisation of what was happening was gutting his wife. They were not going to be able to pack more than the horses would be able to carry and there was no time. They were going to have to abandon the house, the veteran's charity and the vast bulk of their possessions. There would not even be time to say goodbye to good friends.

"We leave everything behind," Marcus cried out savagely. "Pack only the most valued possessions and those that we can carry on the horses. Hurry."

Then, avoiding Kyna's gaze, he turned to Aledus who was standing around looking helpless. Hastily Marcus tapped him on his chest.

"Take one of the horses," he said in an urgent voice. "Ride to Portus. Warn Alexandros and tell him that I need the Hermes ready to sail within a few hours. Tell him that we are coming. Wait for us in the harbour. All right. Go."

"Yes Sir," Aledus replied, as a little colour shot into his cheeks. Then the young man was off, limping out through the doorway. In the hall the two corpses of the slain senators still lay where they'd fallen. Pools of blood had formed around their bodies. There had been no time to move them. Marcus did not watch Aledus leave. Instead he hurried into his bedroom and, reaching under the bed, he pulled out a metal strong box. Inserting a key into the lock, he opened the box, rummaged inside and took out several small wooden writing tablets. Dumping them onto the bed, he fumbled for a stylus pen, opened one of the tablets and began to furiously write onto the thin plywood. The letters were to Paulinus and Lady Claudia, transferring the ownership of his villa and the charity into their joint possession, whether they wanted the buildings or not. The letters would have some legal status, but on their own they would not stop Nigrinus from seizing his property for himself, if he was determined to do so. In Rome he had learned, the law was only obeyed by the ordinary citizens. The rich and powerful more or less did what they liked.

As he signed the final letter, Marcus took a deep breath and gazed down at the documents. It was done. But this was no time for regrets. Slipping the letters into his tunic pocket, he reached out to the remaining wooden writing tablets and hastened back into the atrium of his home. The slaves had nearly finished packing, and the pitiful looking collection of saddle bags sat in the middle of the atrium.

"Come here, all of you," Marcus cried out to his slaves. "Form a line. I wish to speak to you all. Quick."

Hastily the four slaves dropped what they were doing, and half ran up to Marcus and obediently formed a line in front of him. At Marcus's side, Kyna gasped as she realised what he was about to do.

"All of you," Marcus said sternly, as his eyes quickly moved from one slave to the next. "Kyna and I can no longer stay in Rome and we are not going to force you to come with us. I know some of you have loved-ones in Rome." Marcus paused and looked down at the floor. "You have served us loyally and faithfully," he said in a grave voice. "I would like to thank you for this. As gratitude I am making you all freedmen and women. Here are your official letters of manumission. They are official legal documents stating that you are now free men and women."

Silently Marcus went down the line of two men and two women, handing each one of the small wooden tablets. The letters had been written years before and he'd been keeping them for the suitable moment when he would free his slaves and now that moment had come. The slaves said nothing as they took possession of the documents and gazed down at them.

"You are free now," Marcus said in a quieter voice. "Now go. Leave us and get as far away from this house as possible. The men who will be coming here shortly are going to kill everyone they find. It is no longer safe for you to stay here. So, go. All of you. Go."

For a moment the slaves did not move. Then the two men and one of the women quickly and silently acknowledged Marcus and, giving Kyna a swift farewell hug, they slipped out through the door. Marcus watched them disappear. Then he turned and frowned. One of the women was still standing before him. It was the same slave who Aledus had been flirting with.

"Sir," the young woman stammered nervously. "I am on my own. I have no family here in Rome and my mistress seems distressed. She will need me on the journey ahead. So, I shall stay at her side and come with you. This is my decision as a free woman."

Marcus stared at the woman in surprise. Then before he could do anything, Kyna came up to her and gave her a silent hug.

"Sir," Indus suddenly called out from the open doorway. "The horses are ready and prepared. We can go."

"Good," Marcus snapped, as leaving the two women, he quickly grasped hold of the heavily-laden saddle bags and began to drag them across the floor towards Indus. "Pack the bags onto the horses but we don't leave until Ahern gets here."

"Sir, Nigrinus and his men may show up at any time," Indus said quickly.

"No. We wait until Ahern gets here," Marcus said, as he kicked aside one of the corpses that was blocking his path.

***

Marcus, clad in cloak and dark travelling clothes, stood alone in his garden. For a moment everything around him was quiet and peaceful. Fondly he turned to gaze at the tiles, statues, plants and flowers. He loved this garden. There were many happy memories here. How many countless hours had he spent in this place. He couldn't remember. He had created his garden from nothing and now he had to say goodbye. He would not be coming back to this house. He would not be coming back to Rome. This was farewell. With a sigh he wrenched his eyes away and turned to gaze out over the sprawling city of Rome, that stretched away below him. It sure was a great view he thought. The mighty and magnificent temples, domes, columns and buildings seemed to gleam in the sunlight and, out on the Tiber the river barges were ploughing up and down. And as he gazed down at the proud and eternal city, Marcus's expression hardened. For thirty-five years he had served Rome, first in the army and then as a politician. He had done his duty. He had kept his vow. He had given his best and how had Rome repaid his service? They had tried to kill him. They had threatened his family. They had besmirched his reputation. They had mocked him. And now they had run him out of the city, forcing him to abandon everything. As his face darkened, Marcus clenched his right hand into a fist. He was done with politics. Whoever now became the next emperor, Nigrinus or Hadrian, it didn't matter anymore. With enemies on both sides he was fucked either way.

Giving Rome and his garden a final glance, Marcus turned and headed back into the house. Kyna and her freedwoman, both clad in grey travelling cloaks, their heads covered by hoods, were waiting for him in the doorway, and out on the road Indus was holding the reins of the four horses. The saddlebags strapped across the beast's backs bulged outwards.

"We're ready to go Marcus," Indus cried out in his native language.

"Where is that damned boy?" Marcus growled, as he strode out into the road and turned to look down the hill, but the road was deserted.

Avoiding looking at Kyna, Marcus impatiently started to pace up and down in the road. Indus was right. How long could he wait? Nigrinus's men may appear at any moment.

"Shit," he hissed as he glared down the road. Where the hell was Ahern?

At last Kyna cried out and pointed at something down the road, and as he whirled round and peered down the hill, Marcus's heart sank. The slave he'd sent to fetch Ahern was stumbling back up the hill towards him and he was alone.

"Where is Ahern?" Marcus cried out in alarm, as the panting slave came lurching towards him.

"He says he is not coming Sir," the slave stammered, as he gasped for breath. "He says he is going to stay in Rome and finish his steam machine. I tried Sir. I really did but he refused to come with me. He said to tell you that he would be all right. He said that you should go."

Behind him Kyna emitted a strangled shriek, and before anyone could react she was off heading down the street in the direction of the city. Hastily Marcus ran after her and grabbing her by her arm he hauled her back.

"No," Marcus hissed angrily. "No Kyna. We must leave him. There is no time. We must go now."

"He is my boy," Kyna cried out as the tears streamed down her face. "He is my son."

"He is going to be all right. Claudia will protect him," Marcus snapped, as he dragged his wife back to the waiting horses. "We have no choice. We must go Kyna."

Hastily Fergus fumbled for a wooden writing tablet in his pocket and pressed it into the exhausted slave's hands.

"You are a freeman," Marcus growled as he fixed a stern eye on the man. "Go. Don't remain here."

Then gesturing to Indus to saddle up, Marcus forced Kyna up onto one of the horses. "We ride for Portus," he cried as he heaved himself onto his horse. "Now ride. Ride. Ride."

***

As the four of them clattered into the port and headed for the harbour front, Marcus anxiously cast around searching for Aledus. The waterfront was crowded with sailors, slaves, labourers and merchants and around him he could hear a multitude of foreign voices. Out on the water dozens of ships of varying sizes and shapes bobbed up and down within the protective man-made moles that jutted out into the sea. Over his head a bird swooped down on a piece of discarded fish. Twisting on his horse Marcus gazed back at his companions. Kyna looked traumatised and was staring blankly ahead. She had not said a word since they'd fled from their home. Behind Kyna her freedwoman was anxiously clutching the black cat in a sling around her neck. Only Indus bringing up the rear seemed unconcerned.

"Marcus, Marcus, over here," a voice suddenly cried out. Catching sight of Aledus waving his hand, Marcus urged his horse towards the young man.

"Everything all right?" Marcus growled tensely as he slid from his horse.

"Alexandros is ready to sail the moment you are aboard," Aledus said hastily. "His wife Cora is waiting over there with a lighter to take you out to the Hermes."

"Good man," Marcus said, placing his mutilated hand on Aledus's shoulder. "Thank you Aledus," he added in a quieter voice. "But I have another task for you," Marcus said, as he pulled two small wooden tablets from his tunic pocket. "These are important letters. I need you to deliver them to Paulinus and Lady Claudia. The addresses are on the front."

"I can do that Sir," Aledus replied quickly.

Turning to Kyna and Indus, Marcus hastily gestured for them to dismount and start unloading the saddle bags. Then grasping hold of Aledus's shoulder, he led the army veteran aside and turned to him with a grave look.

"I feel that I can trust you," Marcus said carefully. "But when you are done here, there is one final thing that I must ask of you. It's a big favour and I am sorry to have to ask this, but I have no one else to turn to."

"What Sir?" Aledus said frowning.

"I need you to go to Syria and find Fergus," Marcus said quietly. "Find Fergus and tell him everything what has happened. Tell him that his family are in trouble, that we've had to return to Vectis and that I need his help. Will you do this?"

Aledus blinked as he gazed back at Marcus in silence. Then at last he nodded.

"All right I will do it," he said.

"I am going to leave our horses in your possession," Marcus said quickly, as from the corner of his eye he saw Cora approaching. "Sell them or set them free, I don't care. It's up to you. And here - this should be enough to cover your expenses," Marcus said, as he pressed a bag of coins into Aledus's hand. "The last news we had from Fergus was that he'd been promoted to prefect of the Seventh Numidian Auxiliary ala and posted to the desert frontier, but that was some time ago now." Marcus paused as he fixed his eyes on Aledus. "Find Fergus," he said quietly. "Tell him that his family are in trouble and that we need his help. These are desperate times."

Marcus was the last to scramble into the small lighter, and as he took his place at the oars, the little boat began to pull away from the waterfront. In the middle of the boat, beside the pile of saddle bags Cora, Kyna and her freedwoman were silent and in no mood to talk. All three women looked nervous. Casting a glance towards the harbour front as the lighter glided across the water, Marcus caught a last glimpse of Aledus as he led the four horses away into the crowd. Then twisting to look behind him, Marcus took a deep breath as he saw the welcome sight of the Hermes looming ahead.

"Hello old friend," he muttered as he gazed up at the little ship.

Chapter Nineteen – A New Mission

Antioch – Province of Syria – February 115 AD

Fergus lay in bed watching Galena as she slept beside him. His wife's eyes were closed, and her chest rose and fell with a gentle motion. Through the open window the night sky was fading into dawn and somewhere in the city a dog was barking. Galena was still beautiful, despite having given birth to five daughters he thought. Still as good looking as the first time he'd set eyes on her, in the Lucky Legionary tavern at Deva in Britannia, more than ten years ago now. A little mischievous smile appeared on his lips as he watched her. He loved this moment; the hour before dawn - one of the few precious moments, which were his; when all was quiet and peaceful, and no one was making demands on him. Slowly he reached out and ran his fingers across her naked breast and she stirred and muttered something to herself. Then, as he tickled her playfully under her chin, she woke and opened her eyes. And as she recognised him she smiled.

"I had a dream that you were back," Galena muttered sleepily and happily as she turned onto her side. "But it wasn't a dream."

"Ssshhhh. Keep your voice down," Fergus whispered, as he reached out to pull her closer. "Or you will wake our daughters. I think they are all still asleep."

"I am not asleep," a little girl's voice said from across the room.

Fergus groaned and rolled his eyes as he let go of his wife and gazed up at the ceiling. His plan had been thwarted. In the bed Galena giggled, as she stared at him and guessed what he'd been thinking about. A week had passed since he'd returned to Antioch, and Hadrian had mercifully allowed him to spend some time with his family. There had been a lot to catch up on.

"How long do you think you will stay this time?" Galena whispered as she seemed to read his mind.

"I don't know," Fergus replied with a sigh, as he gazed up at the ceiling. "Hadrian says that Adalwolf has gotten himself into trouble, but he hasn't told me what kind of trouble. He says that if I agree to this new mission, he will take Marcus, my father, off his death list." Fergus paused. "I think we should make the best of the time that we are given," he said at last, as a fond little smile appeared on his lips.

"Yes," Galena nodded, as she ran her fingers along his eyebrows. "Yes, you are right. But when this war is done - when Trajan has enough of glory and conquest, I want to take the girls back home to Britannia, Fergus. None of them have seen the land of our ancestors. It's time they did."

"You want to go back to Britannia?" Fergus asked, as he glanced at Galena.

She nodded. "Yes, when this over I want to go home. I would like to see my father if he is still alive. I haven't seen him in eight years. It's time I did."

Fergus remained silent as he stared up at the ceiling.

"What have you been doing whilst I was away," he asked at last, as he turned to gaze at his wife. "I'm sorry. I never asked you."

"Don't worry husband," Galena said with a little mischievous twinkle in her eye. "I haven't been eying up Hadrian's guardsmen. I too have made some important contacts whilst you were away. I am friends now with Plotina and Matidia, Trajan's wife and niece. They are both living at the imperial palace here in Antioch, but we meet as often as we can. They are fun. They are powerful allies of Hadrian. They are confident that he is going to be next emperor of Rome."

Fergus was about to reply, when there was a sharp knock on the door to their room.

"Sir," Flavius, Hadrian's German bodyguard called out from behind the door. "Hadrian wants to see you right now, in his study."

***

Hadrian looked in fine physical and mental health, as he slowly paced up and down behind his desk with a thoughtful expression. His beard was neatly trimmed. He was wearing a fine white senator's toga and he seemed highly motivated. A large pile of letters and documents lay strewn across the desk and, in his hand Hadrian was casually flipping and catching a small knife. The two of them were alone. Fergus had noticed the continued change in his boss's physical appearance and attitude, which had started after the failed assassination attempt in Athens, some eighteen months ago. It was as if Hadrian was physically and mentally preparing himself for the imperial succession. Gone was the flabby, slightly overweight stomach and the lazy attitude. Gone were cups of stale wine left over from the drinking contests the night before. Gone were the embarrassing female and male sexual conquests, which had to be hidden from Vibia, Hadrian's wife, and bundled out of the house. Instead Hadrian looked strong, calm and in complete command of himself. He looked like a leader in waiting.

"Fergus, I have a problem," Hadrian growled at last, as he paused to face Fergus who was standing stiffly to attention in front of the desk.

"I will get straight to the point," Hadrian said, fixing his eyes on Fergus. "I have an important job that needs the skills of a capable, experienced soldier like yourself. That's why I recalled you from the frontier. This is a sensitive dangerous mission. There is no one else who I trust to do this job. Attianus left for Rome a few days ago on important business. So that's why you are going to do this task for me." Hadrian paused as he carefully studied Fergus.

"You are probably wondering what the hell has happened to Adalwolf," Hadrian snapped. "Well he has managed to get himself into a shit load of trouble." Hadrian sighed as he looked down at the small knife in his hand. Then quickly he looked up at Fergus. "Last year whilst you were on the frontier, I despatched him to the city of Phasis in Colchis on the Black sea coast. Phasis, if you don't know, is the terminus of our northern trade route to India and the land of the Chin beyond. The city is full of Indian and foreign traders and merchants. It's a fucking merchant's paradise. You can buy and order anything in Phasis."

"I wanted to provide Trajan with a birthday gift like no other," Hadrian exclaimed. "One hundred Indian tiger cubs. That's what I wanted to give Trajan for his forthcoming birthday. One hundred live tiger cubs. It would cost a fortune but every one of those animals is well worth it. Properly managed, that number of animals would provide enough exotic beasts for the Coliseum in Rome for many years. So, I sent Adalwolf to Phasis to arrange the deal with the Indian merchants. However," Hadrian said, as his tone turned scornful. "Adalwolf seems to have failed in his mission. A month or so ago I received a message from a Parthian prince called Sanatruces who is nephew to the King of King's Osroes. This Parthian prince claims to have captured Adalwolf. He sent me Adalwolf's signet ring as proof. He is demanding a ransom in gold for his release. If the gold is not paid by the end of summer, then the Parthians will execute Adalwolf. Sanatruces says he will wait for the gold at the Albanian city of Derbent on the coast of the Hyrcanian ocean."

Hadrian flipped the small knife up and down in his hand.

"Adalwolf is an old friend," he said at last, in a quieter voice. "He saved my life in Germania. He and I go way back. If he is in danger, then I want him back and I want him brought back home alive and in good health. I have jobs I need him for in the future."

"He is a good man Sir; I know him well," Fergus said hastily, as he stared into space.

"So," Hadrian said sharply, as his eyes bored into Fergus. "I need you to go and negotiate with this Sanatruces. You are to bring Adalwolf back to me alive. I shall provide you with everything that you need, horses, money, supplies. So, as a start, go to Phasis and speak to the Indian merchants who Adalwolf was dealing with. Find out what they know. It may help you. I am going to provide you with a ransom in gold. The exact ransom that Sanatruces is demanding. Guard it well for Adalwolf's life will depend on it," Hadrian said as he smoothly pulled a sealed papyrus scroll from the folds of his toga and offered it to Fergus. "This letter is meant for your eyes only. You are only to open it once you reach Phasis. Is that understood? Only when you reach Phasis."

"Yes Sir," Fergus replied stiffly, as he took the scroll, glanced at the wax seal and then hastily slipped it into his tunic pocket.

"Do this for me," Hadrian said, as he sternly gazed at Fergus. "And I promise that you shall have paid your father's debt and that I shall take Marcus off my death list. But only if Adalwolf is returned alive and well. Clear?"

"Yes Sir," Fergus added quickly. "I understand. But as you said this is an important mission. I would feel more comfortable if I could choose the men who will accompany me. With your permission I would like to take the men and woman from your close-protection-detail with me on this journey. I know them. They are the best Sir."

"You would have me left unguarded?" Hadrian said as his eyes narrowed.

"You have plenty of guards Sir," Fergus replied. "Please, this is going to be a difficult journey. I would be happier with my men around me."

"All right Fergus," Hadrian said, nodding solemnly. "You shall have your men. I will see that all the arrangements are made. You shall leave in a few days."

From behind his desk, Hadrian had laid his small knife down on the desk and was staring at Fergus.

"Don't fail me," Hadrian said in a warning voice. "Adalwolf is an old friend of mine and I want him back alive and in one piece. He is precious. That will be all."

Chapter Twenty – The City of Phasis

Phasis, Colchis, Roman province of Cappadocia - March 115 AD

As he reached the crest of the hill and caught sight of the city of Phasis, Fergus reined in his horse and gazed down at the settlement. It was late in the day, and to the west the sun was sinking into the Euxine Sea. The fresh, tangy sea breeze on his face suddenly reminded him of the beach on the Isle of Vectis and down in the green, pleasant valley he could hear the distant bleating of sheep. They'd made it at last, Fergus thought. Eighteen days after setting out from Antioch on horseback, they had finally reached the Black Sea port unscathed and unimpeded by nature or bandits. Ahead, the flat and wide, green river delta was teeming with flocks of birds and livestock, and the multitude of farms along the river looked well stocked and prosperous. Just beyond the wide and placid river, the stone walls of the city of Phasis rose around the strip of land at the river's mouth, protected from the east by a large inland lake and to the west by the sea. The Greek colonists, who had founded the colony some eight hundred years ago, had chosen a good, easily defended site Fergus thought, as he studied the city. Turning to gaze out to sea, he could make out two ships heading for the port. Their sails were bulging in the wind and they seemed to be racing each other home. Hearing the thud of hooves coming towards him, Fergus twisted round on his horse and glanced back at his eight companions who were strung out along the path.

"So that's it; that's Phasis," Flavius cried out in his Germanic accent as the big German ex-boxer sporting a blond moustache and long blond hair came to a halt beside Fergus and gazed at the city in disappointment. "It looks puny."

Fergus did not reply as he turned his attention back to the city. Before he'd left Antioch, one of Hadrian's Greek advisors had given him a briefing on the lands he would be travelling through. Colchis, the advisor had told him, had once been an independent kingdom until it had been brought into the Roman sphere of influence by Pompey the Great, some hundred and eighty years ago. The ancient port city of Phasis had always been a prosperous Greek city. Now garrisoned by four hundred Roman soldiers it was well placed to take advantage of Colchis's abundant natural resources. Its future had been secured by exporting gold, iron, timber, hemp, linen, salt, honey and Sarmatian slaves from beyond the great mountain ranges to the north - to the resource-hungry cities in Greece. But what had truly catapulted Phasis into the premier league of important cities within the Roman empire and forced its attention upon the great trading houses of Rome, was the Roman discovery that the city was the terminus of the northern trade route to India and China.

"Shut your mouth Flavius," Skula snapped, as he too reined in his horse at Fergus's side and turned to gaze at the city. "You don't know what you are talking about." The bald Scythian with his flat nose had a huge axe strapped across his back and there was an uncharacteristic emotion in his voice.

"What is it Skula?" Fergus asked patiently, as he turned and reached down to check the locked iron box, that was strapped and secured to his horse's back. The box was filled with the ransom gold that Hadrian had provided him with.

"I have been to Phasis before Sir," the Scythian said in a tight voice, as he stared at the city. Raising his hand, Skula gestured towards the north. "My people's homeland lies somewhere beyond the mountains to the north. We are close. Beyond the mountains there are grasslands that stretch to the horizon like nothing you have ever seen before. A sea of grass. It is ruled over by the great horse clans. It's where I was born," Skula declared in a grave voice. "And it is where I shall be buried." Pausing, his bearded face hardened as he seemed to recall a memory. "I was fourteen Sir," he said at last, "when

I joined my father and brothers on my first and last raid on the southern lands. We crossed the mountains intent on plunder. We were after women and gold, but the gods did not smile on me, for I was taken prisoner and sold as a slave. My masters brought me here to Phasis and I thought I had died, for there were things in this city that I had never seen or witnessed before. It was like entering a new world." Slowly Skula turned to look across at Fergus. "Phasis is where I left my youth behind and became a man. It is here, that as a slave, they forced me onto the ship that took me to Athens and eventually to you Sir."

For a moment the three of them were silent as they gazed down at Phasis and the sea to the west, and waited for the rest of their companions to catch up.

"Well just don't get any ideas about leaving us in the lurch and fucking off back to your own country," Flavius growled. "I personally prefer having that great big axe of yours at my side."

Skula's hard face cracked into a sudden grin. "Fear not Flavius," the Scythian replied in a changed voice. "My loyalty is to Fergus. If he had not picked me from that Athenian brothel, I would still be there working the door instead of enjoying the delights of your company. And besides I like getting out to see the world."

Fergus remained silent as he heard the rest of his companions approaching. The thud of their horses' hooves was accompanied by the jingle and creak of their weapons, equipment, and the snorting of the horses. Twisting round, he watched them approach. He had hand-picked them all and they were tough as nails. His companions had all served in Hadrian's close protection team and he knew their strengths and weaknesses. He knew how far to push them. Arlyn, the shy and tall red-haired Hibernian who, in a melancholic mood, liked to sing his sad native Celtic songs. The two Italian brothers, ex legionaries and in their late forties, who delighted in practical jokes. Saadi, the youngest in the group, the small, former pickpocket and only woman in the party, and the two new boys, Numerius a former Praetorian guardsman kicked out of the guard for seducing his commander's wife, and Barukh, the young idealistic Jew from Antioch, who claimed to have fought as a gladiator in the arena.

"Is that it?" Numerius cried out in relief, as he lowered his mud-splattered hood from over his head and gazed down at the city.

"Yes, that's it boys," one of the Italian brothers called out with cheerful excitement. "Phasis, gateway to the unexplored and fabled east. The destination of Jason and his Argonauts and their search for the golden fleece. I hope you are not superstitious. Colchis is where the sorceress Medea lived. You know the one who fell in love with Jason. Better pray to your gods that you don't meet her. The stories say that she killed her own children and swore vengeance on Jason for dumping her. She is one hell of a pissed off sorceress."

"Afraid of a woman are you," Saadi called out, as she gave the brother a mocking look. "And here I was thinking you were a proper man afraid of nothing. My mistake."

"You like me," the Italian brother replied, giving Saadi a seedy wink. "I know you do Saadi. It's not too late to declare your affections for me you know."

"I would rather go to bed with a pig," Saadi retorted as she turned away with a look of disgust.

"Saadi," Skula called out suddenly, as he pointed to the north. "Over there beyond the mountains is my homeland. A sea of grass. You would like my people. For the horse clans of the steppes allow all unmarried women to fight alongside their men. The women I grew up with, were all trained in horsemanship, in hunting, in shooting arrows and in hand to hand combat. They say that when the Greeks first learned of this they called our women, amazons. You would fit in just right I think."

"Amazons," Saadi exclaimed, as a glimmer of interest appeared in her eyes. "That sounds intriguing Skula. You must tell me more about these women from your homeland. I would like to know more."

"I will tell you about them," Skula said in a solemn voice.

On his horse, Fergus gazed up at the sky. It was getting dark. "All right listen up, all of you," he called out. "I don't want any trouble when we enter the city. No picking fights, no visits to whores, no drinking and no boasting about our mission. We have come here to find the Indian merchants, who Adalwolf was doing business with, and that's what we're going to do. Now let's find ourselves a tavern, settle the horses and get some food and rest. We will start looking for the merchants tomorrow."

"Can we have a bath Sir," one of the Italian brothers asked as he raised his hand. "We have been on the road for a long time. Some of us need a bath. I can smell them from a hundred yards away."

"If they have baths in Phasis then you may have a bath," Fergus replied, as urging his horse onwards, he started out for the city.

***

Fergus closed the door to his room and carefully locked it. Outside, through the open window it was dark, and in the street below he could hear the noise of horses' hooves, shouts and the trundle of wagon wheels. They'd encountered no problems entering the city and after some aimless wandering through the streets, he'd found a tavern that had space for them all and stables for the horses. Glancing at the iron box that stood beside the bed, Fergus moved across the room and sat down on the bed. On their long perilous journey from Antioch he had always kept the locked, strong box, containing the ransom gold for Adalwolf's release, close to him. Hadrian was right. If the gold was lost, then Adalwolf would be lost and there had been plenty of bandits and robbers along the roads they'd travelled, who would have eagerly taken it from him, if only they had known about the precious cargo. Rubbing his tired eyes, Fergus reached out and took a quick sip of wine from a cup that stood beside his bed, before searching for something inside his dirt and sweat stained tunic. Pulling forth the letter that Hadrian had given him in Antioch, he studied the scroll with a thoughtful, puzzled look. Hadrian had told him to only open the letter when he reached Phasis. It was a bit odd, but Hadrian could be odd sometimes. With a sigh Fergus broke the seal and carefully unrolled the papyrus. Rising to his feet and moving across into the flickering light of an oil lamp, he gazed down at the neat lettered writing and began to read.

To Fergus from Hadrian. If you are reading this and have obeyed my orders you will have reached Phasis and be ready to receive additional information regarding your mission. Adalwolf is an old and dear friend and negotiating and securing his successful release is your prime responsibility. I have entrusted you with this important task because I believe that you can get the job done. However, I firmly believe that it would be irresponsible to make deals with terrorists who so willingly threaten and kidnap Roman citizens going about their lawful business. As I am a representative, the future emperor and supreme commander of the Roman state, I cannot make any deals with men who threaten Rome with blackmail and extortion. For if it becomes known that Rome is willing to pay for the release of its citizens, then no Roman citizen anywhere will be safe from these bandits. Our policy is clear. We do not negotiate with terrorists. There shall be no negotiation with this Parthian prince calling himself Sanatruces. But that does not absolve you from your duty and responsibility to Adalwolf and to me. Find a way to free Adalwolf. Use your own initiative. How you handle the situation is up to you, but it is imperative that Adalwolf be freed and brought back to me alive and well. And if you fail, do not bother coming back at all, for it will be your fault that Adalwolf is dead and all my responsibilities to you shall be forfeit. Hadrian

Fergus gazed at the letter in shock. Carefully he reread it to make sure he had not missed anything. Finally, he dropped the scroll onto his bed and ran his fingers across his beard as he slowly shook his head in bewilderment.

"You are a fucking coward," he hissed angrily. "You couldn't tell me this face to face in Antioch. You made me read it when I was seven hundred miles away. You weasel. You, outrageous piece of shit."

Abruptly Fergus turned to stare at the iron box, as a horrible thought came to him. Hastily he picked up the box and placed it on the bed before pulling away the key from around his neck, where it hung on a chain, and inserting it into the lock. With a metallic creak the lock opened and quickly Fergus raised the lid of the box and gazed down at two heavy stones that were the box's only contents. Fergus staggered backwards in shock. There was no gold. There was no ransom. All this time he had been faithfully guarding two heavy stones and a useless box. Hadrian had tricked him. He had fooled him. He had made him look like an idiot. With a surge of anger, he sent the box flying across the room where it clattered against the far wall.

"You prick," Fergus snarled, his face flush with rage. "Oh, you are a fine arsehole. I spit on you."

Unsteadily Fergus reached out for his cup and drained the wine in one go. Then heavily he sat back down on the bed and glared silently at the upturned iron box. What was he going to do now? He had to decide. But there was no question of abandoning his mission. Adalwolf was a good friend. He'd known him for ten years. No. There could be no question of leaving Adalwolf to die. And there could be no question of leaving Marcus, his father, on Hadrian's execution list. His father had to be removed from that list. So, he resolved, he would have to do something but what? Hadrian had said that he was to use his own initiative, but that was easier said than done. Hissing in frustration, Fergus's fingers caught hold of the Celtic amulet around his neck. Galena had given it to him when they had first been married. She had said that it had powerful magic that would help ward off evil spirits. Tensely he played with the cold iron as he tried to figure out what to do. Without any gold to buy Adalwolf's release, the only other option was a covert rescue mission. But there was no time to make plans. He only had eight men. He would have to make it up on the go.

***

In the dense, narrow, twisting streets of the original Greek Polis the diversity of the crowds was like no other Fergus had experienced. Accompanied by Flavius, Skula and Saadi, he strode on down the street in search of the Indian trading house with which Adalwolf had been doing business. Most of the inhabitants seemed to be Greeks and local tribesmen, but a significant proportion were foreign merchants and their slaves and attendants. Wherever he looked Fergus saw strange faces, dark skinned Indians, huge bearded Sarmatians from the frozen north, small pale Chinamen with slanted eyes, Greeks, Roman citizens dressed in toga's, Parthians in their baggy trousers, Arabs wearing their headdresses, bearded orthodox Jews, Armenians and Germans. The buzz of dozens of different languages filled the streets, making Fergus wonder how anyone could communicate with each other. It was morning, and as he made his way down the street, he could smell the scent of exotic spices and herbs. Along the side of the alley, the traders had adorned their shop fronts and market stalls with cages in which sat strange animals and birds. Others had laid out their wares on shelves and tables. Fruits, plants, spices, silk, clothes and foods like he had never seen before, were everywhere. But the scale of the shops and businesses was small, and as he pushed on deeper into Phasis, Fergus remembered what Hadrian's Greek adviser had told him. Most of the foreign goods pouring into Phasis along the great northern trade route were destined for onward shipment to the great cities of the empire. Phasis itself was just a small transit port of no more than five thousand souls.

Finally, as he entered a small market place, and turned to look around, Fergus spotted a sign above a simple-looking stone building. The sign had been written in a language and alphabet that Fergus had never seen before but directly underneath were two translations and the last one was in Latin.

"Mahendra's Indian merchant group," Fergus read out aloud. "Finest Indian merchandise. Specialist in the purchase and trade of tigers. Reliable and fast delivery guaranteed most of the time."

"Is that the place where Adalwolf went to do make his deal?" Flavius exclaimed in his Germanic accent as he pointed at the building.

"Yes, that's the right name," Fergus growled, as he started to push through the crowd towards the shop. He had decided to tell no one about Hadrian's trickery and the debacle with the non-existent ransom gold. It would be best for the moment if everyone continued to believe that they were going to negotiate Adalwolf's release. His companions remained silent as they followed and, as Fergus entered the front room he was met with a blast of incense that nearly left him choking.

Hastily a slave appeared from the back room, took one quick look at Fergus, smiled and bowed deeply and gracefully.

"I wish to speak to Mahendra," Fergus said in Latin, as he fixed his eyes on the slave. For a moment the man looked confused. A blush appeared on his cheeks and he slowly shook his head.

"I wish to speak to Mahendra," Fergus repeated in Greek and, as he did the slave suddenly seemed to understand and quickly and silently he vanished into the back room. A few moments later he was back, accompanied by a big, dark skinned, red eyed and black haired Indian man of around forty. For a moment Fergus stared at the trader and the merchant gazed back at him.

"Are you Mahendra, owner of this business?" Fergus said carefully in Greek.

"I am Mahendra," the merchant replied in heavily accented Greek. "How can I help you?"

Fergus turned to glance at his companions who were all staring at the dark skinned Indian in silent astonishment and fascination.

"I am a friend of Adalwolf and work for master Hadrian," Fergus said, speaking slowly as he tried to remember the correct Greek words. "Adalwolf was doing business with you on behalf of his patron, master Hadrian. Adalwolf came to you to negotiate the purchase of ninety-nine live tiger cubs. You were going to arrange the deal for him. But then we heard that Adalwolf was abducted. Hadrian is an important man. He wants to know what happened to Adalwolf? You are one of the few people who last saw him. I need to know what you know about the business deal and the nature of Adalwolf's abduction? Anything that you can tell us will be useful. Please. It's important. Adalwolf is my friend too."

As Fergus fell silent, Mahendra gazed at him with a face that betrayed no emotion.

"The deal was for one hundred tiger cubs," the Indian merchant replied sharply. "And the deal is off. I am sorry."

Fergus looked away. The merchant had passed his little test. He was the right man. "Please, you must know more than that," Fergus said carefully, turning to fix his eyes on the merchant.

Mahendra met his gaze. Then abruptly he looked away.

"It is bad business. Bad business what has happened to Adalwolf," the Indian merchant said slowly, as he too searched for the Greek words. "I have already sent instructions to my people in India agreeing the deal. Now I must send another message telling them to stop work. That costs me my reputation."

"What about the abduction?" Fergus asked with a little encouraging nod. "Do you know what happened to Adalwolf?"

"Ah, the Parthians," Mahendra said with an irritated, dismissive gesture. "Agents of Prince Sanatruces abducted your friend. But it was not done here in Phasis. After making the initial arrangements with me, Adalwolf travelled to the city of Gabala in the land of the Caucasian Albanians. He went there so that he could work out the final details of the deal. Albania is a vassal state of Rome. It lies to the east on the shores of the Caspian. The Albanians charge duties on all trade that crosses their borders. One needs to choose the right ship's captains for the transport across the Hyrcanian ocean. In Gabala he would be closer to the people he needed to speak to. It is in Gabala that Sanatruces's agents found him and took him prisoner. I do not know where they took your friend or whether he is still alive."

"Did anyone else know about the business deal?" Fergus asked.

"Yes," Mahendra nodded solemnly. "In Gabala, Adalwolf said he was going to speak to the Roman ambassador about the deal. The ambassador's name is Licinius. I have met him. He is an influential man with the Albanians, as you would expect. He would have known about the deal. Speak to him if you wish to know more. I have told you everything I know."

Chapter Twenty-One – Roman Diplomacy on the Caucasus Frontier

The Cyrus river was broad and placid as it wound itself through the peaceful valley. On the northern bank, stretching away to the horizon, ranged the green, heavily forested foothills of the mighty Caucasus mountains. Fergus sat on his horse stoically gazing ahead, as he trotted along the bank of the river. It was a cold April morning and his face and travelling cloaks were stained and splattered with mud. The iron strong box was secured to his horse's back, and coming on behind him in single file, were his eight silent companions. Thirteen days had passed since they had departed Phasis on their journey to Gabala, capital of Caucasian Albania. Their path had taken them on a south-eastern course, initially along the Phasis river valley to the Colchian fort at Sarapana and then across the hills to the Cyrus, the great trading river that flowed all the way into the Hyrcanian, Caspian Sea. There had been no paved roads, just rough, muddy farmers' paths and tracks. But the river valleys had been rich and fertile and occupied by numerous farms and villages. Fergus however, had gained the impression that the wild, wooded hills and rugged, trackless mountains to the north were scarcely populated. The forests had been filled with chestnut trees and had teemed with game. Deer, wild boar, bears, foxes, hare, grouse and pheasants had provided ample opportunity for the occasional hunting that had supplemented their rations. And one night, as they had camped out under the open sky, they had heard wolves howling to each other in the mountains. The noise had completely unnerved the horses.

The few native villages they had come across had spoken a language that none in his party had understood and it was only by using his limited knowledge of Greek, that he'd been able to purchase provisions for his companions and their horses. It had felt as if they were nearing the edge of the civilised world. But the people had been friendly, and they had not run into any trouble.

Out on the Cyrus a long convoy of ships and rafts, all tied together by ropes, had appeared around a bend in the river and was slowly making its way upstream. The shouts and cries of the drivers and the snorting and bellowing of the horses and oxen which were dragging the ships upstream, filled the crisp morning air. Gently urging his horse from the path, Fergus drew aside and came to a halt as he watched the convoy approach. The ships and rafts were piled high with what looked like trade goods and on the boats, he caught sight of a few dark-skinned and black-haired men. They had to have come from the east, from India. Fascinated, Fergus stared at the traders out on the water, as behind him his companions came to a halt and did the same. The great northern trade route, Hadrian's Greek adviser had briefed him, ran from Phasis to the Hyrcanian Ocean via the Phasis and Cyrus rivers. The route crossed through the ancient kingdoms and Roman vassal states and protectorates of Colchis, Iberia and Caucasian Albania. From the western shores of the Hyrcanian, in Caucasian Albania, trade goods; gold and silver were exchanged for cottons, pearls, black pepper, Chinese silk, exotic animals; which were transported by ship across the Caspian to the mouth of the Oxus river. From there they were hauled eastwards until they reached a tributary river called the Bactrus, which led to India. The whole journey from India to Phasis took two months, the adviser had claimed. The northern trade route to India and China was the hardest and least used of all the oriental trade routes, the adviser had added. But its great strategic advantage to Rome was that it avoided having to cross Parthia. It allowed direct trade between the Roman empire and India and China, and in times of war with Parthia and when the main silk road was closed, that was particularly useful.

"How far to Gabala Sir?" Arlyn called out.

On his horse, Fergus stirred. "Tomorrow we shall leave the river and head north-east into the hills," he replied. "The peasants in that last village said that it will take two or three more days before we reach the Albanian capital."

"Then what Sir?" Flavius the German said quietly, as he glanced at Fergus. "Where are we going to meet this prick Sanatruces and negotiate Adalwolf's release? How are we going to do this?"

Fergus sighed as he gazed at the traders out on the river. "Patience Flavius," he said in a gentle voice. "I am working on a plan. But I need to speak to Licinius, the Roman ambassador in Gabala before I make the decision. We need more information on where and how Adalwolf is being held prisoner. Right now, all I know is that Sanatruces awaits us and the gold at Derbent. Once we know more we will act."

On his horse Flavius was gazing at Fergus with a thoughtful look. "Now why do I get the feeling that there is something you are not telling me," Flavius said, with a sudden troubled look in his eye.

"Shut up Flavius," Fergus growled, as he kept his eyes on the ships in the river.

"If Adalwolf was trying to purchase one hundred tiger cubs for the emperor, then I think these animals must be rare and expensive," Numerius called out. "But what's a tiger Sir? Have you ever seen one of these beasts? What do they look like?"

"It's a little furry pussy cat that likes to be tickled under its chin," Flavius snapped, twisting on his horse to get a good look at Numerius. "Man, you Praetorians are thick. You were posted to Rome. Did you never visit the Coliseum? They fed Christians to the tigers and lions and please don't tell me you don't know what a lion is. I think I will cry if you do."

On his horse Numerius looked offended. "Well, better to be thick than ugly like you," he retorted with wounded pride. "And I never went to the games."

"Are you calling me ugly?" Flavius snapped as his face darkened and he glared at Numerius. "You will pay for that insult you thick prick."

"Cut it out, all of you," Fergus said sharply. "You remind me of a group of whining, bitching women. So, shut it. You are giving me a headache. Now, let's go."

***

Gabala looked poor and it was small for a capital city Fergus thought, as he walked his horse on through the gateway and into the town. The tall, rounded stone and brick watchtowers, that formed the southern gate into the walled city, were manned by guards. The Albanian soldiers were bearded, clad in chainmail armour and wearing pointed helmets not unlike Syrian auxiliary archers. Glancing up at the soldiers, Fergus saw that they were watching him. The Albanians however remained silent, as clutching their spears and bows, they warmed themselves beside their burning braziers. No one called out or tried to stop them as Fergus continued-on into the city, followed in single file by his weary companions. To the north the high, snow-capped mountain peaks of the Caucasus loomed on the horizon, frighteningly close, dominating the rugged, uneven terrain. The Caucasus had steadily drawn closer as soon as they had left the Cyrus behind, and their sheer beauty was breath-taking. Higher and mightier than the mountains around Lake Van, they seemed to represent a vast wall of rock commissioned by the gods and constructed by giants. Eagerly Fergus turned to look around the town as he nudged his horse on down the narrow, muddy unpaved street. Gabala had been hard to find, tucked away as it was amongst the jagged rocky mountain peaks, beautiful cascading waterfalls and plunging gorges and densely forested valleys. But they had made it at last, and now that he was here, it felt as if he had reached the last outpost of civilisation. For, beyond the mountains to the north and the Hyrcanian Ocean to the east, the knowledge of Hadrian's Greek advisers became sketchy and uncertain.

From the doorways of their simple stone and wood built houses, the local inhabitants paused in what they were doing, to stare at Fergus as he slowly rode on down the street. Most of the men were bearded, tall and pale skinned and some of the women were wearing headscarves. They gazed at him without smiling, their hard faces suspicious and unfriendly. Most were dressed in simple, long flowing tunics made of linen, over which they wore sheepskin or bearskin cloaks. As Fergus pushed on deeper into the town in the direction of a large stone fortress, he passed a small square. A crowd of adults and children had gathered around a solitary performer who was forcing a large brown bear to perform tricks for the audience. Fergus raised his eyebrows as he gazed at the scene in amazement.

"We're not in Antioch anymore boys," Flavius muttered from directly behind him, as he too gazed at the bear.

The Roman ambassador's house and diplomatic compound in Gabala was a large stone fortress-like building arranged around an open central courtyard. Two auxiliary soldiers, clad in chainmail and armed with spears and shields, were standing guard outside the gate into the courtyard. Coming to a halt by the gate, Fergus dismounted and quickly glanced up at the proud Roman banner that fluttered from the battlements. The letters SPQR were unmistakeable.

"I need to speak with Lucinius, the ambassador," he called out in Latin, as he strode up to the guards. "Tell him that I have come from Antioch, on the Legate Hadrian's orders and am here on urgent business. Hurry man."

The guards glanced at each other. Then one of them turned and hastened away into the compound. A few minutes later he was back, and hurrying after him came a well- dressed, clean-shaven man wearing a white Roman toga and accompanied by a few tough looking and hard-faced military men, clad in civilian tunics.

"My name is Lucinius," the man wearing the toga called out in perfect Latin, as he strode towards Fergus. "I am the Roman ambassador here. Did you say that you have come all the way from Antioch? Hadrian has sent you?"

"That's right Sir," Fergus replied, as he took a moment to study Licinius. The ambassador looked to be in his mid-thirties and there was a friendly, affable and disarming attitude about him.

"Well that is a welcome surprise," Lucinius grinned, as he quickly turned to gaze at Fergus's companions. "I don't get many Roman visitors out here. You have reached the end of the world. It will be good to hear your news. You are most welcome. Have you and your men found lodgings for the night?"

"We are here on urgent business," Fergus said, as he slowly lowered the hood from over his head. "Hadrian has sent us to find out what happened to a friend. A man called Adalwolf. I have been told that Adalwolf came to Gabala to finalise a business deal with some Indian merchants, before he was abducted by a Parthian prince named Sanatruces. I understand that you met Adalwolf?"

"Ah yes," Licinius said, as he quickly rubbed his hands together and looked down at the ground. "Yes, a most unfortunate and unpleasant business. You had better come into my home and I shall tell you what I know. You and your men and your horses are welcome to stay here in the compound. We have the space. My advisers here will show you where you can stay. Once you are rested and refreshed, come to my quarters and we shall talk."

"Thank you, Sir," Fergus replied, as he dipped his head in graceful acknowledgment. Turning to his companions Fergus gestured that they should dismount. Then, leading his horse by the reins, he followed the ambassador's advisers into the courtyard and, as he came through the gateway he caught sight of a young woman watching him from the second-floor balcony. The lady's white stola dress fluttered in the gentle breeze and her long black hair cascaded down onto her shoulders. She looked stunning and for a moment Fergus was transfixed.

Wrenching his eyes away from the gorgeous woman, Fergus led his horse over to the stables where Licinius's advisers were waiting for him. As a slave hastily took the reins from him, one of the hard-faced military men sauntered over and caught Fergus's eye before giving him a quick head-to-foot examination.

"That's the ambassador's wife," the ex-soldier muttered quietly. "And from one former soldier to another. Take my advice. Be careful. She's a man eater and a first-class bitch."

***

"So, you have brought gold to purchase Adalwolf's release," Licinius said, leaning back in his chair, as Fergus finished telling his tale. The two of them were alone, sitting in the ambassador's luxurious study. A jug of Caucasian wine and two cups stood on the table and the floors were covered with thick, warm, animal skins. It was evening and, in the flickering glow of the braziers, Fergus could see a small stone bust of emperor Trajan, standing beside the fireplace. Licinius sighed as he turned to gaze at the iron strong box that was wedged in between Fergus's feet. For a moment he seemed lost in thought.

"I can see now why you needed eight companions," Licinius exclaimed. "Transporting that amount of gold is a risky business." Licinius turned to gaze once more at the iron strong box. "I'm afraid we are a long way from Rome. The mountains and forests in these parts are invested with bandits and robbers who prey on the oriental trade going up the Cyrus. And that is not even mentioning the barbarian tribes to the north beyond the mountains. You were lucky not to have been attacked. If I were you I would keep the existence of the gold a closely guarded secret."

Fergus nodded. "You said that you were going to tell me about Adalwolf," he said as he reached out to his cup of wine.

"Yes," Licinius replied with a hasty nod. "Yes. I did meet your friend Adalwolf," he began. "He arrived here from Phasis a few months ago. He sought me out, said he needed my assistance. We had a pleasant evening where he told me all about the business deal he was trying to arrange. One hundred tiger cubs." Licinius smiled disarmingly. "That sort of number of beasts will have cost a fortune, but then again, if Hadrian is paying, then it is nothing."

"What happened?" Fergus asked quietly.

"Well I agreed to help him," Licinius said, raising his eyebrows in exasperation. "Anything to help Hadrian is a worthy cause. I have some contacts amongst the small Jewish community here in Gabala. The Jews are the middlemen in the Indian trade. They are the shipbrokers. The merchants use them to negotiate and charter the ships that take the goods across the Hyrcanian ocean. The actual transport of the goods from India to Phasis however, is mainly done by Albanians, Armenians, Siraces and Aorsi tribesmen etc. Those guys take all the risks and get paid the least."

"And Adalwolf?" Fergus insisted.

"I was going to meet him to introduce him to some of the Jewish brokers," Licinius said with a regretful sigh. "But the meeting never happened. Agents working for the Parthian prince Sanatruces abducted Adalwolf right here in the city. Snatched him from the street just like that. Sanatruces must have got wind of what Adalwolf was doing. There was nothing I could do, and by the time I had informed the King, the agents and Adalwolf were long gone."

"Where did they take him? Do you know where they are holding him?"

Licinius paused as he gazed at Fergus. "Derbent," he said at last. "Sanatruces is at the city of Derbent. He has been there for months. It's about ninety miles from here to the north-east across the mountains. The city sits on the frontier of the Kingdom of Caucasian Albania with the northern barbarians." Hastily Licinius raised a finger in warning. "But before you decide to ride straight through the front gate, you should know that Sanatruces enjoys the protection of the Alans. They are the largest and fiercest of the horse clans that live on the plains to the north. The latest news we have here in Gabala, is that they are encamped at Derbent in strength but are maintaining a peaceful posture for now. But that can change as easily as the weather. Those savage horsemen will not just let you pass without paying them an adequate, let's call it a "an adequate protection fee."

"And the King of Albania," Fergus said. "He tolerates these barbarians entering his kingdom?"

"He says there is no profit in trying to fight them," Licinius replied, in a sour voice. "The King will do nothing unless the Alans directly threaten him and his power."

Fergus looked down at the iron box standing at his feet and for a moment he seemed lost in thought.

"Why have the Alans come to Derbent?" he said at last raising his head to look at Licinius. "And what is Sanatruces doing here anyway? The war between Rome and Parthia is far away to the south on the Tigris and Euphrates. What business has brought a Parthian prince so far to the north?"

"A good question," Licinius replied. with an amused gleam in his eye. "Let me explain the strategic situation here on the Caucasus frontier for I see you are unfamiliar with it. This is a tough neighbourhood but an important one to Rome. The Caucasian kingdoms act as buffer states against the barbarian hordes to the north, just like Armenia was a buffer state between Rome and Parthia. They help protect Roman land. It's my job to ensure that this protection continues. An additional factor is the control of the valuable northern trade route to India and China. Together Caucasian Iberia and Albania control and protect the two-main mountain passes and invasion routes, through which the northern barbarians can attack our interests to the south of the Caucasus. One route passes through the Darial gorge to the north west. It's called the Caucasian Gates. The gorge has been fortified and there is a small Roman garrison." Licinius paused, as he made sure he'd not lost his audience, but Fergus was watching him attentively. "The other invasion route is at Derbent," Licinius exclaimed. "The city dominates the narrow strip of accessible land between the mountains and the shores of the Hyrcanian Ocean. Forty years ago, the Albanians decided to make a deal with the Alans to the north and allow an Alan raiding party to pass through Derbent on their way south, where they devastated and looted Armenia and Northern Parthia. So, you can see why Rome wishes to control these passes."

Licinius paused, as he reached for his cup of wine and took a hefty sip. The ambassador seemed to be enjoying himself.

"Gabala may seem like a sleepy provincial outpost but it's really a hotbed of international intrigue and power politics."

Licinius smiled broadly, as he saw that he had Fergus's attention. "The city is filled with foreign diplomats and spies. Romans, Armenians, Jews, Sarmatians and Parthians, all trying to bend the King to their interests. Now, together with the Caucasian kingdom of Iberia to the west, the kingdom of Albania is currently and officially an enthusiastic vassal state of Rome. Ofcourse they fucking are," Licinius said with a little chuckle. "For we are on the up. Rome is victorious on all fronts and Trajan's conquest and annexation of Armenia and the ongoing Parthian civil war have pushed the Albanians into pledging to be our best friends and loyal allies. They are our dear sworn allies, until they are not. But the King here in Gabala is a shrewd man. He knows that fortunes and times change and, if we were to suffer a reversal in the field or Parthia returned in strength, then his loyalty to us would wain and the influence of the Parthian diplomats at his court would grow. It was always so and always it shall remain. So, you can see how important prestige is Fergus. Prestige buys you friends."

"Which brings me to your question of what Sanatruces is doing at Derbent," Licinius said hastily as he saw Fergus's attention start to waver. "I believe Sanatruces has come to Derbent to arrange a treaty of alliance between the Alans and Parthia on behalf of his uncle the King of Kings Osroes of Parthia." Slowly and ominously the Roman ambassador raised his finger in the air. "But I suspect Sanatruces has even wider ambitions. I suspect that Parthian gold is being used to not only persuade the Alans into war with Rome, but also the peoples further west, the Roxolani and free Dacians on the Danube and maybe even the Germanic Quadi and Marcomanni. If the Parthians can persuade these tribes to attack the Danube frontier, it will cause us problems. Many of Trajan's troops have been taken from the garrisons along the Danube and that sector of the frontier is only lightly held. A serious invasion would mean that legions would have to be withdrawn from the war against Parthia."

"So, the gold that Hadrian is willing to pay to secure Adalwolf's release, will most probably end up helping to subsidize attacks against the empire," Fergus said with a frown.

"I fear so," Licinius said in a grave voice. "It would be a good idea if someone were to kill Sanatruces."

Fergus too suddenly looked grave. "When I was posted to the desert frontier in Syria," he said quietly, as he turned to stare at Licinius. "I came across evidence that the Parthians were using gold to meddle and foment rebellion; unrest amongst the people's subject to Rome. So, if what you are saying is true, then the Parthians are expanding this strategy to the northern barbarians. This is going to cause us trouble. Have you informed Rome of your suspicions?"

"I have sent several urgent letters to Trajan and the Senate," Licinius replied wearily. "There has been no response as far as I know. You have been my only Roman visitor in a long time. It can be a lonely posting out here."

"Well I am grateful for your hospitality," Fergus said with a gracious dip of his head.

Across from him Licinius sighed and ran his hand across his chin. "This war with Parthia must end in a diplomatic settlement," he said. "I do not presume to know Trajan's strategy, but I do know that Parthia is too large and powerful to be conquered. At some point we are going to have to decide on how far to go and what lands to keep and defend. It's a decision that is going to cause considerable disagreement between the Peace and War factions in the Senate. Let's hope it does not lead to civil war."

Abruptly Licinius leaned forwards, his eyes flashing in alarm. "But do you know what really keeps me awake at night. What happens if those millions and millions of barbarian horsemen living on the great plains to the north start to move westwards like the Cimbri and Teutones once did in the time of the Consul Marius. What happens when they start to pour across the Danube and Rhine. I have seen these wild savage horsemen. They scare the shit out of me."

"We will throw them back," Fergus replied sharply. "The Legions can handle anything. But I am just a soldier," Fergus added with a little smile. "My father, Marcus, however is a senator in Rome. He will know much more about such weighty matters of state."

"I like soldiers," a woman's smooth voice suddenly cut in, and as Fergus hastily scrambled to his feet, he saw the young woman he'd noticed earlier in the courtyard. The lady slowly glided across the floor and came to stand at her husband's side. Then she turned to gaze at Fergus and, as she did Fergus was once again struck by her beauty and attractiveness, so much so that it nearly made him blush.

"Soldiers know how to obey. I see that you are enjoying my husband's company," she said in a confident voice. "My name is Julia and I hear that you have come to purchase Adalwolf's release with gold. That is a bold undertaking."

"It is," Fergus replied lowering his gaze.

"Has my husband told you that Sanatruces arrived by ship across the Hyrcanian Ocean and that he is currently anchored off the coast at Derbent. Did he tell you that he holds your friend Adalwolf hostage aboard one of his vessels?"

Fergus raised his eyebrows in surprise as he forced himself to look at Julia. "No, I didn't know that," he replied.

At his wife's side, a blush had appeared on Licinius's face. Half-heartedly he raised his hand in a dismissive gesture.

"I was going to tell him," Licinius said, turning to his wife with a chiding expression. But she ignored him, and her eyes remained on Fergus.

"If you have not done so already, you should invite him to the King's banquet that's taking place in two days' time," Julia said to her husband, as she continued to gaze at Fergus. "His company will be a refreshing change to the usual stuffiness of the occasion. I insist."

At his wife's side Licinius suddenly looked helpless.

Chapter Twenty-Two – Seduction

His companions were already sitting around the long wooden table eating breakfast when Fergus strode into the kitchen. Silently he took his place at the end of the table as Licinius's slaves hastily laid some food out in front of him. Casting a quick glance at his companion's faces, he could see that sleeping in a proper bed and having a roof over their heads had been good for them after spending so many days out in the wilderness.

"Licinius is a good host Sir," Flavius the German said cheerfully, as he turned to Fergus whilst stuffing his mouth with sausage and bread. "He puts on a good feast and this is only breakfast. What will he serve us for dinner?"

Fergus nodded but said nothing, as he quickly glanced at Barukh. The young Jew was staring at Flavius in silent disgust at his eating habits, but the German was blissfully unaware.

"How come Saadi gets her own room whilst the rest of us must share," one of the Italian brothers exclaimed, giving Saadi a mocking wink. "That doesn't seem fair Sir."

"It's for your own protection dickhead," Saadi snapped, glaring across the table at the brother. "I have seen your cock and it's the smallest I have ever encountered. Your mother must have mated with a midget."

Saadi's words were met with a howl of good humoured jeering and cries. Across from her, the brother was grinning.

"I told you she wanted to see my cock," he cried out proudly.

"You two," Fergus said wearily, as he looked up in the direction of the brothers. "Leave Saadi alone and stop picking on her. She is not interested in either of you and she's right. The separation is for your own protection."

"Maybe Sir," Flavius interrupted, his mouth still half full of bread and sausage. "Maybe Arlyn could sing one of his native songs for us tonight at dinner. I always like his songs," the German added, as he pointed his finger at the tall, red haired Hibernian. "They remind me of good times."

Around Flavius the table grew quiet except for a few sniggers.

"You must be the only one," Skula said, breaking the silence with a little disbelieving shake of his head, as he turned to stare at Flavius. "Who actually likes his songs? When Arlyn opens his mouth and sings, the rest of us just want to cry and go to sleep. His songs are so fucking depressing."

"Ah thanks a lot Skula," Arlyn snapped with an offended look, as he chucked a piece of bread at the bald Alan tribesman.

"It's true," Skula exclaimed, raising both his hands. "Ask anyone except the ugly German over there."

"There is no need to call me ugly," Flavius responded.

"No," Numerius suddenly chipped in. "No. But it's all right for you to call me thick is it?"

"That's because you are thick," Flavius retorted, as he looked away in disgust.

In his seat around the long table Fergus rose to feet.

"Barukh," he called out, gesturing for the young Jew to come over. "I need to discuss something with you. It's important. After breakfast. Let's go for a walk."

***

Fergus held out his arms in front of himself and stood still, as the slave fussed around him, carefully straightening and brushing the white toga he was wearing. The toga belonged to Licinius - a spare, but the ambassador had insisted he wear it to the banquet being held by the King of Caucasian Albania, at the royal residence later that evening. As the slave completed his task, bowed and quickly left the room, Fergus frowned and looked down at himself. Wearing a toga was not something he was used to, but if diplomatic etiquette required him to, then he would go along with it. He didn't particularly want to attend the party tonight, but Licinius and Julia, the ambassador's wife, had insisted. They seemed keen on his company and maybe it wouldn't be a complete waste of time if he could pick up some useful information. Two full days had passed since they'd arrived in Gabala and the ambassador had been nothing but helpful and cooperative. Licinius seemed genuinely pleased to have received him and had eagerly interrogated him about all the news from back home. The enforced rest at the ambassador's residence had been good for his companions too, and had raised their spirits. And they were going to need the rest for the long arduous journey ahead, Fergus thought grimly.

"You look very handsome Sir," Flavius said with a grin, as Fergus stepped out into the corridor of the ambassador's house and locked the door to his room behind him.

Fergus nodded without much enthusiasm. "Flavius," he said quietly. "Keep an eye out tonight when I am gone. See to it that there is no trouble."

"Are you expecting any trouble Sir?" the German ex-boxer replied quietly.

For a moment Fergus fixed Flavius with a serious warning look. However, he said nothing as he strode on past his deputy and started to descend the stairs to the ground floor.

***

The banquet was a dreary affair and Fergus was soon bored. In the great hall of the royal residence a long wooden table ran the length of the room, and seated on either side were around a hundred chatting guests. The table itself was covered with plates, jugs of drink and rich food dishes - some the like of which Fergus had never seen before. In the corners and vestibules of the hall, braziers filled with coal were alight, filling the hall with warmth. Along the walls torches lit the banquet in a dim, flickering reddish light. The smell of incense hung thick in the air and the floor was covered with warm furry animal skins. Near the doorways motionless guards and slaves stood pressed up against the walls, staring into space. The King of Caucasian Albania sat at the head of the table on a gleaming throne made of stone, wood, gold and silver. He was a short, fat, vulgar looking man, with a small crown on his head and he was laughing like a hyena. Seated nearest to the King were the most prominent guests and amongst them Fergus could see Licinius. The Roman ambassador too was laughing, as he raised his cup in a toast. Fergus however was too far away to hear what the King was discussing. Reaching out for his cup of wine, he took a sip and sighed. He'd been placed at the far end of the table with all the less important guests, sandwiched in between a drunken Sarmatian whom he couldn't understand and an Albanian woman who had nothing to say. Sitting directly opposite him however, was Julia, Licinius's beautiful wife and she seemed to be enjoying herself. As the dinner had progressed and the mood had grown less sober, Fergus had noticed the attention Julia was receiving from the other guests. It was only natural though he thought, considering her beauty and attractiveness. Turning once more to glance in the direction of the King, Fergus was surprised when Julia suddenly called out his name, speaking in Latin.

"Do you have a wife Fergus?" Julia asked as she fixed him with a stern unsmiling look.

"I do," Fergus replied quickly. "Plus, five beautiful daughters. They await my return in Antioch."

"Ah, Antioch," Julia said with sudden longing, as she took a sip from her cup. "I miss that great metropolis. It's so much better than this primitive shit-hole. Nothing but drunk Sarmatians and entertainers making bears do tricks. That's what this city offers."

"Don't let our host hear you say that," a tipsy guest, seated beside Julia exclaimed, with a grin as he leaned into her. But Julia ignored the man; her eyes were fixed firmly on Fergus. And as she gazed at him, Fergus had to look away, for she was a truly stunning looking woman. Easily the most beautiful he'd ever met, and her attractiveness seemed to be casting a spell over him.

"It must be hard for you and your wife to be apart for such long periods of time," Julia said, as she gazed at him from across the table.

"It is," Fergus replied, as he forced himself to look at her. "But we are used to it and she has five children to take her mind off me."

"And what do you have?" Julia asked studying him without smiling. "How do you cope with being apart from your wife for so long? It must get lonely."

"I am a soldier," Fergus replied quickly. "I do as I am ordered. I have a job to do. I focus on the job, the challenge and the welfare of my men. I try to survive."

For a moment Julia said nothing, as she studied him from across the table. Then her face cracked into a little seductive smile and, as she smiled at him, Fergus blushed like a boy.

"I like you," Julia said quietly. "I like you a lot Fergus."

Fergus turned to look away without replying. Suddenly he gasped as he felt a shoeless-foot gently poke its way into his groin. Across the table from him, Julia looked amused. Hastily reaching under the table with his hand, Fergus pushed the foot away, but it came straight back at him.

"Do I make you feel uncomfortable?" Julia asked as she smiled at him from across the table. "You look uncomfortable Fergus."

"I am all right," Fergus replied stiffly, as he battled the foot under the table with his hand, but again it came straight back worming its way towards his groin. Julia was playing footsie and she was not accepting no for an answer.

"If you are uncomfortable now," Julia said, with an amused smirk; "you will be even more so in a while when this banquet becomes an orgy. That's what usually happens when it gets late and too much wine has been consumed. Fucking is all that the King seems to care about."

Fergus nearly choked, as he hastily reached for his cup of wine.

"So, before a lady of Rome must suffer that indignity," Julia said with a sigh. "I would like to retire to my home. Will you escort me Fergus? The streets can be unsafe after dark."

"Your husband. Surely, he can take you home," Fergus replied quickly, as he turned to gaze down the table. And as he did, he saw Licinius casually glance in his direction.

"No," Julia said sharply. "Licinius shall stay here. He has business with the King that needs taking care of. It will have to be you."

And without waiting for an answer, Julia rose to her feet and prepared to leave. As she came around the table towards Fergus she bent down beside him. "Come on. I am going to fuck your brains out tonight," she whispered into his ear.

***

The Roman embassy compound was quiet and the two guards at the front gate leading into the courtyard, were not at their posts. It seemed as if all had called it a night and had gone to sleep. Silently Fergus and Julia walked into the courtyard and started up the stairs to the second-floor bedrooms. In the courtyard the night air was cool, and in their stables, the soft whinny and snort of the horses was the only noise. Fergus followed Julia up the stairs, and in the light from the flaming torches he had a fine view of her perfect arse. They had spoken little whilst she had led him back to the embassy through the darkened streets of the city. Fergus was struggling with himself. He wasn't sure what he was going to do. Julia seemed to have bewitched him, and his body, overwhelmed with desire, was following her. She was truly, the most attractive woman he had ever come across and no thoughts of Galena seemed to make him immune from a growing and raging desire. Galena would never know. His wife was far away and there was a chance he would not be returning from this mission. Better to have his way with this beautifully hot woman then. But at the very back of his mind something was nagging at him - a tiny warning voice that would not go away. There was something about all this that was not quite right, the voice in his head was screaming.

As they entered the long-dark corridor on the second floor, Julia suddenly turned and pushed him back up against the wall and a moment later her hot little tongue was pressing into his eager mouth. She moaned as her hands flitted over his body and his eager hands over hers, and for a few moments they stood pressed together kissing. Then she broke free, and catching his hand she pulled him towards one of the bedrooms. Kicking open the door, she giggled as she let go of him and stumbled backwards onto a large bed. The room was large and lit by burning lamps fixed to the walls and, in the far wall was an open window. Following her into the bedroom, Fergus paused to gaze at Julia as she sat up on the bed. She was staring at him. Slowly and deliberately she spread her legs, and slowly started to undress herself, as she beckoned for him to join her. Fergus felt his heart thumping in his chest.

It was wrong, but he didn't care. The sight of this woman was driving him crazy. He was going to have her. But the stubborn little warning voice in his mind would not go away and suddenly he hesitated and his fingers reached up to touch the Celtic amulet, hanging around his neck. Galena might never know but he would know. He would know he'd broken the vow he'd made to her. It would be a dishonourable act, however much his body willed him on. Once more he hesitated.

"What's the matter?" Julia purred as she saw his hesitation.

"I am not doing this," Fergus said at last, forcing the words from his lips. "I have a wife."

Swiftly before his resolve crumbled he turned on his heels and headed for the door. But just as he reached the doorway, from the corner of his eye, he caught a sudden movement in the shadows. With a cry, a man armed with a knife launched himself straight at Fergus. He was quickly followed by another armed man. Crying out in shock and fright, Fergus had just enough time to raise his hand and block the man's knife hand, before the momentum of the attack sent them both tumbling and crashing through the doorway and into the corridor beyond.

"Kill him. Kill him. Find the key," a woman's voice screeched. "He has the key on him."

And with a shock, Fergus realised the voice belonged to Julia. On top of him his attacker was grunting and straining as he tried to slice open Fergus's exposed throat. The man was terrifyingly strong. With a howl, Fergus bit the man's hand and was rewarded by a shriek of pain and a momentary slackening of the man's grip. Crying out and with a mighty effort, he managed to roll his attacker onto his back and with a vicious and furious scream head-butted him straight in the face. He was rewarded with a horrible crack as he broke the man's nose. Then someone kicked him in the head and he went crashing backwards onto the floor, his head spinning. Blurrily he saw the second man advancing towards him clutching a knife. The man was cursing as he prepared to finish him off. Weakly Fergus tried to raise his hand to protect himself, but it wasn't going to do him much good.

Suddenly his attacker groaned, stiffened, dropped his knife and slowly sank to the floor, and behind him, in the dim light, Fergus caught sight of Flavius, clutching his bloodied sword. The German's eyes were wild and blazing with fury, as he kicked the dying man. Scrambling to his feet, Fergus steadied himself against the corridor wall as Flavius turned and swiftly despatched the attacker with the broken nose. Unsteadily, his head screaming in pain, Fergus stooped to pick up the discarded knife and staggered back into the room. Julia was still on the bed staring at him in horror. Then with a snarl of rage, she came at him clutching a small knife. But as she lunged he caught her arm, spun her around and savagely slammed her forehead hard into the wall, knocking her unconscious with a single blow. As she collapsed, with blood streaming down her face, her little knife went clattering onto the floor.

Breathing heavily, Fergus turned to look around the room but there was no one else.

"What the fuck is this?" Flavius hissed furiously as he entered the room and, with wide staring eyes, gazed down at the unconscious woman. "What the fuck just happened?"

Fergus raised his hand to rub his head as he tried to focus. His breathing was coming in gasps and his hand was trembling as he realised how close to death he'd come. Silently he gazed down at Julia. The woman had tricked him. She had nearly managed to lure him to his end. But why? Then his face darkened.

"Wake the others," Fergus whispered hoarsely, as he quickly placed his hand on Flavius's shoulder. "Tell them that we are leaving right away. I mean right fucking now. We take the horses and we go. But we do it quietly. And thank you. If you hadn't shown up I would have been a dead man."

"You told me to keep watch," the German hissed. "So, I did. When I heard the commotion, I came right away. What's going on Sir? Why did they attack you? I don't understand. They have been so hospitable."

"They want the gold. They are after Adalwolf's ransom. Licinius and his wife have been planning to rob us from the moment they found out about the gold. And they will murder us to cover their tracks." Fergus snapped, as he turned and hastened away down the corridor.

At his room along the darkened corridor, he hastily inserted the key into the lock, opened the door and cautiously poked his head into the room but as he looked around he could see no one. Pausing to listen, he could hear nothing. That was good. The commotion seemed not to have woken anyone, but Licinius must have a plan. Was he biding his time? Was he planning to kill them all in the courtyard? But he must have been relying on Julia striking first, and that hadn't worked, so maybe they still had time, but he had to hurry. Casting a quick glance around the room, he saw that his few belongings were still where he'd left them, untouched, but as he moved into the room and stooped to look under the bed, he saw that the iron strong box had vanished. They must have stolen it whilst he was at the banquet, but without the key that hung around his neck, it would take them a long time to open it. Hastily discarding his toga, he dressed himself in his tunic and riding cloak, checked on Corbulo's old sword and strapped it to his belt. Then, snatching his few remaining belongings, he slipped out of the door. In the corridor he was heartened to see his companions waiting for him. They looked alarmed but alert and had their weapons drawn.

"What the fuck is going on Sir?" Skula hissed as he turned to gaze at Fergus in confusion. "Flavius says he killed those two men over there. But they are the ambassador's men."

"We have outstayed our welcome," Fergus whispered, as he started down the corridor. At the stairs leading down into the courtyard, he paused to cautiously study the dark courtyard beyond. All seemed quiet and peaceful and he could see no one about. In the gloom he could hear the soft whinny of the horses in their stables. Turning quickly towards the entrance gate, he could see that it was open and unguarded just like when he'd walked through it only a few minutes before. Maybe Licinius was still at the banquet. Maybe he had left the dirty work to his wife and his men? Maybe he didn't have the balls to take on nine armed and experienced fighters.

"We take our horses and we go," Fergus hissed, as he turned to look at his companions crouching behind him. "We don't stop for anything until we are out of the city. Kill anyone who gets in our way."

"But where are we going Sir?" Arlyn whispered loudly. "And where is the box with the gold. I see you don't have it."

"We ride for the Hyrcanian coast," Fergus replied in a quiet voice. "To the delta where the Cyrus flows into the ocean to be precise. I will explain later. And as for the gold. Well there is no gold. Hadrian lied to us. But he still wants us to rescue Adalwolf and that is what we are going to do."

"There is no fucking gold! That box was empty all this time," one of the Italian brothers exclaimed in astonishment. "That's not funny. That's a fucking joke."

"So, this is now a rescue mission," Skula muttered, as a little smile appeared on his lips. "I like it. They snatch Adalwolf. We snatch him back. Fuck you Sanatruces and goodbye. I like it a lot. Let's do this."

"Let's go," Fergus hissed as he rose and hastily started down the stairs and into the darkness.

As he hastened across the dark courtyard towards the stables, Fergus strained to listen, but he could hear nothing unusual. There was no one about. Quickly and as silently as possible his companions found their horses and saddles and began preparing the beasts for the ride. As he finished securing his saddle, Fergus heaved himself up onto his horse and hastily turned to see wherever his men were ready. Seeing they were, he raised his fist above his head and urged his horse out into the courtyard. The darkness remained quiet and peaceful as he, followed by his companions, fled through the open gates and into the night. But as Fergus twisted round to gaze back at the embassy, he saw a solitary man, clad in a white toga and clutching a burning torch, watching them from a balcony.

Chapter Twenty-Three – On the Hyrcanian Ocean

The Albanian village was small and nothing more than a collection of primitive stone huts and shelters with reed covered roofs. It was morning and across the vast, flat, featureless marshes, where the Cyrus flowed into the Hyrcanian Ocean, all was silent except for the solitary cry of a circling bird and the gentle whine of the wind. In the sky a blanket of dull grey clouds obscured the sun and a faint, rotten-egg smell cloaked the delta. On the muddy ground, Fergus dismounted from his horse and turned to glance at the fishing boats, that lay at anchor in the narrow tributary stream, half hidden by the tall green water reeds. A few locals, clad in drab woollen clothes, were sitting beside the shore line mending a fishing net. They were watching him with guarded, suspicious eyes. Carefully Fergus lowered the hood of his cloak from over his head. Five days had passed since they'd fled from Gabala but there had been no sign of pursuit. Licinius seemed not to have had the heart to go after them. Along the narrow path that led away through the marshes, his companions slowly followed his example and dismounted.

"Barukh, Flavius, with me," Fergus said quickly, as he gestured for them to join him. Hastening towards him was a small group of village elders, led by a tall man with a fantastic long white beard.

"Let's hope they speak a little Greek," Flavius growled, gazing at the approaching villagers as he shifted his belt into a more comfortable position. "Or else its back to sign language."

Fergus said nothing as the villagers, studying him cautiously, came to a halt. They did not seem afraid or hostile and, from their posture he guessed that they had encountered foreigners before. But their clothes and homes looked primitive and poor. Wrenching his eyes away from the villagers, Fergus glanced at Barukh. The young Jewish gladiator looked unconcerned.

"We are about to find out if what the Jewish elders in Gabala told you is true," Fergus said quietly.

"I believe they told me the truth," Barukh replied confidently. "The man we need to speak to is called Vusal. He is the fixer. He can get us what we want. In Gabala they said he has a long white beard. So maybe that is him over there. He not only arranges ships for the traders to cross the Hyrcanian, but also physical labour for the trade caravans. Probably the young men from these coastal villages," Barukh said calmly, as he turned to look around the village. "The Jews in Gabala say Vusal is trustworthy, and I know the price he charges the merchants. There is no chance that he is going to rip us off."

"So, fishing is not the only way they make their living around here," Flavius growled.

"Good," Fergus said, as he turned to the tall, white bearded village elder. "Well done. We seem to have found the right place then. But I doubt that these fishermen have ever done what I have in mind."

For a moment Fergus sized up the village elders. Barukh had carried out the instructions he'd given him in Gabala, and had sought out the Jewish brokers in the city, who had told him about Vusal. And on the ride from Gabala to the shores of the Hyrcanian Ocean, a hundred and forty-mile journey to the south-east, he had finally explained what they were going to do. It was a simple plan. But it all hinged on them being able to find a suitable ship.

"Vusal," Fergus called out, as he pointed at the tall bearded elder. "You are Vusal. Vusal?"

"I am Vusal," the man replied in broken Greek, with a grin that revealed a mouth filled with rotting teeth. "You need a ship?"

"A ship and two experienced men who know how to sail her," Fergus replied. "In exchange we shall give you our horses."

Across from him, Vusal turned sharply to look at the horses. For a moment he said nothing as he examined the beasts. Then muttering something to one of the elders, he turned his attention back to Fergus and frowned.

"Where do you want to go my friend?" Vusal exclaimed.

Fergus grinned and pointed his finger towards the east. "To India," he replied. "Where else?"

***

The Albanian fishing boat was nothing compared to the Roman naval galleys, merchant vessels or Liburna's that Fergus was used to. It was a small primitive ship with a single mast and a couple of rowing benches. A pile of old fishing nets lay towards the prow and the hull looked worn and old. The cargo hold smelled of fish and rotting wood and was not very large, but it would do. The owner of the boat, a swarthy looking man of around forty with a moustache, together with his son, a youth of around eighteen, stood watching Fergus in silence. As Fergus finished his inspection he jumped down into the shallow water and waded ashore. His companions were clustered together on the muddy riverbank, watching him sceptically.

"All right, grab your stuff and let's go aboard," Fergus called out. "We're leaving."

In response his companions hoisted their personal belongings up onto their shoulders and started to wade out into the river, towards the fishing boat, all except Saadi who remained stubbornly standing on the shore, her arms folded across her chest. She looked deeply unhappy as she gazed at the fishing vessel.

"Saadi, let's go," Fergus called out as he beckoned to her.

But Saadi shook her head in stubborn defiance. "I am not going on that ship," she replied. "Look at the state it's in. It's going to sink."

"Stop fucking around and get aboard," Fergus snapped angrily. "It is not going to sink."

"It is going to sink. I hate the sea and I cannot swim," Saadi cried.

Fergus groaned and quickly ran his hand through his hair in frustration. He was just about to yell at her again when, Skula suddenly came wading past him. The bald Alan tribesman headed straight towards Saadi.

"I won't let you drown Saadi. Come on. It won't be so bad." Skula called out and there was something in his voice that seemed to reassure her, for after a moment's hesitation, Saadi's shoulders drooped and reluctantly she started to wade out into the river towards Skula.

"Well it must have been the tone of my voice," Fergus muttered to himself in a sarcastic voice as he looked away and shook his head in bewilderment.

***

Fergus stood at the prow of the small fishing vessel, as it slowly nosed its way down the narrow, reed infested channel. The splash of the oars in the water, the creak and groan of the ship's timbers and the gentle moan of the wind, were the only noises. Around him, the flat marsh lands of the river delta stretched away to the horizon, a vast morass of tangled reed beds, water channels and mud flats. But there was still no sign of the sea. High above in the grey cloudy sky birds were circling. Turning to gaze back down the way they'd come, Fergus could see that the fishing village had already disappeared, hidden from view by the tall reeds. The Albanian skipper and his son were standing at the back of the boat clutching the steering bar. They made a stoic, unexcitable team, their dour gaze fixed on the channel up ahead. Early on Fergus had learned that both father and son only spoke their own local language. Communication was going to be difficult, but it couldn't be helped. And in the middle of the boat, on either side of the cargo hold, his companions were manning the oars. Turning to look ahead, Fergus sighed. He was committed now. He had to keep believing in the plan to rescue Adalwolf, even though a multitude of things could go wrong. He had to keep going and be seen to know what he was doing. That was leadership. His companions were relying on him to get this right and not lead them to their death.

At last, after an hour or so, the channel up ahead started to widen, and Fergus caught his first glimpse of the Hyrcanian Ocean. The grey, dreary expanse of water stretched away eastwards and the waves lapped along the shoreline. Eagerly he gazed out to sea, as the gentle swell caught hold of the boat. Not many Romans could boast to have sailed on the Hyrcanian Ocean. It was a semi-legendary place. He'd come to the very edge of the known world according to Hadrian's Greek advisers. Pressing them on their knowledge, the Greek advisers had conceded that they believed that the northern reaches of the Hyrcanian might connect to the outer ocean that encircled all land. But it was just a theory for no one had successfully managed to go there and return. Steadily the small boat began to push away from the land, heading eastwards and out into the open water. At the back of the fishing boat the Albanian skipper suddenly called out in his native language and his son quickly moved forwards and began to raise the ship's sail. Fergus watched the small sail go up, and as it did his companions stopped rowing and pulled in their oars. Catching his eye, Flavius got to his feet and, steadying himself against the hull, he made his way towards the bow.

"Savour this moment," Fergus said as the big German came to stand beside him. "We are on the Hyrcanian Ocean. Not many will be able to boast about that."

"It doesn't look any different to the other seas upon which I have sailed," Flavius replied, as he gazed out across the gentle swell. Quickly he turned to Fergus. "But aren't we going the wrong way Sir? Our course is surely not to the east."

Fergus glanced quickly at his deputy. "You are right," he replied in a quiet voice. "But these are border lands. There may be spies watching us from the shore. I want to make sure that no one suspects our real intentions. Vusal and those villagers," Fergus sighed. "They seem motivated by profit. If they knew what we were planning, what would prevent them from informing Sanatruces and being paid for their service? No. We will sail due east, until we are out of sight from land, as if we were heading for the established Indian trade routes. Then we shall turn north towards Derbent, but only when we can no longer see the coast."

For a long moment Flavius said nothing, as he seemed to be thinking it through.

"You are a crafty and suspicious man," Flavius exclaimed at last. "But one thing is certain. Adalwolf is going to owe us big time after this."

***

It was afternoon when Fergus caught sight of the two ships. Hastily he cried out a warning to his companions and all eyes turned to gaze at the distant vessels. Several days had passed since they had set sail. To the westward the rocky coast was about half a mile away and beyond, clearly visible, the great mountains and snow-covered peaks of the Caucasus rose from the earth; a looming barrier of soaring rock, forest and snow. The galleys appeared to be at anchor, for as he peered at them, Fergus could see metal chains extending down into the sea. They were large, much larger than their own fishing boat, with banks of oars and, as he strained his eyes he could see figures moving about on the decks. The galleys reminded him of the Greek triremes he'd seen in the harbour at Athens. Quickly Fergus shifted his gaze and turned towards the coast. In the narrow two-mile-wide strip of land that separated the sea from the mountain slopes the walls of a city gleamed in the sunlight.

"Derbent?" Fergus cried using the Caucasian Albanian name, as he turned towards the Albanian skipper and pointed at the city walls. "Derbent?"

"Derbent," the captain replied hastily with a little confirming nod. If the skipper was a little baffled with what was going on, he and his son hadn't shown it yet. Their inability to speak Greek or Latin had forced them to keep their silence for these past few days. For a moment Fergus gazed at the settlement. It looked small but its strategic position astride the narrow pass was unmistakable. Then slowly he turned his attention back to the ships, lying at anchor just off the shore.

"Are they Parthian ships?" Fergus asked but the captain didn't understand.

"Do you think they are the galleys on which Sanatruces is holding Adalwolf," Arlyn said as he came to stand beside Fergus.

"It could be," Fergus muttered. Quickly he beckoned for Flavius and Skula to join him. "All right, listen," Fergus said quietly. "This is the plan. We will drop anchor close to those ships and throw our fishing nets into the sea. We are going to pretend that we are just ordinary fishermen going about our business. That will give us a chance to observe them. Flavius, Skula and I, together with the Albanians, shall remain out on deck. The rest of you will take shelter in the cargo hold. This fishing boat is far too small for such a large crew. It could make those Parthian sailors suspicious."

"Then what?" Skula growled.

"I need to get a closer look at those galleys," Fergus replied.

"How?" Skula shot back.

"I am working on it," Fergus snapped, with a hint of annoyance. "Now don't just stand there. Get moving. Get the captain and his son to deploy those fishing nets."

The skipper looked baffled as he sat on the edge of the boat's hull and gazed down into the greenish water. The afternoon was wearing on and the boats nets had been cast into the water and a respectable and growing pile of silver scaled fish, filled an open barrel. At the captain's side, his son was gazing silently at Fergus as he sat with his back leaning against the hull. The youth looked amused, as if he was trying to figure out what was going on. Near to the nets, Skula and Flavius looked bored as they took it in turns to check if they had caught anything. The sun was heading for the western horizon. Around them on the open water, the swell of the sea moved the deck and the creaking of the timbers and the occasional slap of a wave, striking the ship's side, broke the awkward silence. Fergus however was oblivious to his crewmates. His eyes were firmly on the two ships, a hundred or so paces away. The galleys had not moved from their position nor had anyone come out to investigate who they were. The ruse seemed to be working.

"We caught some more fish," Flavius said, as he left his place and came to stand beside Fergus. "So, what's the plan Sir?"

"They are Parthian ships," Fergus replied quietly, as he studied the galleys. "Look at the winged lion painted onto the front of that galley and, over there the two horsemen locked in combat. Those are Parthian emblems all right and they are the only ships out here. They must belong to Sanatruces. But on which one is Adalwolf being held? Fancy taking a guess?"

Flavius remained silent as he turned to gaze across the water at the galleys. For a long moment he said nothing.

"Ofcourse it's just a guess Sir," the former boxer said at last. "But if I were Sanatruces. I would want to keep such an important hostage close to me. So, I would say that Adalwolf is being held on that galley over there. The one with the pennant flying from its mast. The other boat doesn't have one."

Slowly Fergus nodded. "Yes, that's what I was thinking too. But I still need to get a closer look at that galley." Fergus glanced quickly at his deputy. "I am going to need you to act a part," he said sharply.

***

The fishing boat bobbed up and down on the swell as it slowly edged alongside the large Parthian galley. It was indeed a big vessel Fergus could see, with an underwater battering ram at the bow and oar holes along its side. But the rowers had retracted their oars and, at the bow a heavy and solid-looking and expensive iron anchor chain vanished into the sea. A castle like deckhouse occupied the aft and centre of the ship, making it look dangerously top heavy. And looming over him was a tall mast, from which fluttered a solitary purple pennant. From the deck of the galley, suspicious faces were peering down at him. Fergus, clad in an old Albanian fisherman's clothes, stood at the prow and, seeing the men he hastily raised his hand in a friendly greeting.

"Friends," he called out in Greek. "Friends. May I come aboard? We have a sick man on our boat who needs attention. Do you have vinegar or maybe some Fennel? We shall share some of our catch with you."

On the deck of the Parthian galley, no one spoke as the sailors stared down at the small fishing boat.

"Please we need help," Fergus called out in Greek as he turned and pointed at Flavius, who was lying stretched out on the deck covered in a blanket with Skula kneeling beside him. And as if on cue Flavius groaned and rolled his head from side to side, whilst Skula damped his forehead with a damp piece of cloth. At the back of the boat the Albanian captain and his son were looking on in silent disbelief.

"What do you want?" a man suddenly replied in heavily accented Greek, as he pushed his way towards the side of the galley and peered down at Fergus. Catching sight of Flavius lying stretched out on the deck the man's face darkened.

"He is not coming aboard," the Parthian cried out in alarm. "Stay away. We do not want your disease on this ship. Go on. Move away."

"He has no disease," Fergus called out. "He is just ill and all I want is some vinegar or fennel. We will offer you some of our fish in return. May I come aboard Sir?"

The Parthian seemed to hesitate. Then he turned to a few of the men standing beside him and a quick animated conversation took place in a language Fergus could not understand.

"All right," the Parthian shouted, as he turned back to Fergus. "But the sick man stays where he is." The next moment netting made of rope was flung over the side of the galley and splashed down into the water. Carefully Fergus reached out, grabbed hold of the netting, leapt over the side of the boat and began to clamber up towards the deck and, as he did he was conscious of the dozens of eyes watching him. With a grunt he slithered over the edge of the hull and landed on the deck. A posse of armed Parthians were glaring at him. The dark bearded men were wearing Parthian trousers and hip length jackets, fitted with belts and boots on their feet.

"Vinegar or fennel, preferably both," Fergus said quickly, as he turned to face the Greek speaking man. "Please my lord. We shall be very grateful. My friend is not well."

"All right fisherman," the Parthian replied, as he quickly said something to one of the men standing beside him. In response one of the sailors hastened away. "We will give you some of our supplies," the Parthian replied, turning back to Fergus. "But after that you must go."

"We are most grateful my lord," Fergus said with a hasty bow. Then he turned and beckoned for the captain's son to join him with the sack of freshly caught fish. The youth looked amused as, encouraged by Skula he crossed the deck and started to clamber up the rope netting and, as he passed Flavius, the German groaned loudly. On the deck of the galley most of the Parthians who had greeted Fergus had started to drift back to their tasks, but a few remained. As he waited for the Parthians to bring him what he'd asked for, Fergus quickly turned to look around. A solitary guard was standing outside the stern deckhouse doorway, and close by in the middle of the deck, was a dark square hatchway with a ladder leading down into the hull. Further towards the bow another guard was standing atop the roof of the middle deckhouse and gazing out to sea. And beside the main mast was a stack of barrels.

"The name of your lord, Sir?" Fergus said quickly turning to the Parthian who spoke Greek.

"What do you want to know that for?" the Parthian replied with a frown.

"We are simple folk my lord," Fergus said respectfully lowering his gaze. "You have helped our sick comrade. In our prayers to the immortals we shall offer thanks to your lord for this act of kindness."

On the deck the Parthian's eyes narrowed as he gazed back at Fergus. For a moment he hesitated.

"The Lord Sanatruces, nephew to the king of kings, Osroes of Parthia commands this ship," the Parthian exclaimed in a proud voice.

Fergus dipped his head and kept his eyes on the deck. Then, as the son of the Albanian skipper scrambled over the side carrying the bag of fish, Fergus turned to him, took the bag and respectfully laid it down at the Parthian's feet.

"Our sick comrade is of German origin," Fergus said hastily, as he looked up at the Parthian. "He refuses to worship our gods and for this they have struck him down with illness. These Germans are proud and stubborn in their beliefs. When he talks in his sleep we cannot understand what he is saying. It is troubling."

"We have a man like that down below," the Parthian replied, as he spat onto the deck. "A German like your friend. A right arrogant bastard. Never shuts up. Threatens us with eternal fire and damnation."

Fergus nodded as his eyes swept across the galley deck.

"We are grateful for your help my lord," Fergus said, as a Parthian sailor returned with a small jug of vinegar. "We shall honour lord Sanatruces tonight in our prayers."

Then with a final respectful nod, Fergus turned away and was about to clamber back over the side of the galley when the Parthian suddenly said something in a language Fergus did not understand. Startled, Fergus froze. Behind him the Parthian repeated what he'd just said. Shit, a voice screamed inside Fergus's head. Shit, shit, shit. But before he could act, the Albanian skipper's son standing beside him suddenly replied speaking rapidly in his native language and gesturing at Fergus. Fergus stood rooted to the deck. Had the Parthians just discovered that he was not who he claimed to be? Had the Albanian youth just betrayed him? But as he slowly turned to face the Parthian, the man gave him a queer look and shrugged. Without a further word the Albanian youth started to clamber down the side of the galley and hastily Fergus did the same. As he clambered back into the fishing vessel clutching the jar of vinegar, Fergus quickly turned to look up at the Parthian ship, but the Parthians had already disappeared. Crouching down beside Flavius, Fergus placed the jar on the deck and then sharply turned to stare at the Albanian youth. What had the young man just said to the Parthians? What had he told them? But across from him the youth just looked amused, and catching Fergus's glare he responded with a wide smile.

"Well?" Flavius whispered as he lay on the deck with the blanket partially covering his body and Skula kneeling beside him.

"Adalwolf is on-board the ship," Fergus hissed, as he reached for the jar of vinegar. "And I think I know where they are holding him. We are going to go in tonight under the cover of darkness."

Chapter Twenty-Four – Rescue or Not?

The darkness was nearly complete. In the night sky there was no sign of the stars or the moon. A warm south-western wind was blowing, bringing with it the smell of wood smoke from the shore. Across the calm sea the only illumination came from the faint glow provided by Derbent, half a mile away, and the ship's lanterns aboard the Parthian galleys. The rest of the coastline was shrouded in complete darkness. Quietly, Fergus slipped over the side and into the sea and, as he entered the water he gasped at the cold. He was semi-naked wearing just his undergarments and his belt. Tied around his neck was a waterproof pig's bladder that floated on the water. A few moments later there was another quiet splash, and in the faint light provided by the fishing boat's solitary lantern, Fergus saw Barukh's head in the water. The former gladiator too had a waterproof bladder tied around his neck. Gasping for breath, Fergus turned in the direction of the Parthian galley some thirty paces away and began to swim quietly towards it. The current was not strong, and as he drew closer to the big galley, Fergus kept his eyes firmly on the deck of the ship. In the faint glow of the ship's lanterns, he could make out a sentry slowly patrolling up and down on the roof of the deckhouse.

As he reached the galley that was bobbing up and down on the gentle swell, Fergus grasped hold of the solid iron anchor chain and clung to it, as he struggled to regain his breath. The swim had been exhausting and he was freezing. A few moments later a hand grasped hold of his shoulder and then another hastily reached out to clutch the iron chain, as Barukh appeared. For a moment the two of them clung to the chain, resting, as their bodies rose up and down on the swell. At last, with a grunt Fergus reached up and slowly started to heave himself up the chain towards the deck above, using both his hands and feet. The movement of the ship and the chain made it a slow and hard task but at last, after what seemed an age, he managed to grasp hold of the side of the galley, and with a final effort, roll himself over the side and onto the deck. Panting quietly from the exertion, Fergus lay on his back for a moment as he stared up at the night sky. Around him the night remained quiet and peaceful. Hastily he scrambled to his feet and leaned over the side of the galley. In the darkness he could just about make out Barukh, as he tried to climb up the anchor chain. Stretching out his hand, Fergus caught hold of the former gladiator and silently dragged him over the edge of the galley and onto the deck.

Crouching on the deck Fergus turned to look back at the fishing boat and, as he did the boat's solitary lantern suddenly went out, making the vessel disappear into the night. Fergus bit his lip. His companions were acting as instructed. Pausing to listen, Fergus glanced up at the castle-like deckhouse. In the light from one of the Parthian lanterns, he could see a figure. The lookout however, seemed oblivious to their presence. Swiftly Fergus pulled his army pugio from his belt, cut the string that tied the bladder around his neck and pressed the waterproof sack into Barukh's hands.

"Let's go," Fergus whispered, as he crept towards the ladder leading up onto the deckhouse roof.

As silently as he could Fergus went up the ladder. Reaching the top, he paused and carefully raised his head to look out across the flat roof. In the faint light a solitary guard was leaning against the balustrade, gazing out to sea. He had his back turned to the ladder. Quickly Fergus shifted his attention towards the middle and stern of the galley beyond. Beside the aft deckhouse he could just about make out another sentry, but apart from the two-night watchmen the deck seemed deserted. Sensing Barukh waiting on him to move, Fergus took a deep, silent breath. Then in one smooth movement he rose and crossed the roof in two of three silent strides. Slamming his left hand across the sentry's mouth, he sliced open the man's throat with his knife. The Parthian stuttered and choked in shock, but as a torrent of hot blood gushed down his chest and over Fergus's arm Fergus kept his hand firmly clamped over the man's mouth, as he gently forced him to the ground. Crouching on the roof Fergus kept his hand firmly over the dying man's mouth, as he anxiously turned to stare at the sentry at the back of the ship. But the other night watchman had not moved, and all remained quiet. As the seconds passed Fergus's breathing started to return to normal. A little noise made him turn and in the glow of lantern he saw Barukh come up onto the roof and crawl towards him holding the two waterproof bladders.

"You know what to do," Fergus whispered. "Use the lantern. Wait until I return with Adalwolf and you hear my voice. Then you jump into the water on that side of the boat."

In reply the former gladiator nodded as he gazed in the direction in which Fergus was pointing, his body shivering slightly from the cold.

Without any further hesitation, Fergus let go of the dead man's mouth and started down the ladder leading into the middle section of the galley. Carefully keeping to the shadows, he flitted across the deck and crouched beside the square hatchway that led down into the hull. Straining to listen, he paused to allow his breathing to normalise. But in the night, he could hear nothing unusual. Risking a quick peek down the ladder, he could see only darkness. Briefly closing his eyes, he reached out to touch Galena's amulet that hung from around his neck. Then gripping his pugio knife, he boldly slipped his legs down into the hatch and started to climb down into the hull of the galley. As the darkness enclosed him, he suddenly felt his feet reach the wooden deck. Turning to look around, Fergus saw that he was in a long open galley that seemed to stretch the entire length of the ship. On either side were rows of benches for the oarsmen and in between them, crammed into every available inch of space, men seemed to be asleep, stretched out across the benches or curled up in hammocks. Snoring and the occasional cough and fart punctured the darkness.

Where was Adalwolf? Had he miscalculated? Were the Parthians keeping him in one of the deckhouses instead? Then Fergus froze, as he caught sight of a figure slumped on the deck, his torso lashed to the main mast by a rope. The man's arms and legs were clamped together with iron chains and the figure seemed to be asleep. It was Adalwolf. Fergus's eyes widened as he stared at him. Yes, it was Adalwolf. There was no mistake. Hadrian's Germanic adviser looked in a sorry state. His beard looked unkept and he'd lost a lot of weight. But it was him.

Boldly Fergus left the ladder and started to creep down the middle of the galley past the sleeping sailors and oarsmen, towards Adalwolf. As he reached the mast, Fergus calmly knelt beside Adalwolf, and using his knife quickly cut through the rope binding him to the main mast. Adalwolf stirred and Fergus hastily clamped his hand over the old German's mouth and brought his own mouth close to Adalwolf's ear.

"It's me Fergus," he whispered. "Hadrian has sent me to rescue you. You must be quiet. We are going to be leaving now. Can you walk?"

Adalwolf's eyes blinked open and he turned to gaze at Fergus in shock and alarm.

"It's me Fergus," Fergus hissed, as quietly as possible. "I am here to rescue you. Now can you walk with those chains?"

For a moment Adalwolf was unable to reply, as he stared at Fergus in disbelief. Then as his shock seemed to subside and he recognised Fergus, he nodded.

"I can walk a little," Adalwolf whispered. "But these chains make a huge noise. Everyone is going to hear me."

"We are going to get up now. Walk towards the ladder and then up we go," Fergus whispered. "Just do exactly as I say and you will be fine. Now let's go. We are going to get out of here."

And without giving Adalwolf a further chance to say anything, Fergus heaved the adviser onto his feet and started to half drag him across the deck towards the ladder and the hatchway leading upwards. The iron chains clanked and thudded on the deck, making a horribly loud metallic noise, as Fergus and Adalwolf waddled down the middle of the galley. Fergus's cheeks coloured with the effort and the noise, but unperturbed he boldly continued past the ranks of the sleeping crew. But their progress was slow and as he sensed the men being awakened around them Adalwolf suddenly leapt onto Fergus's back, clinging to him in desperation. Nearly stumbling with the additional weight, Fergus groaned as he forced himself down the galley with Adalwolf holding on in piggyback style. They had just reached the ladder when a challenging shout rang out and, from the gloom a man appeared coming towards them.

"Climb," Fergus hissed as he half flung Adalwolf onto the ladder. Then as the man closed with him, Fergus lunged and stabbed him in the neck. With a shriek the sailor staggered backwards, hit the hull and collapsed to the deck. And as he did pandemonium broke out and the dark galley was suddenly filled with shouts and cries of alarm.

"Move, move," Fergus screamed, as he started up the ladder pushing Adalwolf before him. With a cry, the German adviser rolled out onto the deck and into the fresh air. He was followed moments later by Fergus.

"Now Barukh. Now. Do it now!" Fergus roared, as he staggered to his feet. On the roof of the deckhouse there was no immediate reply. Then in the gloom something moved. The lantern was torn from its place and flung onto the floor. As the lamp smashed onto the deck, the roof of the deckhouse suddenly burst into flames that spread like a flash flood racing across the timbers - fuelled by the oil from the two waterproof bladders.

Fergus did not pause to watch. Stumbling towards Adalwolf, he roughly hauled the old groaning man onto his feet. Down below in the galley all hell had broken out. A sudden shout made Fergus turn. A bearded Parthian with a handsome face and clad in a richly decorated jacket but nothing else, was standing in the doorway of the stern deckhouse, no more than six or seven paces away. The man was staring at Fergus in shock and outrage.

For a moment Fergus stood rooted to the deck, as his eyes locked on the Parthian. Then with a furious cry Fergus flung his pugio knife at the man. Without waiting to see the outcome he grasped hold of Adalwolf, lifted him boldly off his feet and with a huge adrenaline fuelled roar, charged towards the edge of the ship and flung Adalwolf and himself overboard and into the sea. They landed in a great splash, and as he went under, Fergus caught a mouthful of the slightly salty water. Surfacing with a splutter he gasped for breath and caught sight of the Parthian galley. One of the deckhouses was on fire and the flames were rapidly spreading. Barukh had done a good job. On-board, the galley men were frantically rushing to and fro and their shouts and screams rent the night. A terrified yelp for help nearby was suddenly cut short, as Adalwolf seemed to take in a mouthful of water and vanish beneath the surface. The German was not going to last long in the water, with those iron chains. Desperately Fergus scrabbled around in the blackness. His hand brushed Adalwolf's head and frantically

Fergus caught hold of him and dragged him back to the surface.

"I have got you," Fergus gasped. "I have got you. Stay still. Don't struggle."

The freezing cold was swiftly sapping Fergus's strength, as he forced Adalwolf's head above the surface and desperately turned to look around in the darkness. He had not been expecting the complication of the iron chains. But it was too late now. The German was retching up water in a continuous stream and he was close to complete panic. Grimly, Fergus held on forcing Adalwolf's to keep his head above the swell.

"We are here," Fergus cried out into the night. "We're over here. We're over here."

In the darkness there was no reply. Then suddenly a lantern flickered into life and Fergus caught the faint outline of a boat.

"We're here," he screamed in desperation.

Nothing happened. Then the boat turned in his direction and the lantern started to draw closer. Fergus cried out again. His strength was nearly gone. He was not going to last much longer. Then close by, something crashed into the water and, as he cried out again, he suddenly felt a firm hand grasp hold of his shoulder and start to drag him towards the fishing vessel.

"I have got you Sir," Arlyn hissed, as he began to drag Fergus and Adalwolf through the water towards the fishing boat. "I have got you, Sir."

***

Fergus sat slumped up against the side of the small fishing vessel. The night was far-advanced, and the small boat was all alone, surrounded by pitch darkness and the vastness of the sea. It was impossible to see the deck he was sitting on.

The sight of the burning Parthian galley had slowly faded, as they had headed away from the coast north-eastwards on the wind. And as the flickering fire had faded away into the darkness the sea swell had grown, as had the strength of the wind. Sitting opposite Fergus, Adalwolf and Barukh were slumped out on the deck, too exhausted to do anything else. Around him in the darkness, Fergus was aware of the rest of the crew. He could sense their tension. No one had spoken much since the successful rescue, for their spirits had been dampened by the changing weather. Steadying himself against the pitching, moving hull Fergus slowly got to his feet and as he did, he felt the force of the wind on his face. Grimly he reached up to touch Galena's good luck amulet. The little fishing vessel was heading into a storm, a ferocious storm and there was nothing they would be able to do about it.

Chapter Twenty-Five – The Storm

With the arrival of dawn, the storm began to strengthen in fury and violence. As the waves grew in height, the small fishing vessel was tossed up and down, a piece of helpless flotsam on an angry, surging sea. Fergus and his companions clung on. At the stern the Albanian captain looked tense, as he held on to the steering bar. His face and body soaked to the bone as he tried to keep the bow aligned with the waves. Fergus crouched beside the mast, holding on to it as he wiped the freezing water from his face. His body was shivering with cold and he was exhausted. The sail had been furled and stowed away in the cargo hold. There was no sign of land. They were completely alone with nothing but the raging waves, the howling wind and the driving rain. Grey, dreary clouds covered the sky in every direction. Grimly Fergus turned to look at his companions. On the sodden, drenched and careening deck, Adalwolf was lying on his side trying to keep warm. His eyes were closed, and the chains were still fastened to his legs and arms. There had been no time to try to pry them loose. Flavius and Barukh clung to the oarsmen benches on either side of the small boat, their expressions grim and hard, as they waited for the storm to pass. There had been no more space in the small cargo hold where the others had sought refuge.

But the storm was not easing; it was growing worse Fergus thought, as he snatched a glance out across the bleak waves. There was no chance of choosing a course. The storm was going to drive them to where it wanted them to go. There would be no arguing with the weather gods. All they could do was try and keep the boat afloat. As he peered out across the sea, a huge wave came crashing over the bow of the boat and struck Fergus full on, nearly tearing him away from the mast and washing him overboard. Spluttering and gasping in shock Fergus wiped the water from his face with wide eyed horror. And as he stared at the next wave, he suddenly remembered the stories Marcus his father had told him about his epic voyage across the western ocean to Hyperborea. Waves as tall as trees; an endless expanse of water; no sign of land for weeks on end; huge black sea monsters spouting water high into the air and strange red painted natives. If it had been anyone but Marcus telling these stories, he would have dismissed them as fantasies but now, out here in the midst of the angry Hyrcanian ocean, he found them strangely comforting. If his father could survive the challenges of the western ocean; then he, Fergus, could do the same out here. The sea was not going to take them he thought, with a burst of determination.

"We're going to be all right," Fergus shouted as he turned to his companions, trying to sound confident and reassuring. "We're going to be all right."

No one replied. The shriek of the wind, the lashing rain and the battering and surging roar of the waves made any communication almost impossible. Fergus gasped as another wave came crashing over the bow, drenching him from head to foot in icy cold water. Grimly Fergus held onto the mast.

It was around noon, with the storm still raging, when another huge wave came crashing over the bow, flooding the deck and with a crack, the boat's mast snapped in two and crashed down onto the deck, narrowly missing Adalwolf. Fergus cried out in shock but Adalwolf was too tired to move. And before Fergus could grasp hold of the broken mast, another wave caught it and washed it clean overboard where it was quickly lost in the boiling, surging waves. Clutching the stump of the mast, Fergus turned to stare at the Albanian captain standing at the stern. Amongst the white spray and howling wind, the man made for a heroic figure as he held onto the steering bar. The loss of the mast had not changed the skipper's expression. All his attention was focussed on keeping the ship's bow pointed at the waves and preventing them from being capsized.

"Fergus. Fergus," a voice was screaming above the noise of the storm. Alarmed, Fergus twisted around and saw Skula poking his head out of the cargo hold. The Alan tribesman looked worried.

"We have a leak," Skula yelled. "The boat is taking on water."

"Fix it," Fergus shouted, as he was drenched by a wave. "Use whatever you have but plug that damned leak. Just do it."

There was no chance of him leaving his position beside the mast to go and investigate. The movement of the boat and the ferocity of the waves made that too dangerous. Quickly Skula's head vanished back into the cargo hold. Grimly Fergus turned to stare out across the sea. How much more of this pounding could they take? How long before the small fishing boat fell apart?

"This is some rescue mission," Adalwolf roared, with a sudden surge of energy as he lay on the deck gazing at Fergus, his drenched body shaking with cold.

"Shut up old man," Fergus shouted, as he twisted his head to look at Adalwolf. "If you hadn't gotten yourself kidnapped we wouldn't be here."

***

It was growing dark when at last the ferocity of the storm started to slacken. Wearily, his body shivering and drenched, Fergus opened his eyes and raised his head to look out across the bleak, grey waves. There was no sign of land and without a mast and a sail they were helpless, forced to drift and go where nature was taking them. His fingers were so numb he could barely feel them. Night was closing in fast, but the sea was calmer, and it had stopped raining. As the whine of the wind started to die away, at the stern of the boat, the captain handed the steering bar to his son and slumped down onto the drenched deck. The man looked utterly exhausted.

Turning to check on Adalwolf, Flavius and Barukh, Fergus could see them also lying slumped on the deck, their eyes closed as if asleep. No one seemed to have the strength or energy to do anything. With a groan he stirred and dragged himself along the planking to the middle of the fishing boat and the small enclosed cargo hold. Peering inside he could see a huddle of faces, Skula, Numerius, Saadi, Arlyn and the brothers. Most seemed to be asleep, too exhausted to do anything else, but they had managed to plug the leak for the dirty, sloshing water at the bottom of the hold didn't look too deep. Catching sight of him, one of the Italian brothers winked in encouragement but said nothing.

Turning away Fergus crawled towards the stern, where the Albanian captain sat on the deck, staring vacantly into space. His son, clutching the steering bar, was peering into the gloom ahead. Edging up against the side of the hull, Fergus raised his fingers to his mouth and blew hot air onto them. Then reaching out, he tugged at the youth's leg and looked up at him.

"You," Fergus said, gesturing at the youth. "What did you tell that Parthian aboard that galley? What did you say to him when we were about to leave?"

The youth looked down at Fergus without understanding and Fergus sighed and looked away. Of-course it was no use. The boy and his father had no knowledge of Greek or Latin.

"Skula," the youth suddenly replied. "Skula. Skula."

Fergus frowned. Was the youth asking for Skula?

"Skula," he yelled turning to the cargo hold. "Come on out here. I think the Albanian boy wants to have a word with you."

For a moment nothing happened. Then a head poked out of the shelter and reluctantly Skula emerged and staggered towards him. And as he did, the Albanian youth said something to him that made the Alan tribesman frown.

"What is he saying?" Fergus blurted out as he gazed at Skula.

At the steering bar the youth spoke again, directing his words towards Skula who suddenly looked surprised.

"He is trying to speak in the language of the Alans, my people," Skula said quickly, as he gazed at the youth. "But he's not very good. He is speaking in single words." And as the youth repeated himself for a third time, Skula translated in a hesitant voice. "On ship. Parthian. Ask. You. Where from. I say. You gift. From Gods. To my village. You Romans. I know. You. No India. You. Fight. Parthians. Good. Me. No like. Parthians."

Fergus grunted in surprise and looking up at the youth, he nodded his gratitude. In reply the boy grinned back at him.

***

It was dawn and there was still no sign of land. The sea was calm, and the stricken fishing vessel aimlessly bobbed up and down on the swell. In the skies the grey clouds still blocked out the sun. Fergus sat on his haunches, using a knife and a piece of wood, to patiently pick away at the iron clamps that held Adalwolf in chains. Hadrian's friend was sitting up, with his back leaning against the hull and gazing vacantly out across the sea. Around them, the crew huddled on the deck, resting and sleeping. Everyone looked exhausted. The weather may have improved but they were now swiftly running out of fresh drinking water and Fergus had enforced strict rationing of the remaining supplies. But what was left was not going to last for more than a couple of days.

"Thank you," Adalwolf said quietly, as he looked at Fergus.

"We are not out of here just yet," Fergus grunted, as he tinkered with the iron leg clamps. "And I didn't do this for you."

"I know," Adalwolf said with a sigh. "But thank you anyway. It can't have been easy finding and rescuing me. I bet Hadrian was not prepared to pay for my release. I know his policy. No negotiation with terrorists. He is right."

"We figured something else out," Fergus said wearily, as he leaned back and gazed at the leg irons as his latest attempt to break them failed.

Adalwolf nodded. "Sanatruces is up to no good," he said. "I know why he came to Derbent. He is trying to enlist the Alans and other tribes into an anti-Roman alliance. He is trying to get them to attack our positions in Cappadocia and along the Danube. And there is more. I learned that the Parthians are encouraging and funding rebellion across the whole of the Roman east. Especially the Jews. The Parthians are plying them with gold and urging them to rise and avenge the destruction of their temple. Hadrian must be told about this at once. If I do not make it, then you must. Hadrian must be made aware of the trouble that is coming."

"Hadrian knows," Fergus said sharply, as he reached out and started working on the iron leg clamps again. "I came across Parthian agents out in the Syrian desert. They were transporting gold to dissident groups. I reported it myself to Hadrian and Attianus. They are aware of what the Parthians are doing."

"Well that's good news then," Adalwolf said in a relieved voice.

"You know you are going to owe us all a huge feast when we get back to Antioch," Fergus said tinkering away with a little smile. "The boys have been telling me what they are looking forward to eating when they get back. It's an expensive list."

"Don't you worry," Adalwolf replied with a smile of his own. "It will be bigger and better than any of you can imagine."

For a while Fergus was silent as he worked on the clamps. Then at last he looked up at Adalwolf.

"My father, Marcus," Fergus said in a tight voice. "As you know, his name appears on Hadrian's death list. Attianus meant it when he said that when Hadrian becomes emperor he is going to have all on that list executed. I must get my father off that list. He's my father - who has just got himself caught up in something that he doesn't really understand. When we get back to Antioch, Hadrian has promised to take him off the list. That's the reason why I agreed to come out here and rescue you."

"We all have our reasons and motifs," Adalwolf replied in a quiet voice. "If our roles had been reversed, I am not sure I would have come to get you either." And as he finished speaking, a little smile started to grow on Adalwolf's lips. Fergus too grinned and then, turning his attention back to the clamps, he forced his knife in deeper, wriggled around and, with a metallic click, the clamp snapped open.

***

It was morning on the following day when a squawking bird suddenly came swooping out of the sky and alighted on the prow of the little vessel. Slowly Fergus opened his eyes and gazed at the creature. He and the rest of the listless passengers lay about on the deck as the craft bobbed up and down on the water. Most of his companions seemed to be asleep, too weakened and exhausted to do much else. But as he tiredly gazed at the bird, Fergus suddenly became aware of a new noise. One that they had not heard before. The crash and roar of waves breaking onto a shoreline. Startled he crawled across to the side of the boat and raised his head over the edge. And there, a hundred or so paces away, he caught sight of a flat, sandy but also rocky coastline. Fergus gasped, and his eyes widened. Hastily he turned to his companions, but no one else seemed to be aware of the land or had heard the boom of the surf. Turning back to stare at the shore, he could see that they were drifting towards the land. His face grew pale. The waves and current were taking the fishing boat straight onto a group of sharp, jagged rocks.

"Land!" Fergus roared with all his strength and his voice boomed out across the water like a centurion training a company of new recruits.

His roar had the desired effect. Staggering onto his feet, Flavius cried out in relief and from the stern a great shout of joy erupted, as the others stirred and started to move. But Fergus's delight was slipping away fast, as he saw the rocks drawing closer and closer. If the boat struck them it would tear the craft apart.

"Hold on," he yelled. "We are being driven onto the rocks. Everyone hold on."

There was nothing anyone could do. With wonderous, terrified eyes, Fergus stared at the rocks as the fishing boat headed straight onto them. Then with a heart rending and terrifying tearing, splintering groan, the boat was thrown onto the rocks and all hell broke loose. The shock of the collision sent Fergus tumbling overboard and into the shallow water. His startled yell was cut short, as he took in a mouthful of water and his arm grazed a rock, scraping away much skin. Then his feet hit the sandy bottom and he burst from the water gasping for breath. Around him, the yells and shrieks of his companions rose above the roar of the surf. The fishing boat however was finished. The force of the waves and the immovability of the rocks had wrecked the boat and already she was sinking at the stern and breaking apart. Gasping and spluttering, Fergus swam away from the rocks and caught hold of Adalwolf's arm. The German looked at the end of his tether. But the sea was not deep and, as Fergus found his feet, he dragged Adalwolf onto the beach. Dropping Adalwolf onto the sand, he turned and headed back into the water but as he waded into the surf he could see that his companions had made it. They had all made it. Some like Arlyn and Flavius looked relieved but Skula was struggling, as he staggered out of the surf with Saadi clinging to his back. The girl was panicking and screaming, her nails digging into Skula's skin.

Wearily Fergus retreated to where Adalwolf was sitting in the sand. The German, relieved of his iron chains, was panting from exertion and he was soaked to the bone. As his companions slowly gathered around him on the beach, Fergus turned as he heard a sudden howl of anguish. The Albanian captain was on his knees, his hands grasping his head, as he stared at the sunken, smashed remains of his fishing boat that was being methodically broken up by the elements. At his side, his son too was gazing at the melancholic scene with horror. Then catching sight of Fergus watching him, the captain's face darkened with sudden rage and before anyone could stop him, he leapt to his feet and stormed towards Fergus. The first furious punch caught Fergus on the shoulder and the second on his chin. Staggering backwards with a cry of pain, Fergus tumbled onto his back. But as the Albanian skipper launched himself again, Flavius and Skula intervened and pushed the man backwards. A furious, hate-filled stream of words followed in a language Fergus could not understand. Raising his hand and pointing his finger at Fergus, the Albanian captain said something to him and spat onto the sand.

"I think he is a little bit pissed off about the loss of his boat," Adalwolf said slowly, as he gazed at the Albanian who Flavius and Skula were forcing away. "I think he blames you for his loss. Can't argue with that. That fishing boat was probably how he made his living. And now it's gone."

"Our horses were a generous trade for his boat and I haven't got anything with which to compensate him," Fergus growled, as he rose to his feet and rubbed his chin with a painful expression. "And I am not responsible for that fucking storm either. But if he tries to hit me again I am going to hit him back."

***

The campfire crackled and roared and around its embrace, warming and drying themselves, sat the crew. It was late in the afternoon and out on the beach the roar of the surf was a continuous dull boom. A thin column of black smoke rose into the clear skies and the broken remains of the boat lay scattered across the rocks and washed up on the beach. Fergus sat, carefully watching the captain. The Albanian too was glaring at him and not bothering to hide his hostility. Around the fire Fergus's companions were passing around the one remaining animal bladder that they'd managed to retrieve from the wrecked ship. The brothers had managed to find a small stream a half a mile inland and were sharing the water they'd brought back.

"So, where the hell do you think we are?" Numerius exclaimed as he looked around the beach.

"I think the storm blew us northwards," Adalwolf replied. "The weather is cooler here and the winds have been coming from the south-west. That still means we could be anywhere. But I can't see the Caucasus. My best bet is that we have been drifting northwards."

"Shit," Numerius muttered, with a sudden anxious expression. "Well, without a boat it looks like we are going to be walking home."

As it was being passed around Fergus was just about to take a swig of water from the bladder, when Flavius suddenly rose to his feet in alarm and cried out.

Hastily Fergus stood up, his hand dropping to the pommel of Corbulo's old sword and turned to look in the direction in which Flavius was pointing. And there on the flat open grassland that vanished away inland, he suddenly caught sight of a small band of stationary horsemen. The riders were no more than forty paces away. They seemed content to observe and made no effort to come towards the fire. Fergus tensed as he stared at the newcomers. They looked like no horsemen he had ever seen before. The men were tall, bearded and with long free-flowing hair. Slung across their backs, they were carrying powerful composite bows and their heads were covered in high pointed caps with flaps over the ears and the nape of their necks.

"They are Alans," Skula suddenly cried out in an excited voice. "They are my people. Let me go and talk with them."

And without waiting for permission, he strode away from the fire and towards the band of horsemen with Fergus and Flavius hastening after him.

As he walked towards the horsemen, Fergus could see that the horses had no saddles and the riders were sitting on saddle cloth. The Alans did not move and remained silent, carefully watching Fergus and his two companions. But as the three of them approached, several of the horsemen raised their beautiful composite bows, notched an arrow and trained their weapons on the newcomers. Abruptly Skula stopped and raised his hands. Then in an excited voice he cried out, spewing forth a stream of words in a language that Fergus had never heard him speak before. Instead of trying to understand the words Fergus gazed at the band of horsemen. Hadrian's Greek advisers had been silent about the Alans during their briefing back in Antioch, except to say that the horsemen who inhabited the vast plains to the north were proud and ferocious warriors who lived to fight. Studying them now, Fergus noticed their richly ornamented leather belts, holding knives, swords and battle-axes. The men's padded and quilted leather trousers tucked into boots and their long-sleeved tunics reached down to their knees. Over this they were wearing felt coats and their fingers were adorned with bone rings. They looked fearsome and proud and completely at ease on their horses.

One of the men suddenly replied to Skula, and for a moment the two of them seemed to be engaged in a conversation, speaking their strange, unintelligible language. At last Skula turned to Fergus.

"It's all right," Skula said hastily. "He says he saw our smoke and came to investigate. He says that we have trespassed on his lord's land. But he can see we had little choice. He is willing to take us to his camp. It's a half a day walk inland. I think we should go with him Sir."

"Tell him that we are Greek merchants," Fergus said, as he gazed at the Alans and the horsemen stared straight back at him. "Tell him that we did not mean to trespass and that we shall gladly go with him to his camp. We are not here to cause trouble. Tell him that we lost our boat on the rocks."

Quickly Skula turned to the Alans and spoke to them, and in reply, one of the horsemen said something and gestured to the south.

"He says," Skula said translating slowly. "That we are lucky to have come ashore in his lord's land. There is trouble further to the south. He says the clans that border the great mountains are not as honourable and generous as his lord."

"Well that is the first bit of good fortune we have had in days," Fergus growled.

Chapter Twenty-Six – The Alani Camp

The plains and gently rolling hills were devoid of trees; just an endless and open expanse of grass and semi-desert. Wearily Fergus trudged along, following the band of Alani horsemen as they crossed the wilderness. It was getting late and across the steppes the temperature was starting to drop. It felt as if they had been walking for hours and, as he turned to look at his companions, he could see that they looked exhausted. But there were no horses for them to ride, so walking was the only thing they could do. Turning his attention back to the Alani horsemen, Fergus had noticed that they didn't seem hostile, but nor did they seem overtly pleased to have found them trespassing in their lands. The exception was Skula. He was fascinated by the wild horsemen as he strode alongside them speaking to his kinsmen. The bald Alani tribesman had come home Fergus thought, with a sudden pang of foreboding. He had been reunited after all these years with his own people.

Dropping back to walk alongside Adalwolf, Fergus nudged the German diplomat with his elbow and nodded in the direction of the Alani.

"What do you know about these people?" Fergus muttered, as the two of them strode along through the grass.

Adalwolf looked up and gazed at the horsemen in silence. "Not much," he replied. "Only that they are numerous and stretch from the Danube to the outer ocean. That they love horses and war. That they don't particularly like Romans."

"Do they have a king of kings like the Parthians?" Fergus asked.

"I don't think so," Adalwolf replied. "I think they are divided into semi-independent clans. Sometimes they unite to fight against foreigners or to go raiding. Most of the time however they seem to be at war with each other."

Fergus nodded and turned to peer out across the steppes. In the twilight he could not see far into this strange land, but in the big open skies above him, the first of the stars had become visible, twinkling and gleaming like tiny diamonds.

"Let's hope they will allow us to go on our way without any trouble," Fergus said as he turned to peer at the Alani. "But I can see now that no one goes on foot in these lands. We need to get hold of horses. On horseback these open plains will allow us to cross large distances very quickly."

"You also need to know in which direction to ride," Adalwolf said sourly.

"The horsemen told us that there is trouble to the south along the great mountains," Fergus said. "That could imply that the mountains are the Caucasus. If so then our journey home lies to the south-west."

"And how are we going to get hold of horses?" Adalwolf asked with a note of scepticism. "All our possessions were lost in the shipwreck. All we have are our weapons and the clothes on our backs."

"I have a plan to get us home," Fergus nodded as he reached up to touch Galena's amulet that hung around his neck. "But I am going to need your help. I need you to find out where we are. But first we must recover our strength. The last few days have exhausted us."

***

The tent-covered wagons that formed the Alani encampment, were like nothing Fergus had ever come across before. It was dawn and across the vast steppes - an endless sea of grass - the sun was rising, a red ball in the east. Stiffly, Fergus got to his feet from the ground beside the tent-covered wagon where he and his companions had spent the night. The night had been cold, and for a moment he allowed the rays of the sun to warm his face. Then he turned to look around. In the dawn light he could see that the camp had been drawn up along the banks of a stream. Amongst the wagons, with their peaked leather and hide-bound tent covers, the Alani, clad in their peculiar padded trousers; knee length tunics; felt and fur coats and peaked caps, were going about their business. There were no houses; no fixed defences; no sign of permanent settlement - just a semi-circle of nomadic wagons and a multitude of animals, horses, oxen, cattle, dogs and sheep. On the opposite side of the stream, a boy was guarding a large herd of sheep. Further along, a herd of cattle was drinking from the stream and, from somewhere out of sight, a dog was barking. A column of smoke was rising into the clear blue sky from a campfire and out on the open grasslands a party of horsemen were riding their horses. The Alani however ignored him, and Fergus found it hard to distinguish men from women, for they all seemed to be dressed in the same manner. The only attention he and his companions seemed to receive was from a group of silent children, who were standing and staring at him from a respectable distance.

As he gazed at the Alani camp, two women appeared and came towards him, carrying pots covered with cloth. Without saying a word or looking at Fergus, they placed the pots on the ground nearby and departed. Curiously Fergus removed the cloth and saw that one of the pots contained what looked like milk whilst the other seemed to be filled with boiled sheep's meat.

"Breakfast is here boys," Flavius called out in a cheerful voice as he raised himself off the ground and approached the pots, sniffing the air hungrily.

Fergus had just finished his meal when a troop of Alans came striding towards him. In their midst, he recognised one of the men who had found them on the beach. Rising to his feet, Fergus turned to face them. The tall nomads with their wild and savage appearance paused and seemed to be searching for Skula. Catching sight of him, one of the men called out.

"What do they want?" Fergus said sharply.

Skula rose hastily to his feet.

"They say we are to come with them to meet their lord," Skula replied.

Without saying a word Fergus wiped his mouth with the back of his hand and quickly handed Arlyn his empty bowl. Then with Skula at his side he set off after the Alans towards one of the tent-covered wagons.

The Alani headman was sitting cross-legged around a campfire, over which a pot of stew was cooking. He was clad in similar clothing to the other Alans and the only thing that marked him out from the others was the gravitas and respect with which his clansmen treated him. On the man's belt, Fergus noticed a finely crafted image of a deer set into a plaque of solid gold. As Fergus and Skula approached, he raised his head to gaze at them with shrewd eyes. Fergus halted in front of the fire and nodded a quick greeting, which was not returned. Then the headman spoke. His words were directed towards Skula but he kept his fierce blue eyes on Fergus.

"He wants to know who we are and what we are doing in his land?" Skula exclaimed as he translated.

"I am a Greek merchant from Athens," Fergus replied, speaking in Greek as he gazed back at the headman. "Tell him that our ship was caught in a storm and that we were shipwrecked on the coast. We are sorry for trespassing on his land but are not here to cause trouble. Once we have recovered our strength we shall be on our way."

As Skula finished translating the Alani headman chuckled and said something to his companions that produced a grin amongst the assembled nomads. Then the headman spoke again.

"He says he has no quarrel with the merchants who cross his land," Skula translated. "Merchants come here often to trade. However," Skula said, clearing his throat. "If you are Romans then matters are more complicated. There is a Parthian prince at Derbent who is promising the clans much gold if they are to go to war against the Romans and their allies. He says that the Parthian prince makes an appealing proposal but that he has yet to decide what to do."

"So, I have heard," Fergus replied carefully. "But I have no interest in politics or war. I am here just for the profit. Profit that I am willing to share with him if we can come to an arrangement."

Skula glanced at Fergus with a quizzical look, as he translated. The Alani headman however raised his hand in a dismissive gesture.

"He says we can speak about this later," Skula translated. "But for now, we are welcome. He invites us to join him and his clan in a feast tonight. The feast to celebrate the end of winter. He wants to know if we will accept his invitation?"

"Gladly," Fergus replied, with a respectful nod towards the headman. "It will be an honour."

In reply the headman nodded as he gazed at Fergus. Then abruptly he seemed to lose interest and as he did, Skula gestured for Fergus to leave. The audience was over.

***

The feast began well before night fall and in a fashion that Fergus had not expected. The whole clan, some thirty-five families making up several hundred people, men, women, children had gathered together on the slope of a grassy hill close to the encampment. Archery targets had been placed out in the steppes and, as Fergus and his companions looked on, horsemen came tearing along on their small, shaggy ponies, whooping and shouting, and began shooting arrows at the targets. The rate and accuracy of arrows striking the targets was remarkable. And Fergus's amazement grew as he saw that there were young women amongst the riders competing with the men. The young women looked fierce, wild, focussed and were clad in similar fashion to the men and they were just as good. The archery contests were greeted with wild ecstatic cries, yells and hollering of encouragement from the crowd. Gazing at the riders, Fergus was reminded of the small Numidian horsemen he'd commanded on the Syrian frontier, but he'd never seen women riding like these Alani. These amazons were a fantastic sight. Glancing sideways at Skula, Fergus could see that he was transfixed as he stared at the competition. Skula had come home and the realisation suddenly made Fergus look down at the grass. He had never seen Skula look as happy as he did right now. The archery duels were followed by a demonstration of horsemanship. Riders came galloping past the crowds at full speed, performing the most amazing acrobatics, and again Fergus saw that the competition did not distinguish between men and women. As the feats of horsemanship came to an end, the crowd started to drift back to the camp of tent-covered wagons beside the stream. A group of older women and children were already busy constructing a large fire. Walking back into the camp with his companions, Fergus saw more women preparing whole sheep for slaughter and cooking.

As darkness fell the feast really began. Over the raging, crackling fire, several sheep carcasses fixed onto iron spits, were roasting, their fat dripping and exploding into the fire. The whole clan had come together and throughout the camp Fergus could hear wild joyous singing, howling and clapping. The Alani had placed him, Skula and Adalwolf close to the headman around the large campfire; a position of honour. In the glow and heat of the flames, the Alani were feasting noisily and boisterously and some were smoking Cannabis. Taking a sip of Koumiss, fermented and slightly alcoholic mares' milk, from his cup, Fergus turned to gaze at the troop of dancers and singers beside the fire. The women and men were singing, shouting, dancing, clapping their hands and kicking, whirling around and stamping their feet and a few of the Alani were playing musical bone plate instruments. Despite not understanding a word, the noise was pleasing, Fergus thought and the dancing, wild, savage and primitive.

As he looked on, the Alani headman gestured to someone and from the shadows a man appeared, pushing a young woman before him towards Fergus. The girl looked sullen and was unsmiling. At Fergus's side the headman turned to him and gestured that he should take the girl's hand.

"He is giving the girl to you," Skula called out to Fergus with a smirk. "Tonight, she is yours to do with what you please. She is a gift from the headman."

For a moment Fergus was speechless as he looked up at the young woman. Then he turned to the headman and nodded his gratitude.

"Skula. Tell him that I am grateful for his generosity and hospitality," Fergus cried out, trying to make himself heard over the boisterous noise. "He is a generous host. Tell him that I shall attend to the girl later tonight. For now, however she should sit and enjoy the feast. Tell him that I would like to discuss an arrangement with him."

"An arrangement, Sir?" Skula replied with a frown.

"Yes," Fergus said. "Tell him that I wish to purchase horses from him for myself and my companions. I shall pay him in good solid Roman gold coins."

At Fergus's side Adalwolf paused from smoking the Alani Cannabis and turned to look at Fergus in surprise.

"What?" Adalwolf said sharply. "You have gold coins on you? Where? I thought we lost everything we had in the shipwreck."

But Fergus gestured for Adalwolf to be silent as he turned to the headman. Skula had translated and the Alani warrior was looking grave as he considered the offer. Then the man looked up and spat into the fire before saying something.

"He will make a deal with you," Skula said in an excited voice. "But first he wants to see these gold coins."

In response Fergus placed his cup of Koumiss down on the ground, pulled his cloak from his torso and began to tear apart the sleeve where he'd stitched several gold coins into the lining. As the coins tumbled into his hand, he held them up for the headman to see before handing them over and as he did, he was oblivious to the watchful gaze of the Albanian captain who was sitting nearby.

"You, sly dog," Adalwolf exclaimed in surprise as he passed his cannabis to Fergus, who took a few quick draws and exhaled as he waited for the headman to reply. "You had a reserve of coin hidden away all this time."

"Have you found out where the hell we are yet?" Fergus said as he took another draw of Cannabis, exhaled and handed it back to Adalwolf.

"More or less," the diplomat growled, as he turned to stare at the dancing, yelling tribesmen and women. "I think we came ashore on the north-western coast of the Hyrcanian. Skula says that the tribesmen tell him that the nearest Roman positions, at the Caucasian Gates, lie some two hundred miles or so to the south-west."

At Fergus's side the headman looked satisfied, as he pocketed the coins and stretched out his hand in agreement.

Quickly Fergus shook his hand and picked up his cup of Koumiss and clinked cups with the headman, before taking a sip.

"We have a deal," Fergus said, turning to Adalwolf as the diplomat puffed away on his cannabis. "Once we are sufficiently rested, we shall set out for home."

"If you say so," Adalwolf said in a vacant, contented voice.

It was deep into the night when the noise and feasting at last seemed to die down. Around the camp fire the flames were burning themselves out and most of the Alani had stumbled away into the darkness or had fallen asleep, or were smoking themselves into happy oblivion. Stiffly Fergus got to his feet. His belly was stuffed with roasted sheep's meat and Koumiss and the cannabis was making him feel slightly dizzy. Beside the dying embers of the campfire, his companions seemed to be asleep, overcome by the food, heat and feasting. And as he turned to find his way back to the tented wagon where he'd slept the first night, he caught sight of the girl sitting patiently on the ground. Despite all around having fallen asleep the girl had waited for him, although she didn't seem too pleased by the prospect. With a sigh Fergus turned towards her and as he did, she quickly rose to her feet.

"Go," Fergus said gesturing for the girl to leave. "Go," he repeated and as she finally seemed to understand, she turned and hastily vanished off into the night.

***

It was evening on the following day and Fergus and his companions were standing about, admiring the herd of small shaggy horses which the headman had given them. The wild looking beasts had no saddles or stirrups, but they seemed tough. Nearby, close to the stream a boy was guarding a flock of sheep and two Alani women were sitting in the grass making arrows. Amongst the tent-covered wagons most of the clan still seemed to be recovering from the feast the night before, but there was no sign of the Alani headman. He had ridden off into the steppes with some of his men that morning and had not yet returned. Idly Fergus stroked the back of one of the horses. Then he paused, as from the corner of his eye he noticed the Albanian youth hastening towards them. The Albanian looked troubled.

"Skula," Fergus called out softly in warning, but the bald Alani tribesman had already spotted the youth and was coming towards Fergus.

The youth hesitated as he came up to Fergus and as he did, Fergus felt a sudden pang of alarm. Turning to Skula the young man said something and as Skula frowned, the youth repeated himself.

"What is he saying?" Fergus snapped as he turned to look at Skula.

"I think he is trying to tell us that we must leave, right now," Skula said frowning. "He has come to warn us. He says that we are in danger. That we must leave now. He is very insistent."

"What?" Fergus blurted out, as he turned to look at the youth in alarm. "Who? Why are we in danger?"

The Albanian spoke again, repeating himself carefully and slowly, as he gazed at Skula, trying to see if he had understood.

"I think he is saying," Skula began. "That his father, the captain, saw you give those gold coins to the Alani headman last night at the feast. His father told him that you should have given those gold coins to him, in compensation for the loss of his fishing boat."

Across from him, the Albanian youth spoke again, choosing his words carefully.

"His father is furious," Skula added, as he quickly glanced at Fergus. "He blames you for the loss of his boat. His father told him that he is going to tell the Alani headman everything when he returns. He is going to tell the headman that we are not Greek merchants. That we are Romans and that we only came here to rescue Adalwolf. That we lied to the headman."

Once again, the youth spoke as Skula fell silent.

Skula's face suddenly seemed to grow pale. "He says his father is going to tell the Alani headman that he could get much more gold if he hands us all over to prince Sanatruces and the Parthians at Derbent."

For a long moment Fergus said nothing as he stared at the youth. "Shit," Fergus muttered at last as he looked down at the grass.

"Where is that piece of shit," Flavius hissed as he stepped forwards, his angry eyes blazing. "I am going to slice open his treacherous throat. Where is that prick? He is not going to be talking to anyone after I am finished with him."

"No," Fergus said sharply, as he held up his hand. "The captain has a valid reason to feel aggrieved but at the same time we needed that gold for those horses. I made my choice. Skula, ask him why he has come to warn us? Why is he doing this? Why is he going against his own father?"

Quickly Skula spoke and as the youth seemed to finally understand, he replied and as he did, he turned to look at Fergus.

Skula raised his eyebrows in surprise. "I think he says that the captain is not his father," Skula exclaimed. "We just assumed he was. His real father was killed by the Parthians. That's why he hates them so much. That's why he is helping us. He says he is a friend of Rome."

As Skula fell silent, the youth quickly spoke again.

"He says we should not hurt the captain. But he says he hopes we kill many Parthians. That we slaughter them without mercy," Skula added.

Fergus gazed at the youth in silence. Then hastily he groped for something in his pocket and produced a solitary gold coin.

"My last coin," Fergus said, as he pressed it into the youth's hand. "I was keeping it for an emergency, but I guess this is one. Tell him Skula, that we are grateful for his help."

The youth looked down at the single gold coin and then quickly his fingers closed over it and he turned to give Fergus a wide grin before hastening away.

"What are we going to do Fergus?" Adalwolf asked as he watched the youth walk away.

"Gather your gear," Fergus said quickly, as he too watched the youth head back into the Alani camp. "I think the boy spoke the truth. We are leaving. We will head south-west towards the Caucasian Gates. With a bit of luck, we should be able to put enough distance between us before the Alani have a change of mind about us. Come on, move, move."

Chapter Twenty-Seven – Three Decisions

It was dawn, and to the south the majestic and massive Caucasus rose from the earth, their jagged, fifteen thousand feet high, rocky and snow-covered peaks clawing at the blue clear skies. Along their barren, but impressive, ridges, glaciers ran down into steep, narrow valleys. The lower slopes of the gigantic mountains were covered in dense, green forests and lush alpine meadows. It was a beautiful sight Fergus thought as he gazed southwards - this barrier between the continents of Europa and Asia. Hadrian's Greek advisers had told him that the two mountains chains, that formed the Caucasus, ran for nearly eight hundred miles from the Black Sea coast to the Hyrcanian Ocean on a north-west to south-east axis. For the moment Fergus was alone. The others were still asleep next to their horses, curled up in the grass beside the river and wrapped up in their warm Alani blankets. He stood at the edge of the wide, placid Terek river which, swollen with spring melt-water, was flowing eastwards from its source in the high mountains to the south. It was a fresh morning and despite it being May, the night had been surprisingly cold. Beyond the river to the south, the flat grasslands and open rolling country seemed to be coming to an end - replaced by forests and the Caucasian foothills. Hearing the lonely cry of a hunting bird high in the clear skies, Fergus turned to look north and back across the steppes. But he could not spot the early morning predator. It had taken them three days and one night to cross the seemingly endless plain of grass from the Alani encampment to the banks of the Terek. Skula had led them. He had claimed to know the way to the Caucasian Gates and they had made good and swift progress on their small and tough horses. There had been no sign of pursuit but despite this, Fergus could not shake the sense of alarm and nervousness he'd felt when abruptly leaving the Alani camp. The scenery might be beautiful, but something was not right. Their journey southwards had been far too easy.

Carefully Fergus knelt beside the river and splashed some of the clear mountain water onto his face. The water was ice-cold, but it tasted good. Straightening up, he turned and strode back to his companions and the horses.

"Come on, wake up, wake up," Fergus called out, as he kicked his companions awake. "We must go. Come on. There is no time to waste."

As his companions silently staggered to their feet and started to gather their belongings, Fergus moved across to the small, blackened camp fire and stamped out the few remaining embers. Then he turned to his horse and carefully reached out to gently run his hand down the horses' nose. The beautiful Alani horses were battle-trained and had been castrated to make them more obedient.

"Excellent cavalry horses aren't they Sir," a voice said behind him and as Fergus turned, he saw Skula standing watching him.

"They are," Fergus replied, turning his attention back to his horse.

Skula hesitated. "I need to speak to you, alone Sir."

And there was something in Skula's voice that made Fergus turn sharply. Gesturing for the Alani tribesman to follow him, he moved a little distance away from the others.

"What?" Fergus growled with a sudden sense of foreboding.

Skula hesitated again. Across his back he had strapped an Alani composite bow and a quiver of arrows. A small, round mirror with fine images of the sun and fire engraved into its edges, hung from his belt on a leather strap. The small mirror was a religious symbol used to honour the Alani sun god, Skula had explained. Suddenly Fergus groaned as he guessed what Skula was going to say. Ever since they had encountered the Alani, Fergus had noticed that Skula had become more and more absorbed by the culture of his own people. It was as if the enforced stay with the steppes people had rekindled something in him.

Skula sighed and he seemed to be genuinely struggling to speak.

"Sir," he said at last, looking up at Fergus, his face grave. "The time has come for me to say farewell to you Sir. I am not coming back with you."

Fergus stared at Skula in silence. Then he looked down at the grass with sudden sadness.

"You are not a slave," Fergus said quietly. "You are a freedman and you are paid for your work. So ofcourse you are free to leave us and choose your own path. But I shall be sorry to see you go Skula. We have been through much together; you, I and the others. What will you do now? Where will you go?"

Hastily Skula nodded. "It is a hard decision Sir," he said in a serious voice. "But I am set on it. I want to go in search of my family. I was fourteen when I last saw them. It is time that I returned home Sir. They may still be alive."

Fergus sighed and turned to look northwards across the grass lands. For a moment he did not move. Then at last his shoulder sagged and he nodded as he accepted Skula's choice.

"It is not far from here to the Caucasian Gates," Skula said quickly, as he turned to gesture at the river. "You do not need me to guide you anymore. All you need to do is follow the Terek upstream and the river will take you home. The Gates are maybe sixty or seventy miles away. Once you reach them, you will enter a very narrow gorge. The cliffs are sheer, some six-thousand feet high, compressing the river gorge to a narrow strip of stony land. The pass is the only way in which to cross the mountains. The Terek's white-water flows straight through it, heading south, from its source. The first and last time I rode through that gorge there was a small fortress, perched high on a cliff, overlooking the narrowest part of the gorge. It was manned by Iberian soldiers but there may be Romans there too. Your people call the fort Cumania. It controls all access through the gorge. Keep following the Terek Sir and it will lead you home."

Fergus nodded as he gazed at Skula. Then he turned to look at the others. They were all standing beside their horses, ready to go, watching the two of them in sombre silence as if they had guessed the purpose of the conversation.

"There is a final thing that I need you to do for me," Fergus said, as he carefully turned to look at Skula. "I need you to stay here until darkness. Find yourself a good observation spot from where you can see the river. If there is any sign of trouble, any sign that the Alani are coming after us, then I need you to warn us. Prepare a fire and make black smoke. In these clear skies the smoke will be seen from miles and miles away. Can I count on you Skula? Can I rely on you to do this old friend?"

"Ofcourse Sir," Skula said quickly. "I will do that."

Slowly a grin appeared on the bald Alani's lips and he threw open his arms and gave Fergus a big farewell hug, gripping him tightly.

"I shall always remember you Sir," Skula said as he let go and stepped back. "I shall honour all of you wherever I go. And when you get back to Antioch Sir. Tell Hadrian, from me. That he is still a prick."

***

The Terek river was wide and deep and along its banks grew tall, river reeds. At a steady walk on horseback, Fergus led his companions in single file along the left bank as they followed the river westwards into the increasingly rough and wild country. To the south, the beautiful snow-covered peaks of the mountains were drawing closer and dark green forests covered their lower slopes like a coat. Closer by, the grass lands had given way to forest, great sturdy oaks and pines. It was mid-morning and the only sign of life they had come across had been a magnificent and solitary stag, standing watching them from the top of a rock. Stoically Fergus gazed ahead, as his horse picked its way along the river bank. Letting Skula go and saying farewell to him had lowered the morale of his companions and no one seemed to be in the mood to talk. Fergus sighed. But the Alani tribesman had made his decision. He could have argued with Skula, pointing out that he'd signed a contract of employment and sworn an oath of allegiance, but it was clear that Skula's heart was in his native land. It would be cruel to insist on him coming with them when he clearly no longer wanted to. Twisting around on his horse, Fergus glanced back at Adalwolf who was following him.

"What do you know about the Caucasian Gates?" Fergus called out.

"Only what Pliny tells us," Adalwolf replied - "That the Gates divide the world between civilisation and barbarism."

Fergus was about to say something else when he froze, and his eyes widened in shock. There beyond Adalwolf, on the horizon, in the direction from which they'd come, a thin column of black smoke was rising into the clear skies.

"Oh no," he gasped.

"What?" Adalwolf asked, as he quickly turned to see what Fergus was staring at. Then as he too caught sight of the black smoke, the colour drained from his face. "Ah shit," the German diplomat cursed in his native language.

"Seems that our hosts have had a change of heart," Fergus snapped in a tight voice, as he stared at the distant column of smoke. "They are coming after us. That smoke is Skula's warning."

"Are you sure it's from him?" Adalwolf asked hopefully. "Could it not be from another source?"

"No," Fergus replied sharply. "We are not going to take that chance. We must assume that the Albanian captain talked. That the Alani are after us." And without waiting for Adalwolf to reply, Fergus raised his fist into the air and cried out to his companions. "Trouble," he yelled as he pointed at the smoke. "Let's ride. Hurry. Move, move, move."

And as he urged his horse into a canter, Fergus wrenched his eyes back to the river as he felt his heart pounding in his chest. He'd been right to feel nervous about the Alani. He'd been right to take precautions. The Albanian fisherman must have convinced the Alani headman that he would be able to get much more gold, if he delivered them to prince Sanatruces at Derbent. The journey to the Caucasian Gates was no longer a leisurely ride Fergus thought grimly. It had become a race between life and death.

It was dusk, and Fergus was leading his men in single file along the banks of the Terek, when an arrow came zipping across the river and struck Numerius in his leg. A split second later a second arrow buried itself into Numerius's horse, causing the beast to rear up and crash onto its side, throwing Numerius to the ground. Shrieking, Numerius went flying and tumbling into the long grass. Frantically, Fergus turned to stare at the opposite bank of the river, and in the twilight, he caught a glimpse of horsemen galloping and flitting through the light forest, parallel to him. And as he stared at them, another arrow went whining passed him.

"There here. Get into cover," Fergus screamed, as he swerved away from the river. But on the open hillside there was no cover. In the gloom the nearest forest was a hundred yards away. In the long grass Numerius was crying out in pain with his hands pressed to the arrow sticking out of his leg. As the others galloped away, Fergus brought his horse to a halt, slid to the ground and raced to Numerius's aid. But Flavius beat him to it. Ignoring the whining arrows, the big German rushed towards Numerius, and together with Fergus, heaved Numerius up and over his horse's back. Close by, another arrow struck the ground.

"Go, go," Fergus roared as Flavius hoisted himself onto his horse and, with one hand holding onto Numerius. started to gallop towards the forest as fast as the horse could go. Hastening back to his own horse, Fergus had nearly reached the animal, when it was struck in rapid succession by two arrows that sent the horse crashing and screaming to the ground. Wildly, Fergus swerved past the dying beast and started to run. Another arrow went whining past, so close he could feel it. Desperately, Fergus started to zigzag across the open meadow as he raced for the forest line. There was no time to look behind him to see whether the Alani had crossed the river. With a yell he burst into the cover of the trees and went stumbling over a tree trunk and rolling painfully onto the ground. Pulling his gladius from its sheath, he leapt to his feet. Ignoring the bruises and his panting, heaving chest, he turned to face the way he'd come. But in the twilight, out on the open grassy slope that bordered the river, he could see nothing. Pausing to catch his breath, he heard Numerius crying out in pain from deeper in the dark forest. Cursing to himself, Fergus pushed his sword back into its sheath and hurried away through the trees in direction from which he could hear Numerius crying out.

The others had gathered around an ancient oak tree, as Fergus came stumbling towards them through the undergrowth. Numerius was lying on the ground and Flavius and Barukh were tending to him as best as they could.

"Muffle him," Fergus said sharply, as he came up to his companions. "His cries are going to give away our position."

Adalwolf caught Fergus by the arm, his eyes wide with shock.

"They were women!" He exclaimed. "Those riders shooting at us. They were women. I saw them. We are being hunted by women - Amazons."

"We can't stay here," Fergus said, as ignoring Adalwolf, he knelt beside Numerius and looked down at his wounded companion. "The darkness will shield us, and the river is too deep for them to cross but there may be a ford further upstream and the night will not last forever."

"How the hell did they overtake us so quickly?" Arlyn hissed in a dismayed voice. "They must have been at least two or three hours behind us when we spotted Skula's smoke. How can they have moved so fast?"

"I don't know," Fergus snapped tensely. "Maybe they knew a short cut. We don't know this land. They do. But it doesn't matter. They have caught up. We must deal with it."

"Well if this is the best that they can do, then they are not very good archers," one of the Italian brothers exclaimed, as he spat onto the ground.

"No," Fergus said sharply, as he looked up at the brother. "If they wanted us dead we wouldn't all be here right now."

"What do you mean?" Arlyn snapped from the shadows.

On the ground, Flavius had forced a piece of wood into Numerius's mouth and the former praetorian guardsman was grimacing, as he bit down on it with his teeth. Carefully Flavius began to pull the arrow from the flesh and, as he did, it came away with a sickening, sucking pluck. Extracting the arrow, Flavius held it up in the dying light, then leaned forwards and sniffed the arrowhead. On the ground Numerius groaned, as Barukh hastily tore a strip from his tunic, poured some vinegar over the wound and began to bind it up with the cloth.

"They want us alive," Fergus said, as he turned in Arlyn's direction. "We only have value to them if they can take us alive. I think they intend to sell us to Prince Sanatruces. That must be their plan. This attack was just meant to slow us down. Those Amazons were probably scouts, riding ahead of the main force."

Amongst the trees his comrades remained silent, as they digested what had just been said, and in the gathering darkness the only noise came from the snorting horses and Numerius's groaning.

"Why would they want to slow us down?" one of the brothers asked as Barukh finished binding up the leg wound.

"Because they already know where we are heading," Fergus said harshly, as he rose to his feet and gestured for Flavius and the older brother to lift Numerius up onto one of the remaining horses. "There is only one way across these mountains and that is through the Caucasian Gates. That's where they will be heading, to cut us off from our escape route across the mountains. So, we must make a choice. Either we use this darkness to push on and hope we make the pass before the Alani do. Or we find a place to rest and recover before setting out again."

"I am with you whatever you decide," Saadi hissed from the gloom.

"You are the boss," Flavius shrugged as he finished hoisting Numerius over the horse. "We do what you decide Fergus."

Fergus was silent as he turned to gaze at the anxious faces watching him. If they pushed on towards the mountain pass, using the darkness as cover, he could be blundering straight into an Alani ambush with exhausted horses and men. But if he sought to hide and rest he would be abandoning all hope of reaching the Caucasian Gates before the Alani caught up. Then their route would be blocked.

"All right," he snapped as he made up his mind. "I reckon that we are probably ten or fifteen miles from the Caucasian Gates, but we are not going to make it tonight. Not in our current state. So, let's use the darkness to find ourselves somewhere to hide and rest. We will figure out what to do, when we have found shelter. We need to move away from the river. Arlyn you will take point. Find us a place to hide. Don't lose sight of the man in front of you and keep quiet. Now let's go."

As the small party started out in single file through the wood heading westwards, Fergus positioned himself at the rear, behind the horse carrying Numerius. Flavius was walking beside the beast, with one hand making sure that the former praetorian did not slide off onto the ground. Numerius was groaning softly and seemed to be slipping in and out of consciousness. It wasn't only the arrow wound, Fergus thought as he followed his companions through the forest and thick undergrowth. The nasty tumble from the horse could have broken bones in Numerius's body and caused internal bleeding. But there was no time to check. Nor was any of them qualified to handle such injuries. Glancing at the horses, Fergus could see that they were lathered in sweat and exhausted from the day's long ride. No, there could be no question of pushing his exhausted men and horses towards the pass without knowing who was in front of him or how far they still had to go. They had to rest and recover their strength. Tomorrow he would think up a new plan.

As they pushed deeper into the dense forest the darkness steadily grew, enclosing them in a veil of perfect and protective blackness. In the night sky there was no sign of the stars and the moon and soon Fergus lost visual sight of Arlyn. The only way he knew the tall Hibernian was still leading them, was Arlyn's occasional soft birdcall to mark his position. At last, after an hour of plodding deeper into the forest, the ground started to slope steeply down into a gorge and as they began to descend, Fergus had to help Flavius steady his skittish horse. At the bottom of the gorge they splashed through a small muddy stream and then a little later, Flavius came to an abrupt halt.

"Sir," a soft voice called out in the darkness. "I think there is some sort of cave ahead. Shall we make camp?"

"All right," Fergus growled as he pushed his way past Flavius - "but there will be no camp fire. We can't risk it."

***

The night was silent, pitch-black and cold as Fergus sat on the ground, his back propped up against a rock. He'd lost his warm, Alani blanket when his horse had been killed and he was sorely missing it now. The cave that Arlyn had found was more an overhanging cliff of solid rock, set at the bottom of the narrow gorge, but it would have to do. At least there was water for them and the horses to drink. Restlessly Fergus gazed up at the dark skies high above. He could not sleep as he tried to figure out what to do next. Close by, a body suddenly stirred, and a hand came out of the darkness and gently prodded him.

"What?" Fergus muttered in an annoyed voice.

"Sir," Flavius whispered. "I didn't want to mention it whilst the others were still awake."

"What?" Fergus repeated.

"We have another problem Sir," Flavius whispered. "That arrow which struck Numerius in the leg. I think it was poisoned."

"Poisoned?" Fergus hissed as he turned to stare in Flavius's direction. "Are you sure?"

"I think so," Flavius whispered. "I had a sniff and the arrow head smelt funny and I remember that Skula once told me that his people used poisoned arrows. It means Sir that we have to make another decision."

"We are not leaving Numerius behind," Fergus hissed, as he shook his head. "I am bringing you all home."

"With all respect I don't think that is up to you Sir," Flavius whispered. "Numerius is already a dead man. That poison will kill him slowly. We should leave him behind. He is going to slow us down and you know it Sir. Those Alani riders knew what they were doing. This is exactly what they want us to do. Taking Numerius with us is just going to slow us down. We have already lost two of the horses. I don't want to leave him behind either. But it is the correct decision Sir."

"No," Fergus said firmly. "No one is going to be left behind. We are all going to get out of this."

Chapter Twenty-Eight – The Caucasian Gates

It was still dark when Fergus woke his companions. In the night the weather had changed, and it had started to rain. In the gloom they silently gathered together around Numerius, who was lying stretched out on the ground. The wounded man seemed to be unconscious, but he was still breathing.

"We're going to try and push on towards the Caucasian Gates today," Fergus said. "It's the only way we're going to get home. We must assume that the Alani have already reached the pass and are waiting for us. So, if we can't fight them, outrun them or hide from them, there is only one thing left for us to do." Fergus paused, as he looked at the huge amount of rainwater that was pouring over the edge of nearby overhanging rocks, like a curtain, into the valley below. "What we are going to do is trick them, he said in a determined voice. I am bringing all of you home. No one is going to be left behind. This mission began with the aim of bringing Adalwolf back home but each of you is as important to me as he is. You are my comrades in arms. You are my brothers. You are my friends. We will try and get as close to the mountain pass as we can. After that we'll figure it out from there. But we are going to get home, all of us. I want you to know that. We are going to do this."

In the darkness no one spoke, and the only noise was the heavy continuous patter of the rain.

"All right, let's move out," Fergus said, trying to sound as confident as he could. "I will take point. Arlyn and Flavius will bring up the rear. We don't have enough horses, so we shall walk and keep to the cover of the forest. Keep your eyes open and keep the noise down. Those Alani are out there searching for us."

***

At dawn the rain seemed only to be growing in intensity. The grey, depressing skies were filled with dark storm clouds and the sun had been banished. Completely drenched, Fergus plodded on through the forest. The terrain had grown rougher and had started to rise steeply and their progress had slowed, as they pushed on in the direction of the towering, snow-capped mountain peaks. Behind him his companions came on, silently winding their way up the hillside. Grimly Fergus peered up the slope and through the trees. He hadn't a clue about how he was going to get through to the Caucasian Gates. His confidence had been fake. Yet he had to pretend that he knew what he was doing. His companions were relying on him to get them home. Their belief and trust in him was the only reason they followed him. It was the essence of command. The responsibility was a heavy burden and his companions' faith could vanish in an instance. But there was no point in dwelling on such matters Fergus thought, as he pushed on through the forest. He just had to get on with the job. He would have to throw the dice and see what he was given. If he failed and the Alani captured them, it wouldn't matter anyway. It would all be over.

It was half way through the morning, when Fergus caught sight of the Terek through a gap in the trees. Hastily he raised his fist in the air and crouched on the sodden ground and, behind him his companions came to an abrupt halt. The storm was still raging, plunging the world into a strange grey twilight and, in the torrential driving rain, Fergus saw that the slopes ahead were open grassland without much cover. The valley seemed to be rising straight up into rugged, rocky terrain. Looming over everything the snow-capped mountains, now very close, cast their shadows over the lush, rain struck alpine meadows and magnificent jagged-rock formations. Carefully Fergus wiped the rain from his forehead, as his eyes slowly traced the course of the river up the valley to where it disappeared behind a cliff. Follow the Terek and it will lead you to the fortifications in the Darial gorge, Skula had told him. But from his position, he could see nothing but the driving rain and the raging white-water torrent that was the Terek. Turning around, Fergus silently beckoned for Adalwolf to join him and as he did so, high above him, a flash of lighting lit up the grey skies, followed a few moments later by the crack and deep roll of thunder.

As Adalwolf, his face and tunic totally sodden, crouched beside him, Fergus turned and pointed at the slopes leading towards the massive mountain barrier of rock and cliff that seemed to bar the route southwards.

"We need to go that way," Fergus said, as another crack of thunder rolled across the mountains. "We need to follow the river. The fortifications blocking the mountain pass are somewhere beyond those cliffs."

"I don't like that open ground ahead of us," Adalwolf grunted, shaking his head. "Once we venture out there, anyone posted on those cliffs will be able to spot us."

Fergus nodded as he peered at the mountain slopes through the trees and the driving rain. "For now, we shall remain here in the cover of the forest," Fergus said. "But you and I are going to do some reconnaissance. I need to know what lies around the corner of those cliffs; the ones behind which the river vanishes."

***

The storm was showing no signs of abating. In the dull, grey sunless skies the rain came hammering into the earth, with a ferocity Fergus had seldom experienced and with it, came an icy northern wind. High above, the lightning flashes and the crack and roll of thunder seemed to be drawing closer. Wiping the water from his face, Fergus peered down into the valley below. Beside him, lying in the sodden grass, Adalwolf too, was staring at the Alani encampment and the narrow river valley, which funnelled upwards towards an even narrower defile before twisting away into the mountains, a half a mile away. The Alani tribesmen were split into two groups, with one on each side of the raging white water river. Most had sought shelter from the storm along the sheer cliff faces. However, a few hardy horsemen were out in the open, guarding the narrow valley leading up to the even narrower rocky defile. Through this the swift, thundering white water of the Terek came careering and surging on its wild, breakneck journey through the mountains and out into the northern plains.

"I count around forty of them," Adalwolf said, as he gazed down at the Alani. "They seem to have brought extra horses. Maybe that is how they managed to overtake us."

Fergus said nothing as he studied the encampment. The Alani had done just as he had expected. They had blocked the valley leading towards the Darial gorge and the Caucasian Gates and, in the confined narrowing mountain valley, there seemed no possibility of slipping past them without being spotted.

"We could just leave them here to stew," Adalwolf said with a sigh. "Surely there must be another way across these mountains."

"No," Fergus replied sharply. "The Alani have the numbers. They have the horses. They know this land. They will track us down eventually. It's just a matter of time. And there are no other passes across these mountains that I know about. No, we have to find a way through them here - and quickly."

"I shall pray to the gods," Adalwolf said with a hint of weary sarcasm in his voice.

Fergus wiped the rain from his face again, as he peered at the Alani. For a while the two of them lay in their observation post without speaking. Then, as another shattering crash and rumble of thunder tore the skies apart, a sudden crack and swift movement caught Fergus's eye. In stunned silence, he watched, as in the valley above the Alani camp, a section of the mountainside came loose and started to slide down the steep slopes. An enormous deluge of mud, rocks and debris went roaring and slithering over the cliff edge and down into the river below.

"Landslide," Adalwolf gasped, as he watched the torrent of debris crashing down into the river. "Fuck me. Have you ever seen anything like that?"

Fergus stared at the spectacle in awe, as a few final rocks went tumbling down the side of the mountain and into the river. The landslide seemed to have blocked most of the Terek's course with a dam of mud and rocks. For a long while the two of them gazed at the freak blockage.

"The debris from the landslide seems to be holding back the river," Adalwolf suddenly exclaimed. "But it looks mighty unstable. That dam is not going to hold forever. With all that river water pressure piling up behind it, there is going to be a flash flood, when it breaks. Have you ever witnessed a flash flood before Fergus?"

"I haven't," Fergus muttered.

"So dangerous," Adalwolf replied, shaking his head. "One moment the river bed is dry. Then within moments a wall of water is upon you, sweeping everything before it. Nothing survives being hit by a flash flood. It just flattens everything and it's so quick. The worst thing is that you have little warning that it's about to hit you."

On the ground Fergus suddenly seemed to perk up. Hastily he shifted his gaze away from the landslide towards the Alani. The tribesmen too had noticed the landslide and, as he looked on, the figures nearest to the river began to move away to a respectable distance.

"They are afraid," Fergus hissed in sudden excitement. "Look. They are moving away from the river. They too, must be worried about that dam breaking."

"I see them," Adalwolf replied. "That's only sensible. When that dam breaks the flash-flood is going to go straight down the river. You don't want to be anywhere near the river when it breaks."

For a long moment Fergus stared at the Alani and the river. Then, despite the driving rain a little colour shot into his cheeks.

"I have an idea," he hissed with sudden excitement. "But you are not going to like it."

***

It had started to rain again, and a bitter cold northern wind was blowing. In the night sky there was no sign of the stars or the moon, banished behind the endless marching rows of grey storm clouds. Cautiously, on foot, Fergus moved across the open valley floor towards the Terek. In the darkness he could barely see further than a few yards, but over the whine of the wind he could hear the river. It was close. Following on behind him on horseback and in a single file, came his companions. A thin rope bound them all together, to prevent them getting separated in the darkness. The horses snorted nervously and here and there they dislodged a stone, that went clattering away down the slope. Saadi, being the lightest, had tied Numerius to her horse and the ex-praetorian's legs and arms dangled from the beast's back. The wounded man still seemed to be unconscious. Bringing up the rear came Arlyn on foot, clutching a sword. Their progress however was agonisingly slow. Anxiously Fergus turned to look up the valley in the direction of the narrow gorge that led towards the Caucasian Gates, but he could see nothing in the darkness. As he reached the edge of the river he paused and crouched, straining to listen. Behind him his companions and their horses did the same. In the night however, the only noises came from the whine of the wind, the patter of the rain and the gurgle of the river. There was no sign of the Alani. But their encampment was not far away.

Still Fergus waited, crouching at the river's edge as he listened and strained to see in the near-complete darkness. The storm and the driving rain seemed to have prevented the Alani from starting any campfires. They would be as drenched as he was, Fergus thought grimly, but their sentries would still be out there, watching.

The plan he'd told Adalwolf was simple and bold. Under the cover of darkness, they were going to go straight up the middle of the river and through the Alani camp and on into the narrow gorge beyond, relying on speed, surprise and the cover of darkness. The threat of a flash flood breaking through the landslide that blocked the river further up the valley, had been noted by the Alani, and in consequence, during the day, Fergus had observed them moving their sentries a little further away from the course of the river.

"You do realise," Adalwolf whispered nervously from the darkness close by. "That if that unstable dam of mud and rock breaks, which it can do at any moment, we are going to be swept away in a deluge of water. This is a fucking big risk we are taking."

"That's the whole point," Fergus hissed. "Down here the water level in the river is low. It will make it easier to move through the river. We are going to use that landslide and the threat of a flash flood to our advantage. If they fear the potential of a flash flood the Alani will keep their distance from the river. That's our chance."

"You can't know that for sure," Adalwolf whispered.

"It's too late," Fergus whispered. "We are committed, and I can't think of any other plan. Just pray that this rain continues. The noise will hopefully help cover our approach."

Swiftly Fergus turned to the others, waiting close by in the darkness.

"Stick to the river," he hissed. "Walk your horses. Control them. The river is going to be slippery and treacherous. But it won't be deep. Once you are beyond the landslide you ride for the gorge with all speed. Do not stop for anything. If we are discovered. It will be every man for himself. You ride for the Caucasian Gates. Good luck boys."

Without another word, Fergus rose and gingerly began to move out into the Terek. The landslide further up the valley had blocked most of the river's natural flow and subsequently the water level in the river had dropped significantly. As he moved out into the middle of the river, to his relief, he found the river current weak. The water only came half way up to his knees, revealing smooth stones and boulders. But Adalwolf was right. If the landslide that was blocking the river gave way, as it surely would at some point, then the flash flood would kill them instantly.

Grimly Fergus started to push on up the river towards the Alani encampment, as behind him his companions cut the rope that had bound them together, and silently urged their horses into the water. The splash of the horses' hooves in the water and the beasts nervous snorting sounded horribly loud. In the pitch blackness of the night it was hard to see anything, and their progress was slow. The river however was their guide, and as they moved on up its shallow course, Fergus muttered a silent prayer to the water nymphs, imploring them to be kind and merciful.

As they steadily drew closer to the Alani camp, Fergus pulled his gladius from its sheath and turned to peer into the darkness on either side of the river. In the night there was no movement, but the patter of the rain and the gentle whine of the wind continued. Carefully, making sure that he did not slip on the smooth stony and rocky riverbed, Fergus moved on. They had to be close now. Tensely Fergus paused, as he suddenly heard the soft whinny of a horse. Turning around to check behind him he could see nothing, and the noise was not repeated. All seemed peaceful and as it should. Reaching up to wipe the rain from his face, Fergus carefully started forwards again.

The minutes passed in tense silence and, as he moved on up through the shallow river bed, Fergus's heart began to beat faster and faster. They were going to do this. They were going to sneak straight through the middle of the Alani camp. They were going to have a laugh about this afterwards. Abruptly ahead he sensed that they had reached the landslide. Pausing in the river, Fergus peered into the gloom ahead as he made out the ugly mass of mud, rocks and debris that had so crudely cut the Terek in two. Trickles and streams of water were already flowing over and past the highly unstable, jumbled barrier. It seemed like the whole mass could give way at any moment. Carefully Fergus started to wade towards the bank of the river. Behind him he heard a horse snort and the gentle splash of hooves in the water. His companions were still with him.

He had just made it to the riverbank when Numerius suddenly shrieked in pain. Fergus's eyes widened in horror, as the shriek rent the night. For a moment he could not move. Before Saadi could stop him, Numerius had cried out again, his piercing shriek of agony sending a chill straight down Fergus's spine. From close by, Fergus heard a sudden shout of alarm and to his horror down along the riverbank something seemed to move in the darkness.

"Ride, ride. Go," Fergus yelled as he turned to his companions.

Frantically he flung himself aside, as in the darkness his companions on horseback came surging past him and noisily shot out of the shallow river and up onto the bank. With a wild scramble and thud of hooves they were off, leaving him behind as they clattered up the valley in the direction of the narrow mountain gorge. There was no time to see what was happening behind him. With wild splashing steps, Arlyn came racing past Fergus and vanished off into the night. In the confusion it was every man for himself now. Hastily Fergus scrambled up onto the riverbank and was just about to follow Arlyn, when he nearly collided with a figure in the darkness. With a startled cry and acting on instinct, Fergus stabbed the man with his sword and felt the blade slice through flesh. A shriek rang out in the night. Close by, he heard voices shouting to each other in a foreign language. Fergus started to run. In the utter darkness it was impossible to see more than a couple of yards ahead and, as his boots splashed through the water-logged, muddy and stony ground, he tripped over a rock and went tumbling. His head hit something sharp and Fergus cried out in pain and shock as he felt blood start to pour down his cheek. Then he was up and running, ignoring the searing pain, his boots crunching across the stones and splashing through the mud. Behind him more shouts pierced the night air and from close by, he heard the whinny of a horse and the thud of hooves.

Wildly Fergus veered around a large boulder and nearly plunged straight into the wide, shallow lake of water, that had formed behind the landslide and which was still blocking the river. Around him, the Alani voices were shouting to each other. They seemed to be everywhere. The number of voices was growing but he could not see them in the darkness. With growing desperation, Fergus sprinted up the gorge whilst trying to keep the course of the river to his left. Suddenly ahead, he sensed something move in the darkness and above the patter of the rain, he heard footsteps rapidly drawing closer. A figure loomed up and crashed into Fergus, tackling him to the ground with a triumphant yell. As he went crashing and tumbling to the ground, Fergus desperately lashed out with his sword and the cold, hard steel hit something - for his attacker shrieked in pain. Ignoring the bruises and blood seeping down the side of his head, Fergus frantically struggled free and back up onto his feet. His attacker made a last attempt to hold on to Fergus's leg, shrieking as he did. Yet fear lent Fergus desperate strength and with a vicious slicing blow, he silenced the man with his sword. Then he was off again, staggering and limping through the darkness and the rain.

The Alani however seemed to be gaining on him. Their shouts and cries filled the night all around him. Pounding up the valley still in the heavy rain, Fergus felt himself starting to tire. His breathing was coming in ragged gasps and he was steadily losing the ability to ignore the pain. If they caught him now it would all be over. No one was coming to rescue him in this pitch-darkness.

With a startled yelp he again tripped over a rock and went crashing headlong into the ground. Groaning, he dragged himself up and started to run again. But his pace was beginning to slow. Close by something clattered into the ground and a dozen yards to his right he heard a shout. But the darkness hid it all from sight. Furiously biting his lip Fergus ran on. How far were the Caucasian Gates? Was he going in the right direction? It was impossible to know. All he could do was follow the river and hope that it led him straight towards the Roman fortifications. As he struggled on up the stony valley, Fergus suddenly found himself thinking about his grandfather. Corbulo had faced many challenges in his life and he had never given up. He had never despaired even when the odds were heavily stacked against him. And if

Corbulo could survive, Fergus thought with a sudden surge of adrenaline and resolve, then so could he.

Less than ten yards away in the darkness, Fergus heard horses galloping past him up the valley. Without thinking he veered away straight into the Terek. Frantically he started to wade across the river towards the other bank, his boots slipping, scraping and striking the smooth river stones. The water was ice-cold. The current tugged at his clothes and body, trying to flush him downstream and as he pushed on deeper, the water started to come up to his knees; then his waist, then his chest. Gasping from the cold he emerged and staggered up onto the far bank and without pausing started to run again. There was no way of knowing whether his trick would work. In the darkness the shouts of the pursuing Alani still seemed horribly close.

Struggling and panting for breath, shivering with cold and half his face covered in blood, Fergus gasped, as suddenly a half a mile or so up ahead, he caught sight of a row of burning torches extending across the narrow gorge. The Caucasian Gates! High above him, he caught sight of more lights, eerily suspended in the darkness. It had to be Cumania, the fortress that guarded the narrow mountain pass. A little cry of relief and pure joy slipped from Fergus's lips, as he ran towards the burning torches.

To his right the crash and roar of the Terek filled the darkness with noise. Slowly the wall blocking the pass drew closer and as it did, the voices of his Alani pursuers started to fall back. When he was less than a hundred paces from the line of burning torches, which seemed to be protected from the rain Fergus cried out again. In the flickering torch light, he caught sight of iron-covered, wooden and stone ramparts, that ran across the length of the narrow gorge. The fortifications looked formidable, blocking all access through the pass. And underneath the section ahead ran the surging, roaring Terek.

Dimly Fergus was aware of movement up on the walls and the warning cries of sentries manning the fortifications. They were not going to open the gates for him Fergus thought with a sudden realisation. Not in this darkness. Not without knowing who was out there in the gorge. That just left one option.

Something hammered into the ground close by and horrified, Fergus realised it was an arrow. The sentries up on the walls were shooting at him.

"Roman soldiers," Fergus roared in Latin and then in Greek. "Don't shoot. Roman soldiers. For fuck's sake stop shooting."

But his cries seemed to go unheeded, as another arrow struck a rock close by and went bouncing crazily away into the air. No, Fergus thought with sudden savage resolve, he hadn't come all this way to be killed by his own side. That was not how it was going to end for him.

The fortifications were very close now and in the dim flickering torchlight, Fergus caught sight of the narrow gap in the barrier, through which the Terek was surging down the canyon floor. The river passage through the fortifications was barely high enough to let a man pass and the river seemed narrower at this point. The flow of water was wilder than further down the valley. As a third narrow narrowly missed him and hammered into the stony ground, Fergus leapt into the raging, surging river and with a defiant snarl, started to force himself upstream towards the gap in the walls. On the riverbank, a couple of rider-less and panic-stricken horses went galloping past in the opposite direction. The strength of the river current was almost overpowering, as the gushing water tried to force him back and wash him down the valley. Snarling and growling with the last of his energy, Fergus furiously battled his way upstream towards the low gap in the iron clad walls. The rushing, ice-cold water was colder than he could have ever imagined and soon he'd lost all feeling in his feet. On the ramparts above him he was aware of shouts and figures moving about in the gloom, but no one seemed to be shooting at him anymore.

Forcing his way through the low gap in the fortifications, Fergus gasped and cried out as he staggered and swayed towards the river bank. Dimly he was aware of shouting and movement on the bank. Then in the darkness he heard the rapid splash of feet coming towards him, and a moment later someone grasped hold of his arm and dragged him out of the water. Shivering uncontrollably Fergus staggered up onto the land, still clutching his grandfather's sword. Torches were bearing down on him from all sides and then he recognised that the men around him were shouting in Latin. Turning to face the man who had dragged him out of the river, Fergus saw that it was Flavius. The German ex-boxer was grinning from ear to ear and a little further away Fergus caught sight of Adalwolf, Arlyn, the brothers, Saadi and Barukh. His companions looked exhausted, drenched and freezing as they sat, huddled together, under the watchful eye of a party of armed Roman legionaries. But for a few scrapes and bruises they looked unharmed.

"We thought we had lost you," Flavius cried out, as he grasped hold of Fergus's head with both hands and, before Fergus could stop him, the German had planted a kiss on Fergus's forehead. "We thought they had taken you," Flavius yelled with genuine relief, as he let go and stepped back. "But they didn't. Those fucking tribesmen failed. We made it Fergus. We made it. What a ride."

Fergus could not stop shivering as he stared at his companions. His body was frozen and the pain in his head was starting to really hurt. From the darkness a Roman centurion, clad in a fine red horse-hair crested helmet and clutching a burning torch, was coming towards him. The officer was accompanied by more legionaries carrying torches that sizzled in the rain.

"Numerius," Fergus gasped suddenly, as he stared at his companions. "Where is he? I don't see him."

"He didn't make it I'm afraid," Flavius replied with a little shake of his head, as he looked down at the ground. "He is dead. We managed to drag him through the river but the poison." Flavius paused. "The poison from that arrow killed him. I am sorry. I know you tried Sir."

"Shit," Fergus hissed, as he looked away and closed his eyes.

"Who the fuck are you? What the hell are you doing here?" the centurion roared as he marched up to Fergus and Flavius.

For a moment Fergus did not reply as he stood with his eyes closed, his body shaking feverishly with cold.

"It's a long story," Fergus stammered, as he opened his eyes and tiredly turned to face the officer. "We are acting on orders from the Legate Hadrian. I am going to need some horses, provisions and a guide to show us the way back to Antioch. And the next time Sir," Fergus said, as he took a step towards the centurion, his body shivering and shaking uncontrollably. "When your men try to shoot me. I will have you transferred to the arse-end of the imperial frontier."

"We're already there," the centurion snapped sourly, as he fixed Fergus with a quizzical look.

Chapter Twenty-Nine – Second in Command

Antioch – Roman province of Syria, Summer 115 AD

Hadrian was standing beside the window of his study, looking out over his garden. He looked thoughtful. His hands were clasped behind his back and, clad in a fine white toga and sandals, he looked tanned, fit and alert. He turned as Fergus marched into the room and stiffly snapped out a salute. In the chair along the wall, Adalwolf rose to his feet and nodded at Fergus. But to Fergus's surprise, Hadrian's adviser looked uncomfortable. And as he sensed Adalwolf's discomfort, Fergus felt a sudden, sharp stab of unease. Four days had passed since he and his companions had returned to Antioch in triumph. But Hadrian had kept him waiting, before at last, this morning, summoning him for the official debrief. The rescue mission had been a success. So why was Adalwolf looking so unsettled? It didn't make sense.

Fergus lowered his eyes as Hadrian gazed at him, and as the silence lengthened it started to grow awkward.

"Stand at ease Fergus," Hadrian said at last in a quiet, neutral voice and in response Fergus relaxed his muscles a fraction.

"My official report on the mission Sir," Fergus said quickly as, keeping his gaze on the floor, he stretched out his hand and offered Hadrian a tightly rolled papyrus scroll. It had taken him nearly a whole day to write it.

Hadrian said nothing as he took the report and, without looking at it immediately passed it to Adalwolf, who hastily and nervously placed it in a drawer beside the desk. The awkward silence returned. Standing in the middle of the room, Fergus at last raised his gaze and looked at his patron, wondering whether Hadrian would actually bother to read his report. As he gazed back at Fergus, a cold, ruthlessness had appeared in Hadrian's eyes and suddenly Fergus had the distinct impression that something had changed since he'd last seen Hadrian all those months ago. This was not a meeting of friends, nor of an employer with employee, or even a master with a slave. No, Fergus thought with sudden insight, this was different. It was as if Hadrian was becoming a different, more remote person. He was distancing himself from him. He was cutting the bonds of friendship and mutual respect that had bound them together for these past ten years. Hadrian was preparing to become emperor of the Roman world and would no longer need his loyalty and service. This was goodbye. Hadrian had not summoned him here for a debrief. He was here to say goodbye, Fergus realised with a shock and, as he did a little colour shot into his cheeks.

"You once told me that you wanted to return to active service in the army," Hadrian said sharply. "Do you still wish for this?"

"I do Sir," Fergus replied stiffly.

"Good," Hadrian said glancing quickly at Adalwolf. "As a reward for your service to me and for bringing Adalwolf back, I have arranged for you to be posted to the Fourth "Scythica" Legion. Their HQ staff are based at Zeugma on the Euphrates. You will join the legion as their tribune laticlavius, their second in command."

Fergus's cheeks burned with a deep and sudden excitement. He was being promoted. Second in command of a whole fucking legion. The blood seemed to rush to his head. Suddenly he was back in the muddy fortress of Deva Victrix in Britannia, as a young, newly trained legionary, dreaming of one day becoming a legionary legate, a commander of a legion. And now his dream suddenly seemed to be within reach.

Hadrian had paused to watch Fergus's reaction.

"I hope that you will understand that this is quite a promotion," Hadrian said sternly. "Tribune laticlavius, second in command of a legion is a fiercely sought after and competed for position amongst the sons of senators. Believe me that there were some very good alternative candidates whom I could have appointed." Hadrian was studying Fergus carefully. "So, count yourself fortunate Fergus that I chose you for this role. I trust that you will not make me regret this appointment and I hope too, that when the day comes, I will be able to count on your support."

"You shall always have my support Sir," Fergus replied hastily, lowering his head in a respectful manner, "I owe you everything and thank you for this posting. You are most generous. I shall make a success of it."

Slowly Hadrian nodded as he gazed at Fergus.

"Adalwolf will hand you my letter of introduction confirming your position," Hadrian said. "Give it to the legionary legate when you arrive in Zeugma. After that you will have re-joined the army and officially left my service. Is that all clear?"

"Yes Sir," Fergus replied.

"Good then, this is goodbye, Fergus," Hadrian said coldly. "You will have to make arrangements for your family to leave my home and move to Zeugma, but I shall leave that up to you. Flavius will be promoted to be my new head of security. I expect you to leave within the week."

Hadrian paused.

"Good luck," he said at last in a tight voice, as he kept his hands firmly clasped behind his back.

"Thank you, Sir," Fergus muttered. An awkward silence followed, as Fergus refused to leave the room. From the corner of his eye Fergus saw Adalwolf fidgeting nervously with his fingers.

"Was there something else you wished to discuss?" Hadrian said with a sudden frown.

"Sir," Fergus said, clearing his throat as he looked up at Hadrian. "The last time we spoke you promised me that if I were to bring Adalwolf back to you alive and well, that you would take my father off your death list. I ask you now to honour that pledge. That promise that I was given."

The room went quiet. From his position beside the window Hadrian gazed silently at Fergus. Slowly he shook his head.

"No Fergus," Hadrian said in an ice-cold voice. "I am not yet ready to forgive those who tried to have me murdered. There will be no compromise. Your father Marcus shall remain on the list until I have heard from Attianus in Rome. That will be all. You are dismissed."

***

"He lied to me," Fergus hissed angrily, as he led his horse along the river bank. It was late in the afternoon and, along the banks of the Orontes the tall reeds swayed in the hot desert breeze. In the distance the walls of Antioch were just about visible, shimmering in the heat. Walking along at his side, leading his own horse, Adalwolf sighed.

"He is Hadrian," Adalwolf said wearily. "He is going to be the next emperor of Rome. He can do what he likes."

Above the two men and their horses, in the blue sky, the fierce, hot sun beat down on the earth.

"I don't care who he thinks he is," Fergus said bitterly. "A promise is a promise. A man who breaks his word has no honour."

"Careful Fergus," Adalwolf replied in a warning voice, glancing sideways at Fergus with a disapproving look. "He is Hadrian. There is no man like him. That's all I can say."

Fergus muttered something to himself and turned to gaze at the Orontes as it wound its way towards the distant metropolis. He had thought it prudent to take the horses, to get out of the city and to go for a ride along the river, before giving Adalwolf a piece of his mind. The fewer eyes and ears the better, for Antioch was rife with informers and spies. Out on the water a solitary fishing boat was gently bobbing up and down on the current and, in the forested mountains to the east, a large flock of birds had risen and taken to the clear skies.

"You could change his mind," Fergus snapped, turning to Adalwolf. "He listens to you. You are his adviser. This is my father's life that we are talking about. I can't just not do anything. I was promised that his name would be taken off that list. A fucking solemn promise was made."

But Adalwolf wearily shook his head. "I am your friend Fergus. I already tried to get him to change his mind, but he won't do it," the adviser said. "The memory of the assassination attempt still haunts him. He wants vengeance and he is going to get it."

"My father had nothing to do with the assassination plot," Fergus snapped. "He is not the kind of man who would have taken part in such a thing."

"He must have known about it though," Adalwolf shot back. "And for Hadrian that is enough. You father is a member of the War Party. They are our political rivals. You know this. Hadrian cannot afford to show weakness. Not now that the emperor's health is starting to deteriorate."

"Trajan's health is deteriorating," Fergus said sharply, as he turned to stare at Adalwolf in alarm.

"Yes," Adalwolf muttered. "I am not supposed to tell you this, but Hadrian has received reports from the emperor's doctors. It's nothing specific but Trajan is succumbing to old age. The reports are top secret you understand. Not a word of this must get out."

Fergus nodded, and for a while he said nothing as the two of them walked their horses along the river bank.

"If Trajan's health is deteriorating then the matter of his succession is becoming more urgent and with it the fate of the men on that list of death," Fergus said. Turning to look at his friend, Fergus took a deep breath. "I am running out of time. Please old friend," he pleaded. "Speak with Hadrian again on the matter of my father. I beg you. You owe me. I saved Hadrian's life twice. Don't make me regret this."

But once again Adalwolf shook his head.

"You have no choice but to accept what he says," Adalwolf said firmly. "Be thankful for your army promotion. It is what you wanted after all. And have hope that Hadrian will show leniency and mercy when he becomes emperor. It is possible."

"So, you want me to trust a man who has broken his promise to me," Fergus said in a sarcastic voice.

"Hadrian is preparing to succeed Trajan," Adalwolf said in a serious voice as he ignored the jibe. "He is steadily moving his supporters into senior positions within the legions and the army. Soon he hopes to be officially appointed as Trajan's deputy. In command of all military units in the eastern provinces of the empire - effectively in charge of the war with Parthia. When that happens his control of the eastern legions will be complete. If Nigrinus wishes to challenge Hadrian he will have to rely on the legions in the west, but it's doubtful they will support him. Our agents are at work amongst them too. The tide is turning against Nigrinus and the War Party. Your father would do well to switch sides whilst he still can. Maybe you should tell him this."

Fergus looked down at the ground as he walked along. "My father is an honourable man," he replied at last. "Once he has chosen a side he will not change, not even when faced with death. There is no chance that I could convince him to change sides and I will not try. He would think me weak if I tried."

Adalwolf nodded as he gave Fergus a quick sideways glance.

"There is something else that you should know," Adalwolf said. "I am not supposed to tell you this either so not a word to anyone you understand." Fergus nodded and Adalwolf continued. "Remember those intelligence reports you gave to Hadrian concerning the Parthian attempts to ferment rebellion in our provinces and amongst the Jews."

"What about them?" Fergus murmured.

"Well Hadrian is not going to act on them," Adalwolf said smoothly. "He is going to let it all play out. He hasn't even passed on the information to Trajan. No special counter measures are being taken."

"What?" Fergus exclaimed as he turned to look at Adalwolf in astonishment. "Hadrian is going to do nothing. But there have been several confirmed reports. Prince Sanatruces was in fucking Derbent precisely for this purpose. I myself saw Parthian spies in the Bedouin camps out in the desert. This is sheer madness. Counter measures must be taken. To do nothing is to invite disaster. It's criminal."

But Adalwolf shook his head. "No," he replied patiently. "It is called politics. Hadrian is set on doing nothing. Your reports and others have been buried. Hadrian does not want to know."

"Why?" Fergus blurted out.

Slowly Adalwolf turned to gaze at Fergus. Then he sighed. "Because Hadrian does not believe in this war with Parthia," he replied. "Because the Peace Party believe that the empire has reached its natural limits. When Hadrian becomes emperor the age of conquest will end and will be replaced by retrenchment. Trajan may wish to follow in the footsteps of Alexander the Great and conquer the world, but Hadrian knows that even an empire like Rome has its limits. He will use the coming rebellions to justify his policy."

"He will do what?" Fergus said as he came to a halt and stared at Adalwolf in astonishment.

"If serious rebellion breaks out amongst the eastern provinces," Adalwolf said calmly. "It will mean the end of the war with Parthia, for the troops will be needed closer to home. It will give Hadrian an excuse to make peace with Parthia and return to a more sensible frontier."

For a moment Fergus stared at Adalwolf in stunned silence. Slowly he shook his head in bewilderment.

"You talk lightly of these coming rebellions," he hissed. "But you do not have a wife and five daughters who may be caught up in it all."

***

The excited shrieks of the girls playing in the swimming pool filled the garden of Hadrian's villa. It was nearly noon and under the blazing hot sun, Fergus sat watching his daughters playing in the pool. At his side, lounging in her own chair, Galena had stripped to her sunhat, bra and undergarments, as she sunned herself whilst keeping a watchful eye on her girls. But she did not look amused. She looked furious.

"There is nothing I can do," Fergus said quietly as he ran his fingers lightly across his wife's naked skin. "So, I have accepted the posting. Zeugma is not far from here. I am sure that the town and fortress have adequate facilities for the family of senior officers. It won't be so bad."

"I am not concerned about the facilities in which we shall live," Galena retorted, speaking in her native Briton language. "It is

Hadrian that I am upset with. He made you a promise and he broke it. The man is worthless. We have served a worthless man all these years and it makes me sick."

Fergus sighed and looked away.

"What would you have me do?" he murmured.

"I want to return to Britannia," Galena said sharply, as she turned to look at her husband. "It is time we went home."

"We will return to Britannia but just not yet," Fergus said in annoyed voice. "I have been promoted and have accepted my posting. This is important to me. We discussed this. Don't make this difficult."

Looking frustrated, Galena turned to stare at her daughters in the pool and, for a while she said nothing. At her side Fergus sighed again. He could sense that she was thinking something through - some plan, which she was keeping from him. Then at last Galena turned to him, her eyes flashing angrily.

"No man shall betray my husband like this," she hissed in her native language, her fury flowing through her voice. "If Hadrian thinks he can treat you in such a manner then he is gravely mistaken. Gravely mistaken. Such betrayal angers not only me but also the gods."

As she finished speaking and turned to gaze at her children, on cue, the peaceful day was suddenly rent by a deep rumble and for a moment the whole world seemed to shake and sway beneath them. Alarmed, Fergus leapt to his feet, but the swaying movement had already died away. In the pool his daughters had fallen silent and were staring at him with confused, frightened eyes.

"It's all right," Fergus called out to them, trying to sound reassuring. "It's just an earthquake. That's all."

Chapter Thirty – An Unexpected Intervention

Fergus's head hurt as he slowly made his way down the stables, pausing now and then to stroke the noses of the horses. It was morning and his last day in Hadrian's service. Tomorrow he and his family would be leaving Antioch and heading for Zeugma on the Euphrates. The farewell party that his companions had organised for him had gone on long into the night and he still wasn't sure how he had managed to find his way back to his quarters in Hadrian's villa. The one thing he did remember was the warmth from Galena's naked body, as he had slipped into bed beside her. Out in the courtyard of the large villa complex, Galena's slave girls were packing the family's belongings into a horse-drawn wagon. Fergus groaned as he tiredly rubbed his face and turned back to gaze at the horses. Tribune laticlavius, second in command of a legion! He would be one of the principal advisers and deputies to the legionary legate who was in command of five and half thousand men. It was a very senior rank, the first ambition of every senator's son. The position as senior tribune of a legion was only open to the senatorial class, a privileged rank that gave the holder a taste of army life and prepared him for a further career in the senate or the provincial administration. Fergus sighed as he stroked the horses nose. If only Titus and Furius, his former commanding officers in the Twentieth could see him now. As he thought about his old comrades a sudden nostalgia seemed to take hold. Muttering a short silent prayer, Fergus turned his gaze to the straw-covered ground. If only his grandfather Corbulo could see how high and far he'd risen, he thought. Corbulo in his twenty-five years of service had never risen above the rank of tesserarius, company watch-commander but Fergus was sure he would be proud today. He would be proud of what his grandson had become and as he thought about it, Fergus smiled, a warm contented smile. All those years ago, back in the legionary camp at Deva as a young new-recruit, he had resolved to make his grandfather proud and he had never wavered in that ambition.

The sound of someone entering the stables made Fergus look up, and as he did he saw Adalwolf accompanied by Galena, coming towards him. Both looked serious and both were not smiling. Fergus straightened up as Adalwolf came up to him and for a moment Hadrian's adviser studied him in silence.

"I have come to inform you, old friend," Adalwolf said in a stiff, awkward voice. "That Hadrian has reconsidered and has decided to take your father, Marcus, off his death list. Your father is no longer an enemy of Hadrian."

And with that, Adalwolf abruptly turned around and marched out of the stables leaving Fergus alone with Galena. Stunned, Fergus watched him go. Slowly he switched his gaze to his wife. Galena was looking at him with a sudden mischievous smile.

"What just happened?" Fergus exclaimed in confusion.

"I told you that Hadrian was gravely mistaken," Galena purred, her eyes twinkling.

"This was your doing?" Fergus said with sudden insight. "You managed to get Hadrian to change his mind? How?" he snapped, frowning, his insight turning to suspicion.

Galena stepped up to her husband, smiled, and fondly ran her fingers across his cheeks.

"Oh, you can be so blind sometimes, husband," she said with a little chuckle.

"What did you do?" Fergus exclaimed.

"Do you remember when you were here in February," Galena replied, as she looked up at him. "I told you that I had become friends with Plotina and Matidia. They are Trajan's wife and niece, important supporters of Hadrian. Well I went to see them at the imperial palace and I told them how Hadrian had broken his word and his promise to you. I told them that Hadrian had acted in a disgraceful manner and they agreed. They said they would speak to Hadrian directly and make him keep his promise. And they did, and now Marcus is no longer an enemy of Hadrian. You saved your father, Fergus."

Fergus looked down at Galena in stunned silence, as she smiled sweetly back at him. Then Fergus shook his head in amazement.

"No, you saved him," he said quietly. "This is fantastic news."

"It doesn't matter who did it," Galena replied. "The important thing is that Marcus is no longer on that awful list of death."

Fergus gazed down at his wife. Then abruptly he caught hold of her shoulders, spun her around and pulled her into him, before kissing her neck. In response Galena moaned, arched her back and laid her head into his shoulder, as Fergus's hands groped her breasts before his fingers started to move down her stomach.

"I am going to have you right now and right here," Fergus whispered, as he pulled her into one of the empty stables. Galena giggled in delight as the two of them tumbled into the straw.

***

It was around noon when Fergus, whistling a cheerful bawdy tune to himself, strode out through the gates of Hadrian's home and started out in the direction of the Agora, the market place. The hundred and seventy-mile long road to Zeugma was nothing compared to the marches he'd undergone with the army. But his family would need some supplies for the journey tomorrow and he also had to treat his girls after his long absence. In the streets outside Hadrian's villa, only a few people were about, and it was quiet. The scent of Galena's perfume still clung to him, and suddenly distracted, he pictured her lithe, naked body lying in the straw of the stables. In the clear blue sky, the fierce sun beat down on the metropolis, encouraging its inhabitants to seek shelter from the sweltering midday heat. But as Fergus came out through the gates a solitary figure, with a hood covering his head, swiftly rose to his feet, from where he'd been sitting against a wall and hastily limped across the street towards him.

"Fergus," the stranger suddenly called out in Latin. "Fergus is that really you?"

Fergus stopped in midstride and frowned, as he turned to face the stranger. Slowly the man lowered his hood and grinned with relief.

"Aledus," Fergus exclaimed in surprise. "Aledus, what the hell are you doing here?"

Aledus grinned broadly and with relief, before taking a step forwards and quickly embracing his old army buddy. As he stepped back, Fergus shook his head in bewilderment and disbelief. This was turning out to be a day full of unexpected surprises.

"Good to see you, old friend," Aledus said, ignoring Fergus's question. "How long has it been? I seem to remember that you left our company at the end of the Dacian war."

"Nine years," Fergus grinned as he stared at Aledus. "Holy shit. That's how long. And it's good to see you too. But why the limp and the civilian clothes. I take it you are no longer in the army then?"

Aledus sighed and looked down at his leg. "You are right," he replied. "Got a nasty leg wound that gave me this limp. Can't run and couldn't keep up with the boys on the march. So, the army gave me a medical discharge. That was about two years ago now."

"Shit, that's bad luck," Fergus said, grinning from ear to ear as he gazed at Aledus. For a moment he was silent as he studied his friend in amazement. "What a coincidence that we run into each other here in Antioch of all places," he said at last.

A sheepish look appeared in Aledus's eyes. "Well actually it isn't a coincidence," Aledus said with a weary sigh. "I have been in Antioch for over a month now, trying to find you. They said that you lived in Hadrian's villa, but the guards would not let me in or confirm that you were in residence." Aledus paused. "I was sent to find you and pass on a message."

"By who?" Fergus exclaimed sharply.

"By your father, Marcus," Aledus replied quickly, as he turned to look around the near deserted street. "He sent me to find you. I have come all the way from Rome. It's been a long journey and you are not an easy man to find." Aledus paused and then turned to Fergus with a serious expression. "Look we need to talk," he said quietly. "Do you know a good place where we can go? Preferably one that serves quality wine. This heat is killing me, and you are buying, because I am running out of money."

***

"I am sorry Fergus," Aledus said as he finished recounting the message that Marcus had tasked him with delivering.

Across the small corner table in the quiet city taberna, tavern, Fergus was staring down into his mug of clear water. For a long moment he said nothing as sombrely he took in what Aledus had just told him. Marcus and his whole family were still in mortal danger. They may have got out of Rome and fled to Vectis, but even in Britannia they would not be safe. Nigrinus was one of the most powerful men in Rome and his reach, and that of the War Party, would be long. The triumph of getting Marcus removed from Hadrian's list had been replaced by a new, unexpected danger much closer to home. A danger, which he Fergus was ill-equipped to deal with.

"Thank you," Fergus said at last, as he looked up and gave Aledus a nod. "My father was right to trust you. You have been a good and most loyal friend."

"Your father is a good man and I had nothing else to do," Aledus said raising his hand. "After the army discharged me I drifted back to Londinium for a while to see my family. But I couldn't settle, I was restless, directionless, without motivation. I missed the army life, but they would not have me back. Jobs came and went as did the women. So, last year I decided to go to Rome and seek my fortune in the city. Rome is where the money is and it's so much more interesting than provincial Londinium."

Fergus frowned, as he studied Aledus from across the small table.

"But the gold that we took from Dacia," Fergus said, lowering his voice. "Surely you had enough to live out a comfortable life?"

"You would have thought so," Aledus replied with a little embarrassed chuckle. "I gave some of my fortune to my family, but I lost the rest." Aledus shrugged and looked away. "Whores, girl-friends, wine, gambling. It all went in the end. I lost it all unfortunately. I am as broke as an ugly whore."

"Fucking hell," Fergus swore as he shook his head. "Tell me that you enjoyed yourself at least."

"I did," Aledus grinned. "More than you can imagine. I can fill your head with the most outrageous stories Fergus, but I have never been any good with money."

Across the table, Fergus grinned. Then he raised his cup and the two of them clinked their mugs together.

"So, what are you going to do?" Aledus asked leaning forwards across the table.

Fergus sighed and looked down at his mug of water. "Hadrian has arranged for me to become the Tribune laticlavius of the Fourth Legion," he said quietly. "I am leaving for Zeugma tomorrow. It's on the Euphrates."

"They have appointed you second in command," Aledus exclaimed, as his eyes widened in shock.

"They have," Fergus grinned.

Aledus leaned back in his chair and exhaled sharply. "Shit Fergus, how the hell did you manage that? It only seems like yesterday that you and I were running errands for Furius in Deva."

"Hadrian arranged it all," Fergus growled. "It helps when you have a powerful, influential patron and your father is a senator. They open doors for you."

"No doubt," Aledus replied, as he gazed at Fergus with renewed respect. "Well I am glad that one of us has made something of himself."

"And Catinius, what has become of him?" Fergus asked quickly.

"He lives," Aledus replied. "At least he did when I last saw him. He is still with the Twentieth at Deva. They have made him an optio. He is doing well I think." Aledus paused as he gazed at Fergus. "So, you still banging the wife? The tavern owner's daughter who owned the Lucky. What was her name; Galena?"

"I am," Fergus replied with a little smirk. "She has given me five daughters."

"Five daughters," Aledus grinned and shook his head. "Well done you. Well done Galena. That's going to cost you when they get married."

Fergus waved the comment away with a good-natured movement of his hand. For a while the two of them sat without talking, content in each other's company as they savoured the old memories each had rekindled. Then at last Fergus looked up, his face suddenly serious looking.

"Will you return to the Isle of Vectis and seek out my father?" he said gazing across at Aledus. "I will give you money for the passage. Tell him to have hope. But if you have other plans I will understand."

"Ofcourse I will go to Vectis," Aledus said, without hesitation. "Like I said, your father is a good man and I am sure he will have a job for me. Besides," Aledus paused, as a little private smile appeared on his lips. "There is someone in your father's household who has caught my fancy. One of your mother's slave girls. Finest specimen of woman that I have ever encountered. We have something together. Maybe I will even marry her. If your father agrees to set her free."

Fergus looked away, his face sombre. "My father is more than capable of looking after himself and his family," Fergus continued, in a quiet, sober voice. "But he is also stubborn to the point of foolishness and proud. He will need your help in defending his farm. I fear he has bitten off more than he can chew this time. He is not the kind of a man who will abandon his property without a fight. If Nigrinus sends men to Vectis, my father will fight them. He is not going to run away from his farm."

Fergus sighed and for a moment he struggled to speak.

"I will ask Hadrian to write to the Governor of Britannia, asking for the Governor to extend his protection to my family. I think the present governor is a supporter of the Peace Party, but I can't be sure of that. That's the best way in which I can help them."

"Will that work?" Aledus replied, looking down at the table.

"I don't know," Fergus said in a weary voice. "I don't know whether Hadrian will agree to send the letter. I am not entirely sure the governor in Britannia is on our side and maybe it will all come too late, but it's the best I can do."

Across the table Aledus slowly nodded.

"I will go to Vectis, Fergus," he said in a calm voice. "You can rely on me, old friend. I have missed a good fight. I have missed being part of something."

Fergus nodded and slowly extended his arm across the table and, as he grasped it in the legionary fashion, Aledus grinned.

"Then we shall meet again at my father's farm on Vectis," Fergus said with a heavy heart. "And we shall see you married to that slave girl. May the gods protect you and ensure a safe journey. Tell my father and my family to have hope."

Chapter Thirty-One – The Fourth "Scythica" Legion

The blue waters of the Euphrates dazzled and glinted in the fierce noon sunlight; a most refreshing sight amongst the stunted trees, prickly bushes and arid semi-desert of the surrounding countryside. It was noon and it was sizzling hot. Above, in the clear blue skies there was not a speck of cloud to be seen. The Roman villa stood alone on a small rocky hill overlooking the wide, sluggish river just outside the city of Zeugma and from the garden top terrace the views were magnificent. A pair of tall Greek-style stone columns adorned the main entrance and the roof was covered in neat red tiles. Down the bottom of the rocky, terraced garden, where the lazy river water lapped up against the bank, Fergus's daughters were excitedly exploring their new home under the watchful gaze of one of the slave girls.

On the villa's terrace, Fergus, wearing his legionary armour and clutching a horsehair crested helmet in his hands, was standing still, as Galena and another slave fussed over his uniform and splendid red cape with its broad purple border. The broad purple stripe was a symbol of his new rank as second in command of the Fourth Legion. Today was going to be his first day officially back in the army. His excitement however was tempered by the news Aledus had brought and it had been with a heavy heart that he'd left Antioch to take up his new post. Sombrely and silently, Fergus turned to look at the stone terrace floor. The news from Rome had presented him with a choice and he'd made it. He had chosen to remain in the east and continue his army career. Had Marcus expected him to return to Vectis and Britannia right away? Was his father expecting him to come and help defend the farm against Nigrinus? Part of him had wanted to go but what would he be able to achieve? He would be putting Galena and his daughters in danger. If Marcus needed men to defend himself and his farm, then he would find them closer to home. His father had contacts amongst the Batavian veteran's community. He had defended his farm before. No, he had resolved, his best chance at helping his family was to use Hadrian. To get him to write a letter to the governor of Britannia, asking him to extend his protection to Marcus. But Hadrian had refused to see him before he'd left for Zeugma. Instead he had been reduced to speaking to Adalwolf, who had agreed and promised to raise the matter. However, there was no guarantee that Hadrian would agree or act on his request. There was no way of knowing whether his plan would work or whether it would come too late. So, he had left Antioch for the Euphrates, worried, helpless and ignorant to his family's fate, a world away on Vectis. And that worry would be his burden to carry; his alone.

Out on the Euphrates a couple of local fishing boats had dropped anchor and cast their nets, Downstream, through the shimmering noon heat, Fergus could see the bridge of pontoon boats that stretched for several hundred yards across the river. It reminded him of the bridge across the Danube that he'd crossed at the start of the invasion of Dacia. The pontoon bridge connected Zeugma on the right bank with its twin town of Apamea on the left and eastern bank. Fergus sighed as he stood still, feeling the relentless heat from the sun beating down on him. Hadrian's Greek advisers had given him a short but concise briefing before he had departed from Antioch. They had explained that the Euphrates had long formed the eastern frontier of the Roman empire. Zeugma they had told him was an important city of eighty thousand people. That was why the Fourth Legion had its base near the town, for Zeugma controlled one of the few crossing points on the Euphrates. A place of great strategic importance. The river itself also marked the cultural border between the Mediterranean world and that of the Near East. Hadrian's Greek advisers had explained that the lands on the eastern bank of the river belonged to the Kingdom of Osrhoene, a Parthian vassal state which, under Roman pressure and surrounded on three sides by Roman territory, had recently switched sides, pledging its allegiance to Trajan and to Rome. The capitulation had meant that the frontier had shifted hundreds of miles to the east and south, to the Chaboras river and the line of hills and ridges that ran eastwards towards the city of Singara, captured only a few months before by Lusius Quietus.

Beside Fergus, the slave girl respectfully stepped backwards and lowered her eyes. Galena too had stopped fussing and was smiling at her husband, her face radiant and beaming with pride.

"You look magnificent," Galena purred, casting an approving eye over her husband. "A senior legionary commander must look the part." Then a mischievous twinkle appeared in her eyes. "And just as handsome as the first day that I caught you staring at me in my father's tavern in Deva."

***

As Fergus approached the city gate on horseback, the tall walls of the city of Zeugma reflected the sunlight, trying to blind him. Stoically Fergus pushed on, ignoring the annoying flies that buzzed around his sweat-drenched head. The city partly abutted the banks of the Euphrates and, high up on a hill that dominated the town, he could make out the citadel, home to the barbarian goddess Tyche and the HQ of the Fourth Scythica. Casting his gaze towards the river he could see wagons, horses and figures crossing the pontoon bridge. The war it seemed had not disrupted trade and along the walls he could see no obvious defensive preparations. The city's inhabitants seemed to be at ease, confident that the Parthian and Armenian threat was far away. And that was just as well for the villa, that had been assigned to his family, was beyond the protection of the city walls.

The city gate was open and guarded by the local city watch. The armed, bearded warriors, clutching round shields and spears, stared at him as he trotted on into the city, but no one attempted to challenge or stop him. Ahead, the regular Greek style city blocks opened into a broad colonnaded avenue, similar but much smaller than the main thoroughfare that ran the length of Antioch. The familiar noise of the advertising cries of the merchants and traders rang out in the street, mixing with the thud of horses' hooves, laughter, the tramp of boots and sandals, barking dogs, the trundle of wagon wheels and the impatient mooing of cattle. As he pushed on down the colonnaded avenue, Fergus caught sight of some legionaries drinking and gambling in the shade of a tree. The men's helmets, shields and spears lay carelessly discarded on the ground and the soldiers appeared to be drunk. With a disapproving look, Fergus turned his gaze away. From the buildings, the fatness of the inhabitants, the quality of their clothing, the abundance of food and other goods and the busyness in the streets, he could see that this was a prosperous town. A little further up the main street he caught sight of a queue of legionaries waiting patiently to enter a whorehouse. A he gazed at the scene, a stark-naked woman suddenly appeared in one of the second-floor windows, seductively rubbed her vagina with a cloth and tossed it down into the queue of soldiers. In the street the soldiers cheered and a mad, undignified scramble to claim the soiled cloth broke out in full view of the passers-by. Fergus looked away in disgust. At the camp in Deva in Britannia, amongst the men of the Twentieth, the weak, effeminate and low quality of the legions based in Syria had been a source of deep contempt. And Fergus could see why. The wealth and easily available pleasures of a town like Zeugma seemed to have influenced morale and discipline.

The squad of legionaries on duty at the gate into the fortress, atop the steep hill on the edge of the city, nevertheless saluted smartly as they caught sight of him. Passing into the citadel Fergus came to a halt in a square courtyard and dismounted, handing the reins of his horse to a slave boy who came running up to him. Apart from the slave, there was no one about in the courtyard. No one to welcome him and, for a moment, Fergus looked lost as he gazed around. Above him, the fierce sun beat down and all was silent. The fortress was far too small to house an entire legion, but this was the place where he'd been told to report to the legionary legate. With a grunt Fergus headed for one of the dark doorways that led into the stone buildings. In the passage way beyond, several doors led into small rooms filled with stale, hot air. A few soldiers looked up as he passed on by but only a few rose stiffly to their feet to salute him.

"Where can I find Gellius, the legionary legate," Fergus snapped, as he came face to face with a legionary in the dimly lit corridor.

"He's not here," the man replied, as he brushed on past without a glance at Fergus.

"The Praefectus Castrorum then?" Fergus snapped. "Where is the Camp Prefect?" But the legionary had already disappeared around a corner.

Annoyed Fergus turned to look down the dimly lit corridor. From somewhere deeper in the maze of corridors and passageways of the old Seleucid Citadel he suddenly heard a peel of laughter. As he approached the source he heard it again and, coming around a corner, he caught sight of two legionaries standing beside the entrance to an office. They had their backs turned to him and were sniggering as they peered at something in the room beyond. Marching up to the doorway Fergus cleared his throat and, as the two soldiers turned and saw him they hastily sprung aside and resumed their guard duty on either side of the entrance. Stepping into the spacious room Fergus paused. A young semi-naked woman was slowly performing an elaborate striptease for the benefit of the four legionary tribunes who were splayed out across the comfortable looking couches. The tribunes, all of them young, barely out of their teens, were grinning from ear to ear. But as they caught sight of Fergus standing in the doorway the grins abruptly vanished. For a moment the large room became very still.

"Holy shit," one of the young equestrian officer's exclaimed, his cheeks blushing furiously, as he finally recognised Fergus's uniform. A mad panicked scramble followed, as the four young staff officers leapt to their feet and saluted. Their young faces were flush with embarrassment.

"Get out," Fergus snapped as he turned to the stripper.

"She hasn't been paid yet," one of the tribune's protested.

"Get out," Fergus roared with real fury in his voice, and as he did the woman hastily gathered up her clothes and fled from the chamber. Fergus waited until she was gone before turning his attention back to the young staff officer's. The four tribunes stood stiffly to attention before him, staring into space, their arms pressed tightly against the sides of their bodies and they were suddenly sweating. The men looked flabby, unfit and their uniforms were in a state of disgrace.

"My name is Fergus. I am the new Tribune laticlavius," Fergus growled, as he examined the officers. "Now can someone tell me where I can find Gellius, the legionary legate?"

"He is not here Sir," one of the tribunes with blond hair replied swiftly. "He has left on a tour of inspection of some of our garrisons on the other side of the river. We are expecting him back tomorrow or the day after Sir."

"And the camp prefect, where is he?" Fergus snapped.

"He should be back at nightfall Sir," the blond tribune replied staring into space. "He has taken the first cohort on a route march across the desert. A training exercise Sir."

"Well it's good to see that someone in this legion is doing something worthwhile," Fergus growled. For a moment he paused. This was not the welcome he'd expected. In the absence of the legate he was now the most senior commanding officer of the Fourth Legion.

"So," Fergus said in a dangerous voice, as he took a step towards the four staff officers, his eyes flashing angrily. "All the senior officers are out of camp and you decide to use this opportunity to entertain yourself with a stripper. Is that how you a military Tribune, a Tribune augusticlavii are supposed to act?"

"No Sir," came the hesitant, embarrassed replies.

"You are all a fucking disgrace," Fergus roared. "You are supposed to be legionary officers. You are supposed to set an example to the men. This is the fucking army that you have joined. Not some privileged whorehouse. If you don't take your work seriously then how can you expect the men to do the same. This legion only works when we have discipline and professionalism and it's your fucking job to provide that discipline." Fergus paused, looking furious. "If you think that you must only bear this posting for a year before you can return to your pampered, privileged lives, then you are wrong. Things are going to change. They are going to change right now and if any of you don't like it I shall arrange for you to be sent home to your families in disgrace and you can kiss your careers goodbye. Have I made myself clear?"

"Yes Sir," the tribunes barked as the sweat ran down their faces.

"Have I made myself clear?" Fergus roared in a furious voice.

"Yes Sir," the tribunes roared back.

Silence descended on the room and as it did, Fergus turned to look around. "A legion has five Tribune augusticlavii," he said in a calmer voice. "I count only four of you. Where is your colleague?"

"There are only four of us at the moment, Sir," the blond-haired tribune replied hastily. "They promised us a replacement, but he has not yet arrived."

"Is the legion understrength?" Fergus said with a frown.

"Somewhat Sir," the blond tribune replied. "There are only two cohorts and the legionary cavalry here in Zeugma. The rest of the legion is spread out across the cities of Osrhoene on garrison duties. But all cohorts are understrength. They promised us replacements, but they still haven't arrived."

Fergus grunted as he took in the news. "Very well," he growled at last, as he looked up at the young tribunes. "We will get to work right away. I am going to need cohort strength reports, the disposition of our garrisons, the state of our food supplies and the most recent combat and intelligence reports. In the absence of the legate I shall take over his office. I will need your names and personnel files on my desk right away and when the camp prefect returns with the first cohort, he is to report to my office immediately. You," Fergus said, pointing a finger at the blond Tribune. "What is your name?"

"Britannicus Sir," the tribune replied quickly.

"Britannicus," Fergus exclaimed raising his eyebrows in surprise. "You are from Britannia?"

"Yes. From Londinium Sir," the staff officer said quickly. "My father is a wool merchant."

"Then you are far from home," Fergus replied, switching to his native Briton language. "I too am from Britannia but not from Londinium."

For a moment Britannicus looked surprised and unsure how to proceed.

"That is good to know Sir," he replied haltingly, in the Briton language. "And welcome to the Capricorn legion Sir. I am sorry about the stripper. Please don't tell the legate. It won't happen again Sir."

"I need you to arrange for a general inspection of all legionary units that remain in Zeugma," Fergus said, ignoring the request and switching back to Latin as he gazed at Britannicus. "I want to inspect the men. Have them ready for inspection at dawn tomorrow with all their equipment, horses and weapons. And for fucks sake, smarten yourselves up. You are officers in the Roman army."

Chapter Thirty-Two – "Welcome back to the War"

The legate's office in the heart of the ancient Seleucid citadel was silent, oppressive and stuffy. There were no windows and little ventilation. It was evening and Fergus sat behind the desk waiting patiently for the Praefectus Castrorum, the camp prefect and third in command of the legion, to finish reading his letter of introduction which Hadrian had given him. On the table between them, he'd placed his magnificent crested helmet and his red cape was draped over the back of the chair. The camp prefect was a short man of around fifty, with short grey hair and a hard, grizzled face. Carefully Fergus studied the man, trying to figure out how he was going to handle him. The officer had served for twenty-nine years in the Fourth Legion and was a battle-hardened, no nonsense veteran who had climbed the ranks the hard way. So Britannicus, the young Tribune, had informed him. There was not a more experienced or respected soldier to be found in the whole legion.

"Seems to be in order," the camp prefect said at last in a gruff voice, as he handed the letter back to Fergus.

Silently Fergus placed the letter in a leather satchel. Then he turned his gaze back to the camp prefect.

"May I ask what happened to my predecessor?" Fergus said.

"He died of the plague," the camp prefect replied.

Fergus raised his eyebrows. "Plague," he exclaimed. "Where was this? In Zeugma?"

"No, not here," the camp prefect said. "In one of the towns beyond the river. A few months ago, there was an outbreak of the plague. It killed the laticlavius and took half a company of men with it before the outbreak vanished."

"I am told that you are the longest serving member of the Fourth Legion," Fergus said, abruptly changing the conversation. "You must have seen many tribunes come and go. You have read my letter. You have seen my army record. How do I compare to the previous occupants of this position?"

For a moment the grizzled camp prefect hesitated and gazed at Fergus guardedly.

"I have seen twenty-three men occupy your position in my time with the legion," the camp prefect said sharply. "A few of them were all right but most were not much more than boys, amateurs with no real interest in the fortunes of the Fourth or the men under their command. The restoration of the pride and reputation of the Fourth is my only concern. And as regards to you," the camp prefect said as he hesitated again, his watchful eyes examining Fergus. "I would say you were either Hadrian's cocksucker or a genius or just damn lucky to have got your position."

In his chair Fergus grinned as he gazed at the camp prefect. Silence descended on the stuffy office as Fergus turned to look down at the desk.

"I am the second in command of this legion," Fergus said at last in a calm, measured voice as he looked up. "You are third in command. Together our job is to advise the legate. The old grizzled veteran legionary who climbed the ranks and the young son of a senator, a political appointee. We are the legate's senior team. That's how it's supposed to work isn't it? Gellius will depend on us and it's vital for the effectiveness of this legion that we work well together."

Fergus paused as he gazed at the camp prefect.

"Now I called you here because I believe it is important that we make a good, effective team. Division and rivalry at the top will filter down into the ranks and I do not want that to happen, nor I am sure, do you. Like you I want the Fourth to be the best. I mean that. So," Fergus said with a sigh. "I thought we could take this opportunity to mark out how we are going to work together. So, tell me your thoughts, your concerns."

Across the desk the camp prefect remained silent as he gazed at Fergus and Fergus could see that the officer had been taken by surprise by his comments. At last the old warrior cleared his throat.

"I am the most experienced soldier," the camp prefect said gruffly. "I know this legion, its officers and men inside out. This is my legion. I may come from a humble, ordinary family Sir, but I do not leave after a year like you do. I will continue to advise the legate on the day to day management of the cohorts, all training issues, discipline, promotions and logistics," the camp prefect snapped. "You," the prefect hesitated. "You with your connections to Hadrian however seem better suited to advise him on politics, diplomacy, deployment and intelligence issues. If the legate asks your opinion, then you will back me up and I shall do the same with you. If we have a dispute we discuss it separately. Like I said the reputation and the pride of the Fourth is my only concern."

"As it is mine," Fergus said quickly. "All right, agreed," Fergus added. "But if there is a need for an independent battlegroup or vexillation, I shall be given its command and you will defer to me."

"Eager for battle, are you Sir?" the camp prefect replied sharply.

"I am," Fergus replied, lowering his gaze. "And I have taken command of such formations before. It was my troops who broke through the Bitlis pass last year and it was I who killed the Armenian king. I am not here to admire the scenery. I have come here to fight and make a name for myself."

"Then welcome back to the war," the camp prefect said in his gruff voice.

***

The fifteen hundred or so legionaries of the First and Second Cohorts of the Fourth Legion stood stiffly to attention on the dusty parade ground of the legionary fortress on the outskirts of Zeugma. On their right flank, the hundred and twenty legionary cavalrymen, clad in their full gear, ceremonial facemasks and mounted on their horses, stood drawn up in four turmae, squadrons, waiting patiently for the inspection to begin. It was dawn and the infantry, wearing their army uniforms, belts, hobnailed boots, gleaming body armour and legionary helmets with wide cheek guards, stood arrayed according to their individual company and cohort formations. The men were clutching their pila, spears. Their large, oval legionary shields, emblazoned with lightning bolts, were resting and leaning against their legs on the yellow sandy ground. Standing proudly to attention in front and behind each century were the company officers, the centurions, optio's, company second in commands, cornicen, trumpeters and the signifer's, clutching their proud unit's standards. Across the parade ground not a sound could be heard except the gentle moan of the warm morning breeze.

Slowly and steadily Fergus made his way along the massed, silent and motionless ranks, examining the officers and men as he did. The legionaries were staring rigidly into space and not a word was said as Fergus took in the state of their weapons, uniforms, equipment and the bearing of the men. He was closely followed by the camp prefect, the four tribune augusticlavii and the primus pilus, the legions most senior centurion and commander of the First cohort. They were followed in turn by the standard bearer of the legion, clad in a magnificent lion's head that was drawn over his helmet and proudly holding aloft the gleaming aquila, the sacred and precious eagle banner of the Fourth Scythica.

Fergus said nothing as he moved on down the ranks, his quick alert eyes passing across the faces of the legionaries. There had been no news from Gellius, the legate and no one at HQ seemed to know when exactly to expect him back, for he'd been given contradictory reports on that issue. So, he would just have to get on with the job without his boss, Fergus thought, and the first task was to see for himself the state of the men and their equipment, for his initial impression had not been positive. As he reached the cavalry squadrons, Fergus paused and turned to the camp prefect and the primus pilus. Both men were old enough to be his father and both had served in the army far longer than he had, but they lacked the senatorial rank and social standing to rise any higher. Fergus took a deep dissatisfied breath as he fixed his eyes on the two senior officers.

"Listen, this is not good enough," he said, lowering his voice so that the cavalrymen could not hear him. "These units are a disgrace. Some of the men look fat and unfit. Many are missing vital pieces of equipment and armour. I counted several men without their pugio knives. Helmets are dirty, uniforms look shabby and unwashed. Do the men not take pride in their companies? Do we have a shortage of equipment? Some of the shields that I saw looked like they were falling apart and since when do we tolerate beards in the army. If we were on campaign, I would understand but we are at our home base now. There is no excuse for this shit."

"Hadrian has a beard," the primus pilus replied in a sour voice. "And I can assure you Sir that the First cohort are fit and battle ready. The camp prefect took them on a route march through the desert only yesterday."

"The overall standard is not good enough," Fergus snapped. "Maybe some of the men are up for battle but many others look they couldn't handle a mob of outraged geese. It is not acceptable. I want every single man up to standard. That means turning out with all the proper gear and equipment. And if that means additional training exercises then so be it. There is a fucking war going on gentlemen and we are not going to win it looking like this."

"Maybe we should wait until the legate returns before making hasty decisions," the camp prefect said, as he gave Fergus a perplexed look.

"No," Fergus growled in an annoyed voice. "In the legate's absence I am in command of this legion and my orders will stand. We are going to repeat the whole inspection again at dawn tomorrow and this time I want to see an improvement. And if tomorrow I see the same load of shit, that I have just witnessed, then all leave will be cancelled, and as an example I shall have one man from each company flogged in front of all his comrades. We are either a proper fighting-fit legion in the imperial Roman army or we are nothing. Discipline starts with how a man maintains himself and his equipment. See to it that your officers and men get the fucking message."

***

Gellius, the legate was a tall handsome aristocratic man of around thirty-five. A white focale, neck scarf was tied around his neck to mop up body sweat, and he was wearing a scarlet paludamentum, cloak, fastened to one shoulder. Fergus stood before his commanding officer waiting for Gellius to finish reading his letter of introduction. At his side the camp prefect was looking down at the ground with a dour look. The legate's office was quiet except for the rustle of the papyrus scrolls and the creak of the chair in which one of the junior tribunes was sitting. Several days had passed since Fergus had ordered the troop inspections and, despite considerable improvements on the second inspection, he was still not entirely happy. Titus, his old centurion back in Twentieth would have made both the First and Second Cohorts run around the walls of Zeugma as punishment for the neglect the men had shown.

"Good, welcome to the Fourth Legion Fergus," the legate said at last, looking up at Fergus as he handed Hadrian's scroll to a tribune. "I am glad you are here. We have been rather short staffed since your predecessor died." Gellius frowned as he took his time examining Fergus. "So, what news from Antioch? I expect you will be happy when Hadrian is finally appointed as the emperor's deputy and commander in chief of Rome's eastern legions? I hear the appointment is imminent."

Fergus hesitated as he sensed the trap. Gellius was asking him where his political loyalties lay, and he would have to answer without knowing where the legate himself stood regarding Hadrian and Nigrinus and the War and Peace parties. If he got the answer wrong, it was going to cause friction.

"I served Hadrian as his head of security for many years Sir," Fergus said. "Hadrian deserves the promotion. He deserves to be the next emperor."

Across from him Gellius grunted and turned to look away and for an awkward moment silence, returned to the office.

"Well you certainly have done well from being in Hadrian's service," Gellius said at last in a neutral voice. "But I also see that last year you served under Lusius Quietus and Task Force Red. I believe they were deployed around Lake Van. My brother served with the sixth legion as their second in command. Maybe you know him?"

"I am sorry Sir," Fergus replied. "I did not meet him. I was away most of the time on detached service, hunting Armenian rebels in the mountains. And later I opened up the Bitlis pass into northern Mesopotamia."

"Yes, yes," Gellius said smoothly, "I saw all that in your letter." The legate paused to examine Fergus carefully again. "Normally the tribune laticlavius that they send us are rich well-connected boys, without any military experience. You

Fergus, however seem to be an exception. I can't understand it. You started out with the Twentieth at Deva as an ordinary legionary from an insignificant family. Service in Britannia followed. Ten years ago, you are transferred as part of a vexillation to the German frontier where you claim to have saved Hadrian's life. After that you take part in the Dacian war, which you successfully conclude, by being appointed Hadrian's head of security. And suddenly your father strikes it rich; so rich that he can afford to join the senatorial class. That is one hell of a rise up the social ladder Fergus."

A little smile had suddenly appeared on Gellius's lips as he took a step towards Fergus. "Seems to me," Gellius said, lowering his voice. "That the key moment for you and your family's fortunes came during the Dacian war. What did you do? Rob some wealthy Dacian of all his gold and silver? Find yourself a little goldmine? A man does not go from being an ordinary farmer to so quickly becoming a senator without some dirty secrets. So, what are yours Fergus?"

"With all due respect Sir," Fergus said stiffly. "That is none of your goddamn business. I am here to serve this legion. I am here to fight Parthians and make the Fourth great again. If there is some misunderstanding regards my role I will be glad to inform Hadrian of the matter."

The office went very still and in the corner, the junior tribune sitting at a desk seemed suddenly to be holding his breath.

Gellius was staring at Fergus. Then just as the silence became intolerable, the legate threw back his head and laughed.

"Good Fergus, good," the legate exclaimed as his laughter subsided. "You passed my test. I can see that you are the honest, no bullshit type of officer. Most men who have stood where you are standing have tried to worm their way out of the question and the worst ones have simply lied. But you, you gave it straight back to me on the chin. I like that. You've got balls. We are going to get on, you and I."

"Yes Sir," Fergus said in a patient voice.

Gellius nodded and then turned back to his desk with a sigh. "I understand that you have had the First and Second Cohorts out on parade twice this week. From now on I want the camp prefect to take care of such inspections. It's his job to supervise training and disciplinary issues. Is that understood?"

"Yes Sir," Fergus replied stiffly.

Gellius sat down in the chair behind his desk and looked down at the paperwork that lay scattered across it. Then he looked up at Fergus.

"The Fourth is not where I would like them to be," the legate said in a grave voice. "Some of the cohorts are first class, made up of veterans but others are not. We have had too many new and raw recruits and little time to train them. Most of the cohorts are also understrength. Our best units are the First cohort and the cavalry turmae. Both are fit for active service. The rest however are only fit for garrison duties. That's why they are spread out across the kingdom of Osrhoene."

"I understand Sir," Fergus said. "We need time to integrate the new recruits and prepare them for battle."

"We don't have time," the camp prefect interrupted sharply. "The war is not going to pause for us. My men are spending nearly all their time on the frontier building roads, forts, supply depots, watch towers and on garrison, guard and escort duties. There is no fucking time to train them."

"The camp prefect is right," Gellius said with a sigh. "With the capture of Armenia and northern Mesopotamia, Emperor Trajan has ordered the construction of a new fortified frontier and all the army's efforts are going into this. That's why there have been no large military campaigns planned for this year. The army is busy but not with conquering new land. I also have it on good authority that Trajan believes us not to be first class or combat ready. He doesn't think that the Fourth is high quality enough to take an active part in the war."

The legate paused as he looked from Fergus to the camp prefect and back again. "Our job is to prove Trajan wrong," he growled at last. "I intend to show that the Fourth has fully and finally removed the stain of dishonour and defeat that we inherited. That is my ambition and that will be your ambition."

"Dishonour and defeat Sir?" Fergus said raising his eyebrows.

"Yes," Gellius replied with a little nod. "Fifty-five years ago, during the reign of emperor Nero, the Fourth was forced to surrender to the Parthians. It was an ignoble and devastating defeat and the Fourth has never really recovered from it. The stain on our honour and reputation still lingers but I am determined to erase it once and for all and this current war with Parthia is our opportunity."

"That is only true Sir," the camp prefect said gruffly. "If Trajan still wishes to go further and conquer the rest of Mesopotamia. From everything that I have heard, it seems that the emperor is content to just consolidate his new frontier. Maybe large-scale fighting and campaigning is already over."

"Maybe," Gellius muttered as he looked down at his paperwork on his desk.

"Trajan's health is starting to fail," Fergus said suddenly. "I learned this in Antioch Sir."

Behind his desk Gellius looked up at Fergus and, for a moment he said nothing. Then he frowned.

"You know this for certain?" the legate said as at Fergus's side the camp prefect too had turned to gaze at him in surprise.

"Yes, my source would not lie about such a matter. They are keeping it secret. So the news should not go beyond this room," Fergus replied.

"Shit," Gellius said at last, as he looked away. "So, the struggle between the War and Peace factions is coming to a head. Soon we're going to be fighting this war with one eye on the Parthians and one eye on our rear."

"That is one way of looking at it Sir," Fergus said. "But there is another. In his heart I believe that Trajan has always been a soldier. If he knows that his time is nearly up and if I were a betting man, which I am, I would wager that Trajan is planning one final campaign; one final conquest. He wants to be known as the greatest. The lure of following in Alexander the Great's footsteps is just too great. He will want to go where no Roman army has ever been before. That's why I reckon that in the coming campaign season, he will throw caution to the wind and stake all on the conquest of Mesopotamia. This last campaign shall be his legacy to Rome."

Chapter Thirty-Three – Marching Orders

Autumn 115 AD, Zeugma, Province of Commagene

Fergus to Adalwolf, greetings old friend. I pen this brief letter to you as a reminder of the dire situation that my family finds itself in. Did you manage to raise the matter of my father and Nigrinus with Hadrian? It is of utmost importance that you do so. Please write to me as soon as you can with news.

These past weeks and months have been very busy, and I have not been able to see much of Galena or the girls. My duties have taken me right across the old kingdom of Osrhoene to visit and inspect our scattered garrisons. The men are working tirelessly to build the new frontier and much good work has already been completed. Morale is high, but I sense that the locals are less impressed by our presence, although none dare to show it to us. The local traders and merchants who dominate these caravan cities seem to want their world to remain politically divided but economically unhampered. It is under these conditions that they can flourish. So, they are not happy to find themselves at the mercy of a single, highly organised financial system that taxes their profits and lays down new rules. There is trouble coming for our garrisons and I am trying to prepare them as best as I can.

Near the city of Edessa where emperor Trajan so recently held court I happened to come across my old friends from the 7th Auxiliary Numidian Cavalry Alae but there was only time for the briefest of greetings with Hiempsal. In the wooded district of Mygdonia I too saw legionaries and auxiliaries cutting down trees and constructing portable boats. If this is a sign of the things to come, then I believe I shall soon be receiving my marching orders and further letters will have to wait.

Write soon old friend with news and please remember that my family's fate weighs heavy on my heart. I am returning to Zeugma soon and shall await your reply. Do all that you can. Fergus to his dear friend Adalwolf.

***

"Fergus, Sir," Britannicus, the young tribune called out in his native Briton language, hastily saluting as he caught sight of Fergus wearily dismounted from his horse. "The legate wishes to see you right away. I am to take you to him now."

It was late in the afternoon, in the courtyard of the old Seleucid citadel and HQ of the Fourth Legion in Zeugma. Annoyed, Fergus turned to gaze at Britannicus as he handed his horse over to a slave.

"What? No time to even wash my face" Fergus snapped in an irritable voice. "I have just got back. What's so damn important?"

"There has been news," Britannicus said with excitement in his voice. "We have received orders Sir."

Fergus frowned as he stared at the young tribune. Then without saying a further word, he started out in the direction of Gellius's office, hastily followed by Britannicus. In the dark corridors of the old fortress the legionaries smartly saluted, but Fergus seemed oblivious to their presence.

The legate was in his office going over some paperwork when Fergus marched in and rapped out a quick salute. Fergus's red cape with the broad purple boarder were stained with dust, as were his boots and body armour. After his long journey he had been hoping to go home and see Galena and his girls, but those plans seemed to have been dashed.

"You wished to see me Sir," Fergus said quickly, as he sensed Britannicus standing behind him.

"Yes," Gellius said as he gave Fergus a quick glance. "Whilst you were away we received new orders. The Third Cyrenaica legion has been tasked with the capture of the city of Doura-Europus and they have requested reinforcements. Trajan have ordered us to put together a vexillation. I am putting you in command. The boys from the Third are mustering at our outpost in the town of Circesium on the Euphrates. Doura-Europus is about fifty miles further downstream on the right bank of the Euphrates, but it's in Parthian hands. We're going to have to fight for it. After you have made the necessary sacrifices to the gods, you are to take the First cohort and our cavalry and leave as soon as possible. My written orders are to follow. Once you have joined the Third Cyrenaica, you are to report to their legate for further instructions. You will be remain under his temporary command until you receive further orders. Am I clear?"

"Yes Sir, I understand," Fergus replied in calm voice. "May I make one request Sir?"

"Go on," the legate said sternly.

"That I can take Britannicus with me Sir," Fergus replied. "He is proving to be a good, competent staff officer. However, he has never seen combat and I know he is desperate to see some before he is sent home."

"Found yourself a young protégé have you," Gellius said quickly.

Gellius paused as he examined Fergus. Then he cast a quick glance at Britannicus whose cheeks and ears were glowing.

"Granted," the legate said at last in a stern voice. Gellius then turned his attention back to Fergus. "So, it seems that you are going to have your wish and lead the men into battle." Fixing his eyes on Fergus, Gellius straightened up and continued speaking. "I expect you to lead your men in a manner that will bring pride to this legion. If you can't manage that, then don't bother coming back. War tests a man like nothing else. That will be all Fergus. May fortune ride with you."

Chapter Thirty-Four - The March South Begins

The Euphrates had widened and had grown more sluggish the further south and downstream they had gone. Along the river's lazy banks, green reeds, isolated tufts of grass, prickly bushes and a few stunted trees fought for life in the harsh, stony and featureless Syrian desert that stretched away to the horizon. It was late in the afternoon and, in the clear blue sky, the sun glared down on the long Roman column that was spread out on the march along the west bank. The faces of the stoic legionaries, loaded down with sixty pounds of equipment plus spears, body armour, entrenching tools, helmets and their large shields, were covered in dust and fine desert sand. Their marching packs containing food, blankets, water-pouches, spades, cups, cooking utensils and spare weapons were slung over their shoulders, suspended on wooden rods. In between the marching men, some of the legionaries were leading mules loaded down with leather tents, firewood and sharpened wooden stakes.

Fergus, clad in his red cape with the broad purple border and wearing his magnificent crested helmet, rode on his horse at the very front of the column with Britannicus at his side. The junior tribune was clad in a similar red cape but with a thin purple border. He looked excited and keen. Behind Fergus came the primus pilus of the First cohort, the cornicen, trumpeter and the cohort standard bearer holding up the square vexillation standard of the Fourth Scythica. Idly Fergus turned to look towards the west. The flat, stony Syrian desert stretched away to the horizon and there was nothing to see. The view reminded Fergus of his patrols with his half savage Numidian riders of the 7th Auxiliary Cavalry Alae. He hadn't known it at the time, but he realised now but those had been good days. Great days. Tearing around the desert on their small shaggy horses and lording it over the wealthy, pompous trade caravans that had used the road from Palmyra to Sura. Once he'd gained their respect those hardy north-African horsemen would have followed him anywhere. With a sigh, Fergus turned to look towards the east. Out on the Euphrates, a convoy of boats manned with oarsmen was keeping pace with the slow plodding column of heavy infantry, archers, engineers and cavalry. The boats were piled high with vital supplies for out here in the desert, there would no chance to go foraging. On the eastern bank the desert stretched away to the horizon. One day out from the Roman outpost at Circesium and they had entered a wasteland, which would have swallowed up whole armies if it wasn't for the reassuring presence of the wide tranquil river. Twisting around in his saddle, Fergus gazed back at the stoic, plodding column that was following him. The legate of the Third Cyrenaica had ordered him to lead the advance on Doura-Europus. It was a gesture of respect that Fergus had gratefully accepted. As he gazed back at the long columns, Fergus could see that the battlegroup of seven thousand men, including the whole of the Cyrenaica and an attached cohort of Syrian archers, had created a dust cloud that would be seen for miles and miles. They were not going to take Doura-Europus by surprise.

"Sir, riders approaching," Britannicus cried out excitedly, as he raised his hand and pointed at something out in the western desert.

Calmly Fergus turned to gaze in the direction in which the young tribune was pointing and there on the horizon, he suddenly made out figures on horseback racing towards the long, dusty column. Behind him the two squadrons of legionary cavalry stirred, as they too caught sight of the approaching horsemen.

"Well," Fergus growled, as he turned to glance at Britannicus. "Your eyes are better than mine. Are they ours or the enemy?"

Britannicus hesitated as he squinted and raised his hand to shield his eyes.

"Ours Sir," he exclaimed at last. "Looks like the recon squadron. Shall I order our horsemen to intercept them Sir?"

"No, let them approach," Fergus replied, as he stared at the distant figures with a thoughtful expression.

"Why are they returning Sir?" Britannicus asked.

"I don't know," Fergus replied with a frown. "But I don't think this is good news. They had orders to return only if they spotted trouble."

As the lead horsemen rode up to Fergus, he recognised the decurion in command of his recon squadron. The man had a Bedouin scarf wrapped around his head that half obscured his face, and both he and his horse were covered in dust.

"Parthian horse archers," the decurion cried out, as he slowed his horse and trotted towards Fergus. "We spotted them about four miles to the south. They will be here shortly. No more than two or three hundred of them, but they are moving fast."

"Any cataphracts amongst them," Fergus called out quickly. "Did you see any heavy shock cavalry?"

"No Sir," the decurion cried, as he lowered his Bedouin scarf. "Only horse archers but they looked dead set on intercepting us."

"Good," Fergus said hastily. "Rest your horses and form up with rest of the cavalry." Anxiously Fergus turned to peer into the desert to the south, but he could see nothing.

"What can two or three hundred light horsemen do to us Sir," Britannicus exclaimed in a puzzled voice, as he too peered towards the south. "There are seven-thousand of us. Surely, they are not going to attack us. That would-be madness."

"Ride back to the legate of the Third and warn him that we are about to make contact with a force consisting of two or three hundred enemy horse archers," Fergus snapped at Britannicus, ignoring the young tribune's question. "Tell him that I believe the enemy to only consist of horse archers. Go!"

For a moment Britannicus looked confused. Then, as a little colour shot into his cheeks, he turned his horse and galloped away down the column of plodding legionaries. "Centurion," Fergus cried, as he twisted round to stare at the primus pilus of the First cohort. "Have your men prepare to receive mounted archers. But we keep moving forwards - you understand."

"Yes Sir," the officer said quickly, as he too peeled away from the front of the column.

"Are we not overreacting a little," the standard bearer said in an arrogant voice. "These Parthians are probably just on a reconnaissance mission, out to learn our size and composition. They won't dare to attack us."

"Shut up," Fergus hissed in an annoyed voice as anxiously he turned to gaze to the south. "You are a fool. The Parthians will have spies in all these desert cities. They will have already known our intentions and everything there was to know about us before we even left Circesium."

"Sir," the cornicen suddenly called out in a tight voice as he pointed at the horizon, and as he did, Fergus hastily turned to gaze in the direction the trumpeter was pointing. And there on the horizon, small fast-moving clouds of dust were being whipped up into the air. The dust clouds seemed to be on a collision course with the Roman column. Hastily Fergus turned to the sixty cavalrymen mustered behind his staff. "Form a wedge," he yelled. "If those bastards get too close we will have them, but no one moves until I give the order."

Further down the dusty Roman column a trumpet rang out. It was the signal to prepare to receive cavalry. The Parthian horsemen were indeed moving fast Fergus could see. The horse archers had formed a single line and were bearing down on the Roman column at an angle. When they were a hundred paces away or so, the angle of the assault changed, and the Parthians went racing and galloping down the Roman flank. With a whirring noise a hail of arrows slammed into the column and here and there a trooper tumbled from his horse and a legionary collapsed to the ground. Shrieks and cries broke out amongst the Roman ranks, as the Parthian horse archers veered away into the open desert in a lazy figure of 8 manoeuvre. Along the banks of the river, the ordered Roman column had broken up as the legionaries had come to a halt and had raised their shields against the menace. Warily the heavily laden legionaries watched the Parthian horsemen as they came around for another pass.

"Keep moving, keep moving," Fergus roared, as he turned to the men of the First cohort. "Sound the signal to advance," Fergus yelled at his cornicen. "They are trying to slow us down. We must keep moving."

A moment later a trumpet rang out. Grimly Fergus gazed at the Parthians as they came racing in for another attack. The riders had no armour and were wearing loose fitting tunics. The horsehair plumes atop their helmets were streaming behind them and a quiver of arrows and a spare bow hung from their belts. As the whining, whirring arrows slammed and hammered into shields, horses, men and the ground, a cavalryman close to Fergus suddenly groaned and toppled backwards from his horse with an arrow protruding from his body.

"Shit," Fergus cursed as he gazed at the enemy riders. The Parthian horsemen looked like they were superb riders who knew exactly what they were doing. Some of the men seemed to be riding with both hands free. At his side, one of the cavalrymen hastily thrust a small round shield into Fergus's hands.

"What are we waiting for Sir?" one of the cavalry decurion's cried in a frustrated voice. "Let us go after them. We can take them."

"No," Fergus replied sharply. "Stay in formation. We don't have enough cavalry to overwhelm them. They are faster and more mobile than we are. If we leave the column they will simply envelop us and mow us down. We won't even get close to those horse archers. We stay in formation unless they make a mistake."

Tensely Fergus turned to look down the column. The legionaries had started to move again but the pace had slowed, and the men were watching their desert flank warily, their large shields protectively raised around their bodies. In the corner of his eye Fergus suddenly caught sight of Britannicus racing down the Roman column towards him. As the young tribune reined in his horse beside him Fergus could see that the boy's cheeks were flushed with excitement.

"Sir, the legate orders you to keep advancing. We are to keep moving," Britannicus gasped. "He is going to send us a company of Syrian archers and a company of slingers. They are coming up the line now Sir."

"Good," Fergus growled. "The sooner those bastards get a taste of their own tactics the better. When the archers and slingers get here, I want them to take up positions amongst the legionaries. The heavy infantry with their shields should provide them with some protection. See that it is done."

"Yes Sir," Britannicus said hastily, as he turned to peer at the Parthian horsemen out in the open desert.

"What are they trying to do Sir?" Britannicus exclaimed.

"They are harassing us," Fergus snapped, as he too stared at the Parthian column. "Trying to slow us down. Wear us out. It suggests that the enemy do not have the strength to contest our advance and meet us in a pitched battle. But they are going to make us fight for Doura-Europus nevertheless."

***

It was dark and along the banks of the Euphrates the long Roman column had come to a halt for the night. The only light came from the moon and the beautiful clear carpet of twinkling stars in the night sky. Fergus stood beside a horse-drawn wagon sipping a cup of posca, as he gazed in the direction of the western desert. The legate in command of the battle group had forbidden the lighting of campfires to conserve precious supplies of firewood and to prevent the fires from being used as markers for the Parthians. There had been no question of building a regular army marching camp, for in the desert there was nothing that could be used to build the camp. Instead the Roman battle group lay strung-out along the river's edge, protected by pickets and the sharpened wooden anti-cavalry stakes the soldiers had brought with them. A few army tents had been erected but most of the legionaries had opted to get some rest under the stars amongst their comrades, mules and wagons. But if they had expected to get a good night's sleep they were mistaken. As Fergus raised his cup to his lips and gazed into the darkness, he could hear the Parthian horse archers shouting and hollering. The noise was followed by trumpet blasts and from the darkness the occasional thud of approaching hooves and an arrow hammered into the Roman camp, a reminder to the legionaries of the ever-present danger lurking out in the desert.

"Bastards are not going to let us get any sleep," the primus pilus growled, as he appeared from the darkness and placed his hands on the edge of the wagon. "I have been around the camp. The men are on edge and frustrated Sir. They want to know when we are going to deal with these horsemen."

Fergus nodded as he took another sip of posca. Then he turned to gaze in the direction of the river, where the convoy of heavily laden flat-bottomed barges and boats had beached themselves for the night.

"Any suggestions?" Fergus growled.

"No Sir," the primus pilus replied with a sigh. "We can't see shit in this darkness and the enemy are far too fast and mobile. Attack them and they will run away and still shoot at you. I don't want my men blundering around in the night chasing ghosts. We will just have to endure it. That's what I have been telling the men."

Fergus was about to agree with the primus pilus when Britannicus suddenly spoke up in the darkness close by.

"Sir," the young tribune said hesitantly. "I have spoken with our Palmyran guides and scouts. They know this stretch of the river better than anyone. They tell me that about three or four miles downstream there is a fracture in the earth, an old dried-up water channel. It's not very long, deep or wide and it runs parallel to the river. The Palmyran's say that the gully is just deep enough to hide several hundred men."

Britannicus hesitated. "So, I was thinking Sir. What if we sneaked in say two companies of Syrian archers and slingers with maybe a company of legionaries in support. We could hide them in the gully and ambush the Parthians as they approached?"

Fergus frowned as in the darkness he turned to gaze in Britannicus's direction. At his side the primus pilus grunted in surprise.

"The boy may have something there," the old warrior muttered cautiously.

"We would need to move the men under the cover of darkness," Fergus growled. "How would we do that without the Parthians noticing?"

"We use the boats Sir," Britannicus replied hastily. "We move the troops down river in the darkness and get them into position before dawn."

"You would need some bait," the primus pilus growled. "Something to attract the Parthian's attention. Something significant enough to lure them into the ambush."

"We could use a few legionary squads as bait," Britannicus said with growing excitement. "Say a recon patrol scouting ahead of our main force. We place them in full view but close enough to the gully. Then as the Parthians move in, our archers and slingers reveal themselves at the right moment and cut down the enemy."

In the darkness Fergus looked down at the ground. "It's a risky plan," he said at last. "What happens if the Palmyran guides have got the lay of the land wrong? What if in the darkness, we miss the correct landing ground? Our men would be isolated and far from help if it goes wrong. What happens if we run into a larger Parthian force? We cannot afford to lose those archers and slingers."

"It could work Sir," the primus pilus said. "Some risks are unavoidable. But if it means getting these bastard horsemen off our backs then it's worth it in my view."

Fergus remained silent as he thought it through. "All right," he said at last. "The legate will need to approve the plan. Britannicus, you and I will go to him and explain the operation. If the legate gives his approval, then I will…"

Fergus stopped in mid-sentence. He had wanted to say that he would command the ambush himself, but that would be wrong. As tribune laticlavius and vexillation commander he had wider responsibilities now. His primary duty was to manage the whole vexillation, not just to lead a small part of the battle. This was now a matter of delegation. Awkwardly Fergus cleared his throat.

"Britannicus," Fergus snapped. "If the legate gives his approval, then you will lead the troops down river and set up the ambush. Take an experienced centurion with you. If you are successful signal, us with a trumpeter. I shall ask the legate to delay our march by an hour to give the ambush a chance. After that we shall continue downstream towards your position. Are you ready to take on such a task?"

"I am Sir," Britannicus said from the darkness in a voice dripping with tension and excitement.

"The boy has no combat experience," the primus pilus growled. "Maybe you should send someone more experienced to do the job Sir?"

"No," Fergus said in a harsh voice. "It's his plan and he must learn. He must start somewhere. He will either make a success of it or he will die."

"Along with our precious archers and slingers," the primus pilus muttered unhappily.

***

Tensely Fergus sat on his horse and gazed southwards along the Euphrates. Dawn had come and gone, and the thousands of legionaries, horses, wagons and mules stood waiting for the order for the advance to resume. They wouldn't be able to wait much longer. At Fergus's side his staff too were peering southwards, but along the green river banks and out in the stony desert, there was no sign of the enemy. And there had been no signal from Britannicus and his men.

"We can't wait any longer Sir," the primus pilus said sharply, as he sat on his horse at Fergus's side. "If they were successful we should have heard their signal by now. Doura is still a day's march away. We need to reach it before nightfall."

Fergus sighed wearily and nodded.

"Very well," he said. "Have the cornicen sound the advance. We will know soon enough, what has become of Britannicus and his ambush."

A few moments later a trumpet rang out and the long Roman column began to move. On the river the barges and boats did the same. Idly Fergus turned his gaze to the open desert on the column's right flank. The Parthian horse archers were nowhere to be seen and that gave him hope. For surely if Britannicus had failed, the Parthians would have been here to harass and slow down the Roman advance, as they had done yesterday and throughout most of the night.

It was a half an hour into their advance when Fergus suddenly heard a distant noise and his heart leapt. Had that been a Roman trumpet? Straining to listen, Fergus suddenly heard it again. The noise was coming from the south. Then ahead along the river bank he caught sight of horsemen galloping towards him. From the banner they were holding up it looked like the recon cavalry squadron were returning, or at least a few of them were. As the horsemen raced towards him, every eye in the Roman vanguard turned to stare at them. The Roman cavalry men's faces were half obscured by their Bedouin style scarves and they seemed to be in a hurry.

"Sir," one of the cavalrymen cried out as he recognised Fergus and swerved towards him. "The decurion sent me Sir. The banks of the Euphrates up ahead are littered with dead Parthian horsemen and horses. There must be at least one hundred enemy dead. Shot to pieces by our archers and slingers. The ambush worked Sir. The rest of the enemy have fled."

An excited stir ran through Fergus's staff at the news.

"What about Britannicus and his men?" Fergus called out hurriedly. "What has happened to them?"

"They are well Sir," the cavalryman replied. "Britannicus has withdrawn his men back onto their boats for safety. He awaits our approach in the middle of the river. He has even managed to take a few prisoners."

"Our casualties?" Fergus snapped.

"Minimal Sir," the cavalryman grinned in triumph. "A few wounded as far as we could see. The road south to Doura-Europus is open Sir."

As the Roman column began to pass the first of the fallen Parthian horse archers, a strange satisfied muttering and hissing seemed to make its way down the ranks of the marching legionaries. A few of the men, perhaps those who had lost comrades in the earlier attacks, broke formation to spit on and defile the Parthian dead until they were called back by their officers. Fergus however, had no time for the dead. His eyes were on the Euphrates and the collection of flat-bottomed barges. The recon riders had been right. Britannicus had wisely withdrawn his men into the river in case the Parthians had brought up reinforcements. The boats, having spotted the advancing Roman column, were already heading into the reed-infested shore and as he gazed at them, Fergus spotted Britannicus standing proudly at the front of one of the craft. As the young tribune recognised Fergus, he raised both his fists in the air and roared in ecstatic triumph and around him his men did the same.

***

It was late in the afternoon when the dull, rhythmic crunch of thousands of pairs of legionary's boots, the thud of horses' hooves and rumble of wagon wheels was disturbed by a sudden crack. The next moment a small geyser of water erupted, close to one of the boats in the river. Startled, Fergus turned to gaze at the convoy of boats that was following the Roman column. What the hell was that? Out on the Euphrates the sailors were shouting to each other in alarm. Another crack followed and a moment later another small geyser of water shot upwards, close to the convoy. Fergus rubbed his tired eyes and stared out across the river.

"The boats are under attack Sir," Britannicus cried out, as he pointed at the left bank of the Euphrates. "Look, Parthian artillery on the eastern bank. They are shooting at our boats. They are trying to sink our supplies."

Fergus said nothing as he too caught sight of the Parthian ballistae drawn up on the left bank of the river; a battery of three heavy-wheeled catapults. Britannicus was right. The Parthians were targeting the slow-moving boats. As he stared at the scene transfixed, the cracking noise came again. A dark object went hurtling through the blue sky in a graceful arc and instantly burst into flames as it slammed straight into one of the heavily laden, defenceless barges. On the river, the screams of the sailors rose up and as he gazed in horror at the unfolding scene, Fergus saw some of the boats men leap into the water.

"Let me take a company of legionaries and capture those catapults Sir," Britannicus hissed eagerly, as he quickly turned to look at Fergus. "Look they are undefended by infantry Sir. If we can get across the river those artillerymen will be defenceless. But if we do nothing they are going to wreak havoc amongst our boats."

Fergus was staring at the unfolding scene with quick alert eyes. Something didn't seem quite right, but Britannicus had a point. If he did nothing the Parthians would have a field day with the battle group's boats.

"Silence those catapults. Do it," Fergus growled at last, nodding at the young tribune. As Britannicus hastened away Fergus quickly turned to the primus pilus who was riding beside him. "Have the boats men bring their boats into the cover of the reeds," he snapped. "We must save those barges at all costs."

"Yes Sir," the primus pilus growled, as he too hastened away.

Tensely, Fergus turned his attention back to the river. Another barge had been hit and was burning and drifting out of control. A thick column of black smoke was rising into the clear blue sky and in the water, men were desperately screaming for help. The Parthians had to be using incendiary projectiles. Fergus bit his lip. There was no question of the battle group engaging in an artillery duel with the Parthians, for the Roman artillery had been dismantled at the start of the march and would take time to reassemble. Time, which he did not have. Turning his attention to the boats, Fergus saw that Britannicus, leading a company of eighty legionaries, had taken over two barges and they were rowing furiously out into the middle of the Euphrates. And as he watched the mad dash develop across the river, geysers of water erupted close to the boats, showering the soldiers with water. "Come on, come on, come on," Fergus muttered tensely as he watched the furious race across the Euphrates. On the far bank he could just about make out the Parthians, running around reloading their catapults. Another cracking noise reverberated across the sluggish river and a dark projectile went arching away, before plunging into the water and narrowly missing one of the supply boats. On the left bank Britannicus and his men seemed to have finally made it to the shore, for as he peered at the unfolding scene Fergus caught sight of the Roman legionaries pouring from their boats and storming ashore. Amongst the Parthian catapults, a final defiant projectile went flying across the river and landed in the water with a great splash. Then as the legionaries closed in on their position, the Parthian artillerymen turned and fled, running for their lives into the desert. And as they did Fergus felt a tug of sudden unease. Would the Parthians really have left a battery of highly valuable catapults alone like that, without protection? His unease suddenly grew. Something was not right.

On the far shore Britannicus and his men had taken triumphant possession of the catapults and seemed to be milling about, having given up on chasing the Parthian artillerymen. Urgently Fergus turned to his cornicen, his trumpeter.

"Sound the recall," he snapped. "Do it now man."

Flustered, the cornicen raised his trumpet to his lips and blew. Then he blew again. The noise rang out across the river and the desert beyond. There was no way Britannicus could not have heard the signal. But on the far side of the river, the Roman legionaries did not seem to be responding. Suddenly Fergus gasped in dismay. From out of nowhere a line of Parthian horsemen had appeared and were galloping straight towards Britannicus and his men. And as he caught sight of the enemy, a flush spread across Fergus's cheeks as he realised that he'd been had. The Parthians had struck back with an ambush of their own. The artillery position had been bait. He had swallowed it whole. On the left bank the small band of legionaries were isolated and about to be slaughtered.

"Sound the fucking recall again," Fergus yelled at his cornicen, as he stared at the drama unfolding on the opposite side of the river. In response another furious trumpet blast rang out. On the opposite shore Britannicus had at last spotted the approaching threat, and as Fergus looked on, the legionaries turned and began sprinting back to their boats. But the Parthians were already upon them. Fergus groaned as he saw the small fast horses and their riders racing across the stony desert. A hail of arrows struck the fleeing Romans, mowing them down. Bodies went tumbling to the ground, arms went flailing and the shrill shrieks of panic drifted across the water, but Fergus was helpless to intervene. All he could do was watch in horror.

At the water's edge a group of legionaries had managed to get one of the boats afloat and were desperately piling into it. Others were screaming as they raced towards the riverbank, only to be cut down along the shore, their bodies tumbling and spinning onto the ground and crashing into the river. On the boat the survivors were desperately trying to put some distance between them, but the merciless hail of Parthian arrows kept coming, picking off men and sending them tumbling into the river where the weight of their armour ensured that they went straight to the bottom.

At last the one-sided fight seemed to come to an end and the Parthian horsemen stopped shooting arrows and turned to rob and mutilate the Roman dead and dying that lay scattered along the riverbank. Fergus said nothing as the single boatload of survivors came drifting back into the right bank. And amongst the desperate, traumatised men aboard, he caught sight of Britannicus. The young tribune looked utterly shaken, humbled and distraught as he gazed into the water.

"They killed half a company of my men Sir," the primus pilus hissed, as he gave Fergus an angry, resentful look. "And for what? I am going to make sure Gellius hears of this disaster."

Chapter Thirty-Five – The Assault on Doura-Europus

The crack of the Parthian catapults was greeted with warning shouts and cries from the Roman siege fortifications. Fergus stood in his command post some distance behind the foremost Roman positions, gazing at the western wall of Doura-Europus. Columns of black smoke were rising from within the settlement. All morning from within the besieged city, the Parthian artillery had been targeting the line of Roman trenches and sharpened wooden anti-cavalry stakes that methodically cut the city off from the outside world. As he stared at the scene, another Parthian projectile came hurtling through the clear noon sky, landing in the open desert with a crashing thud and releasing a foul-smelling stench. In a reflex response, Fergus and the men standing around him raised their Bedouin style scarves to their mouths and noses. The Parthians, the battle group had learned to its cost, had started hurling poisoned gas projectiles at them as soon as the siege had begun a few days ago. The projectiles, sealed jugs filled with bitumen and sulphur crystals, were igniting to create deadly poisonous gases.

A little way behind the Roman field fortifications, a battery of Roman onagers and ballistae were shooting back at the besieged city. The twang of their twisted ropes and the sharp kick back, as the war machines released their large stones, reverberated across the open desert. Along the Parthian walls Fergus could see the defenders manning the battlements and stone towers and from one of the redoubts, a proud Parthian banner fluttered in the breeze. A day's worth of Roman bombardment had not made much visible impact on the defences.

Stoically and silently Fergus allowed his eyes to take in every detail of the besieged city. Doura-Europus rested on an escarpment that rose three hundred feet above the right bank of the Euphrates. To the north and south the city was protected by deep, impassable ravines and to the east by the river, leaving only the western wall as the most exposed to attack. From his vantage point Fergus could just make out a thin and flat island in the middle of the Euphrates. Beyond the blue waters, on the eastern bank of the river, he could see lush, green cultivated fields, a welcome change to the bleak, barren desert that dominated the landscape. At the intelligence briefing before the battle group had started out from Circesium, the Palmyran guides and scouts had explained that Doura was a caravan city. A multi-cultural city of Macedonian Greeks, Jews, Parthians, Bedouin and Arab peoples with close ties to Palmyra to the west. It was not so much a stronghold, they had explained, but more a desert trading post that lay on the east-west and Euphrates trade routes, controlling an important river crossing. But from his vantage point the size and strength of the city's western wall begged to differ with that interpretation, Fergus thought sourly.

From the corner of his eye, Fergus noticed a runner approaching his command post. "Sir," the soldier gasped as he came to a halt before Fergus and rapped out a quick salute. "The legate has called an O group meeting. You are to report to his HQ right away."

Fergus nodded quickly and turned to Britannicus who was standing close by. "Let's go," he snapped.

***

The battle group's command post was nothing more than a square, half a yard-deep dugout, hacked out of the desert. In each corner a wooden pole was holding up a large cloth roof that flapped around in the breeze and shaded the legate and his staff from the burning sun. A legionary stood guard at the entrance.

As Fergus and Britannicus entered the command post, Fergus saw that the legate had gathered together nearly all his senior commanders. The legate of the Third Cyrenaica looked around forty and he had closely cropped white hair and a deeply tanned face and arms. A tense, strangely excited atmosphere seemed to pervade the HQ as the officers, clad in their dusty and stained uniforms and cloaks, stood around waiting for the legate to speak.

"All right, listen up," the legate called out at last, as he turned to look at the stern, hard faces around him. "Our Palmyran allies have returned from the city. They say that the Parthians have rejected our final offer to surrender. Negotiations have ended. The Parthians are going to fight. Now I haven't come here to conduct a long drawn out siege. My orders are clear. Take Doura-Europus as quick as possible. So, we are going to take the city today. We are going to storm the walls and finish this."

The legate paused as he turned to a mock-up of Doura-Europus and the western wall that had been created out of sand. With his fasces, the bundle of rods and a single axe head, denoting the legate's power to hand out capital punishment, he indicated the left half of the Parthian wall. "The Sixth and Seventh cohorts will lead the assault on this sector of the wall," the legate said. "Fergus, your men shall lead the assault on the sector to the right. Our boats and scorpion bolt-throwers will ensure that any escape across the river will be made impossible. The attack shall begin with our Syrian archers moving forwards to provide cover for the legionaries. Each cohort will be issued with assault ladders. You are to storm the walls, clear the enemy from the ramparts and capture the western gate. Once we have the gates the rest of our forces will pour into the city."

The legate paused and turned to look at his officers with a serious expression. "I want all of you to remind your men that the first soldier who makes it up onto the enemy wall and plants his unit standard there shall be rewarded with the corona muralis. I shall personally place the golden crown on his head." The legate paused to again to let that sink in. Then he turned his attention back to the sand mock-up. "The Palmyran's believe that there are no more than five or six hundred armed defenders inside the city," he exclaimed. "Once we have possession of the gates and are into the city, anyone who continues to fight shall be killed. But," the legate said sharply raising his hand. "If the civilian population surrenders they are not to be harmed. They are to be treated with respect. Make sure that your men understand that any looting, raping or murder will not go unpunished. Trajan is very clear. He doesn't want to capture a devastated, ruined and hostile city. We are going to need Doura-Europus as a staging post for the advance into the heart of Mesopotamia. Have I made myself clear?"

"Sir," one of the centurions of the Third Cyrenaica said. "I understand the reasons to treat the civilian population leniently, but they have refused to surrender. The laws of war dictate that they face the consequences of their decision. When the first battering ram or assault ladder touches the enemy wall, the lives of the people in the city belong to us. My men will not be happy that they have been prevented from taking what should rightfully belong to them."

"I have been clear. The civilian population are not to be harmed unless they put up resistance. Any man caught disobeying these orders shall be punished," the legate growled.

***

As Fergus made his way back to his command post he turned sharply to look at Britannicus, who was walking beside him. His young protégé seemed unusually quiet and despondent.

"I am putting you in command of our attack," Fergus said. "Divide the First cohort into two assault groups. You will lead the first. I will lead the second. Once you reach the wall do not hesitate. I want our boys to be the first to capture those gates."

"Sir, would it not be better to put the primus pilus in command of the assault," Britannicus replied in an uncertain voice. "The First cohort are his men after all and he has the experience Sir."

"No," Fergus snapped switching to his native Briton language. "You are going to lead our men. You have the courage and you are a leader. I recognised that back in Zeugma. And there is only one way in which you are going to gain experience. By doing the fucking job."

"But the disaster with the Parthian catapults Sir..." Britannicus's voice trailed off.

"Listen," Fergus said sharply as he came to a halt and rounded on the young tribune. "Every man makes mistakes. Shit happens," he growled. "When officers like us make mistakes, men die. Sometimes many die. It is just how it is. But if one day you want to be a professional soldier, a legionary officer with your own command. Then you are going to have to get used to sending men to their death. There is no room for sentiment. Your job is to get the job done, nothing more. You are going to make more mistakes. You are going to get more men killed. That's war. But you do not have the right to give up just because of one or two setbacks. You keep going until you either win or die. When you lead your men up onto that fucking wall remember that they will be looking to you for inspiration and leadership. And that's what I too expect to see from you."

***

The trumpet signalling the start of the assault rang out across the desert and from behind their fortifications, officers rose to their feet shouting orders. Hastily the Syrian archers and Balearic slingers began to move forwards, carrying their large light wood screens. Tensely Fergus watched the start of the attack from his command post. The wooden screens would provide enough protection from arrows and spears but could not stand up to a direct hit from one of the Parthian catapults. Luckily the enemy seemed to have only a limited number of war-machines. As the archers and slingers moved towards the western wall of Doura-Europus, the defenders up on the ramparts unleashed a hail of arrows and sling shots at the advancing Romans. From his vantage point Fergus could hear the defiant howls and furious screams of the defenders and the thud and clatter of missiles hammering into the wooden screens. In the open ground a Parthian projectile exploded into a cloud of poisonous vapours. Doggedly the archers kept on moving forwards. Then as they had reached missile range, they lowered their wooden screens to the ground and started to shoot back at the defenders up on the walls. On the left flank of the Roman assault, one of the defensive screens had received a direct hit from an incendiary projectile and was burning fiercely, sending choking black smoke wafting across the battlefield.

Seeing that the archers and slingers in his sector had reached their advanced positions, Fergus quickly turned to his cornicen.

"Order the legionaries to commence their assault," he called out.

A moment later the signal for the general assault to start rang out across the desert. From their trenches where the men had been waiting, the first wave of five hundred men from the First cohort surged forwards in small groups. The legionaries, protected by their shields and those of their comrades, rushed forwards carrying their long wooden assault ladders. Here and there a man was caught by a Parthian arrow and tumbled to the ground, but the cover provided by the Syrian archers was keeping the Parthians from effectively impeding the Roman assault. Fergus bit his lip as he watched the legionaries, led by their officers, storm towards the walls. The moment when the assault would either succeed or fail was rapidly approaching.

Fergus grunted at the sight that had started to unfold before him. Across the open desert in front of the western wall of Doura-Europus, over a thousand heavily-armed legionaries were storming the Parthian defences. The air was thick with missiles whining and whirring in both directions and the shrieks, screams and shouts of thousands of men. As he gazed at the scene, a Parthian projectile went hurtling straight into a small, tight knot of legionaries blowing them apart. The horrible, high-pitched screams of the wounded were clearly audible. Out in front, the first of Britannicus's men had reached the Parthian walls and were raising their ladders against the ramparts. Up on the wall, the Parthian defenders were throwing everything they had at the legionaries below.

"Are the second group ready to advance?" Fergus snapped, as he turned to the primus pilus who was standing beside him watching the assault.

"They are Sir," the commander of the First cohort replied. "But I would advise you not to deploy them yet until we see how your young protégé performs. I do not want the rest of my men being caught out in the open."

Fergus said nothing. The primus pilus was being an arsehole. The officer had been annoyed and jealous that Fergus had not chosen him to lead the assault. For if the attack succeeded, the glory and increase in reputation would be considerable for the officers involved.

At the base of the walls several assault ladders had been pushed up against the defences and the first of the legionaries were scrambling up them, under a murderous and frantic Parthian aerial attack. And amongst the hard-pressed legionaries Fergus suddenly caught sight of Britannicus, distinguishable by his helmet and red cape. The young officer was clutching the banner of the First cohort.

Tensely Fergus gazed at the furious battle that was developing for the walls of the city. On the left flank of the attack, the first of the legionaries seemed to have managed to reach the top of the wall. Hand to hand combat had broken out with the desperate defenders but, as he peered at the fighting, Fergus could not see any Roman unit banners atop the defences.

"Look Sir," the vexillation standard bearer suddenly cried out, pointing to the walls. "That's our banner. It's on the top of the wall. He's done it. The young whelp has done it Sir. He is the first to make it up onto the enemy ramparts. I am sure of it. The corona muralis is his."

Fergus blinked as he stared at the Parthian walls. Then he grunted and raised his eyebrows. The standard bearer was right. The standard of the First cohort of the Fourth legion was being held up atop the walls of Doura-Europus.

As he stared at the fighting more and more legionaries appeared on the walls, scrambling up their ladders and the barrage of Parthian missiles seemed to slacken. On the ramparts the shrieks and screams of desperate men could be heard and as he stared at the scene, a Parthian tumbled from the ramparts and fell screaming to his death.

Fergus had seen enough. Quickly he turned and strode out of his command post in the direction of the dugouts, where the second half of the First Cohort were patiently waiting for the order to advance. As he hastened towards his men, his staff, the primus pilus, cornicen and the standard bearer, clad in his lion's head and holding aloft the square vexillation standard of the Fourth, hurried after him. The centurion in command of the four hundred or so men in the second wave looked surprised as he recognised Fergus. In their dugouts the legionaries were anxiously and silently watching the fate of their comrades up on the walls.

"We go when you see those gates start to open," Fergus snapped, as he knelt on one knee beside the officer and turned his attention to the western gate into Doura-Europus. "Remember the legate's orders. Anyone who surrenders is to be spared. No looting, no raping, no murder of civilians. We are going to need these people to be on our side soon."

The centurion grunted but said nothing, as tensely he turned to stare at the fighting.

Up on the walls of the city the Parthian missile barrage had come to an end, apart from the odd desultory arrow. The Syrian archers and slingers were surging forwards across the corpse littered ground towards the assault ladders in support of the heavy infantry. As he knelt on one knee and stared at the gates, Fergus suddenly saw them start to open. And as they did, a Roman trumpet rang out. A surge of satisfaction went coursing through him. Britannicus and his men had captured the gates. They had done the job they'd been tasked with.

"Follow me," Fergus roared in a loud voice, as he rose to his feet and drew Corbulo's old gladius from his sheath. The steel blade gleamed in the sunlight. Raising it in the air, Fergus started to run towards the city gates and as he did, a great triumphant roar rose from the Roman lines and the four hundred legionaries in the second wave rose and went charging after their commanding officer. As he came through the gates, Fergus was met by a scene of devastation beyond. Black smoke was rising into the clear blue sky from numerous fires. Corpses, pools of blood and discarded weapons lay scattered across the densely packed city streets immediately beyond the walls, and the screams and shrieks of the wounded filled the city with noise. A defiant old woman was perched on the roof of her house, furiously flinging roof tiles down at the Romans in the street. As Fergus looked up at her a Syrian archer sent an arrow straight into her chest, toppling her from her perch. In the narrow streets small groups of legionaries were finishing off the last of the defenders and fanning out into the city. The Parthian resistance looked like it had been broken.

Fergus halted just inside the gates as more and more heavily-armed Roman legionaries poured into the city. Then he caught sight of Britannicus. His protégé was tending to a wounded comrade who was lying in the street coughing up blood. The young tribune too was wounded and bleeding from a cut to his left arm, but it didn't look too serious. In his right hand Britannicus was still clutching the standard of the First cohort. Catching sight of Fergus, Britannicus straightened up. The young officer's face was streaked with sweat and dust and more blood was smeared across his body armour. Hastily he crossed the street towards Fergus.

"We took the gates Sir. Like you ordered us to," Britannicus said quickly. "Doura-Europus is ours Sir."

Chapter Thirty-Six – Trajan's Plan

Spring 116 AD

The narrow twisting city street was crowded and noisy. Shopkeepers stood on the doorsteps of their small dwellings displaying their wares and doing business with the townsfolk whom had come out to buy their daily provisions. Beggars, clad in filthy lice infested clothes sat propped up against walls holding up their hands and dogs were sniffing amongst the piles of discarded rubbish in the alleys. It was morning and in the skies above the city of Doura-Europus a solitary desert hawk was gliding on the air currents, hunting for its next meal. Fergus, clad in his helmet, body armour and wearing his Tribune's cloak, strode on down the busy street followed by Britannicus and his staff and as he did, the haggling townsfolk fell silent and hastily moved out of his way. Fergus however was oblivious to the guarded looks he received from the inhabitants. All throughout the winter that had followed the capture of Doura, the army had kept the vexillation of the Fourth and the whole of the Third Legion in the city on occupation duties. There had been little trouble from most of the locals, whom had swiftly adapted to their new circumstances, all except the priests of a temple whom had publicly denounced the Roman occupation. In retaliation the Roman legate had ordered that the doors to their temple be taken down. And there had been no sign of a Parthian counterattack. The Parthians, it appeared from the intelligence reports, were weak and hopelessly divided by their ongoing civil war. The men from the Third Legion had even found time to erect a triumphal arch on the road, north of Doura-Europus, dedicating the city's capture to the Emperor Trajan. As if it had been the Third who had taken the city, Fergus thought contemptuously. If he remembered correctly it had been Britannicus and the men of the First cohort who had captured the gates and sealed the city's fate. The corona muralis, the golden crown should have belonged to Britannicus. However, as the events of the battle were disputed by a centurion from the Third Legion, the legate had found it expedient to award the decoration to both Britannicus and the centurion from the Third. Still the battle honour won by Britannicus had significantly improved the morale and pride of his men and that was a good thing Fergus thought. Most of the legionaries had been housed in tents outside the city's walls. The legate of the Third Cyrenaica and de facto commander of the city had however chosen to base his HQ in the city home of the former Parthian governor, who had reputedly fled before the assault.

Doura-Europus was not a bad posting Fergus thought, as he made his way towards the Roman HQ, but he missed Galena and his girls. During the winter he'd been granted just ten days leave in which to see them in Zeugma. The blessed time had been far too short. But what was worse was that there had been no news from Adalwolf, nothing at all. And despite writing several times, Galena too had had no news either from Kyna or Dylis on far away Vectis in Britannia. There had been no news from Vectis for over a year now. The lack of news unsettled him but there was nothing he could do about it. At night, in the privacy of his quarters, he'd prayed to every god he knew, imploring them for their divine protection. But the immortals too had remained silent and had provided little comfort. The best thing he'd discovered was to just throw himself into his job.

And he was just about to find out what that job was going to be. For the legate in command of the Doura battle group had, it seemed, that morning received important news and had called all his senior officers to an urgent council of war. Maybe the long-anticipated conquest of Mesopotamia was about to begin.

***

The Roman HQ was located inside an imposing, fortified house, originally built in the Seleucid Greek style, but the newer wings were of Parthian origin. A squad of legionaries stood around the entrance on guard duty. The men's body armour and helmets reflected the sunlight and they seemed to be in a good mood. As Fergus followed by Britannicus, the primus pilus and the eight-man legionary escort strode through the entrance into the building, the guards snapped out a quick, well-practised salute. The officers iron hobnailed boots crunched and rasped on the stone mosaic floor. At the door leading into the HQ conference room more legionary guards were on duty, and this time the decanus in charge stepped forwards and held up his hand, blocking the way.

"Only you Sir," the corporal said quickly addressing, Fergus. "Legate's orders. I am only to allow the senior officers into the room. Your staff will have to wait outside."

Fergus turned and gave Britannicus and the primus pilus a quick little nod. Then he stepped on into the room and the guards closed the door behind him. The legate of the Third Cyrenaica and some of his senior officers were already present, pouring over a large map that had been laid out across a table. In the large room colourful frescoes, depicting hunting scenes, adorned the walls. The window shutters had been closed and in the dim light from burning oil lamps, Fergus caught the scent of incense. Marching up to the legate, Fergus quickly saluted and turned to look down at the map.

"You are probably wondering about the unusual secrecy of this meeting," the legate said, glancing quickly at Fergus and then at the others. "Well there is a reason for that. This morning an imperial courier arrived at my HQ. He has brought with him Trajan's plan for the conquest of Mesopotamia. We are going to be on the move southwards very soon."

The legate paused. "Secrecy, gentlemen, is of the utmost importance. What we discuss here right now shall not be shared with anyone outside of this room. You are not to tell anyone, not even members of your own staff. The men shall only be informed of our destination once we are on the march. Is that clear?"

Around the large table, the officers nodded in agreement.

"Good," the legate continued, gesturing at the map with his fasces. "Please look at the map and refrain from commenting until I am finished."

For a moment the legate remained silent as he gazed down at the map. Then he cleared his throat. "Our offensive has already begun," he said. "Here in the north around Singara, Hatra and Lake Van, Lusius Quietus and the Consul Maximus together with four legions and auxiliaries, have already crossed the Tigris into Adiabene and routed the Parthian vassal king Mebarsapes near Gaugemela. These forces are now poised to advance on Ctesiphon from the north, along the banks of the Tigris. Trajan has arranged for a lookalike of himself to be present in the army, to give the Parthians the impression that he intends to follow the same route, along the Tigris to Ctesiphon, that Alexander the Great used four hundred and fifty years ago. Quietus's and Maximus's secondary task is to conquer and pacify Adiabene and Assyria. But their primary task is to act as a diversion. To keep the eyes and attention of the Parthian King of Kings Osroes firmly on the threat from the north."

"For the real blow, the mortal blow that is going to knock the Parthians out of the war, will not come from the north," the legate snapped. "It is going to come from the west and we are going to deliver it. The despatch that I received says that Trajan secretly left our northern armies over two weeks ago. The emperor is hastening to join us here at Doura-Europus, with a second army, consisting of four fresh legions and auxiliaries - together with us a force of thirty-five thousand men. We are to expect his arrival within a week or so. Once the emperor gets here we are to join forces with him."

The legate paused to look at the stern, expectant faces around the table.

"Once Trajan joins us with his army and supply fleet, we are to descend the Euphrates until we reach the Royal river here at Fallujah. The speed of our advance is going to be crucial. Nothing must be allowed to delay us. Trajan wants to strike at the heart of Mesopotamia before king Osroes is even aware of our approach. From Fallujah the Royal river, which is actually a man-made canal connecting the Euphrates to the Tigris, will lead us into the very heart of Mesopotamia and Babylonia. Our objectives, gentlemen, are the great cities of Seleucia, here on the west bank of the Tigris and the Parthian winter capital Ctesiphon, directly opposite Seleucia on the east bank of the Tigris. Make no mistake. These cities together are huge, over twice the land surface of Rome. Their walls are mighty. No Roman army has ever taken them. They are said to have a population of six hundred thousand people and the fertile farm lands between the rivers could support another half-a million inhabitants. These cities form the major Parthian population centres. Ctesiphon is the centre of their government. Once we capture both cities it is only logical that Parthia as a state will collapse and the war will be over."

Chapter Thirty-Seven – Reconnaissance

The sun beat down on the stony, featureless desert. Along the wide, sluggish Euphrates, a thin strip of lush green vegetation provided a welcome relief from the endless monotony of the desert. Fergus, his face half covered in a Bedouin style keffiyeh, sat on his horse peering ahead as he walked the beast down the desert road. To the east along the course of the great river he could make out a dust cloud in the clear blue noon sky. It seemed to be drawing closer. Behind him, coming down the road the two hundred and forty Roman cavalrymen of reconnaissance group "Scythica" also seemed to have spotted the approaching dust cloud. It could mean only one thing, Fergus thought with a frown. People. Turning in his saddle he raised his fist in the air, calling the small column to a halt.

"Britannicus take half the men and move out into the desert," Fergus called out to the tribune who was riding directly behind him holding up the square vexillation banner of the Fourth Scythica Legion. "If they are hostile, prepare to take them in the flank. No prisoners. We can't handle them."

"Do you think they are hostile?" Britannicus asked as he warily studied the approaching dust cloud.

"I don't know," Fergus replied. "But I am taking no chances. Be professional and polite with the civilians but make sure that you have a plan to kill everyone you meet. Now go."

Quickly the young tribune turned his horse and, shouting an order to the four Roman cavalry turmae, squadrons who were following him, Britannicus started to move out into the desert. Calmly Fergus kept on moving down the road towards the dust cloud as the remaining four squadrons reformed around him. A week had passed since Trajan had arrived in Doura-Europus and the advance south down the Euphrates had begun. The sight of four complete legions and a dozen auxiliary cohorts, some of whom had come from as far away as the German frontier, had been a magnificent and splendid occasion. Thirty-five thousand soldiers and a huge fleet of supply boats had descended on the small desert trading post and amongst them, Fergus had caught a glimpse of emperor Trajan himself, clad in his splendid purple imperial robes. And with the emperor's arrival, news had come that the senate, faraway in Rome, had granted Trajan the honorary title of Parthicus for his conquest of Osrhoene and northern Mesopotamia. It had been an auspicious start to the campaign. The start of the Roman advance on Seleucia and Ctesiphon had been preceded by a general council of war, the outcome of which had been to assign Fergus command of one of the two cavalry reconnaissance groups that would precede the main Roman force. The two hundred and forty troopers, the combined cavalry components of the Fourth and Third legions, together with a small band of Palmyran guides and Parthian translators, had been formed into recon cavalry group "Scythica". Their task was to scout ahead of the main Roman army, keeping to the west bank of the Euphrates whilst the second cavalry recon group "Parthica" had responsibility for the east bank.

Warily Fergus fixed his eyes on the approaching dust cloud. Only a considerable body of men could create such a cloud. His orders were clear. He must avoid any contact with strong Parthian forces and report back any problems or threats to the main force that was descending the Euphrates, half a day behind him. But from the cloud of dust it was hard to tell what was coming towards them.

"Form up into a wedge," Fergus cried out as he twisted round and shouted at the troopers massed behind him on the desert road. "Two squadrons on either side of the road."

In response the cavalry decurions, officers, repeated his orders and the Roman reconnaissance group began to form up in tight V shaped formations, with their officers right up at the front. Out on their desert flank, Fergus could see that Britannicus too had formed his men into a V shaped wedge and was moving parallel to him. At Fergus's side his cornicen shifted in the saddle of his horse and brought his trumpet up into a more comfortable position. Fergus kept walking his horse down the road. Ahead, the dust cloud was closer now and in the distance, he could make out figures, horses and camels. As the two parties steadily approached each other along the road, Fergus frowned as he saw that many of the camels were roped together and heavily laden with boxes, sacks and amphorae. The men leading them were bearded, dressed in long white robes and their heads were covered in Bedouin style keffiyeh.

"Looks like a desert trade caravan Sir," the cornicen, said as he gazed at the newcomers. On the road a hundred yards away, the foremost horsemen and camels had come to a halt and were staring at the Roman cavalry patrol. Raising his fist in the air, Fergus motioned his men to come to a halt. For a minute the road remained silent as both parties eyed each other warily. Out in the desert, Britannicus had turned his squadrons towards the road and was slowly moving in on the trade caravan's exposed flank. With a grunt Fergus beckoned for one of his Parthian translators to approach. The man, a swarthy looking Greek from Doura, bowed hastily as he came up to Fergus.

"Come with me. Do exactly as I say," Fergus said sharply as he urged his horse forwards towards the stalled caravan. And as he did, one of the traders did the same, moving out to meet Fergus half way. Cautiously Fergus examined the man on horseback who approached him. The trader's face was half hidden under his keffiyeh and he looked tense. His eyes darted from Fergus to the Roman troopers out in the desert.

"Ask him who he is and what he is doing here?" Fergus growled as he brought his horse to a halt.

Obligingly the Greek translated the message and in response the merchant gabbled something in an alien language and quickly pointed at Britannicus's troopers, who were slowly moving in towards the caravan.

"He says that he is a merchant from Charax bound for Palmyra," the Greek translated. "He says he has a valuable cargo from India for the merchants in Palmyra. He doesn't want any trouble but your men out in the desert are making him nervous."

"Tell him that we shall have to search his men and his animals," Fergus snapped, as he eyed the man. "Tell him that if he complies willingly, that no harm will come to him, his men or cargo."

Hastily the Greek translated, and the merchant replied quickly, turning to look at Fergus with a surprised, questioning look.

"What are you looking for?" the Greek said. "He wants to know what you are looking for?"

"That is none of his goddamn business," Fergus replied sharply. "Now no more nonsense. Have him tell his men to dismount and get down on their knees. My men will inspect his goods. If he cooperates I promise him that all will be well, and he will be free to continue on his journey."

As the translator translated Fergus's words, the trader started to look distinctly unimpressed and annoyed, but he had the good sense not to put his feelings into words.

"He agrees," the Greek said triumphantly as the merchant turned and bellowed something to his own people.

***

As Fergus watched the trade caravan moving away up the road, he sensed Britannicus riding towards him. The young tribune too was gazing at the merchants and their heavily laden pack animals.

"Was that wise Sir to let them go like that?" Britannicus said as he came to a halt beside Fergus. "They could report what they have seen. There could be spies amongst them."

"Sure," Fergus replied nodding, "There is a chance of that. But news of our approach is going to be impossible to hide and we can't kill everyone we meet. I think they were a genuine caravan. The Palmyran guides spoke to the leader and they seem satisfied he was speaking the truth and we found no weapons amongst their trade goods." Fergus paused, as he gazed at the disappearing caravan. Then he turned his attention back to the road leading eastwards. "Come we must keep moving," he growled. "There is still some way to go before we reach Fallujah."

The village nestled amongst the green, cultivated fields that bordered the blue waters of the Euphrates. It was getting late, as Fergus leading his troopers approached the small settlement of mud brick huts and bleating goats. The village was the first that they had come across. A goat-herder holding a stick was the first to see them and after a moment's hesitation, the boy went racing into the village followed moments later by a barking dog.

Cautiously Fergus kept to the road as he eyed the small cluster of mudbrick huts and reed covered roofs. The village looked poor but the fertile fields that surrounded it were filled with an abundance of crops, wheat, barley, millet, rice and date palms. A few women, wearing head scarves were bent over; at work in the fields. They straightened up as they heard the barking dog and gazed impassively at the approaching Roman column.

Suddenly a furtive movement beside one of the huts caught Fergus's attention. A man stepped forwards whirling something above his head and a stone bullet smacked into the shield of one of his cavalrymen. The attack was followed by another man carrying a bow, who stepped out of the cover of another hut and released a solitary arrow that thudded into a horse's flank sending the beast crashing and screaming to the ground and throwing its rider.

"Britannicus take a squadron around the edge of the village," Fergus roared as another stone sling shot went whizzing past. "Cut off their retreat. The rest of you follow me!" And without waiting for an answer, Fergus turned his horse, pulled his long cavalry Spatha sword from its sheath and went galloping towards the village. He was immediately followed by a mass of charging Roman horsemen. Amongst the cluster of mud-brick huts, Fergus caught sight of six or seven men frantically sprinting across the fields towards the blue waters of the Euphrates. Amongst their crops the women too were running but back towards their homes. They were screaming as they ran. Swerving amongst the huts, Fergus urged his horse on after the men who had attacked them. The bank of the river was protected by a long man-made dyke, to prevent flooding, and as he galloped across the fields ahead of him, one of the running men tripped, but as he rose to his feet he was swiftly cut down by a sharp Roman sword. The foremost fugitives had reached the dyke and were desperately clambering up it, when Britannicus and his men came charging along the top of the dyke, their long steel swords gleaming in the sunlight. One man was nearly decapitated before the remainder sank to their knees and raised their hands, crying out in terrified, pleading voices.

Grimly Fergus slowed his horse as he came up to the survivors. The men were looking up at the Roman cavalrymen and pleading with them in their unintelligible, alien language.

"Where is the fucking translator?" Fergus bellowed as he turned to look around.

"I am here Sir," the Greek cried out in a hasty voice, as he rode up to the group of angry, frustrated looking Roman horsemen.

"Ask them why they attacked my men," Fergus hissed, his face dark with anger as he turned his attention to the captives. "And tell them that if I don't like their answers. I will burn their village and hang each one of them from those trees over there."

As the Greek translated, the kneeling survivors seemed to all speak at once, their desperate terrified faces turning to look from one Roman to the next.

The Greek translator cleared his throat as he prepared to translate the answer. "They were told that you Romans," the Greek translator paused. "That you would eat their infants and drink the blood of their women. They were ordered to fight and resist you."

"Who ordered them to do this?" Fergus snapped as he stared at the captives.

"The King Sir," the Greek replied at last. "They say that the King of Kings, Osroes, has ordered everyone to resist and fight the invaders. He has issued a proclamation across all the lands between the two rivers. Any man who fails to resist the invaders is a coward; to be cast out of his village and home."

"And where is the king now?" Fergus growled.

"They don't know Sir," the Greek said at last, after he had finished listening to the panic-stricken voices of the men kneeling on the ground. "They are just simple farmers. But they say that the king is more afraid of his internal enemies than of the Roman invasion. They say that the king of kings is a weak man."

"Ask them if they know where the main Parthian army is encamped?" Fergus snapped.

As he finished translating and listening to the reply he received, the Greek shrugged and turned to Fergus.

"They say Sir," the Greek said carefully. "That as far as they know there are no significant Parthian forces between here and Seleucia. Most of the fighting men are away fighting Osroes's rival in the east."

"Are they saying that Seleucia and Ctesiphon are unprotected?" Fergus said as he raised his eyebrows in surprise.

"Yes Sir," the Greek replied. "That seems to be what they are implying."

Chapter Thirty-Eight – Bluff or Desperation

On both sides of the narrow Royal river the columns of marching Roman legionaries and auxiliaries stretched away to the horizon. The rhythmic tramp of their heavy boots, the thud of horses' hooves, the mooing and braying of pack animals and the groan and creak of dozens of wagons, filled the morning air. Out on the canal Fergus could see a long convoy of boats, tied together by thick ropes and piled high with supplies and provisions. All were heading eastwards towards the Tigris. The sight of the Roman army on the march was magnificent. Looking tired and unshaven, Fergus led the cavalry troopers of his reconnaissance group in the opposite direction, as he searched for the legate of the Third Cyrenaica and his HQ staff. The cavalry troopers were walking their horses in a long single file, their uniforms and horses soaked with sweat and stained with dried mud. Around them in the pleasant, green, muddy and irrigated fields that had replaced the desert, a vast abundance of crops could be seen and amongst the greenery Fergus could see villages of mud-brick with reed covered roofs. The locals had paused in their labours in the fields to stare in silence at the foreign invaders.

A sudden commotion on the other side of the narrow canal caught Fergus's attention. On the far bank a column of legionaries, at least a thousand strong had come to a halt and were turning to face something in the fields to the north. The harsh cries of the legionary officers rang out, drifting across the canal. Fergus frowned. What was going on? The legionaries seemed to be forming a battle line. Then he gasped, as amongst the green fields to the north, he suddenly caught sight of a band of horsemen clustered around a man who was holding up a banner. The horsemen were Parthians but there were only thirty or forty of them. Fergus raised his eyebrows in surprise as across the canal the small band of Parthian horsemen slowly started to form a wedge and move towards the Roman line.

"What the fuck are they doing," Britannicus called out, as he too stared at the scene. "Are they going to attack? That is madness, suicide."

Fergus said nothing as he stared at the approaching band of horsemen. Down the column of Roman cavalrymen following him, every eye had turned to stare at the small band of Parthian riders. On the other side of the canal, the Roman legionaries had formed a line, three deep with the first ranks down on one knee, their spears and shields forming a barrier of steel and wood. In the fields the Parthians had begun to pick up the pace as their wedge moved towards the Romans and, as he gazed at them, Fergus suddenly saw their target. Amongst the mass of legionaries, he caught sight of the gleaming eagle standard, the Aquila of the Third Gallica. The Parthians were going to make a glorious but foolish attempt to capture the legionary eagle. It was madness, sheer desperation. The Parthian holding up his own banner must be a local lord and the riders with him his men at arms. There could be no other explanation.

On the other side of the canal the brave band of Parthians suddenly cried out. Raised their weapons in the air and broke into a gallop as they charged the Roman lines. Fergus slowly shook his head in wonder. As the Parthians with their proud lord at the very point of the wedge came charging towards the Romans, they were met by a murderous volley of spears that brought down every single man and horse in a horrible, screaming tangled crashing mess. From the Roman lines a roar rose, as the legionaries swiftly ran forwards to finish off their fallen enemies. The fight was over. Slowly Fergus turned to look away. What madness had infected men to so needlessly sacrifice themselves? And as he thought about it, an uneasy realisation came to him. The local population did not want the Romans here.

***

The legate of the Third Cyrenaica and his staff were mounted on horses and were leading a column of legionaries along the bank of the canal. Catching sight of the gleaming golden eagle standard, Fergus hastened towards them.

"Sir," Fergus cried out as he rode up to the legate and saluted. "I received your message to report to you in person. You said you had new orders for us."

The legate glanced sideways at Fergus as he kept moving. "Yes," he growled. "Parthica are away on the other side of the canal screening our northern flank. That means Scythica get the honour of being the first to reach Seleucia. I want you to take your men and ride ahead to the city. Trajan wants Seleucia to fall quickly and preferably without a fight. You are to convey a message to its citizens from the emperor. If the city opens its gates to us, the inhabitants shall be spared and treated with respect. However if they close their gates to us, then they shall perish, their city shall be stormed and burned and the survivors sold into slavery. They will probably tell you to fuck off, but Trajan thinks it's worth a try. Is that clear tribune?"

"Yes Sir," Fergus said with a nod. Then quickly he turned his horse away and calling out to his men to follow him, he started out at a trot heading south-eastward along the Royal river.

***

The walls of Seleucia were like nothing Fergus had ever seen before. Huge blocks of stone had been hewn and precisely fitted together, forming an imposing and formidable defensive barrier two or three miles long. Mightier and higher than those of Antioch, the walls were reinforced by huge towers and on the battlements, Fergus could see small figures and proud, streaming Parthian banners fluttering in the warm western wind. From within the city a horn suddenly rang out. Raising his fist in the air Fergus brought his two hundred and forty cavalrymen to a halt along the banks of the canal. The royal river seemed to end not far from the city. It was morning and as he gazed at the Mesopotamian metropolis, Fergus could see that Seleucia occupied a gridiron space along the western banks of the Tigris. In the flat flood plains around the city, the lush muddy irrigated fields were filled with crops and toiling labourers. Once more the horn rang out from within the city and this time the workers in the fields, catching sight of the Roman cavalrymen, broke into a sudden mass panic. Abandoning their animals and tools, the people started to run, fleeing towards the nearest city gate which was still open. Calmly, without moving, Fergus watched the mass panic he'd caused. Switching his gaze towards the city gate he could see that armed men had appeared just outside the entrance. They however seemed few in number and more concerned with the fleeing civilians than with the Roman cavalry patrol.

"The gates are still open," Britannicus exclaimed in an eager voice. "Should we not try to rush them now Sir?"

"Rush them," Fergus replied with a frown, as he watched the fleeing populace. "Those are not our orders. This is a city of around three hundred thousand people. You want to capture such a huge place with just two hundred and forty men?"

"It crossed my mind Sir," Britannicus said with a confident grin.

"No," Fergus said quietly. "There is only one way in which to capture a city of this size with the men that we have."

"I don't understand Sir," Britannicus said.

Fergus sighed. It was time to let the young tribune in on the plan he'd been concocting and refining on the ride towards Seleucia.

"We are going to be the ones who capture Seleucia," Fergus said in a quiet, determined voice, as he turned to his protégé.

"History shall record that it was us. That's going to be my achievement and I am going to do it with a ruse."

"They are closing their gates on us Sir," the cornicen cried out, as he raised his hand and pointed.

"So, they are," Fergus muttered, as the huge iron-reinforced gates began to close. Not all the civilians had managed to pass into the city and the unfortunate ones now turned, fleeing and hurrying away southwards in the shadow of the massive fortifications. In the fields an abandoned cow was mooing loudly.

"Come, let's introduce ourselves and see if my ruse works," Fergus growled, as he gestured to his small escort and urged his horse towards the city gate. "The rest of you stay here out of missile range. Britannicus, raise the white flag and keep an eye on those archers up on the walls. Let's hope they understand the meaning of a white flag."

Cautiously Fergus rode up to the city gate, keeping a tense eye on the bowmen he could see up on the walls. Behind him Britannicus, holding up the white flag of truce, remained silent as he too gazed up at the Parthian defenders. But as the small party of Roman horsemen approached the gates, no one took a shot at them and all remained quiet. Pausing a few yards from the massive sturdy-looking iron-reinforced gates, Fergus examined them. It would take a battering ram some considerable time to break them down and, from the construction of the gates he could see specially designed holes in the roof, from which the defenders could hurl boiling oil and other incendiary material. Raising his head, he looked up at the defenders peering down at him from their fortifications.

"Translate," Fergus snapped as he turned to the nervous looking Greek translator sitting on his horse behind him. "Citizens of Seleucia," Fergus called out in a loud voice.

"Emperor Trajan and his army approaches your city. We are many. We are powerful. We have defeated your armies. We have come to end this war once and for all. Your king Osroes has agreed to an armistice and has agreed to surrender your city. Under the agreed terms you are to open your gates to us and allow my men to enter your city. In exchange you and your city shall be spared and treated with respect. Your leading citizens will retain their privileges and rank. Your merchants may go about their business unhindered. But defy us, defy the solemn agreement that your king has made, and your city shall be raised, and its population sold into slavery. Your city rights and privileges shall be forfeit. You have an hour to make up your mind and open your gates. After that, if your gates remain closed, we shall consider you in breach of the recently signed armistice."

As the Greek finished translating the message in a loud voice, Fergus patiently made him do it again in Greek and then Aramaic. From the walls of Seleucia, the reply was silence. Gesturing for Britannicus and his small escort to follow him, Fergus turned to give the defenders up on the walls a final glance. Then slowly he turned and coolly started to walk his horse away from the gates and back to where the rest of his recon group were waiting.

"I didn't know an armistice had been signed," Britannicus murmured from the corner of his mouth.

"No armistice has been signed," Fergus muttered. "It's a complete fabrication that I just invented but the question is, do the people of Seleucia know this. Do they risk going against the wishes of their king of kings?"

For a moment the young tribune looked shocked. Then a grin appeared on his lips and slowly he shook his head as the small cavalry troop re-joined their comrades.

"Let's see if the ruse works," Fergus muttered, as he turned to gaze back at the city. "Unless Osroes is himself inside the city, which I doubt, the citizens will have no time to find out the truth. They must decide now whether we are telling the truth or are bluffing. They will be taking a decision without knowing all the facts. Do they risk defying us and their king or do they surrender? We will know within the hour how much faith these people have in themselves and their king."

***

Within the hour Fergus triumphantly clenched his hand into a fist, as he saw the gates into the great metropolis slowly start to open. Amongst the Roman cavalrymen an excited stir swept through the ranks. Peering at the gates, Fergus saw a small party of mounted Parthians coming out of the city. One of the Parthians was holding up a white flag. Urging his horse towards the Parthians, Fergus, accompanied by his staff and a small escort, rode towards the men, slowing his mount as he came up to them. The Parthians were clad in armour, helmets and had long black beards. They looked stern, sullen and unhappy, as they gazed at Fergus and his men. Patiently Fergus waited for the emissaries to speak first.

Across from him one of the Parthian's, clad in fine rich robes, was the first to speak, doing so in a harsh, unapologetic sounding voice.

As the man finished speaking, the nervous Greek from Doura seemed to be struggling to translate the Parthian's words.

"He says Sir," the translator stammered. "He says that he is the governor and military commander of the great city of Seleucia and that he surrenders the city to you. He asks only that your men do not enter the city until your emperor arrives. He asks you to confine your men to guarding the city gate. He also wishes to obtain guarantees that his soldiers will be treated with respect and honour as is customary for an honourable, defeated foe."

Slowly and coolly Fergus nodded his acceptance.

"Tell him that I accept his surrender and his terms," Fergus replied. "Trajan shall be here soon. Tell him that he has made the right decision."

Chapter Thirty-Nine – Across the Tigris

The legionaries had stripped to the waist, discarding their helmets, weapons and body armour and were sweating and groaning as bare-chested, they struggled to lift the portable boat up on to the wooden rollers. Close by, teams of ox and water buffalo stood ready to drag the flat-bottomed boat from the Royal river to the welcoming waters of the Tigris, a half a mile away.

"Come on, come on, put your backs into it," a centurion roared as, clasping his vine staff, he strode along the teams of straining legionaries and huge horned water buffalo, which were hauling the boats through the fields. Fergus surrounded by his staff, stood watching the progress from the shade of a palm tree. It was morning and a day had passed since Seleucia had capitulated and Trajan and the main Roman force had arrived. The surrender of such a great city should have been a huge moment but apart from a pat on the shoulder from the legate of the Third Cyrenaica, Fergus had received no official recognition for his triumph. And the reason was clear. There was still much work to be done. Trajan and the senior officers were busy. Directly opposite Seleucia, across the Tigris on the eastern bank, the Parthian winter capital of Ctesiphon was still in enemy hands. But not for much longer, Fergus thought with grim satisfaction. Along the western bank of the Tigris, below the protective dykes, parties of legionaries were preparing to cross the wide, sluggish river. Under the palm tree, Fergus at last stirred, turned and followed by his staff he started out through the lush, waterlogged fields towards the earthen dykes that marked the edge of the Tigris river.

A mile to the north, the massive walls of Seleucia reflected the bright morning light and everywhere he looked he could see Roman soldiers, army tents, cavalry mounts, campfires, pack animals and wagons. There was no sign of any of the locals, who had been working these fields only yesterday. The crops that they had been tending had been trampled underfoot, ruined and squashed by the work parties, dragging their boats overland towards the Tigris. As Fergus approached the earthen dykes that ran along the western bank of the river, he could see the men of the First cohort sitting around, resting in small groups. At his command post close to another clump of palm trees, the cohort standard had been driven into the soft ground and the standard bearer seemed to be asleep, his back leaning against the wooden shaft. The legionary guards saluted smartly as Fergus entered the rudimentary shelter.

"How long before we go Sir?" Britannicus called out in a cheerful, excited voice.

Fergus glanced quickly at his protégé.

"Soon," he growled. "They are hauling the boats across to the river now. Get some rest. It's going to be a long day."

"Have you ever taken part in a river assault Sir," Britannicus asked as he pulled his pugio knife from his belt and turned to examine the gleaming steel.

"I crossed the Danube during the Dacian war. Does that count?" Fergus replied, as he sat down on a chair that had been taken from a nearby village and wearily rubbed his face with his hand.

"Do you really believe that the war will be over when we capture Ctesiphon Sir," Britannicus said as he replaced his pugio in his belt.

"Shut up," Fergus growled tiredly, as he closed his eyes.

Fergus's chance at catching a quick nap however was short lived, for soon a hand was shaking him awake. It was Britannicus.

"Sir, message from the legate," Britannicus said quickly.

With a sigh, Fergus rose to his feet and turned to the soldier standing in the entrance of his command post. Hastily the tribune from the Third Cyrenaica saluted. The boy could not be any older than nineteen or twenty.

"The legate sent me Sir," the young staff officer said in a stiff, posh accent. "I am to show you your objective once we cross the Tigris."

"Show me," Fergus growled.

Following the young officer out of his command post, Fergus climbed up the earthen embankment that prevented the Tigris from flooding. On the top of the dyke he had a clear view of the wide, slow moving river. Along the water's western bank, the first of the Roman assault boats were being floated and the cries and shouts of the engineers and work parties was clearly audible. For a moment the young tribune from the Third Cyrenaica gazed at the Tigris in silence. Across the water the massive, imposing walls of Ctesiphon looked very similar to Seleucia. It was Fergus's first look at the Parthian capital and for a moment, he allowed his eyes to linger. But beyond the stone walls and huge towers there was not much else to see. Raising his hand, the staff officer from the Third suddenly pointed at a cluster of buildings on the eastern bank, that lay a mile or so outside the city walls. In the harbour of what looked like a suburb of Ctesiphon, Fergus caught sight of a small man-made harbour crowded with Parthian fishing boats and transports. Amongst them Fergus could see figures moving about.

"See that settlement Sir," the tribune said in his posh voice. "That is one of the suburbs of Ctesiphon and an important harbour for the river traffic on the Tigris. That is your objective. You are to lead your men across the river and take the settlement and its river harbour. The legate wants you to capture those boats intact. So, you will have to move fast," the staff officer said. "Under no circumstances are the Parthians allowed to escape or burn their boats. We are going to need them afterwards. Is that clear Sir?"

"Any idea of the resistance that we are likely to face?" Fergus growled, as he studied the suburb across the water.

"No," the young staff officer replied. "But judging from the weak resistance we have encountered so far, I wouldn't say it will be a problem."

And with that the tribune from the Third saluted smartly and turned away leaving Fergus standing on the top of the dyke gazing out across the Tigris.

***

As the Roman trumpet rang out Fergus turned to Britannicus. "Take half the men and land them south of the harbour," he snapped, speaking in his native Briton language. "I will take the remainder and land north of the settlement. We will meet you in the middle. Treat the civilians with respect but have a plan to kill everyone you meet. And Britannicus, make sure that the Parthians don't burn those boats. The legate says we are going to need them."

"Yes Sir. Good luck Sir," Britannicus said hastily, in an excited voice. Then he was hastening away along the top of the earthen dyke, shouting orders to his men. Fergus watched him go. Then he scrambled down the side of the dyke, and with his staff and escort following, he scrambled into a boat. All along the western banks of the Tigris the nine hundred odd men of the First cohort of the Fourth Legion were surging down the side of the dyke and piling into their assault boats. As he pushed his way towards the stern and found himself a place right up at the prow, Fergus tensely turned to gaze at the eastern bank. There was no visible sign of the enemy, but they had to be out there. Surely, they would make a stand in defence of their capital. In the river, two legionaries stripped to the waist, were standing in the water holding the flat-bottomed boat in position against the weak current. They were the last to scramble aboard, as the legionaries manning the oars in the packed assault craft began to row out into the river.

Tensely Fergus turned to look downstream where the score of Roman assault craft were rowing furiously for the opposite bank. The boats were packed with heavily armed legionaries. The soldier's shields, body armour and helmets gleamed in the morning sunlight and the creak and groan of timbers and the splash of the oars in the river were the only noise. Out on the river there was no sign of enemy ships. On the extreme left flank, Fergus caught sight of the proud standard of the First cohort. That was Britannicus's boat and he was doing as ordered, leading half the assault force towards the south of the settlement.

"Faster, faster," a centurion at the back of the boat shouted, as he turned on the rowers manning the oars.

From one of the neighbouring boats a sudden warning cry rent the relative calm, and the next moment a fountain of water shot up into the air in between the Roman boats. Fergus gasped in shock. Another warning cry and suddenly he caught sight of a dark projectile arching towards them. The Parthian projectile landed in the river with a great splash, so close that it drenched some of the rowers.

"Fuck," Fergus swore as quickly he turned to stare at the eastern bank. The Parthian catapults were beginning to find their range.

"Move it. Move," the centurion at the back screamed at his men. In the packed assault craft, the stoic legionaries, unable to move, remained silent as all stared tensely at the approaching river bank. If they were to be hit and sunk there would be no chance of rescue. The weight of their body armour would take them straight to the bottom of the river. In the river another fountain of water erupted, as a boat survived another near miss. Fergus growled in frustration as he tried to locate the Parthian catapults on the eastern bank, but he couldn't see them.

"Row boys. Row. Fucking row," the centurion screamed, as the officer grabbed a spear and began to push it into the river in a futile effort to make them go faster.

The eastern bank was getting closer. Out in the river two more fountains of water shot up into the air, as the huge rocks being hurled by the Parthian artillery slammed down into the Tigris. But so far, they had missed their targets. From the packed Roman boats, Fergus could hear shouts and cursing. The rowers were going full out as the small armada raced towards the shore. Then with a harsh grating noise the boat slid up onto the sandy bank, and with a great cry of relief the legionaries surged over the side, splashing into the shallow water. Fergus too leapt down into the water and as he did, he drew his gladius, Corbulo's old sword from its sheath. Along the river bank to the north of the cluster of buildings, the remainder of the Roman boats too were coming into land. Hastily Fergus turned to look southwards along the river bank, but the buildings and the course of the river prevented him from seeing what had become of Britannicus and his men. Splashing through the water, he clambered up the earthen dyke, as along the bank his men were doing the same.

Beyond the dyke he caught sight of irrigated fields that separated the suburb from the massive walls of Ctesiphon, a mile away. The fields were covered with crops and they seemed deserted.

"Take your men around the edge of the village," Fergus roared at a centurion. "Find and silence those catapults. Then re-join us at the harbour. Go."

With a quick nod of acknowledgement, the officer turned and began shouting orders to his company. Fergus too hastened away, leading his remaining men towards the buildings. In the riverside suburb he could see nobody. The place looked completely deserted. Quickly the four hundred men with him, began to form a battle-line centred on their companies and squads and led by their officers. The pace of their advance however slowed as they approached the settlement. Where were the Parthians? Was it really going to be so easy Fergus thought, as his wary eyes darted from one building to the next. In the eerie silence the crunch, clank and creak of the Roman legionary's armour and boots was the only noise. Warily, clutching their shields and spears and led by their officers, the Romans began to enter and fan out into the suburb as they headed for the harbour. Fergus paused at a cross roads between two streets and was about to turn to his cornicen, when ahead of him a Roman voice suddenly shouted a warning.

The next moment all hell seemed to break out. From doorways, windows and the roofs of the buildings around them, a barrage of stones, arrows, roof tiles and stone slingers bullets came raining down on the Roman troops in the streets. Cries and screams rent the still morning air, as Fergus caught a glimpse of the furious, screaming defenders, who had appeared from their hiding places. In the road ahead, a legionary sank to his knees and collapsed sideways into the street, bleeding heavily from a face wound. Another soldier staggered backwards against a wall, dropped his shield and reached out to clutch his throat, which had been torn open and was spewing forth blood. Fergus too cried out in pain and shock as something struck him hard on his shoulder armour and bounced away. Instinctively he went crashing sideways into the relative cover of a wall. His shoulder ached but there was no time to feel the pain. Around him, the quiet streets had turned into a shrieking, bloody ambush. A few legionaries were lying motionless in the street as the hail of projectiles showed no sign of abating.

"House to house, no prisoners," Fergus roared over the din, as his eyes darted from doorway to roof top. "House to house. Clear the fucking street."

There was no way of knowing whether his men had heard or understood him. With a savage, furious cry Fergus turned and kicked down the flimsy door into the nearest building. Then he was into the dark building. In a room immediately to his right, a shape seemed to come at him and without thinking, Fergus stabbed him, feeling the steel slice into flesh, as behind him his staff came piling into the home. Fergus was rewarded by a deep groan. In the dim light he saw a man stagger backwards, still clutching a small knife. The man had no armour or helmet and looked like a civilian. Ahead down a short corridor, a flight of stone steps seemed to lead up onto the roof of the building. Storming up it, Fergus emerged into the clear bright daylight and was just in time to see a young man, no more than a boy, whirling a sling and targeting a squad of legionaries in the street below. As the boy turned and caught sight of Fergus his face went pale with fright and shock. Silently and swiftly Fergus lunged and before the boy could react, he sent the slinger flying and yelling down into the street below, where he landed with a painful thud.

In the house below a woman was screaming in a high-pitched wailing voice. Startled, Fergus felt something whizz past his head. Turning to stare down the street, he saw a girl and a boy crouching on the neighbouring roof. The pair were hurling roof tiles at the legionaries in the street below. Hastily Fergus retreated down the stairs and as he did he met his cornicen, standard bearer and legionary escort. The woman's wailing had abruptly come to an end and a large pool of blood was spreading out onto the dirt floor.

"We go house to house," Fergus roared as he pushed past his men. "Kill everyone we meet until the resistance ends. Follow me."

Emerging into the daylight Fergus was met with screaming, shrieking chaos. In the street across from him, a squad of legionaries were pressed up against a wall, pinned down, as they sought shelter from the barrage of missiles. Further down the street of terraced buildings, another squad of eight men were kicking down doors and entering the homes. Inside the buildings the furious shouts and yells from the Roman legionaries were clearly audible, as they savagely and brutally silenced the occupants. Pressing himself up against the wall of the house, Fergus gazed across the street at the squad of legionaries who were pinned down by a hail of missiles. And as he stared at them, a furious woman, clad completely in black, came rushing out of a doorway holding a rock with both hands. The woman seemed intent on using it to crush a soldier's head but before she could get close, she was brought down by a Roman spear. With a grunt Fergus leapt away from the wall and went sprinting across the intersection and straight at the doorway of a building. And as he did so, something struck his helmet nearly knocking him off balance.

With a savage cry he launched himself at the door and went straight through, crashing on into the hallway beyond. As he recovered his balance and his sword swept around him in a defensive reaction, he saw that he was alone. Behind him he heard shouts and the sound of running boots. As his eyes adjusted to the dim light inside the building, he saw that he was in a rich man's home. Frescoes adorned the walls and comfortable looking couches and a fine wooden table furnished the main room. In a corner an oil lamp was still alight, and the smell of incense hung heavy in the air. The home seemed deserted, but as he caught sight of the stairs leading up onto the roof, he saw that they had been barricaded with broken pieces of furniture and rocks. Above him he could hear shouting in a foreign language and the thud of feet.

"Burn the house down," Fergus yelled as he turned to his men, who had followed him into the house. "Set them on fire. If they refuse to surrender they shall burn."

Emerging out into the street, Fergus saw that the Roman squad who had been pinned down had managed to extricate themselves and were busy kicking down doors and going house to house. The hail of missiles too seemed to have died down, but not the shrieking, wailing and screaming. Behind him he heard voices cursing and then the unmistakeable crackle and roar of fire.

"We keep moving," Fergus cried out. "We need to reach the harbour. The Parthians are not to be allowed to destroy those boats."

Taking a quick peek down the street, he darted out of the shelter of the doorway and went racing down the street in the direction of the harbour. Crouching in the shade of a wall, Fergus's eyes darted from doorway to roof top, as he waited for his men to catch up with him. From the street, down which he'd just come, thick black smoke was pouring out of the doorway and windows of the rich man's house. And as he turned to stare at the burning building, he heard a heartfelt shriek and a man tumbled from the roof overcome by the smoke. A moment later another man, his body alight, came staggering out of the doorway into the street only to collapse and die with the hungry flames eating away at his body.

Grimly Fergus turned to peer down the street ahead. The suburb was not large and in the distance, he thought he caught a sudden glimpse of sunlight reflecting on armour. Were those Britannicus's men? It was impossible to tell. Behind him his men were crouching along the wall, clutching their shields and swords. To his right a column of black smoke was rising into the air, as another building went up in flames. Down an alley he could hear Roman voices shouting to each other. The defenders had not been soldiers, Fergus realised with a shock. They had been civilians defending their homes. Surely, they must have realised that they didn't stand a chance? What madness had induced them to stay behind and fight?

Moving forwards, Fergus kept to the side of the street as behind him his men followed, their hobnailed boots crunching on the stone paving stones. The resistance seemed to have faded away and suddenly as he came around a corner, he saw that he had reached the harbour. In front of him, drawn up on the muddy river bank, were dozens and dozens of Parthian fishing boats and transports.

"Shit. We made it," Fergus cursed, with a sudden surprised look.

Chapter Forty – Parthia Capta

The whirring crack and wild kick back from the Roman onagers and ballistae was continuous as the Roman artillery targeted the mighty walls of Ctesiphon. It was morning and Fergus stood waiting patiently at the entrance to the command post occupied by the Third Cyrenaica legion. A week had passed since the capture of the river harbour and the start of the siege of Ctesiphon. During the day in which he and the men of the First cohort had secured the harbour, thousands of legionaries and auxiliaries had poured across the Tigris on the boats which they had dragged from the Royal river. The Parthian capital had however closed its gates on the Romans, refusing to surrender and forcing Trajan to order a siege.

As he stood waiting for the legate to see him Fergus turned his gaze to the Roman siege fortifications that surrounded the mighty city. The legionaries had dug defensive trenches and had lined their front with sharpened wooden stakes and littered the ground outside the main city gates with caltrops, small iron anti-cavalry spikes. And for the past week nothing had come in or out of the besieged metropolis. Fergus sighed wearily as he rubbed his unshaven cheeks. His men and he needed some proper rest but there could be no question of that until Ctesiphon surrendered. The legate of the Third Cyrenaica had assigned the sector covering the Royal road to him and the vexillation from the Fourth legion. His men had spent the last few days manning and strengthening their siege works. The Royal road, the ancient Parthian highway leading from the city of Susa, far to the south-east, via Ctesiphon to Sardis, a distance of some sixteen hundred miles, was now barred.

"He will see you now Sir," one of the young Tribunes from the Third legion said as he appeared and gestured for Fergus to enter the army tent. Fergus nodded and the legionary guards at the entrance to the command post saluted as he pushed passed them. Inside the large tent a wooden table had been placed in the centre and around the edges were stashed a camp bed and the legate's personal belongings. The legate of the Third was without his armour and was holding up and reading a scroll of papyrus. Seeing Fergus, he rolled up the scroll and gestured for Fergus to take a seat on a looted Parthian chair.

"Some wine," the legate said offering Fergus a cup. "We captured a vast supply in Seleucia. It's not bad either."

Gratefully Fergus took the cup and sniffed at it. Then he took a sip and sat down on the Parthian chair.

"You wished to see me Sir," Fergus said in a tired voice clutching his cup.

"Yes," the legate replied. "How are your men? How is morale? Are they getting the supplies that they need?"

"Morale is good Sir," Fergus said with a little nod. "Our rations are adequate Sir. No complaints have been brought to my attention."

"Good, good," the legate said sounding pleased. "I thought I would take this opportunity to update you on our situation. Trajan is concerned about morale. He has asked all his commanders to report to him on the matter. It's been a long and hard journey from Doura."

"Parthian resistance has been light Sir," Fergus said. "The men do ask me when we shall face them in a proper pitched battle. They are keen to finish this war." Fergus paused as he gazed at his commanding officer. "Has there been any news on the whereabouts of the king of kings, Osroes?"

"Nothing specific," the legate shrugged. "We believe that he fled Ctesiphon before the siege began. He probably went east. There is no Parthian field army to speak of within a hundred miles of here. That's what our scouts and spies report. The

Parthians seem to be more concerned with their civil war than with us."

"But Ctesiphon refuses to surrender," Fergus said frowning as he took another sip of wine. "Who is command of the city if not the king of kings?"

"Ah yes," the legate nodded. "That's a delicate matter. We believe that Prince Sanatruces is the military commander inside the city."

"Prince Sanatruces," Fergus exclaimed in a surprised voice. "Are you sure of this?"

"I said we believe he is in command in the city, yes," the legate replied. "Why? Do you know this man?"

"I have had dealings with him," Fergus muttered as he looked away.

For a moment the tent fell silent as Fergus considered what had been said.

"Well the facts are these," the legate said at last. "Such a large, populous city as Ctesiphon will soon run out of food. They are going to starve. Most of the population know it. Trajan believes that Sanatruces and a few supporters want to hold out and continue to resist. However most of the leading citizens want to surrender the city and negotiate with us. It's a delicate balance. But to swing it towards us Trajan has agreed to announce that a bounty of one hundred thousand denarii has been placed on Sanatruces's head. Trajan wants Sanatruces captured, dead or alive." A smirk appeared on the legate's face. "Let's see how long our dear prince survives inside Ctesiphon once his compatriots realise the reward they can gain by handing him over to us."

***

It was night and Fergus was just about to settle down to sleep on his camp bed in his command post, just behind the Roman siege fortifications, when he heard a sudden loud commotion. The noise was coming from outside and amongst the uproar he heard the thud of hooves and the whinny of horses.

"What the hell is going on out there?" he shouted at the legionary guard posted outside his tent. For a moment there was no reply. Then from outside Fergus heard the noise of running boots coming towards his tent. Annoyed he had just risen from his bed and was groping for his cloak and army belt when the flap to his tent was thrown aside and Britannicus appeared in the gloom, holding up a burning oil lamp. The young Tribune was clad in his full armour and his young face looked flushed.

"Sorry Sir," Britannicus gasped. "But there has been an incident. The night watch report that a small party of horsemen have just broken out from Ctesiphon. They were upon us and away before the men could stop them."

"What?" Fergus growled with a frown. "Are you saying that a party of Parthian horsemen just rode straight through our defences and no one stopped them?"

"That's right Sir," Britannicus replied looking down at the ground with sudden shame.

"Well where the fuck are they now, these horsemen?" Fergus snapped.

"They are gone Sir. Fled into the night heading away down the Royal road. My men tried to stop them, Sir, but they took us by surprise and it was difficult to see in the darkness. I am sorry Sir."

"Shit," Fergus hissed as he turned to look away. Then with a weary sigh he slowly pulled on his cloak and fitted his army belt around his waist. Making sure his belt with his sword was firmly secured he reached for his boots and pulled them on.

"Any idea who they were?" Fergus growled unhappily.

"No Sir," Britannicus replied stiffly. "But we managed to capture one of the riders. His horse impaled itself on one of the sharpened stakes and threw him to the ground. He's badly hurt but he is conscious. Shall I take you to him Sir?"

"Yes please," Fergus said in an annoyed voice as he fastened his cloak to one shoulder and moodily stomped out of his tent and into the night. "And fetch the fucking Greek translator."

Outside in the night, stretching away into the darkness in a giant semi-circle that vanished away behind the dark walls of Ctesiphon, hundreds of Roman camp fires lit up the darkness. Stomping across the field towards the front line of the Roman field fortifications, Fergus was silent as he gazed at the besieged city beyond. Inside the city and along the walls a few pin pricks of light were visible. As he approached a group of legionaries one of the Roman's raised a torch and in its flickering light Fergus caught sight of a man lying on the ground. The Parthian was groaning softly in pain and his eyes were closed. Nearby lay the corpse of his dead horse.

"Where is the damned translator?" Fergus bellowed. In the darkness he heard footsteps hurrying towards him.

"I am here. I am here," the Greek from Doura called out hastily.

Fergus grunted as he caught sight of the translator hurrying towards him. With an annoyed gesture he pointed down at the wounded Parthian.

"Ask him who he is and what he thinks he is doing," Fergus snapped in an annoyed voice. "Tell him that if he cooperates we shall give him medical attention. If not, he will die where he now lies. Go on, tell him."

Quickly the Greek translated. On the ground the Parthian groaned and muttered a few words one of which that made Fergus frown.

"What was that?" Fergus growled. "What did he just say?"

"He says Sir," the translator replied hastily. "He says Sir that he is one of prince Sanatruces's bodyguards. He says that he has fulfilled his oath and does not fear death now that he has helped the prince escape."

"Sanatruces," Fergus bellowed as his eyes widened in shock. "That was prince Sanatruces, nephew to king Osroes whom just rode straight through our lines? We have allowed the prince to escape?"

Amongst the group of legionaries no one answered him.

"Fuck," Fergus hissed as he spun round on his heels and start to run back to his command post. "Where is the stand-by cavalry squadron? Tell them to prepare to ride out immediately," Fergus roared as Britannicus and a centurion appeared from the gloom. "Those horsemen included Prince Sanatruces. He's only the nephew to king Osroes and military commander of Ctesiphon. I am going after him. Where are those fucking cavalrymen?" Fergus roared again.

As the thirty cavalrymen of the night watch, on permanent stand-by, came hurriedly rushing up to his command post Fergus ordered one of the men to dismount. Swiftly he swung himself up onto the horse instead and with a shout he was off charging away in the direction of the Royal road and bellowing at the cavalrymen to follow him.

***

It was dawn. To the east the sun was a red rising ball on the horizon when Fergus finally reined in his tired mount and paused to gaze up the road at the dead horse lying abandoned beside the edge of the gravelly road. In the darkness it had been impossible to see much but he had managed to keep to and follow the Royal road southeastwards for maybe twenty miles. There had however been no sighting of Prince Sanatruces and his escort. For a moment Fergus gazed at the dead beast in silence and without moving. In the dry, brown, waterless, hilly countryside on both sides of the road he could see a few stunted trees and isolated bushes. Slowly at a walk Fergus urged his horse onwards down the road towards the dead animal. The horse seemed to have slowly bled to death judging by the trail of blood that stained the dusty track. And as he approached Fergus saw the tell-tale wounds left by spiky anti-cavalry caltrops. This horse had been there at the breakout from Ctesiphon.

"Sir look," one of the Roman cavalry troopers called out as he pointed at something a hundred or so paces from the road. Turning in the direction in which the sharp-eyed cavalryman was pointing Fergus suddenly caught a glint of reflected light. As he peered at the stunted tree he saw two figures lying propped up in the shade of the tree and one of them looked like a woman.

Carefully Fergus nudged his horse off the gravelly track and began to walk his beast towards the two figures and as he drew closer he saw that one of the figures was a young woman of around eighteen or nineteen. Slowly and silently the Roman cavalry troopers surrounded the pair and Fergus dismounted. The woman looked like she had badly twisted her ankle for it was red and horribly swollen. Maybe from falling from the horse Fergus thought. She was gazing up at him in silence but the defiance in her posture was clear and she seemed fearless. The other person, an elderly man of around fifty, with thick Egyptian style dark eye shadow around his eyes was watching Fergus carefully. There was an intelligent gleam in his eyes and he too seemed unafraid. He was unarmed except for a coiled whip tucked into his belt.

"Who are you?" Fergus said speaking in Greek as he took a step towards the girl. The two strangers however did not answer, warily watching Fergus's every move. "Can you walk on that leg?" Fergus snapped in Greek as he reached out and grasped hold of the girl's arm. In response she cried out in an outraged, unintelligible language and before Fergus could react the girl bit him in his arm. With a cry of surprise and pain Fergus lashed out and struck the girl in the face knocking her to the ground. Then he stumbled backwards and stared down at the teeth marks left in his skin.

"What the hell did you do that for?" he roared in Latin.

On the ground the girl was nursing her bruised face with her hand as she stared up at Fergus with fierce defiance and hatred. Beside her the elderly man rose to his feet and raised his hands in a sudden calming gesture.

"It is forbidden for you to touch her," the man said quickly in near perfect Latin. "My name is Volagases. I serve my mistress, daughter of the king of kings Osroes. I demand that you treat the king's daughter with respect."

***

It was well into the afternoon when Fergus finally caught sight of the outlying Roman pickets on the Royal road. Directly behind him, her hands tied behind her back and her head blindfolded, escorted on both sides by several cavalrymen, rode the daughter of king Osroes and her loyal servant. He had placed both of them on the same cavalry mount. Fergus had blindfolded both and had tied their hands, but the precautions seemed unnecessary for the prisoners had made no attempt to escape. In fact, both seemed oddly relieved that their ordeal on the Royal road had come to an end. Fergus had interrogated Volagases about the whereabouts of Prince Sanatruces but the old man had been reluctant to talk except to say that they had got separated early on from the prince and his men. It was a disappointing end to the chase, to know that Sanatruces had managed to escape, but the surprise capture of Osroes's daughter would make up for it to some extent.

As he trotted down the road towards the Roman pickets, Fergus caught sight of the walls of Ctesiphon in the distance. Something seemed different. Closing in on the Roman positions Fergus frowned. The legionaries were standing around with their weapons raised in the air. They seemed to be in a jubilant mood. Then Fergus felt a tingle run down his spine as he heard the cries coming from the Roman camp. The words were being taken up by more and more soldiers.

"Parthia Capta. Parthia Capta. Parthia Capta," the men were crying out in triumph as they hugged each other in delight.

And suddenly a grin appeared on Fergus's lips as he realised what must have happened. Ctesiphon had surrendered. The Parthian capital had fallen. The war was over.

Chapter Forty-One – Thoughts of Home

Late summer 116 AD – The Roman occupied city of Seleucia, Roman province of Mesopotamia

The night sky looked amazing. Fergus stood alone on the top of the vast flat roof of the former governor's palace in the heart of the great city of Seleucia. It was late and in the dark, balmy summer air he could hear music and laughter drifting up from the streets far below. The large fortified residence, which had been turned into the HQ and barracks of the thousand strong Roman garrison, abutted the massive outer walls of the metropolis and was protected on the other side by a canal and several bridges which separated it from the rest of the city. Raising his cup of wine to his lips Fergus took a sip and turned to gaze up at the fantastic carpet of stars that stretched away across the night sky. He had never seen such a clear view of the stars and as he took another sip of wine he marvelled at their beauty.

Several months had passed since the fall of Ctesiphon and the capture of the daughter of the king of kings. Osroes it seemed had in his haste to abandon his capital left behind his throne and one of his daughters. It was the action of a weak and cowardly man Fergus thought with a sigh. But if he and the rest of the Roman army had believed that the war was over they'd all had a rude shock. The Emperor Trajan, overcome by the greatness of his achievements and flattered by the shower of congratulatory messages he'd received following the capture of Ctesiphon, may have decided to take a leisurely pleasure cruise down the Tigris to the port city of Charax in the far south, but the war had continued, and no Parthian peace offering had arrived. Instead, Fergus thought sourly as he took another sip of wine and gazed up at the beautiful twinkling stars, the emperor had seen it fit to place him in charge, as provisional military governor of the city of Seleucia. It was supposed to be a reward for the ruse with which he'd helped capture the metropolis, but it didn't feel like a reward. Fergus sighed as he turned to look out across the vast city. Trajan had ordered him to garrison and occupy the city with the men from his vexillation from the Fourth legion. He was there as an occupying force. To impose Roman rule and taxation. It had not been a new experience but the fragility of his position, with just a thousand men to control a city of three hundred thousand potentially hostile inhabitants worried him. There was no love lost between his men and the inhabitants of Seleucia and what was worse, his men had little in common with the townsfolk whom spoke a completely different language and whose customs and culture were alien to the legionaries.

Banishing the seriousness of his current position from his mind Fergus grunted and took another quick sip of wine before turning his eyes once more to the heavens. There was something far weightier on his mind that was dampening his spirits. Slowly his fingers reached out to touch the letter in his pocket. It had arrived a few days ago aboard a supply convoy all the way from Doura-Europus. It was from Galena. His wife had written that she and the girls were doing alright at Zeugma and that they missed him. Galena had spoken about her daily routine and that of the girls, trying to sound as if everything was alright. But it had been her last paragraph that had got to him. Despite writing several more times and paying generously for the delivery there had been no news from either Adalwolf in Antioch or Marcus, Kyna, Dylis and the others, faraway on the isle of Vectis in Britannia. No news, nothing but silence. No one had heard from his family in Britannia. There had been no news now for eighteen months and the silence and uncertainty were slowly eating away at him. Had Nigrinus had them all executed? Had he taken over the farm and erased the very memory of their existence? Wearily Fergus stirred and took a deep breath and closed his eyes as he allowed the balmy Mesopotamian breeze to touch his face. What had happened to his father and his family? The lack of news was growing harder to bear by the day.

Author's Notes

The Roman grain annonae (Cura Annonae) and the famous idea of, "Bread and Circuses," did exist and constitutes one of the earliest organised social security systems in the world. Its main purpose was to maintain the prestige of the Emperor and the State and to prevent riots from a starving populace. The loss of the Egyptian grain fleet in my book "Rome and the Conquest of Mesopotamia" is fiction but no doubt such disasters did occur. Their consequences would have been severe. It leads me to conclude that the ancient Romans had to contend with many of the same problems and challenges that we must deal with today in our modern world. From paying for and maintaining an expensive social security net, to large scale immigration, foreign threats and wars, organised crime, identity theft, runaway inflation and yes eventually even climate change. How the Romans tried to handle some of these challenges could provide valuable insights for us today. Their empire did after all manage to survive for nearly twelve hundred years in the West and much longer in the East.

The contemporary historical sources on Trajan's Parthian War are thin on the ground. We simply do not know exactly what happened or even the exact chronological order of events. In "Rome and the Conquest of Mesopotamia" I have based my story on F.A Lepper's analysis and account of the war. His book "Trajan's Parthian War" (1948) is well worth a read.

Emperor Trajan's motives for going to war are also fiercely debated. The ancient view was that he wanted to conquer Mesopotamia (modern Iraq) for the glory and to rival Alexander the Great. A more modern theory is that Trajan ordered the conquest because he wanted to secure lucrative trade routes to India and China. We are not even entirely sure which route to Seleucia and Ctesiphon Trajan actually took although Lepper provides convincing evidence for the Euphrates route. The fact that both Seleucia and Ctesiphon fell quickly during the initial campaign suggests to me that they surrendered quickly. There is no evidence that Fergus took Seleucia by using a ruse. That's pure fiction. However, we do know that one of the daughters of the king of kings Osroes was captured during the fall of Ctesiphon.

Finally, there is some evidence and suggestion that the Alani and Sarmatian tribes did indeed use Cannabis.

"Rome and the Conquest of Mesopotamia" is book eight in the Veteran of Rome series. VOR 9 will be published later in 2018 and will be the final instalment of the series.

William Kelso, London, January 2018

MAJOR PARTICIPANTS IN ROME AND THE CONQUEST OF MESOPOTAMIA

Marcus and Fergus's family

Kyna, Wife of Marcus, mother of Fergus.

Corbulo, Marcus's father, Fergus's grandfather

Ahern, Kyna's son by another man. Jowan forced to adopt him.

Elsa, Orphaned daughter of Lucius, but adopted by Marcus and his family.

Cassius, Elsa's husband and Marcus's secretary

Armin, Orphaned little brother of Elsa

Galena, Wife of Fergus

Briana, Fergus and Galena's first daughter

Efa, Fergus and Galena's second daughter

Gitta, Fergus and Galena's third daughter

Aina, Fergus and Galena's fourth daughter

Athena, Fergus and Galena's fifth daughter

Indus, Marcus's Batavian bodyguard in Rome and ex-soldier

Aledus, Friend and army buddy of Fergus

Dylis, Marcus's half-sister, adopted by Corbulo

Cunomoltus, Marcus's half-brother, illegitimate son of Corbulo

Imperial family

Marcus Ulpius Traianus, Emperor of Rome (Trajan) AD 98 - 117

Plotina Pompeia, Empress of Rome, Emperor Trajan's wife

Salonia Matidia, Trajan's niece.

Members of the Peace Party

Publius Aelius Hadrianus, (Hadrian) Leader of the peace party

Adalwolf, German amber and slave trader, but also guide, advisor and translator for Hadrian.

Vibia Sabina, Hadrian's wife

Publius Acilius Attianus, Hadrian's old childhood guardian (Jointly with Trajan)

Marcus Aemilius Papus, friend of Hadrian

Quintus Sosius Senecio, Soldier and supporter of Hadrian

Aulus Platorius Nepos, Roman politician and soldier

Admiral Quintus Marcius Turbo, close friend of Trajan and Hadrian

Members of the War Party

Gaius Avidius Nigrinus, Senator, leading citizen in Rome and close friend of Trajan. Leader of the war party and potential successor to Trajan

Lady Claudia, A high born aristocrat and old acquaintance of Marcus

Paulinus Picardus Taliare, One of Rome's finance ministers, in charge of the state treasury

Aulus Cornelius Palma, Conqueror of Arabia Nabataea and sworn enemy of Hadrian.

Lucius Pubilius Celsus, Senator and ex Consul; bitter enemy of Hadrian.

Lusius Quietus, Berber prince and Roman citizen from Mauretania in northern Africa, a successful and popular Roman military leader.

Marcus, Fergus's father, senator and supporter of the War Party

Members of Fergus's close protection team

Arlyn, Hibernian bodyguard of Hadrian

Barukh, Jewish bodyguard of Hadrian, recruited in Antioch.

Flavius, Blond Germanic bodyguard and Fergus's deputy

Saadi, only female and youngest member of Fergus's protection team

Skula, A bald Scythian (Russian) tribesman. One of Hadrian's guards.

The two Italian brothers, ex-legionaries and bodyguards to Hadrian

Numerius, bodyguard to Hadrian, recruited in Antioch.

The Armenians and Parthians

Osroes I, King of Kings of Parthia

Parthamasiris, Nephew of Osroes, who became king of Armenia.

Volagases III, rival Parthian king to Osroes, rules in eastern Parthia

Sanatruces, nephew to the king of kings Osroes

The Fourth "Scythica" Legion

Gellius, legionary legate of the Fourth legion.

Britannicus, A young Tribune augusticlavii with the Fourth legion

Hiempsal, Numidian officer with the Seventh auxiliary cavalry alae of Numidians

Other Characters

Cunitius, A private investigator and one-time enemy of Marcus

Heron of Alexandria, A Greek mathematician, engineer and inventor.

Similis, Ex-prefect of Egypt, placed in charge of all security matters in Rome whilst Trajan is away in the east.

Blaikisa, Cassius's freedman

Alexandros, Greek captain of the ship Hermes that sailed to Hyperborea with Marcus

Licinius, Roman ambassador in Gabala, Caucasian Albania

GLOSSARY

Adiabene, region in north-eastern Iraq

Aerarium, State treasury for Senatorial provinces

Aesculapius, The god of healing

Agora, market place and public space

Albania, Roman client kingdom at the southern foot hills of the Caucasus

Aila, Red sea port now called Aqaba in Jordan

Alae, Roman cavalry unit

Alani, A Scythian people living on the steppes to the north of the Caucasus

Antioch, Near Antakya, Turkey

Arabia Nabataea, modern day Jordan and northern Saudi Arabia

Araxes river, also known as the Aras. Former border between the USSR and Iran

Artaxata, ancient capital of the kingdom of Armenia

Athena, Greek goddess and protector of Athens

Agrimensore, A land surveyor.

Armorica, Region of north-west France

Aquincum, Modern Budapest, Hungary

Arcidava, Fort in the Banat region of Dacia

Argiletum, Street of the booksellers in ancient Rome.

Asses, Roman copper coins, money

Babylonia, region around Babylon, Mesopotamia

Ballista, Roman artillery catapult

Banat, Region of Dacia, Romania and Serbia

Berzobis, Fort in the Banat region of Dacia

Bonnensis, Bonn, Germany. Full name.

Burdigala, Roman city close to modern Bordeaux, France

Bostra, a Roman occupied town in Jordan

Capitoline Hill, One of the seven hills of ancient Rome

Carnuntum, Roman settlement just east of Vienna, Austria

Carrobalista, Mobile Roman artillery catapult

Castra, Fort.

Caltrops, small spiked metal anti cavalry and personnel weapons

Cappadocia, Roman province in central and eastern Turkey

Caucasian Gates, Darial Gorge Georgia/Russia border

Centurion, Roman officer in charge of a company of about 80 legionaries

Cella, internal space in a temple

Chaboras river, now known as the Khabur river, tributary to the Euphrates

Charax, near modern day Basra

Cilicia, Roman province in modern Turkey

Circesium, a town now called Buseira in Syria

Classis Pannonica, Roman fleet based on the Danube at Carnuntum

Cohort, Roman military unit equivalent to a battalion of around 500 men.

Colchis, land around the south-eastern part of the Black sea

Colonia Agrippina, Cologne, Germany.

Contubernium, Eight-man legionary infantry squad. Barrack room/tent group room

Corona Muralis, Roman military decoration

Cornicen, Trumpeter and signaller.

Cuirassed armour, Expensive chest armour that followed the muscles of the chest

Cyrenaica, eastern part of Libya

Currach, Celtic boat

Cataphract, type of heavily armoured cavalry

Ctesiphon, Parthian winter capital, near modern Baghdad

Dacia(n), The area in Romania where the Dacians lived.

Decanus, Corporal, squad leader

Decurion, Roman cavalry officer.

Demeter, Greek goddess of agriculture

Denarii, Roman money.

Derbent, claims to be oldest town in Russia, on the Caspian-sea

Deva Victrix, Chester, UK.

Domitian, Emperor from AD 81 – 96

Draco banner, Dacian coloured banner made of cloth

Doura Europus, Near to Salihiye in eastern Syria

Edessa, Sanliurfa, now in south eastern Turkey

Emporium, Marketplace

Elegeia, Armenian town in the region of Erzurum

Eleusinion, Temple of Demeter, Athens

Eponymous Archon of Athens, The city's ruler and mayor

Equestrian Order, The Order of Knights – minor Roman aristocracy

Equites, Individual men of the Equestrian Order.

Euphrates, major river in Iraq, Syria and Turkey

Falx, Curved Dacian sword.

Fibula, A brooch or pin used by the Romans to fasten clothing

Fiscus, The Roman state treasury controlled by the emperor and not the senate

Focale, Roman army neck scarf

Fortuna, The Goddess of Fortune.

Forum Boarium, The ancient cattle market of Rome

Forum Romanum, Political centre of ancient Rome, area of government buildings

Frisii, Tribe of Frisians who lived in the northern Netherlands

Gabala, ancient capital of Caucasian Albania

Gades, Cadiz, southern Spain

Garum, Roman fermented fish sauce.

Gladius, Standard Roman army short stabbing sword.

Greaves, Armour that protects the legs

Hatra, Hatra in Iraq

Hengistbury Head, Ancient Celtic trading post near Christchurch, UK.

Hibernia, Ireland.

Hispania, Spain.

Hyrcanian Ocean, Caspian Sea

Hyperborea, Mythical land beyond the north wind.

Iberia, Spain but also a small Roman client kingdom south of the Caucasus

Imaginifer, Roman army standard bearer carrying an image of the Emperor

Imperator, Latin for commander/emperor, used to hail the Roman emperor

Invidia/Nemesis, God of envy and vengeance

Insulae, Roman multi-storey apartment buildings

Janus, God of boundaries.

Jupiter Optimus Maximus, Patron god of Rome

Kaftan, Parthian dress, a long traditional outer garment

Kostolac, City in Serbia

Keffiyeh, Traditional Arabic headdress

Kushan Empire, Afghanistan, Pakistan and parts of India

Lares, Roman guardian deities

Iazyges, Barbarian tribe, roughly in modern Hungary

Legate, Roman officer in command of a Legion

Liburnian, A small Roman ship

Limes, Frontier zone of the Roman Empire.

Londinium, London, UK.

Lower Pannonia, Roman province in and around Hungary/Serbia and Croatia.

Ludus, School

Lugii, Vandals, barbarian tribe in central Europe.

Luguvalium, Carlisle, UK.

Mars, Roman god of war

Marcomanni, Barbarian tribe whom lived north of the Danube in modern day Austria

Mardi, Armenian tribe that lived around lake Van

Massalia, Marseille, France

Mausoleum of Augustus, Mausoleum of Augustus in Rome

Mesopotamia, modern Iraq

Middle Sea, Mediterranean Sea

Mogontiacum, Mainz, Germany.

Mons Graupius, Roman/Scottish battlefield in Scotland

Mosul, Mosul northern Iraq

Munifex, Private non-specialist Roman Legionary.

Noviomagus Reginorum, Chichester, UK.

Numerii, Germanic irregular soldiers allied to Rome.

Nero, Roman emperor 54-68 AD

Nike, Greek god of victory

Nisibis, Known now as Nusaybin in south-eastern Turkey

Numidians, one of the Berber tribes of northern Africa

Nymphaeum, monument consecrated to the water nymphs

O group meeting, Modern British army slang for group meeting of officers

Onagers, Heavy Roman artillery catapults

Optio, Roman army officer, second in command of a Company.

Ostia, Original seaport of Rome

Osrhoene, a Roman client kingdom around Edessa

Palatine Hill, one of the seven hills of Rome. The Imperial palace there.

Palmyra, Palmyra in Syria, ancient city partially destroyed by IS

Panathenaea, Ancient Greek festival in honour of Athena

Parthian Empire, Iraq, Iran and parts of Saudi, Syria and central Asia

Parthenon, The temple of Athena on top of the Acropolis in Athens

Peplos dress, traditional dress presented to the goddess Athena

Peristyle, open space surrounded by vertical columns

Petra, Petra, Jordan.

Pilum/pila, Roman legionary spear(s).

Pistorum, college of bakers

Porolissum, Settlement in northern Dacia/Romania

Portus Augusti, The new seaport of ancient Rome

Portus Tiberinus, Rome's Tiber river port

Posca, watered down wine with added spices

Praefecti Aeranii Saturni, Rome's finance ministers

Prefect, Roman officer in command of an auxiliary cohort or civil magistrate.

Praetorian Guard, Emperor's personal guard units

Principia, HQ building in a Roman army camp/fortress.

Propylaia, ancient monumental entrance gate into the Acropolis

Pugio, Roman army dagger.

Quadi, Germanic tribe living along the Danube

Resafa II, Fictitious Roman fort near Sergiopolis

Rosia Montana, Ancient gold and silver mining district in Romania/Dacia

Roxolani, Barbarian tribe in eastern Romania

Rutipiae, Richborough, Kent, UK.

Sacred Way, Important road in the ancient city of Rome

Satala, east of Sadak in Turkey on the ancient border with Armenia

Sarmatians, Barbarian allies of the Dacians

Sarmatian cataphracts, Heavily armoured Sarmatian cavalry

Sarmisegetusa Regia, Capital city of ancient Dacia

Saturn, God of wealth

Saturnalia, Roman festival in late December

Scythians, Barbarian tribes, modern Ukraine and Russia

Singidunum, Belgrade.

Sirmium, The ancient city of Sirmium on the Danube

Singara, modern Sinjar in northern Iraq

SPQR, Senate and People of Rome.

Stola, Woman's cloak

Stoas, covered walkways

Styx river, Mythical river of the underworld.

Stylus, Roman pen

Subura, Slum neighbourhood in central Rome

Sura, ancient city on the Euphrates river in Northern Syria, west of Raqqa and north of Resafa

Tapae, Dacian fort at the entrance to the iron gates pass

Tara, Seat of the High King of Hibernia, north-west of Dublin, Ireland.

Tesserarius, Roman army watch/guard officer, third in line of company command

Tessera tile, A small stone carried by the Tesserarius on which the daily password was written down

Testudo formation, Roman army formation and tactic

Tibiscum, Fort in Dacia

Tigris, major river in Iraq

Tribune (military), A senior Roman army officer

Trireme, A fast agile galley with three banks of oars

Tutela, the duties of guardianship

Urban cohorts, A kind of anti-riot police force in ancient Rome

Island of Vectis, Isle of Wight, UK

Velarium, Retractable canvas roof over the Roman colosseum.

Velum, Parched animal skin used as writing paper

Vestal Virgins, Female priestesses of ancient Rome

Vespasian, Roman Emperor 69-79 AD

Vexillatio(n), Temporary Roman army detachment.

Viminacium, Roman town on the Danube in modern Serbia

Via Traiana Nova, Roman road between Bostra and the red sea port of Aila (Aqaba)

Printed in Great Britain
by Amazon